S+A

A qualified parachutist, Harvey Black served with British Army Intelligence for over ten years. His experience ranges from covert surveillance in Northern Ireland to operating in Communist East Berlin during the Cold War, where he feared for his life after being dragged from his car by KGB soldiers. Since then he has had a more sedate life in the private sector as a director for an international company and now enjoys the pleasures of writing. Harvey is married with four children. For more from Harvey, visit his website at www.harveyblackauthor.com. For more about the *Devils with Wings* series, photos and maps visit: harveyblackauthor.org.

D1643055

Also by Harvey Black:

Devils with Wings Book I
The Green Devils assult on Fort Eben Emael

Devils with Wings Book II
Silk Drop
The airborne invasion of Crete

HARVEY BLACK
FROZEN SUN

SilverWood

Published in 2012 by SilverWood Books
30 Queen Charlotte Street, Bristol, BS1 4HJ
www.silverwoodbooks.co.uk

Copyright © Harvey Black 2012

The right of Harvey Black to be identified as the author of this work
has been asserted by him in accordance with the Copyright,
Designs and Patents Act 1988.

All rights reserved. No part of this publication may be reproduced,
stored in a retrieval system, or transmitted in any form or by any means,
electronic, mechanical, photocopying, recording or otherwise,
without prior permission of the copyright holder.

This novel is a work of fiction. Names and characters are the product
of the author's imagination and any resemblance to actual persons,
living or dead, is entirely coincidental.

ISBN 978-1-78132-039-6

British Library Cataloguing in Publication Data
A CIP catalogue record for this book is available from the British Library

Set in Bembo by SilverWood Books
Printed on responsibly sourced paper

To my four children
Elaine, Lee, Darren and Annabelle

Introduction

The reputation of the Fallschirmjäger alone is worth some divisions.
(Field Marshal Albert Kesselring, Frascati, Italy 1943)

In the early days of the Second World War, the German paratroopers, or 'Green Devils' as they were more commonly known, were one of the guarantors for victory. They saw action in all theatres of the war: on Crete; in Russia; Normandy; the Ardennes; on the Oder; in the Reichswald; in Africa and on Sicily; in the Battles of Monte Cassino and the Futa Pass; at Narvik; and in Tunisia and Austria.

A lot has been written on the history and image of the German Fallschirmjäger so I will not be covering that here. On one of my bookshelves, there is a 'Military Intelligence Bulletin' dated September 1942. The bulletin was printed by the US Military Intelligence Service throughout World War II and was designed to inform officers and enlisted men of the latest enemy tactics and weapons. Inside there is a small article on the Fallschirmjäger that says more about them than I could ever do. I recommend it to you.

A good many American fighting men have said that they would like to get a clearer mental picture of German parachutists; what they look like, how they train, what their standard tactics are and, in general, how they do their job.

A common mistake is to imagine that the German parachutist is an ordinary infantryman who, on landing, goes into combat as a guerrilla fighter operating by himself, with help from any fellow parachutists he may have the luck to meet. Actually, a German parachutist is a thoroughly trained specialist who fights as part of a well-organized unit. The German Army teaches him to believe that his is the most important of all jobs; that he is even more valuable than the German Air Force aces. After he has had a long, tough training in a parachutist school, he is prepared not merely to jump well but also to fight well. In fact, teamwork is the German parachutist's guiding principle.

In choosing men who are to be sent to a parachutist school, the German Army selects candidates who are young, athletic, quick-witted and aggressive. Many of them are chosen for their special abilities and skills, e.g. medical, engineering and so on. These are needed just as much in parachute operations as in any other force. During the training, emphasis is placed on exact procedures. For instance, a man packs a parachute with special care if he knows that he himself is going to use it. After proper physical conditioning, the candidate works from a jumping tower, practising landing methods under different conditions. The school also requires and develops fearlessness. To illustrate this, in a transport plane any sign of hesitation at the command "Jump!" may cost the candidate his membership in a parachute company. However, parachute jumping is only a small part of the candidate's training, inasmuch as the German Army hopes to make him a useful member of a wider crack combat organisation. He must know how to take part in what is called a 'vertical envelopment'; that is, the capture of an area by airborne troops.

Here is a translation of a document captured from a German parachute trooper who was taken prisoner in Greece. Its title is *The Parachutist's Ten Commandments*:

1. *You are the elite of the German Army. For you, combat shall be fulfilment. You shall seek it out and train yourself to stand any test.*
2. *Cultivate true comradeship, for together with your comrades you will triumph or die.*
3. *Be shy of speech and incorruptible. Men act, women chatter; chatter will bring you to the grave.*
4. *Calm and caution, vigour and determination, valour and a fanatical offensive spirit will make you superior in attack.*
5. *In facing the foe, ammunition is the most precious thing. He who shoots uselessly, merely to reassure himself, is a man without guts. He is a weakling and does not deserve the title of parachutist.*
6. *Never surrender. Your honour lies in victory or death.*
7. *Only with good weapons can you have success, so look after them on the principle 'first my weapons, then myself'.*
8. *You must grasp the full meaning of an operation so that, should your leader fall by the way, you can carry it out with coolness and caution.*

9. *Fight chivalrously against an honest foe; armed irregulars deserve no quarter.*

10. *With your eyes open, keyed up to top pitch, agile as a greyhound, tough as leather, hard as Krupp steel, you will be the embodiment of a German warrior.*

These commandments were written by Generaloberst Kurt Student and were distributed shortly before the assault on Crete.

Following the battle for Crete in May 1941, Hitler refused to undertake any further large-scale airborne operations due to the high casualty rate. The Green Devils subsequently took up a new role as elite 'line' infantry. Their performance in such hard-fought battles as El Alamein and Monte Casino reinforced their reputation as some of the toughest troops of World War II. By 1944, they had lost their elite status and were no longer trained as paratroops due to the realities of the strategic situation. By the end of the war, the series of new Fallschirmjäger divisions extended to over a dozen, with a concomitant reduction in quality in the higher numbered units of the series.

62,756 Green Devils were killed during the war and over 8,300 are still listed as missing in action. May they rest in peace.

To learn more about the Green Devils in World War II, I can recommend the following titles:

Franz Kurowski, *Jump into Hell: German Paratroopers in WWI*, ISBN 978-0811705820 (2010)

Jon Sutherland, *Fallschirmjager: Elite German Paratroops in World War II* ISBN 978-1848843189 (2010)

Hans Martin Stimpel, *Die deutsche Fallschirmtruppe – 1936-1945 Innenansichten von Führung und Truppe* ISBN 978-3813209075 (2009)

Gunther Roth, *Die deutsche Fallschirmtruppe 1936-1945: Der Oberbefehlshaber Kurt Student – Strategischer, operativer Kopf oder Kriegshandwerker und das soldatische Ethos – Würdigung.Kritik. Lektion* ISBN 978-3813209068 (2010)

Robin Schäfer

Chapter One

Paul stepped into the barn, brushing aside the curtain as he entered. A blackout was in force. His platoon commanders and NCOs were waiting inside for him, the buzz of conversation stopping instantly as Feldwebel Richter brought the room to attention. Paul waved them down and they all looked at him expectantly. He could feel the tension of the moment.

"Well, sir," blurted out Leeb. "Put us out of our misery. Is it on?"

The confident, slim and wiry officer was standing next to one of the barn supports that were precariously holding up a hayloft above. His uniform and his mousey hair were already flecked with strands of straw, so many of which seemed to constantly float in the air, landing on the first surface they encountered. Leeb had been with Paul since Poland where he had served in Paul's platoon as a troop commander. He was part of the glider force that landed on the impregnable Fort Eben Emael, an action that resulted in a promotion to Leutnant. He commanded one of Paul's platoons during the assault on the Corinth Canal and later the massive airborne invasion of Crete.

Paul stood in front of them, looking over their expectant faces. The flickering light from the oil lamps gave them a look of spectres. Leutnant Leeb was in the centre; to his left, the commander of second platoon, Leutnant Dietrich Nadel and to his right, the commander of three platoon, Leutnant Viktor Roth. Behind them, taking their places back on the bales of straw pulled out earlier for seating, the three platoon NCOs: Unterfeldwebels Eichel, Fischer and Kienitz. With them, the commander of the mortar troop, Unterfeldwebel Loewe. The unit had been commanded previously by the now Company Feldwebel: Richter.

Paul moved towards the centre of the semi-circle of straw bales. One had been placed there for him. He took off his Fallschirm and unslung his MP40, placing them both on the bale. As he ran his hand across his fair hair, he touched the scar above his left eye, the consequence of an explosion that had wounded him on Fort Eben Emael.

The tension was palpable.

"Yes, it's on," said Paul, putting them out of their misery.

The barn buzzed with speculation and he waited for it to die down before he continued. "Army Group North has passed the code word 'Dortmund' so Operation Barbarossa starts tomorrow."

The buzz restarted, but this time Paul called for silence as it seemed unlikely they would settle down of their own accord, such was the excitement of the moment and the prospect of being in action again. "When you're quite ready, gentlemen."

The hum died down and the troops quickly switched their attention back to their company commander.

"The artillery barrage will start at three fifteen, lasting up to an hour in our sector, followed by Luftwaffe attacks on the Soviet forward positions and airfields."

"What time will we move out, sir?" asked the impatient Leeb.

"All in good time, Ernst," admonished Paul, halting him with a wave of his hand.

"Pull your seats in closer. I want to run through our timings again."

Bales of straw were dragged into position, forming an even tighter semi-circle around Paul, kicking up a light film of dust as they were moved. Once this task was finished, the troops were again attentive, waiting for more information to be released to them.

"As briefed yesterday, we will be under the auspices of 4th Panzer Group and will be attached to 6th Panzer Division of XLI Corps. We'll move up under the cover of the artillery bombardment, close behind their reserves."

"Do we not have a task then, sir?" declared Nadel. The usually pale-faced officer was still sporting the vestiges of a tan from his time in Crete that, as for all of them, was starting to fade. Although still with a pinched mien, he looked fit and healthy, like all of those who had fought in Crete.

"Nothing has changed, I'm afraid. We are to stick close to the Division until called upon."

There was a groan from the assembled group.

Paul silenced them, something Max would have done had he been there. He looked across at Richter, the newly promoted Company Feldwebel, the replacement for the still recovering Max Grun, the previous holder of the position. Max had been Paul's platoon sergeant when he took his first command back in Poland, where under fire for the first time, Max had saved Paul's life. During the more recent action in Crete, Max had been badly wounded and wasn't fit enough to join them on this latest task.

"Listen to me."

They immediately grew silent, sensing their commander's frustration.

"Between us and the Gebirgsjager, we suffered nearly six thousand casualties on Crete. That was a mere four weeks ago. We have lost a number of our Kameraden and we've had little time to settle in our replacements with the unit. Don't wish an action on us too soon, gentlemen. We may have had some rest but, believe me, we are far from fully recovered."

Paul shifted uncomfortably on the straw bale; the spikes from some of the shorter stalks were penetrating the fabric of his trousers. He looked at each of his officers in turn. They looked very young. He smiled to himself. He was not even twenty-four yet. Then he looked at each of the NCOs, the true backbone of his company, their heads nodding in agreement. Although bravado required them to want to be in a fight, deep down they knew they still needed some time to fully recuperate.

"Most of you were with me in Crete and earned the Iron Cross Second Class. Don't be so keen to rack up the next one just yet."

This brought a laugh from the gathering. All of the Fallschirmjager fighting in Crete had been awarded the Iron Cross Second Class, under the instruction of the Fuhrer.

"The impending invasion of Russia has no equal in history. Our Army Group North alone has some 800,000 men. Striking across their borders tomorrow, we'll have three armoured divisions, three motorised divisions and twenty infantry divisions, not forgetting the three security divisions. It will be a battle to surpass all, and the Soviets will not give up without a fight. We'll have plenty of opportunities to go into battle, believe me."

"Have we got a fire brigade role then, sir?" asked the cherub-faced Roth. His nose was still scarred from when it had been badly burnt by the cruel Cretan sun; his fair skin suffered more than most. The men had nicknamed him *Rudolf, mit der roten nase.* They meant well; he was highly respected by his platoon.

"You could call it that, Viktor. Let's just hope there aren't too many fires."

The men grinned.

"What next then, sir?" enquired Leeb.

"We move up to the line under cover of darkness, so I want all of the trucks loaded by 2200 tonight. But no movement before 2000, understood?"

They all nodded, knowing the importance of keeping the movement of nearly 800,000 men under wraps.

"Feldwebel Richter."

"Yes, Herr Oberleutnant."

"Make sure the drivers have taped over the lights. I don't want anything giving away our position."

"Is it still one rear light, sir?"

"Yes, one rear light. Make sure the right one is taped over though."

"Yes, sir."

"I will conduct a final inspection at 1800, so be ready. Right – status, by platoon. Ernst?"

"All present and correct, sir. Ammunition and rations allocated and distributed, weapons and kit checked. We're as ready as we'll ever be, right, Unterfeldwebel Eichel?"

"Yes, sir," the charismatic Unterfeldwebel from first platoon agreed with his commander. "The boys know the importance of being ready. The veterans have been helping out the new boys, making sure they're up to speed."

"Viktor?"

"If Unterfeldwebel Kienitz and I go over their kit again, it will be worn out before they move out, sir," exaggerated the impulsive commander of third platoon, bringing laughter from the rest of the company.

"Dietrich, you and Fischer as equally up to speed as Leutnant Roth?"

"Of course, sir," affirmed Leutnant Nadel, the more deliberate of the two officers. "Packed rucksacks and readied weapons containers, sir." He quoted the Fallschirmjager mantra.

"Unterfeld Loewe, your mortars packed up and ready?"

The new commander of the mortar platoon, a replacement for Richter who was now the company sergeant, stood up. A giant of a man, like Max, Paul wondered how the soldier had cajoled his way into the Fallschirmjager. His expressive eyes gave an insight to his confidence, yet his scowl could put the fear of God into a subordinate.

"My troop is ready, sir," responded the 'Lion', as he had been nicknamed.

"Thank you, Loewe."

Loewe sat back down beside Fischer. They were like chalk and cheese. The short wiry NCO was completely dwarfed by Loewe, but in size only. A confrontation early on had resulted in a showdown between the two of them and, to the amazement of the company, Fischer had held his own. Since then, the two had become inseparable and good drinking companions.

Paul checked his watch. It was 1600, 21 June 1941.

"I'll leave you to your last-minute preparations, although by the sound of it they've already been done. But I will still be doing the rounds at six and talking to the men. Remember light discipline at all costs. Dismissed."

"*Aufstehen*," bellowed Richter, bringing the men to attention as Paul stood up.

"Carry on. Feldwebel Richter, remain behind please."

The officers and NCOs shuffled out of the barn, kicking up a fine mist of dust, the last man out ensuring the blackout curtain was in place. Although still light outside, Paul had wanted the blackout discipline initiated immediately. Besides, it would be dark very soon. The slim, dark-haired Feld strode over to Paul and came to attention in front of him.

"Sir."

"Stand easy, Feld. You're my Company Sergeant. You can relax a little when no one else is around."

"Thank you, sir," acknowledged Richter, his body slackening slightly, his piercing eyes focused on Paul, awaiting his orders.

Although Richter was an outstanding soldier, proving his worth as the commander of the mortar troop in Crete and becoming an excellent company sergeant, he and Paul had yet to settle into a comfortable status quo. Paul had to get used to to not having Max around and accepting Richter in his new position as the most senior NCO of the company. They were big boots Richter was stepping into and, although the company had accepted him wholeheartedly, he was not Feldwebel Max Grun.

"I'm sure they won't need it, but check that company HQ is up to speed. Ensure Fleck has extra medical supplies, particularly dressings."

"You think there are going to be heavy casualties, sir?" asked the NCO.

"Nobody knows, Feldwebel. But with nearly a million men seeking a resupply at some point, we could find ourselves running short of essentials. We're also dependent on another echelon and not our own 7th Division. We may not be the priority."

"Will do then, sir."

"As for Bergmann and the rest, just keep them on their toes. We don't want our own HQ letting the side down," Paul said with a smile.

"I'll be on them, sir."

"Anything I've missed, Feldwebel?"

"Nothing springs to mind, sir. The platoon commanders seem to be pretty thorough."

"Make sure you do some checks yourself."

"But—"

"No buts. The platoon commanders aren't infallible. They would like to think they are, but they're not."

"Understood, sir."

"Anyway, you know soldiers. They can be quite adept at pulling the wool over their officers' eyes when they choose to."

"That they are," replied Richter, grinning.

"I want you with me at 1800. You have a key role to play in this unit."

"Understood. Is that all, sir?"

"Yes. Thank you. Carry on."

Richter left the barn, leaving Paul on his own. This was the base for the company HQ so no doubt it would fill up again soon, thought Paul. He moved over to one of the bales of straw, sat down and pulled a letter from his tunic pocket. He rubbed the scar above his left eye again, a habit he had acquired after he was wounded during the assault on Fort Eben Emael. It was usually a sign that he was internalising his thoughts and concerns about the forthcoming action. Had Max been here, he would have recognised the signs and teased out any concerns his commander had so he could put them right, or at least try.

Paul opened the now crumpled letter, probably the last he would get for some time, and read the disturbing news again. His mother was ill and, although his father had assured him that she would recover, Paul still worried about her. He had just skipped to the last paragraph when the door to the barn creaked open. Paul turned towards the entrance and saw Helmut step through, holding the blackout curtain aside to allow the battalion commander, Major Volkman, the Raven, to pass through unhindered, quickly followed by Oberleutnants Fleck and Bauer. Paul immediately stood up.

"Here you are, Brand," established the Raven, his dark eyes peering down his slightly hooked nose and into the gloom at Paul. Even in full battledress, he looked ever the aristocrat.

"Just finished a final briefing with the men, sir. Any changes?"

"Good, good. I've had it confirmed that we are travelling out as a battalion, so I want our units to stick close together. It's going to be a bloody traffic jam out there when things start moving. If the Heer require our services, I want us to be instantly available as a coherent unit," he decreed, catching the eyes of his other three officers. "Do I make myself clear?"

"*Jawohl*, Herr Major," they all replied in unison.

"Don't they have anything for us at the kick-off, sir?" complained Helmut.

"Unfortunately, Janke, despite our success at Eben Emael and Crete, the Landser are still sceptical about our capabilities. They appear to want to go it alone."

There was a groan from the four company commanders.

"But we've seen as much action as they have, sir, if not more," piped up Erich, Paul's closest friend next to Max and Helmut.

"I understand your frustrations, gentlemen," the Major replied, tapping his *knochensack* tunic (boneshaker) with the ever-present swagger stick, "but we shall have to just wait. Use this opportunity to train and settle in your new recruits but be ready when we are called upon. I have spoken to General Major Landgraf personally and he assures me that we are being retained until there is a task that befits our skills. I assume your companies are ready?" The question was rhetorical.

"Make sure there are no lights giving away our positions when we move out. I don't want Popov's bombers picking us out. We'll have the Chain Dogs carrying out their traffic duties, so don't give them an opportunity to jump on you." Volkman glanced quickly at Paul as he said it, obviously referring to Paul's clash with the Feldgendarmerie in Poland. In Poland, he had come across two Feldgendarmerie bullying the local population and had inervened. The local Feldgendarmerie commander hadn't taken kindly to Paul's interference.

"Any questions?"

"Is the rest of the Division ready, sir?" queried Paul.

"They still have some supply issues, but the Panzers will be ready to move out as soon as the engineers have done their work.

Then the tanks can start to clear a route through the minefields."

"What about our fuel supplies, sir?" asked Manfred. "We'll be in competition with the rest of the Division. Those Panzers are thirsty buggers."

"It's a worry for me too, so I've had the Adjutant acquire additional stocks of fuel. We have two trucks packed with extra cans."

"We'll need to keep our distance from those two then, sir," piped up Helmut cheerfully.

"Quite, Janke, quite. As you're so concerned for their safety, I will attach them to your company seeing as you are last in the column."

Helmut reddened and Paul, Erich and Manfred stifled a smile.

"One last thing, Brand. We're short of experienced Feldwebels in the Division so I'm transferring Feldwebel Richter across to one of the other battalions. I don't like to do it at this stage of the proceedings, but Division has insisted."

"But, sir, he's only been in post for a month. It would prove disruptive to replace him now."

"I hear what you say, Brand, but nevertheless I have made my decision."

"His replacement, sir?" The frustration in Paul's voice was obvious.

"He's waiting outside. It's done, Oberleutnant Brand, so live with it."

Volkman turned to the other three officers. "Anything else? No? Right, the Chain Dogs will guide us out of the woods onto the road and will be strategically placed along our route."

"No running them down then, sir," declared Helmut, already biting his tongue as the words left his mouth. The look from the Raven was enough.

"I want you with your vehicles by 2100 and ready to move out. Dismissed."

The Raven turned on his heel and left the barn, no doubt to get any final instructions from General Student, Commander of the 7th Flieger Division, not forgetting his temporary commander, Generalmajor Brandenberger.

Paul's fellow officers gathered around him.

"How can he do that?" exclaimed Paul. "We're about to go into battle."

"All our Felds are up to speed, Paul. I'm sure it won't be a problem," Erich consoled him.

"Stop whining," added Helmut, slapping Paul on the back and practically knocking him over. "We've got bugger all to do anyway but eat Panzer dust."

"The Raven will get us mixed up in something; you can guarantee it," said Manfred.

"I don't know about you guys but I'm going to find some grub before it all kicks off. We don't know where the next meal will come from," Helmut continued.

"Panzer dust not enough then?" teased Erich.

"You'll not be smiling when the supply wagons fail to turn up. Have you seen some of those nags?"

"They happen to be Panje horses," said Paul. "They're quite hardy creatures."

"Well, if we run out of food, horse steak will be on the menu," responded a disgruntled Helmut. "Right, I'm off," he said, slapping Paul on the back. "See you guys on the road."

"Me too," added Manfred, following his colleague to the exit. "See you in hell."

His blonde-haired, six-foot friend Erich patted Paul on his arm. "Don't worry, it'll sort itself out. Shall I send him in?"

"Who?"

"Richter's replacement, of course."

"Oh right, yes, send him straight in."

Erich left the barn leaving Paul alone with his thoughts. He moved back to his straw bale, rubbing the scar with his left hand, thinking through what to say to his new company sergeant. At that moment, the gloomy interior of the dust-filled barn seemed to darken further and doubts about the days ahead started to descend and cloud Paul's thinking.

Chapter Two

Raising himself slowly from the bale of straw, Paul walked over to the radio set, which Bergmann had quickly placed on a temporary table made up of two rough planks of wood across two of the many straw bales lying around. The radio had been switched off. Radio silence was to be maintained until the battle commenced. The Soviets were not to be given even an inkling of what was about to be unleashed upon them. To the right of the radio was a bona-fide table, probably acquired from the nearby farmhouse or other home in the close vicinity. Its surface was covered with maps and photographs. One map showed the entire expanse of the Soviet Union, whereas another just extended to Leningrad and an even larger scale map of the immediate area. Paul ran his finger along the route they would be taking. Once the engineers had cleared a way through the minefields and the artillery had finished their potent barrage of destruction, 10th Panzer Regiment and 8th Panzer Grenadier Regiment would punch their way through the Russian lines, followed by the rest of the Division and the Raven's battalion.

Paul heard the barn door creak again as it was pushed open and the lamps flickered, caught by the gentle breeze wafting through, the curtain thrust aside. He turned to meet his replacement Company Feldwebel, his thoughts on needing to speak to Richter and thank him. He turned to face the Fallschirmjager standing by the entrance. As he did so, his jaw dropped open in disbelief.

"Max!"

The heavy-set sergeant slammed his heels together with a crack and saluted. "Permission to join the company, Herr Oberleutnant?" The stocky, square-jawed face was barely able to suppress a grin at seeing the look on his commander's face.

Dispensing with returning the salute, Paul strode over and clasped Max's powerful shoulders, looking down at his familiar company sergeant. "I don't know what the hell you're doing here, Feldwebel Grun, or how you got here, but it's bloody good to see your ugly face again."

"Ever the flatterer, sir."

Paul shook Max's shoulders, the effort barely moving the sturdy NCO, before he pulled away and, grasping Max's arm, propelled him over to the semi-circle of bales and sat him down. They sat opposite each other, Max placing his MP40 at his side and removing his *fallschirm* to join it.

With his fair hair and slightly olive-toned skin, he looked well, thought Paul.

"Well, tell all, Max, for God's sake."

Max's grin widened and he rubbed his battered nose. He was as pleased to see his commander and to be back with the unit.

"That hospital was doing my head in, sir. I was pansying around in bloody nightclothes all day. That's no way for a soldier to behave, so I left."

"You haven't got one of the nurses in trouble, have you, Max?" Paul's question was genuine. "And now you're on the run?" He burst into laughter, realising what he had just said and how absurd it must have sounded.

"You've mistaken me for someone else, sir," Max responded, a feigned mortified look on his face.

"So how did you get here?" Paul thumped Max on the knee.

"They shipped me back home to Hamburg when they realised what a pain in the arse I was going to be. Then I got wind that something was going on in the Division and pestered them until they agreed to ship me out here."

"But no one knows where we are, Max."

"Well, the clerk, she found me kind of cute… "

Paul looked at Max, bewildered. "I'd hardly call you cute. They probably thought I was the only one that could put up with you."

"The Raven… I mean, Major Volkman said something similar, sir, along the lines of 'better that he knew where I was'. Can't possibly fathom out why."

"How are your wounds? Are they fully healed?"

"Top half is fine, sir. Get a few twinges in my side occasionally. But sitting around on my arse isn't going to make it heal any quicker."

"You're not fit to fight yet, Max," said Paul, thinking aloud.

"I'll soon show these Landser how to fight, sir."

"That I can believe, Max, that I can believe. At least if you're with the unit I can keep an eye on you."

"So, what's the score then? I get the gist that something big is kicking off tomorrow."

"Come over here." Paul got up from the bale and headed over to the map table. He lifted one of the lanterns off a hook nailed into a supporting post and placed it on the edge of the table, pulling out the middle-scale map.

"6th Panzer Division will be pushing through here," he said, pointing to a position on the map showing Tilsit and the River Memel, referred to as the River Nemen by the Russians. "They will then push on to Taurage, Dünaburg and then Pskov."

"The ultimate goal, sir?"

"The big prize, Max, is Leningrad."

"That's some distance, sir. Anything for us?"

"Not just yet."

"Just as well," mused Max. "I'm not convinced the unit is fully recovered. We've had less than a month to catch our breath. Another month would have been welcome."

"Does that include you, Feldwebel Grun?" asked Paul with a smile.

"Of course not, sir. Invincible me, you know that."

"Yeah, yeah," Paul was not entirely convinced.

"It's because of you I'm alive and here today, dragging me back through enemy lines. You saved my life, I'll not forget that."

"You would have done the same for me. In fact, you have done the same for me. Anyway, I'm glad you're here. The company is complete now."

"I saw Feld Richter on the way in, sir."

"I must speak to him. He's done a good job while you've been away, Max."

"So I gather, sir, but he's still in the battalion at the moment and he's happy with that."

"He had 'big boots to fill' was how he put it to me."

Before Max could respond, the barn door creaked open again and in piled Helmut, Manfred and Erich, closely followed by Paul's platoon commanders and their platoon NCOs. They immediately crowded around the stocky ex-Hamburg docker and backslaps were the order of the day.

Helmut stood back with Erich and said. "The Rottweiler is back in the fold!"

"Yes," responded Erich. "I feel much more relaxed with him back in the company. They make a tough team together and I suspect

22

Paul's going to need him in these coming days."

"I think the coming days are going to be tough on us all," replied Helmut.

"I agree. Anyway, let's go and welcome Feldwebel Grun back into the family," Erich said, steering Helmut over towards the throng.

Helmut made his way through the welcoming party and, gripping Max's hand firmly, shook it. "Back home, eh, Feld?"

"Wouldn't want to be anywhere else, sir, but you could have come up with some more salubrious surroundings." Max grinned as he gave the barn the once-over.

"Well, Oberleutnant Brand, it appears you've got the original Feldwebel Grun back. His grumblings haven't lessened any."

"We can cope with him," defended Paul, a hand on Max's muscled shoulder, secretly ecstatic to have his NCO, fellow paratrooper and friend back.

Once the furore of Max's return had died down, he requested Paul's permission to do a tour of the company, to reacquaint himself with the troops and meet the new recruits. Paul agreed and Max, along with the NCOs, left the barn, leaving Paul alone with his fellow company commanders.

"It's great to have Max back," echoed Manfred, "but I'm sorry you have to lose Richter. He's a top NCO. Your loss is my gain. I've managed to nab him."

"What's happened to Fink?" queried Paul.

"We're not really sure but he's got the shits real bad and a raging temperature. He looks like hell and smells worse."

"What are they going to do with him?" asked Helmut. "We're moving out in a few hours."

"Ship him home. The medics think it will be some time before he's fit to fight."

"Well, I shall leave you women to natter. Meanwhile, I'm going to find Feld Richter."

"I told him you'd want to see him," Manfred informed Paul. "He's waiting at my HQ."

"You mean that bloody circus tent?" sneered Helmut.

"You two might have ended up in luxury, but the real soldiers have had to rough it."

Paul and Helmut joined in with their laughter. The group then split up, Paul to find Richter and the rest to complete some final checks on their respective units.

Chapter Three

Paul, accompanied by Max, made his way along the dry, dusty track that snaked through the tall pine trees like sentinels on either side, leading him to where his company was stood to. They would all be close to their vehicles waiting for the order to embark and move out.

A Feldgendarmerie stood alert in his standard M36 combat dress. A partially luminous half moon-shaped gorget was suspended from his neck by a flat chain. The *rinkragen*, the Feldgendarmerie trademark, glinted as the moon occasionally broke through the clouds, reflecting off its silver grey surface. The man had an MP40 slung around his neck, the handle and stock gripped ready to use. He was there to act as security, but also to ensure noise was subdued and light discipline maintained. He challenged Paul and Max, who, having given the correct password, were cleared to continue on their way.

The Fallschirmjager had vacated their tented encampment which had been set amongst the gaps in the trees. In the early hours of the morning, the equipment and spare ammunition had been silently loaded onto three-ton blitz trucks, one of the workhorses of the German Army. These four-wheel drive, petrol-engine vehicles would take them into battle. Paul came to the first truck in the long column of vehicles stretching back into the depths of the forest and was met by Leutnant Ernst Leeb of number one platoon. He was grinning with barely suppressed excitement at the impending battle, his white teeth clearly seen in the darkness. Leeb had served with Paul in Poland, in the attack of Fort Eben Emael, Belgium as a troop commander, and later as a platoon commander in Greece and Crete.

"Your men ready, Ernst?" Paul whispered.

"They're ready, sir. I think they'll just be glad to move out of here. It's a bit claustrophobic."

"The waiting will be over soon. Has the personal ammunition been issued?"

"Yes, sir, sixty rounds per man for the Kar 98s and one hundred and eighty for the MP40s."

"Good, we'll go and check on the rest of the company."

"Good luck, sir. You too, Feld."

"It's the Soviets who'll need the luck, sir," growled Max.

Had it been lighter, Max would have seen both officers smiling, thinking to themselves, Feldwebel Grun is back! Paul, Max and Leeb moved along the slatted sides to the rear of the lead truck, where a group of Fallschirmjager had congregated by the tailgate. Some of the men were taking the opportunity to grab some food – something you learnt to do in these situations. A couple were digging into their iron rations looking for tins of meat; others were spreading processed cheese on a crispy, cracker-like hard bread. They were forbidden from using their esbits, solid fuel stoves, due to the blackout which meant heating water for ersatz coffee was out of the question. Uffz Fessman, commander of number one troop, who had been supervising some last-minute relocation of equipment, approached the officers and NCO.

"Your men all set, Unteroffizier Fessman?"

"Yes, sir," responded the wiry troop commander, "itching to get on with it."

"It won't be long, Walter," suggested Max. "This is one show that has to start on time."

"My boys are ready, Feld," affirmed Fessman.

"Don't forget," Max whispered to the larger group, "you are the chosen ones of the German Army," quoting the first line of one of the Fallschirmjager's ten commandments.

They left the first vehicle and groped their way to the next, the transport for the second troop of first platoon, commanded by Uffz Konrad. A similar conversation ensued before they continued on to third troop, leaving Leutnant Leeb then with his men.

Paul and Max made their way along the line of darkened vehicles making contact with Leutnant Nadel of second platoon, Leutnant Roth of third platoon; then to the end of the line where the mortar troop, commanded by Unterfeldwebel Loewe, was situated before working their way back to the head of the column.

They reached the front of the convoy. Paul would be in the lead vehicle, Max in the second. The company HQ, along with their medic Fink, would be on the truck fourth in line. All they could do now was wait. The battalion commander, situated near the middle of the convoy with Oberleutnant Bauer's second company, would send a runner at the appropriate time.

Paul and Max were standing at the front of the lead Opel Blitz and both looked up when two Chain Dogs, Feldgendarmerie, patrolled past, checking that soldiers and officers were respecting the 'no smoking' and 'no lights' orders sent down from high command. The baleful eyes of the paratroopers, who saw them as rear echelon and not real soldiers, watched the military policemen as they moved past.

Max sniffed the air; the almost antiseptic smell of the pine trees and pine needles on the ground filled his nostrils.

"It seems peaceful enough at the moment, sir," whispered Max to Paul. "It doesn't seem like we're on the verge of another war."

"It's peaceful all right, but it will be good to move out of here and out into some space."

Max peered into the forest above him. Although it was not light enough to see the tops of the trees, the impression of height was there. The trees were packed tightly either side of the track and Max understood his commander's desire to move out. A truck could either move forwards or reverse but certainly not turn round.

"I hope to God a truck doesn't break down. It'll be a right bloody mess then," said Max almost to himself.

"Moreover, Major Volkman will be even less pleased, Max."

The forest seemed to close in even tighter around them. They were situated some four kilometres from the town of Tilsit and four and a half kilometres from the River Memel where they would need to cross today. They were not the only ones tucked away secretly in assembly areas hidden from the eyes of the Soviet army. Some three million German soldiers were as close to the Soviet front line; some of the assault troops were even closer... All were waiting for the order to advance. Even now, troops were moving to the edge of the Memel, quietly observing the sleeping giant across the other side.

The air was thick and still. All that could be heard was an occasional cough or the bark of a Chain Dog reprimanding a soldier for some minor offence, ordering silence or a cigarette to be extinguished; the sporadic clink of metal as the paratroopers made last-minute adjustments to their equipment or shifted position. Each soldier did what they could to make the time pass quickly. Some slept; some ate; others sat and whispered to their *kameraden* or sat in their own reverie thinking of their families and loved ones at home. Some dared to think of the days and weeks ahead.

"Listen, sir," hissed Max

"What... what is it?"

"Over there." Max pointed high up and to the West.

Paul cupped his hand to his ear, straining to hear the sound Max had referred to. Then he heard it: a distant drone, slowly growing louder.

"Aircraft, Max."

"It's going to kick off pretty soon, sir. No turning back now."

Paul looked at the luminous dial of his watch: it was two thirty-five in the morning and it would not be long before the Soviets received a wake-up call, he thought. Above them, flying at five thousand metres, Heinkel He 111s and Dornier Do 17-7s headed west, their targets airfields, headquarters and communication centres. Shatter the Russian Air Force, isolate the army and make them leaderless. Special force units would already be springing into action. Units, such as the Brandeburgers, would be moving into position, securing bridge crossing points and attacking communication lines in readiness for the main assault that would follow.

As Paul looked up, searching for the aircraft above him, he was sure he could just make out the darker shadow of the tops of the trees against the slowly lightening sky. Dawn was a mere hour and a half away.

A runner came panting to the front of the truck, his lungs heaving as he caught his breath. "Oberleutnant Brand?"

"Yes."

"Major Volkman's compliments, sir. You are to move out at two forty-five."

"Understood, return to your unit."

"*Jawohl*, Herr Oberleutnant," the runner responded and ran back down the line of trucks to his unit, second company.

A Feldgendarmerie approached and snapped, "Who's in charge here?"

"I am, Feldwebel," Paul answered.

The military policeman saluted. "Right, sir, when you move out you are to follow me to the end of the track. It's about three hundred metres. When you get there, you'll be met by an R75 and sidecar. Turn left and they will lead you to the road junction, about a k and a half. Turn left and then you're on your own."

Paul acknowledged his instructions and the Chain Dog moved about ten metres down the track, ready to lead the convoy.

"Right, Max, let's go."

Max quickly moved down the line of vehicles giving orders

for the troopers to embark and to turn their engines over. The paratroopers clambered onboard, scoffing the last of any food they had in their hands and making themselves as comfortable as possible on the hard wooden bench seats inside the canvas-topped vehicles.

"More comfortable than Tante Ju," one trooper whispered, referring to the Junkers Ju 52, tranpsport plane.

The engines coughed and spluttered into life, the combined noise of the column of over fifty trucks shattering the silence of the forest. The drivers revved their engines gently, warming them up but conscious of the need to still keep noise to a minimum.

Max jumped up into the cab of the second Opel and Paul hauled himself up into the cab of the first in line. He looked at his watch, his heart pounding. The minute hand flicked to the nine and he ordered the Luftwaffe driver to pull forwards slowly.

The vehicles showed no lights, just a single, darkened red at the rear. The Feldgendarmerie, who almost spectre-like could just be made out, looked over his shoulder at the slowly advancing Blitz truck before stepping off the narrow track, the Fallschirmjager battalion attached to 6th Panzer Division following him.

"Stick with the Feldgendarmerie, but take it easy," Paul ordered the driver. "We have the rest of the battalion behind us."

The young driver, barely nineteen years old, put the Opel Blitz into gear and started to crawl forwards, immediately followed by Max's vehicle carrying the second troop of first platoon. Travelling at less than ten kilometres an hour over the rutted track, it took them five minutes to get to the junction where the military police BMW motorcycle and sidecar waited for them.

As soon as Paul's truck nosed its way onto the track that cut across in front of them and they turned left, the rider gunned his motorbike and their speed picked up to twenty kilometres an hour. This track was a little wider and not as rough. In places, though, logs had been laid across where heavy vehicles and tanks had gouged deep furrows earlier in the week. Some of the logs had sunk or shifted and the steering wheel was wrenched from the driver's hands as a front wheel caught a half-submerged log, jarring the vehicle and causing Paul's teeth to gnash together.

A kilometre and a half later, they reached the end of the forest track. There was a metalled road crossing west to east in front of them. East would take them towards Tilsit, only four kilometres away. The Chain Dog waved them to the left and the driver turned onto the road, maintaining a speed of no more than thirty kilometres an hour at Paul's instruction. After a kilometre, Paul ordered the driver to slow down and pull over to the side of the road, close up against the forest treeline, giving the rest of the convoy a chance to escape the forest and join him. With over fifty trucks, it was probable some had only just reached the first junction.

He checked his watch: it was three ten, five minutes until 'H hour' when all hell would break loose. Opening the window of the cab, he leant out. By now, the air was quite warm. Looking up, he saw a glint of the moon appear from behind the steely grey clouds. He peered round behind him and could see and hear the other vehicles pulling up behind him as they had been instructed by the Raven.

"This waiting, sir, it's worse than being in a dentist's waiting room," suggested the driver.

Paul turned his head and looked at the young man who was licking his lips and fumbling with a pack of cigarettes. He was obviously a smoker who was suffering as much from the lack of a smoke as he was waiting for the impending battle.

"The way you drive, I feel that I need the dentist! It'll kick off soon enough," Paul reassured him. "Then we'll all be wanting it over." He opened the door and stepped down from the cab.

Almost immediately he was joined by Max. "The gunners will be doing their stuff soon, sir."

"Yes, they will. The Group's guns will be pounding for all they're worth."

Max did not have a chance to respond for, just at that moment, the first salvos of shells were launched mercilessly at the Russian positions, shattering the stillness of the early dawn. Paul looked west and could see the rapid flashes of gunfire against the pale dawn sky. He knew that, in Army Group North's sector alone, an orchestra of over a thousand big guns would be pounding the Russian positions opposite and along the entire Barbarossa front. Up to seven thousand artillery pieces would be unleashing a hailstorm of death and destruction. The screaming shells could be heard overhead as they were propelled towards the enemy. It was easy to imagine the devastation they would be causing to all those sons of Mother Russia.

When he turned to the east, towards the town of Tilsit and beyond the River Memel, he could see the oily black and yellow smoke billowing up into the emerging sky. A never-ending stream of projectiles continued to ply their way overhead. More and more clouds of swirling smoke filled the morning sky marking the spot where death and human destruction was being played out; a signature of war but one that was needed to bring success ever closer.

"*Scheisse*, sir. I've not seen the like before."

"I'm glad I'm not on the receiving end of that lot," responded Paul as he flinched at some shells as they ripped through the air just above their heads.

"I hope to God the arty boys know we're here," uttered Max who had also involuntarily ducked. He turned round and patted Paul's shoulder. "We've got company, sir."

Paul followed Max's gaze and his eyes rested upon what he thought was a *kubblewagen* bouncing along the road, following the line of the parked up trucks. The vehicle came to a halt; the swirl of dust that was following behind catching up and settling on the occupants and anyone else in the immediate vicinity.

"Bloody country," swore Volkman as he heaved himself out of his VW Jeep, dusting himself down. Even when dressed for combat, the battalion commander looked immaculate, almost as if on parade, his swagger stick endlessly tapping his leg. He had chosen to wear a four-pocket Tuchrock, in preference to the Fliegerbluse or Knochensack, along with his combat trousers and highly polished number two pattern jump boots. Bachmeier, his orderly, had clearly been busy. His tunic was adorned with the ribbon of the Iron Cross second class and, pinned to his left pocket, the Iron Cross first class. He also displayed his Luftwaffe ground assault badge and, taking pride of place, his parachute badge.

"Getting a bit of a hammering, aren't they, Brand?"

"So long as they soften them up for us, sir," retorted Max.

"Softer the better, eh, Feldwebel Grun?"

"When are we going to get in the fight, sir?"

Paul flashed Max a warning glance.

"Not just yet," replied the battalion commander, used to Max's impromptu comments. "Landser work isn't for us. Our masters are no doubt saving something special for you, Feldwebel Grun. How are the new recruits settling in?"

"We could have done with a bit more time to shake them out a little, sir," declared Paul, "but we have plenty of experience in the unit to hold their hand."

"Not too much hand holding, eh, Feldwebel Grun?"

"Of course not, sir," responded Max with a grin.

A sudden explosion of sound made them all duck as the artillery fire, which had seemingly been unsynchronised, were suddenly in tune with each other, a large number of shells bracketing the enemy with their devastation.

"When do we move out from here, sir?" asked Paul

"Patience, Brand, you're worse than the Feld here. The engineers have got to do their bit first."

"Have the bridges been secured?"

They involuntarily ducked again as more shells flew low overhead. More death and destruction heading east.

"They've been secured and, once the engineers have dealt with any mines and removed the explosives from beneath the bridge, the forward unit will push through."

"Who has that pleasure, sir?" inquired Helmut who, along with Manfred and Erich, had joined the group gathered around the lead vehicle.

"The 114th Motorised Infantry Regiment has that pleasure, Janke. I doubt it will take them long to push a channel through the enemy positions. The Russians are starting to crumble all along the line."

"This artillery will be giving the Russians a hammering, sir," chipped in Manfred.

"It will give them a headache, that's for sure," added Erich.

"Sir, sir," called Amsler, the battalion radio operator who was sitting in the back of the Jeep, "Division is after you."

"Right, gentlemen." Volkman looked at his watch which showed three forty-five. "The barrage will be finishing in about thirty minutes and the Division's follow-up units will pass through here. So, back to your vehicles. We'll be moving out at four thirty. I will give you your final instructions nearer the time, Brand." Wishing them luck, he smacked the side of his leg with his stick and strode off back to his command vehicle to take the radio message from Division. Once he had spoken with divisional command, he climbed into the VW and the *kubelwagen* did a one hundred and eighty degree turn and sped off back down the side of the parked up convoy.

"Well, boys, it's kicking off now."

"Don't get too excited, Helmut. We've still to get caught up in the fighting," cautioned Paul.

Just when Helmut was about to respond, they suddenly heard the sound that had struck fear in so many of their enemies: a steadily

31

increasing growl mixed with the piercing squeal of tortured metal and heavy chains. They all turned and looked to the west, the artillery bombardment forgotten as they saw the first of the armoured vehicles heading towards them. The lead tank was a Panzer II. The ten-ton tank, bristling with a twenty-millimetre gun and co-axial MG34, rolled towards them, the first in a long line of death machines. They could now see its flat-topped hull, its short but broad silhouette coming into view; the heavy clanking of the tracks running around the five bogie wheels getting louder. A jet of exhaust shot out of the rear as the driver picked up speed as it passed them, smoke and dust billowing behind it, the Fallschirmjager showered in grit.

"Just as I thought," uttered Max as he spat on the floor. "Eating bloody Panzer dust all the way to Moscow."

Helmut patted him on the back. "We're not going to Moscow, Max."

The group laughed, knowing though that Max had in fact spoken for them all.

A second Panzer II approached them, the tank commander's upper body out of the turret, his black tanker's uniform and beret distinctive in the rapidly improving light. "When we've mopped up the Russkies," he shouted over the noise of the tank's engine, "we'll give you a call." Then he laughed.

"We'll look after your girlfriends while you're away," Max shouted after the passing tank, his hand cupped round his mouth so he could be heard above the din of the six-cylinder petrol engines.

"You wouldn't want to. She's ugly," shouted the tank commander of the third tank as it growled past them.

A fourth Panzer II followed, then another. The sixth tank that followed the lead elements of 11 Panzer Regiment of the 6th Panzer Division was much larger. At around twenty tons, the Panzer IV AusF, was twice as heavy and half the height again of a man and sported a 7.5 cm gun. Its turret swung away from the watching paratroopers as it roared past, its V12 engine drowning out all conversation. Tank after tank thundered past the watching Fallschirmjager who were standing alongside the waiting convoy. Thick clouds of gritty dust covered the men and caught in the back of their throats causing them to spit and clear their mouths.

"Christ, the Russkies are in deep shit," exclaimed Helmut.

"Never mind the Russians," added Erich. "They put the fear of God into me."

The ground trembled beneath their feet as the tanks pressed on towards their objective: the eastern side of the River Memel. They accelerated, exhaust fumes forming a blue cloud that engulfed the convoy they were passing. Once the Panzer IVs left the watching soldiers behind, Panzer 35(t)s took their place. When the German Army occupied Czechoslovakia in 1938, over two hundred LT-35 tanks were incorporated into the Panzer tank units and redesignated Panzer 35(t). This ten-ton tank, with its 37mm armament, was the mainstay of 6 Panzer Division's armour. The paratroopers stared in awe as tank after tank passed them, three battalions in total. Hot on their heels was the 4th Motorised Infantry Regiment. The 114th Motorised Infantry Regiment, along with the 57th Panzer Engineer Battalion and the 57th Panzer Reconnaissance Battalion had already fought their way across the bridge and were moving deeper into Lithuania. The rest of the Division, 6th Motorcycle Battalion, 76th Panzer Artillery Regiment, 41st Panzer Jaeger Battalion, with their 37mmm and 50mm anti-tank guns, 76th Flak Battalion and the 82nd Signals Battalion, would be moving by a different route, but the objective was the same: Russia.

"Christ, this is never bloody ending." Max shouted his frustration above the pandemonium.

"Let the Panzers do some of the hard work for a change," chorused Helmut and Erich.

"We'd better get back to our units. See you in hell, Paul," shouted Helmut as he headed back towards his company, joined by Erich and Manfred, careful to keep tight into the side for fear of getting knocked down by the armour thundering by.

Paul looked at his watch; it was now four fifteen. The battle for Russia had been going for an hour, yet it already felt much longer. The follow-up elements of the Division had been passing for thirty minutes, the column never-ending. A *Kubelwagen* suddenly shot out from between two vehicles carrying the infantry from the 4th Regiment and slowed to a halt just ahead of Paul's truck. The Raven leapt out.

"Here, Brand."

Volkman moved to the far side of the cab of the vehicle and proceeded to unfold a map onto the grey-blue bonnet of the truck. "6th Division is making good progress. The 114th have secured their objectives and now it's up to the Panzers to exploit the gap which I'm sure they'll do admirably. We move out after the 4th have passed so you'll need to get out sharpish. We then stick to their tail like glue to Taurage." He tapped the map. "We're not going through the centre. We'll follow this road east for about three kilometres until we get to here, in between these two small wooded areas. Here you need to turn south. Understood?"

"Yes, sir," acknowledged Paul, his eyes frantically scanning the map, making marks on his own map in front of him.

"Once you turn south, you follow the edge of this small lake here until you get to the end, then head east. That will take us straight over the bridge."

Volkman looked at his young Oberleutnant, who was clearly suppressing the excitement he felt, although the battalion commander could see it in his eyes.

"Once over the bridge, we stick with the landser until we get to Taurage. It's about thirty kilometres. I reckon you have about thirty minutes, Brand. Any questions?"

"Will we have any task assigned to us, sir?"

"No, not yet. The Panzers will be pushing their way through and the infantry will be mopping up. But there could possibly be scattered Russian units, separated from their main force, so be prepared to react."

"How will I know the last vehicle has passed, sir?"

"There will be a Feldgendarmerie outrider. They know where you are and will indicate for you to pull out. There will be a gap before the next unit, the motorcycle battalion, comes through, but you'll need to be damn quick." He slapped his swagger stick against his leg again. "Right, Brand, let's go and good luck."

Chapter Four

The waiting was over; the last truck of the motorised infantry regiment finally passed. The Feldgendarmerie pulled up in a *Kubelwagen*. The Hauptmann, commanding one of the military police troops responsible for the control of the traffic heading towards the eastern front, leapt out and called over to Paul. "Oberleutnant, you need to get your vehicles moving quickly. The next unit is less than five minutes behind me."

"*Jawohl*, Herr Hauptmann," responded Paul. "*Schnell*," he shouted to his driver. "Get the engine turned over now."

He looked back as the Feldgendarmerie Hauptmann jumped into his Jeep and sped off. Then he turned to the second truck and signalled to Max to move out, pumping his right fist up and down in the air.

"We're moving!" he shouted as Max stuck his head through the door window. "Let's go."

Max pulled his head back into the cab and quickly patted the driver on the shoulder. "Right, let's get this battle wagon moving."

Paul leapt back into the cab of his truck and the driver immediately slammed the vehicle into gear and pulled out onto the road, the sound of the Opel Blitz trucks racing their engines behind them competing with the incessant noise of the shells still flying overhead making their way to their targets.

The Blitz crawled up the shallow verge and away from the trees, rocking the cab and its cargo of paratroopers as its front wheels edged onto the metalled, dusty road. Once the wheels found solid ground, the driver gunned the engine and it lurched forwards, shouts of "be bloody careful" coming from the back.

Paul looked into his wing mirror and, to his satisfaction, saw Max's truck angled on the road just straightening up, others also pulling out to follow Paul's lead. He looked up and through the windscreen saw four Stukas flying low overhead, their swept back, gull-shaped wings ominous and threatening, heading east towards the front. Their bomb loads were visible, ready to hit the enemy hard in support of the troops on the ground. They were the Panzer's airborne artillery.

Ahead, Paul could see the *Kubelwagen* had caught up with the tail end of the Infantry convoy, the one they were to follow. He squinted as the low sun's rays flashed from behind the clouds of the rapidly brightening day.

"Floor it. Stick close to that unit ahead," ordered Paul, impatient to get moving and not wanting to lose contact with the battalion in front of them. He unfolded his map and pressed it down on the dashboard, smoothing it out, refreshing his memory of the route the Raven had instructed him to take.

Crump, crump, crump.

Paul flinched as the explosions erupted two hundred metres to their right, in the open fields. The driver flicked the steering wheel, nearly causing the truck to swerve onto the right-hand verge, bringing it back on line just in time.

"Careful," yelled Paul, "keep it on the road. They're firing blind; they haven't got a target." He could imagine the curses in the back as they were thrown against the slatted, wooden sides.

"The Russians have woken up and are trying to hit back," he murmured.

Checking his wing mirror again, he instructed the driver, "Move over to the left. I want to check behind us."

The driver eased the Blitz over to the middle of the road and, using the driver's wing mirror, Paul scanned his charges following behind, satisfied that at least the front element was sticking close.

"We've caught up, sir," the driver informed him.

They were now within ten metres of the *Kubelwagen* and twenty metres of the last troop carrier of the 4th motorised infantry regiment. They crossed a railway bridge, the railway running south to north curving east to join the main railway siding in the town of Tilsit. After about a kilometre, they left the arable area and the forest and moved into the suburbs of the town, leading them briefly to another small forest before exiting out the other side. Paul checked his map again; it was already coated by the never-ending dust. The long, heavily laden convoys heading east were churning up a maelstrom of debris in the dry conditions making it dangerous for the drivers behind, enveloping them in a cloud of dust and often forcing them to drive blind. It was not unknown for vehicles to find themselves crashing into the one in front. Paul's driver needed to stay alert.

Trailing his finger across his map, Paul compared their location with that on the map and was satisfied that he knew where they were. They shot out of the trees and were back in the suburbs, Paul scanning right looking for a road that would take them off the main route and parallel with a small lake.

"We'll be coming off right soon, so get ready."

The truck and the Feldgendarmerie ahead suddenly turned off in a swirl of dust.

"There, there," instructed Paul, pointing, "stick close to them."

"*Jawohl.*"

They swung right, onto a much narrower and even poorer quality road, running towards the lake to their southeast. They crossed over a narrow tributary that fed the small lake then tracked left, keeping the lake on their left. They continued north-east, just catching glimpses of the lake as they drove alongside the treeline. Another kilometre found them at a T-junction by the north-eastern tip of the water. Turning left, the road took them across an overpass and they were then back on the other side, the River Memel now on their right. Paul instructed the driver to turn right immediately and they crossed over heading directly towards the river. Keeping up with the leading unit, the driver suddenly slammed on the brakes as they skidded to a halt less than a metre from the vehicle in front, throwing Paul forward against the windscreen. He turned to the driver, his look being enough.

A motorcycle and sidecar roared up to the *Kubelwagen*. An Unteroffizier got off and spoke to the Hauptmann and after two minutes was back on his motorcycle and roaring down the length of the convoy behind them.

"Wait here, but keep the engine running," ordered Paul as he eased himself out of the cab, dropping to the ground, quickly joined by Max.

"Bogged down already, sir?"

"We'll soon find out. Wait here." He approached the *Kubelwagen* up ahead on the right. "Is there a problem up ahead, sir?"

The Hauptmann turned to face him, smiling, unusual for a military policeman. "Itching to get into the fight, Oberleutnant?"

"Just fed up with all the hanging around, sir, same as everyone else."

"It's just a traffic jam. One bridge and half a division to get across, plus what's following behind us."

"How long, sir?"

"Shouldn't be more than five minutes. They're just moving some tanks and supplies through and then it's our turn. Seems the division is running out of ammunition already. Must have been some fight. They need infantry upfront. The Russians are crumbling so fast, we can't keep up with them."

"That's good news, sir."

"Well, you know what the Fuhrer said, 'Kick in the door and the entire rotten structure will fall in'. You'll get your chance soon, Oberleutnant."

"I hope so."

The truck drivers ahead started to rev their engines in preparation to move out.

"This is it, Oberleutnant. Good luck."

Paul saluted and returned to the cab of his lead truck, pulling himself up into his seat, Max looking up expectantly.

"Your question is answered, Max, we're off again."

Max rushed back to his vehicle and Paul slammed the cab door. "Let's go."

The driver selected a gear and the Blitz pulled forward trailing the lead convoy again. Crawling along the road, heading towards the River Memel directly ahead, they reached a quadrangle, leading to the bridge access.

"Bloody hell, some traffic jam," declared the driver.

"You're not kidding," rejoined Paul, his eyes wide at the volume of vehicles all converging on the access point to the bridge.

"If those bombers come back now, we're stuffed," the driver said.

Paul ignored his outburst, scanning the roads joining the square. Opposite, the road had a line of Krupp-Protze Kfz.81s, the Flak 38s mounted on the rear of the six-wheeled artillery tractor. Opposite and left, a line of towed Pak 36s, 3.7cm anti-tank guns and, to their immediate left, a mass of support vehicles jammed into three lines. There were trucks, wagons, bicycles, motorcycles; an endless line that went back as far as Paul could see. The driver is right, he thought, a tasty target for the Russian Air Force. He looked up, quickly scanning the skies for any more black dots.

Then it was their turn. The engine roared as the driver picked up speed and, within moments, they were on the bridge, crossing the Memel at last. They were quickly across, the bank on the other side scattered with 2cm flak guns, the barrels pointed upwards, the commander of the battery scanning the skies for any potential threat.

Once off the bridge, they passed through a scattering of farms on both sides of the road; then it was wide open spaces, kilometres of meadows and pastures, along with cultivated fields, some of golden young wheat. In the sunlight, it almost looked beautiful.

They raced towards Taurage, some thirty kilometres away, the fields spread out either side as far as the eye could see on this now bright and sunny day. They continued north-east, Junkers ground attack aircraft growling overhead. The road was wide enough for two vehicles side by side and, if hard over, even room for small vehicles to travel down the centre. Looking out in front, Paul could see clouds of dense smoke billowing up into the sky, the Luftwaffe bombing their targets relentlessly as the advance elements of 6th Panzer Division fought the Russians for control of Taurage.

Within a matter of minutes, they came across the first unequivocal signs of the destruction of war that day. In front, a choking black cloud of oily smoke blanketed the road. Like a stranded turtle, a Soviet tank, a BT-7, lay in front of them upside down, its thirteen tons and 45mm gun rendered completely impotent. The unlucky crew of three, trapped inside, had clearly experienced an excruciating and horrific death. Behind that, a second tank, the same type, its turret fifty metres away. The tank's hull was just a burnt-out shell. Bodies were lying close by, their faces contorted, no longer human. No longer someone's son.

"They've had a hammering by the looks of it, sir," pointed out the driver as he maneouvred the truck through the dense smoke, crawling past the shell.

"Yes," agreed Paul, "but we haven't had it all our own way." He indicated the totally demolished PzKpfw 35(t) immediately beyond and on the right; it was hardly recognisable as a tank.

The convoy continued at a steady speed of between five and fifteen kilometres an hour, the sounds of battle getting louder the closer they got to Taurage. They left the wide open space for a short while, driving through the forest near the town of Bubliske. Once clear, they bore right after three kilometres. Up until now, they had been heading just east of north, now they were heading north-east, again across open country, more cultivated fields partly obscured by the constant clouds of choking dust being kicked up by the infantry vehicles ahead of them.

"What's that, sir?"

"What are you looking at?"

"There, sir," the driver pointed, "up there."

"I can't see anything," responded Paul, impatiently peering through the dusty and grimy windshield.

"There, sir." The driver pointed again, trying to hide his exasperation. "Four of them, do you think they're ours?"

"I see them now. Yes, they must be ours. There are three, not four."

Paul now tracked the black specks but the dusty window made it difficult to identify the growing black dots. I must clean this windshield when we next stop, thought Paul, frustrated at not being able to pick them out clearly.

"They could be those Stukas we saw earlier, sir," suggested the driver, crashing through the gears as the convoy picked up speed again, "on their way back from bombing the Russians."

Paul couldn't take his eyes off them, determined to identify the German planes as they got closer. They dropped lower and suddenly seemed to be coming straight at the convoy, their speed of over three hundred kilometres an hour bringing them rapidly within striking distance.

"They could be Stukas," mused Paul anxiously, "but the wings—"

He did not get any further as flashes of light shot from the front of the nearest aircraft, its two companions lined up behind, directly along the column of the motorcade.

"*Scheisse*," screamed Paul. "Pull over now."

The driver wrenched the steering wheel over to the right and the truck's front wheels ploughed up and onto the verge.

"Out, out, get some cover."

Paul leapt out of the cab, the driver throwing himself across the seat close behind his officer to join him outside. Making his way quickly to the back of the truck, Paul shouted to his men and banged on the slatted sides of the canvas-covered truck. By now they clearly knew something was wrong. "*Schnell, schnell*, out, out, aircraft, get to cover now."

As he got to the tailgate, his men piled out over the top, throwing themselves down onto the verge, seeking the small dip on the other side. They had come under fire from aircraft before; they had no intention of staying with the vulnerable vehicles.

Herzog, Petzel and Stumme tore past him, Petzel already setting up the MG34. Stumme, his number two, fed a fifty-round belt of ammunition into the tray. Placing the barrel on the top of a fence, Petzel crouched down and, aiming high, opened fire hoping to stop the airborne onslaught, but to no avail.

The 23mm and 7.92mm rounds fired by the enemy aircraft, smacked into the vehicles near the front of the convoy, kicking up slivers of the stony road, some rounds striking the landser as they flung themselves onto the verge, gripping the tufts of grass, pulling themselves in, hoping to escape the attack.

The first aircraft screamed overhead, its liquid-cooled V12 engine roaring as it clawed the plane of death through the air. The pilot was far from finished. As Paul turned to follow its path, a black shape separated from the aircraft's belly and he went cold knowing instinctively what it was and what would happen next as the six hundred kilogram payload was released. The resulting explosions rocked the air about them, the shockwaves and ferocious heat felt by Paul and the men close to him.

The zip of Petzel's MG34 could be heard along with others, making it difficult for the Russian pilots as another plane screamed over, its red star emblazoned wings defying the German army to bring it down.

Max threw himself by Paul's side. "Fuckers! Where the bloody hell is the Luftwaffe when you need them?"

"We're about to find out, Max," said Paul, pointing east.

A dozen black specks could be seen in a line high up. The lead plane banked over, followed by its comrades, screaming down towards the enemy planes that, seeing the danger, were reluctantly breaking off from their attack. The Ilyushin aircraft scattered. Outnumbered and vulnerable, and pressed by the German hunters, they sought to escape. None made it home that day.

Max jumped up and blew his whistle. "Report, all units report." He moved down the line checking with his men, gathering information on their status so he could report back to his commander.

Paul looked back down the line of vehicles. Grey clouds of smoke filled the sky and flames leapt up into its midst as the fire looked for more fuel to feed its voracious appetite.

"I think the battalion's taken a hit," he called to Max.

"It's right at the other end, sir," Max shouted back. "Probably Oberleutnant Bauer or Janke. At least it's not the fuel trucks. We'd have known about it otherwise," he added before continuing down the line, calling for the platoons to report. The sound of a *kubelwagen* sliding to a halt could be heard on the other side of the truck, and the Raven quickly joined them.

"Your company intact, Brand?"

"Feldwebel Grun is checking now, sir, but I don't think we've taken any hits. The landser upfront may have taken a few knocks. What about the rest of our battalion?"

"Bauer's lost two trucks, but the men were out in time so only a few minor injuries."

"Thank God. That was close, sir."

"Yes, Brand, exactly. We'll be moving again soon, so be ready. They've taken Taurage, so we'll stop over there, regroup and I'll issue new orders."

A motorcycle combination roared up alongside the truck, using the gap created as a result of the vehicles having pulled over to the side. The passenger shouted across, "Get back on the road. Move now, but keep to the right. We'll be bringing vehicles alongside you. Shift." Then, with a roar from the BMW engine, he was off, shouting instructions as he went west down the line of vehicles.

"Right, Brand, do as he says. Once you find somewhere in Taurage where you can pull over, do so. Then we can regroup."

"*Jawohl*, Herr Major."

Volkman hurried back down the unit lines. After reporting to Paul that the company was intact, Max went to his vehicle and Paul climbed back up into the cab of his truck, the engine was already running. Paul instructed the driver to pull out and catch up with the vehicle in front that was already disappearing in a cloud of dust.

No sooner were they off the verge when they were joined by a number of other vehicles: a Horsch cross-country ammunition carrier; a Krupp-Protze Kfz.81 towing a 3.7cm pak; medical vehicles and SdiKfz.221 light-armoured reconnaissance vehicles jockeyed for position along the narrow stretch of road. At times it was wide enough for the two columns and also a central area where smaller vehicles could force their way through to the front. Other times, the trucks were almost touching. The traffic concertinaed, stopping and starting, passing burning tanks and vehicles that had been pushed off the road. Black smoke blinded the drivers causing them to brake suddenly for fear of hitting the vehicle in front. Sometimes their speed was barely a crawl, occasionally a respectable speed of twenty kilometres an hour; the driver continually working his way expertly up and down the gears.

Paul looked out to his right to a battery of 150mm s.FH18 artillery pieces in an expansive meadow which were packing up to move further forward having completed their task of lobbing shells into the enemy earlier in the day as part of the softening up process for the capture of Taurage.

It was three in the afternoon and his eyes were heavy with sleep. The warm air and often rhythmic movement of the Blitz were dragging at his eyelids, pulling them down, tempting sleep as they approached the outskirts of Taurage. He rubbed his eyes and turned to the driver who was doing the same, peering forward, concentration evident, so he did not pile into the vehicle in front or one of those alongside.

"We'll be stopping soon," Paul encouraged him. "Then you can have a break."

"I'm ready for it. My bloody arms are dropping off. Sorry, sir."

"That's OK, not long now. Stick with it for a while longer."

They had been advancing for the last hour at a gruellingly slow pace, shunting forwards every few seconds. The reason became apparent as they arrived at the approaches to the town. The bridge over the River Juna was down. The steel-arched bridge had collapsed in the middle, its back broken, destroyed during the heavy fighting to occupy the town. The engineers had erected a makeshift bridge spanning the fast-flowing river and were already working on a second that was, as yet, incomplete. This meant that only single-lane traffic could cross, creating the traffic jam they were now leaving behind. They rattled over the bridge, now merging with other units as the two lanes became one. The driver changed gear, the engine straining as it suddenly had to find the speed and power to pull its three-ton load up the embankment. Once at the top of the embankment, they continued along the road, passing burnt out houses, most with blown out windows and no roof, a testament to the fierceness of the battle that had been fought there. They had entered their first major town in Lithuania. The road flattened out, the convoy remaining in a single column, trees bordering the road to the right, alongside a deep ditch. To the left was a line of telegraph poles spaced out and still standing, the wire intact. Ahead of them, they could see more clouds of smoke, some of the buildings still ablaze together with wrecks of tanks and other forms of equipment. The Stukas had clearly been busy, and effective, thought Paul.

Once deep into the town, he ordered the driver to pull over to the left, by a row of bombed out buildings. On the opposite side, more houses had been either destroyed by bombs, shells or tank gunfire. The picket fences were still standing, but the buildings were mere skeletons. It did not really matter; the German army now occupied the town.

They had stopped next to a three-storey block, no windows, no door and no floors and the top floor was open to the sky.

"Switch off," ordered Paul, and he jumped down from the cab, the Raven's battalion lining up behind him, the other vehicles shooting past. "Wait here, but stay with the vehicle. Try and grab some kip if you can. We don't know how long we're going to be here."

The driver did not need any persuading; he was exhausted. His head was back against the seat, his mouth open, and he was asleep in seconds.

A *kubelwagen* careered to a halt alongside Paul after swinging in front of the lead truck, bringing a cloud of dust with it. It carried his battalion commander and adjutant.

"Brand, thirty kilometres already and our troops are still pushing forward." The Raven was rubbing his hands together almost with glee.

"What's next for us then, sir?"

"We are to wait here for further instructions. Division will be on the radio within the hour, so you need to find us a building we can use as a temporary battalion HQ. Then I want the officers and senior NCOs brought together for a briefing." Volkman looked at his adjutant, Hauptman Bach. "Yes, Major, twenty hundred?"

"Yes, but if there's any change I'll inform you."

The adjutant turned to Paul. "Make sure you get your men fed. There's a field kitchen back there. They have instructions to provide us with a meal and hot drink."

Paul licked his lips at the thought of a drink, his mouth gritty from the constant invasion of dust. "That will please Oberleutnant Janke, sir," he joked.

The Raven gave him a stern look. "We're not here to feed Janke's eating habits. Twenty hundred then." He turned on his heel, leaving the two Fallschirmjager officers alone, until Max joined them.

"What's the score then, sir?"

"We need to find a temporary HQ, Max. I'll leave that with you."

"Will do, sir," replied Max and he set off to complete his task.

"Join me, Paul," said the adjutant. "We can brief the rest of the company commanders as we move down the column."

Chapter Five

There were no buildings in the near vicinity that had a roof, but they did manage to find a building, although open to the sky, that had solid walls and seemed to be stable. Once the troopers had cleared away some of the rubble, it was satisfactory for the battalion commander to use to brief his men.

The company commanders, Paul, Erich, Helmut and Manfred were perched on a couple of tables salvaged from the bomb-damaged local buildings. The platoon commanders and NCOs were less comfortable resting on blocks of bricks and upturned bits of furniture, Leeb managing to find a three-legged chair to balance on. They were all chatting about the day's events, the first full day of Operation Barbarossa, and the close call with the Russian bombers.

"Shun," called Oberfeldwebel Schmidt as the battalion commander entered the gaping hole where the door used to be. It was now dark and he used a shaded torch to pick their way through the rubble. It was the end of a long summer's day and full lights had been banned due to the risk from the Russian Air Force, who were still flying the odd sortie.

Volkman could just pick out the pale faces of the troops in the dim light. "I'm sorry the surroundings aren't more salubrious, but it seems the Luftwaffe have been a bit heavy-footed as usual."

This brought a laugh from the group, one of the rare moments of humour from the Raven.

"The next stage," he said, giving his usual slap of the thigh with his swagger stick. As he continued to speak, there was the occasional distant explosion, reminding them all that some poor bastards were out there fighting as he spoke, and some would never see the next day.

"Now we're across the Memel and Juno, the next step is to punch through to the Dvina and force a river crossing." Volkman paused for a moment, collecting his thoughts.

"We will go via Raseiniai and Panevezys. It is a three hundred kilometre push. The days will be long and the nights short. With the current speed of 6th Division's advance, we will have to drive all through tomorrow if we wish to keep pace with them." He looked at his watch with a shielded torch. "It is twenty hundred hours now, we will pull out of here at o four hundred. Questions?"

"What about fuel, sir?" asked Paul. "We've only gone about thirty kilometres but have burnt up a lot of petrol."

"Good point, Brand. Hauptman?"

Kurt Bach, the adjutant, cleared his throat. "Fuel will be available tonight, so you need to make sure your drivers get their trucks topped up. Are our reserves still intact, Oberleutnant Janke?"

"Yes, sir, just glad the Russkies didn't hit any of those trucks."

"Thank you for your wise words, Janke," responded the Raven, but with the trace of a smile behind his normally stern face.

"How far forward are our advance units, sir?" questioned Erich.

"Division informs me that Panzer Regiment 11 are approaching Raseiniai, supported by the 114th motorised infantry regiment, with the 4th regiment not far behind," answered Bach. "The reconnaissance battalion is already pushing out a screen seeking out the enemy positions and further weak spots."

"What about the bigger picture, sir?"

"I'll answer Oberleutnant Bauer's question," interrupted the Raven. "Elements of the 18th Army have pushed forwards to our north as deep as sixty kilometres and 8th Panzer Division as much as eighty, capturing crossing points over the Dubysa River at Ariogala."

There were gasps of surprise from the group present. All felt that the Soviets would be defeated quickly, but none of them expected to have pushed so deep in just one day.

"As to the larger picture, it's still sketchy but both Army Group Centre and Army Group South are making good progress."

"Have we a task yet, sir?" asked Paul, almost pleading.

Just then sudden crashes of artillery fire ripped through the air close by. Flares launching skyward lit up the building in an eerie light, scintillating through the vacant windows, flickering over the Raven and giving him an almost manic look. His eyebrows shaded the light from his eyes, which remained dark and deep-set.

"As I've said before, Oberleutnant Brand, we will get an opportunity to make our contribution. Until then, don't be overly keen to get involved with the first fight that comes along. Take the time to acclimatize. A fight will come to us soon enough."

"But it will all be over in a few months, sir," piped up Manfred.

Volkman remained quiet, reflecting on how he was going to respond to these types of questions. "Why are my officers so keen to get into the thick of it?" he said in a slightly exasperated tone. "The Soviet Union, gentlemen, is immense, the Russian Army huge. Yes, it may seem weak at the moment. It may lack the expertise of the German Army, but it is not going to roll over and die without a fight. They have close to three and a half million soldiers waiting to make every German soldier pay the price for every metre of ground we take."

The men shuffled uncomfortably, clearly taken aback by their commander's lack of enthusiasm, having been led to believe the forces of the Third Reich were invincible and that the enemy would crumble quickly. But they also trusted their leader, Volkman.

Recognising the effect his words had on his men, he added, "But we are the German warrior incarnate." He quoted from one of the Fallschirmjager Ten Commandments. "With us supporting our advancing armies, we will have victory."

Pride swelled up inside his officers and NCOs.

"Right, gentlemen, we move out at four. Dismissed."

"Shun," called Oberfeldwebel Schmidt and the men came to attention as Volkman and Bach left the bombed out building.

Paul sought out Max, his bulk easy to pick out in the shadows of the darkened house.

"Nice speech, sir. Do think the Russians are aware that we're coming?"

"Watch it, Max, you'll go too far one day," chided Paul as he punched the iron-like arm then wishing he had not.

Leeb, Roth and Nadel joined them.

"The priority is fuel first. I want all the trucks topped up then the men can get some food, but not before, understood?"

"*Jawohl*, Herr Oberleutnant," they all responded.

"Feldwebel Grun, suss out where the field kitchen is. I'm sure the divisional echelon will have something organised."

"Will do, sir."

"The men need to stay close to their trucks. We may be counter-attacked at any time. Ensure you have platoon sentries and I want a company watch; a half troop patrolling the length of our section of the convoy throughout the night."

"But, sir," protested Roth, "the Russians will be kilometres away by now. "

"I would hope so, Viktor, but I'm not taking any chances, understood?"

"Yes, sir."

"Feldwebel Grun, Leutnant Roth's platoon has volunteered for the company duty."

"Understood, sir."

"So, vigilance. Think back to Crete: the unit we bounced because they didn't think we were there; the counter-attack that later bounced us. Right, get to it. Feld, let me see the duty rosters and patrol timings once the platoon commanders make them available."

"Yes, sir."

"Get to it then. Fuel! Dismissed."

The officers returned to their platoons and Max walked back to the lead vehicle with his company commander.

"A bit uneventful so far, sir, apart from the Russian bombers."

"But is it the quiet before the storm? The battalion commander clearly doesn't think we're in for a walkover."

"Once they give us our head, sir, we'll soon sort them out."

Paul patted Max's shoulder. "You're a one-man army all on your own, Max," he said, laughing. "Get those lists for me then we can get some food and kip while we can."

"And a nice backdrop to lull you to sleep, sir," said Max pointing towards the east and the regular flashes of gunfire and the occasional larger explosion.

Uffz Daecher, the commander of the Pzkpfw 35 (t), leant his shoulder against the turret hatch, scanning the area about him. It was just light enough to enable him to see about half a kilometre ahead. To the left and right, other tanks of his platoon belonging to the 6th Panzer Division and 11th Panzer Regiment crawled forward across the open ground towards their objective: Raseiniai.

His platoon was the advance element and, although it had been a tough fight so far, he reflected that the Russians were being pushed back relentlessly.

He was thrown forward as the tank jerked suddenly. "Bloody hell, be careful down there," he called down to his driver.

"Sorry, Uffz, these bloody gears and this bloody tank are all crap," the driver shouted back above the noise of the engine.

As the Uffz looked up again, he saw a flash in the distance. Almost instantaneously, an armoured piercing shell caught the Panzer's twenty-five millimetre thick hull with a glancing blow, the round whining off into the distance.

"Fuck!" yelled Daecher. "Back, back, back."

The driver, having heard the impact of the solid round hitting their tank, was prepared for the order. He slammed the gears into reverse and powered the one hundred and twenty horsepower petrol engine, hauling the ten-ton monster backwards, desperately trying to escape the attack ahead of them.

"Kluge, tank, five hundred metres, anti-tank," screamed Daecher to his gunner below. He dropped down into the turret, pulling the hatch down after him, his body thrown from side to side as the retreating tank raced to get away. Peering through the episcopes situated around the cupola, he sought out the enemy who had fired at them, determined to get revenge. The tank shook violently, an eruption to their left rocking the suspension.

"Fuck, what was that?" Daecher called out, peering through his left episcope. "*Scheisse*, it's Willi. He's been hit."

Willi's tank had erupted in flames, its turret blasted upwards as a Russian KV-1 destroyed it. The 3rd Mechanised Corps of the Russian Army was counter-attacking.

"Up," yelled Kluge, having thrust a 37mm round into the breech.

"Identified," called Daecher, as he spotted the Russian behemoth through his periscope. "Stop!"

The driver braked, halting the tank from its rearward flight, the chassis rocking on its leaf-spring suspension.

The second it was stable, Daecher sighted the main gun and pulled the trigger. "On way."

"*Meier*, move out, reverse," he ordered the driver again. "The bloody thing just bounced off."

The engine screamed as the driver attempted to get them away from the rapidly advancing Russian tanks, out of range and to safety.

"Up," yelled Kluge, informing his commander that another shell had been loaded.

"Identified, stop!" Daecher yelled. He laid the gun on target and fired again. "On way".

"*Scheisse*… move out. For fuck's sake, move out," screamed Daecher, panic in his voice. "It hasn't stopped it." He peered out of his right-handed episcope to check on the other tanks in his platoon.

He saw a Panzer 35 (t) just as it was hit; the turret skewed to the left as the armoured piercing round from the KV-1 sliced through it. He looked on in horror as he saw his *kameraden* climb out of the high turret, flames engulfing their bodies as they clawed their way out only to have their bodies flung around like dolls as the 7.92mm rounds from the KV's two DT machine guns ripped into them. Thankfully a cloud of dust from his retreating tank blocked out their last final moments.

For the first time he felt fear and ordered another stop as he fired again, to see yet another attempt fail as the round just bounced off the seemingly impregnable monster.

Suddenly his world went silent, just a ringing in his ears. A piece of the tank's armour, blasted at high speed by the armoured piercing round that had punched its way through the turret ring just below the barrel, had shattered, a deadly rain of splinters whipping into the crew. One lethal piece had gouged through the side of his neck, a second shard sliced through his leg. The loader to his left was unrecognisable; he had taken the full force of the blast. Smoke started to form inside, quickly filling the tank with its choking, toxic fumes.

"Out, out," screamed the radio operator, "my legs are burning."

Daecher flung open the hatch gasping for air, smoke billowing around him as he heaved himself up out of the turret, throwing himself backwards onto the rear engine deck of the tank, screaming as he fell on his shattered leg and rolled heavily onto the ground beside the now stationary tank. He heard the driver cry out as the machine-gun bullets started to slice him in two, causing him to fall back into the tank on top of the radio operator. Neither would leave the burning tank again. Some of the last sounds Daecher ever heard were the radio operator's screams slicing through his heart like a knife and the thought of his wife and two-year-old daughter.

As he lay on the ground in his last few moments, both legs at unnatural angles, blood hemorrhaging from the wounds on the side of his head and neck, he saw the tracks of a huge forty-five ton KV tank coming towards him, its armour three times thicker than the opponent it had just crushed, the 76mm gun spitting fire as it attempted to roll up the advancing Panzer Regiment's flank, seemingly unstoppable.

Then Daecher's world went black.

★

The Fallschirmjager officers gathered around their battalion commander in the large farmhouse, just a few yards off a narrow lane, a couple of hundred metres off the main road where the convoy had parked up and forty kilometres south-west of Raseiniai. The building had been appropriated by the Fallschirmjager to use as a covered location in which the briefing could be conducted. They had congregated around a large kitchen table in the open-plan farmhouse. In the background, two battalion HQ clerks were busy pulling together a meal and cups of coffee for the officers present. The solid oak table was strewn with maps. Paul, Helmut, Manfred and Erich looked on intently, waiting for the Raven to speak.

"We've reached the River Dubysa, gentlemen, and the advance units of the Division have swung towards Raseiniai. Unfortunately Panzer Regiment 11 has been counter-attacked by elements of the Soviet 3rd and 12th Mechanised Corps."

"Our units can handle that surely, sir," Helmut chimed in. "We have a full Panzer Division."

"You are quite right, Janke, but they seem to have come up against a new type of Russian tank and our own tanks are proving pretty ineffective against them." Volkman slapped his thigh with his stick as if to emphasise the point.

The assembled officers were aghast. Their Panzer regiments were invincible!

"But how can we stop them, sir? They could just plough through our flank," added Paul.

"It is a risk, Brand, and, even as we stand here and talk about it, there is a colossal tank battle going on now between 6th Panzer Division and the two army corps. It seems that our anti-tank guns are equally as ineffective. Only the flak 88s appear able to penetrate their armour and the Luftwaffe from Luftlotte 1 is making life exceedingly difficult for them."

"So, what's next then, sir?" asked Erich.

"Sir," shouted the battalion radio operator before Volkman could answer his officer's question, "I have Division for you."

"Study the maps, gentlemen. Familiarise yourselves with our current position. We'll be heading for the River Dvina once I've taken this call."

Volkman made his way over to the Torn.Fu.d1 radio, the transceiver set mounted on top of the battery and accessory case, which in turn was mounted upon a wooden stool. The radio was linked to a high rod antenna which had been set up outside, its distinctive horizontal, cruciform antenna on top of the pole. The radio operator handed Volkman the headphones and microphone.

Volkman removed his *fallschirm* and placed one of the headphones against his left ear. "Anton, this is Casar, over."

There was a delay as the operator at the other end of the airwaves sought out whoever it was that wanted to speak to the Fallschirmjager battalion commander.

"This is Anton. Can you read me, Casar? Over." The speaker not up against Volkman's ear crackled.

"Loud and clear, Anton. Over."

The speaker crackled again.

"What size, company or battalion? Over."

More crackling in response.

"Right, sir. We'll pick up the messenger at the agreed location. Over."

The Raven listened closely.

"Yes, sir. Best speed. Understood. Casar out."

Volkman pulled the headphone from his ear and, along with the microphone, handed them back to the radio operator. Then he walked back to the table and placed his *fallschirm* on the edge before dragging a map over towards him. He tapped the map.

"You will have to grab your food and eat on the way, gentlemen. We need to move to here as quickly as possible." His finger pointed to the town of Dvinsk. "Division needs to secure the Dvina bridges."

"Is that our task, sir?"

"No, Brand. It seems they have something else planned for us, but it can't be discussed over the open airwaves. So, we are to head north-east, circumventing Raseiniai and link up with our advancing units." He tapped the map again, this time with his stick. "But we need to head north first. Division has to secure this area and smash the counter-attack, so we need to stay well clear."

"Are they getting any assistance, sir?"

"Yes, Janke. 1st Panzer Division is coming up behind them and onto their flank, trapping them in a pincer movement."

"It shouldn't take long for them to wrap it up, sir."

"I'm not so sure, Bauer. One of their larger tanks, a KV-2, has seemingly held up the advance of our Panzers for best part of a day. Not our concern at the moment though."

He pushed the maps aside and looked at his officers one by one.

"We still have plenty of light left, so I want to push on now. Same order as before, but you need to be alert, particularly you, Brand. We're moving into unknown territory and don't know what enemy elements are still lurking out there. I suggest you have your lead troop one hundred metres ahead of the convoy. At least then you will have some warning if you come up against an ambush or the tail end of a retreating Russian unit."

"Understood, sir."

"IA drills on contact, sir?" asked Erich.

"Brand's company will hold position, your company left flank. Bauer, your company right flank. Janke, your unit in reserve. All clear?"

"*Jawohl*, Herr Major," they chorused.

"Dismissed."

They headed for their trucks, to brief their men and head deeper into hostile Russian territory.

Chapter Six

Paul and his battalion commander approached the large municipal building in the centre of the small town of Zarasai, some thirty kilometres south-west of Dvinsk. The battalion was spread throughout the town having joined other units ready for the big push across the River Dvina. It was 24 June.

They had travelled over three hundred kilometres, following the advancing army as it smashed its way through the Russian defences. Days of continuous driving through the long Russian summer days; nothing but dust and flat, open country about them. Their aim: to meet up with the headquarters elements of the XLI Panzer Corps who finally had a task for the Fallschirmjager battalion attached to them.

The landser sentries came to attention, their Kar98s slapped against their shoulders as they saluted the two officers. Passwords were exchanged, and Volkman and Brand were allowed to enter the headquarters building. They walked up a set of steps and through a wide doorway into the darker confines of the building. A clerk manning the door shuffled through his paperwork and, finding what he was looking for, confirmed their names, checked their identities and, once satisfied, escorted them to a large room at the end of the corridor.

They pushed their way through the door into a smoke-filled room, poorly lit by generator-powered lights. The windows opposite were blackened to prevent any light filtering out and giving away their position, although the Russians had an idea where the German Army was. Once inside the room, adjusting to the dim lighting and thick cigarette smoke, they looked ahead in astonishment. At the far right end of the long oak table that ran down the centre of the room stood an Oberst, a Colonel, in a Wehrmacht woollen tunic, his collar tabs showing him to be infantry. He wore grey jodhpurs and highly polished jackboots; a grey, leather greatcoat was thrown over a chair in front of him. To his left were what could only be described as two Russian officers.

Paul immediately raised his MP40. His battalion commander placed his gloved left hand on the barrel, pushing the weapon down so it faced the floor.

"All is not as it seems, Brand." Volkman advanced to the end of the table and saluted the Oberst.

Paul, following close behind, followed suit. He looked the Russians over. There was a real contrast in their uniforms. Paul was in his full combat regalia, including his splinter pattern *Knochensnack* and combat trousers, his commander in his preferred *tuchrock* and combat trousers. The Russians were similar to each other but their colours were very different. The nearest one, just to the right of the Oberst, wore a green army officer's M35 field shirt, with green collar patches piped crimson. His jodhpurs were tucked into black knee-length boots and he sported a brown leather belt carrying an M38 holster and a map case with supporting straps. He wore a green, peaked service cap. His colleague was wearing a dark blue peaked service cap with a dark red band and crimson piping. His shirt was also very different: a general officer's light grey field shirt with crimson collar and cuff patches, also piped in crimson. His shirt hung over his dark blue jodhpurs, piped in crimson and tucked into high, black, well-polished boots.

The German Oberst returned their salutes then came forward and shook Volkman's hand, followed by Paul's.

"Thank you for getting here so promptly, Major. This must be Oberleutnant Brand you spoke about."

"Yes, Herr Oberst. He's my best company commander."

Paul's eyebrows shot up in surprise at such a compliment from his hard-nosed commander.

"Well, I shall introduce you to my other two guests: Starshiy Major Apraxin of the Russian State Security, the GUGB, and Kapitan Chernekov from the NKVD frontier troops."

Paul gaped as the Raven shook hands with the enemy.

"Catching flies, Oberleutnant Brand?" asked the Russian Major.

"But you—"

"These officers are in fact from our Brandenburg unit," interuppted the Oberst, smiling, "and will be assisting us in our task. You can relax, Brand. They're on our side."

"And what's the task?" asked the Raven.

The Oberst pulled a map forward and they all gathered round; the Wehrmacht Colonel in the middle, the two Russian officers on his right and the Fallschirmjager on his left.

He tapped the map with a pencil he had picked up from the table. "This is the town of Dvinsk and this is where we need to secure the two bridges that service it."

"I will need more than just a company, sir," suggested Volkman, his mind already running through the difficulties of taking such a target.

"That won't be your role, Major. Major Apraxin and his colleagues will deal with that. They will secure the bridge to allow you passage, along with the follow-up forces that will hold it. But we have an issue."

He pointed to an area about five kilometres north-west of the town. "Stretching from here to here," he dragged his finger across the map in a straight line back to the river, "a railway line crosses the railway bridge and goes beyond the area I've just shown you. This is a major railway line and in the north-western sector and the eastern sector are multiple sidings."

Paul and Volkman peered closer, absorbing all the information.

"Here," the Oberst tapped the north-west sector again, "the Russians have at least two armoured trains. Major Apraxin?"

The Russian Major took over the brief and both Paul and Volkman could smell the strong scent of Russian tobacco on the officer's uniform. The remarkably fresh-faced forty-year-old GUGB officer placed a photograph on top of the map.

"This is," he said with a distinctly Russian accent, not a trace of his Germanic roots, "a PL-37 artillery wagon. The black and white photograph doesn't show it but it is heavily camouflaged; black and sand coloured patches over its usual olive-green base. There are two of these, one either side of an armoured locomotive. We can look at pictures of the locomotive later. These are two artillery wagons; each have two 76.2mm guns, in turrets, one at each end of the wagon, along with six machine guns. Either side of these wagons are two anti-aircraft batteries, again on wagons, and, either side of those, two control cars."

He pulled a second photograph from under one of the maps and placed it in front of Paul and his commander. "Unfortunately that's not all. This beast is an MBV-2 armoured cruiser, part of the 14th Independent Armoured Train Battalion of the 23rd Army. It has three T-28 turrets and four Vickers machine guns."

"These two make a small army in their own right, sir," uttered Paul.

"Yes, they do, Oberleutnant. Their presence will make it

difficult for us to cross the bridge and we want your unit, Major Volkman, to solve it for us."

"We shall be glad to oblige. The Oberst and I agreed earlier that I would allocate a company to this operation and it will be Oberleutnant Brand's. When do you propose making the attack?"

"The early hours of 26 June."

"Well, I need to get back to my battalion. I'll leave Oberleutnant Brand under your temporary command and I suggest you brief him fully now. He can bring me up to speed later."

Paul, Volkman and the Oberst exchanged salutes; there were none from the Brandenburgers. After a quick chat with Paul, Volkman left and the briefing re-started, this time for Paul's benefit.

Paul's men grouped around their commander at one end of the interim conference room, darting glances of suspicion at the two Russian officers. There was an undercurrent of excitement though at the thought of finally being given a task worthy of them and their specialist skills. However, as yet, they did not know what that might be.

Paul coughed and Max barked, "Listen in, you lot." The chattering ceased.

Paul looked around the room at the paratroopers he had brought in for the task ahead: the First platoon, commanded by Leutnant Leeb. "I will introduce the officers with me presently but, first, the reason I have assembled you all here is to give you the outline of the mission that has been entrusted to us."

He moved back, away from the group. Some of them were sitting on the edge of the table, others on a jumble of chairs plucked from various rooms of the municipal building. More sat on the grubby floor near the front while the rest stood. He turned to the maps that were pinned to the wall behind him and, with a pointer he had acquired, tapped the river and the town cupped within its curve.

"The town of Dvinsk, gentlemen, and the River Dvina that partially surrounds it; the barrier that prevents us from moving into the town and advancing further east. There are two bridges crossing the river: a road bridge here in the south and, further west, a rail bridge. You can look at the map in more detail later but, for now, you should be able to make out the railway line travelling north-east from the rail bridge where it hits a crossroads. Here the line splits, continuing north-east but also branching off to the north-west and south-east. We're interested in the line as it continues north-east."

Paul moved further along the wall until he was adjacent to a large black and white photographic montage. His men stared intently, now drawn into the plot that was unravelling in front of them, keen to know what it meant for them.

"Just before the line exits the town, there are large railway sidings, some thirty or more lines. In fact, Dvinsk is a major railroad junction."

He walked back towards the table, closer to his men, catching Max's and Leeb's eye, the excitement at the prospect of battle palpable. "It's the railway sidings we're interested in and, more importantly, what we will find there. I will now hand you over to Starshiy Major Apraxin of the Russian State Security."

There was a mild lapse of discipline as the Fallschirmjager looked at the Russian officer, then around at each other, registering their surprise at what they had just heard.

"Quiet," called Max, bringing order back to the room.

"Major Apraxin is naturally not a Soviet citizen but a member of our elite Brandenburgers," Paul continued. "I won't go into any more detail than that, other than to remind you that their role is absolutely secret." He tried to catch the eye of as many troopers as possible, pressing home the importance of what he had just told them. "For those of you that were with me at Fort Eben Emael, you will understand the consequences of this type of information leaking out. Major."

The tall Major, his height matching Paul's six foot two, stepped forward. In his general officer's light grey shirt and dark blue jodhpurs with piped crimson tucked into high black boots, he cut a very different figure from the green of the 'Green Devils' uniform. "First, I would like to say that your unit's reputation has preceded you and I can't think of a finer group of soldiers to work alongside in this task."

The Fallschirmjager, without exception, swelled with pride.

"We have to get across the road bridge on the morning of 26 June, a task that has been given to other members of my unit. They will pose as NKVD, under the command of an NKVD officer, similar to my colleague Kapitan Chernekov."

The chunky officer standing behind him, in full NKVD uniform, nodded his head in acknowledgement.

"But, we have a problem," the Major continued.

He pointed to the sidings that Paul had mentioned earlier. "Here, we have some very dangerous Russian weapons that could seriously interrupt the crossing of the bridge by the follow-up forces once we have completed the task of securing it."

He moved the pointer he acquired from Paul to a group of black and white photographs pinned to the left of the montage.

"This beast is a PL-37 artillery carriage," he said, rapping the photo showing an armoured railway wagon, supported by two railway bogies, with a turret at each end.

"Each turret contains a 76.2mm field gun and as you can see from this picture." He moved to a photograph pinned below it, showing a configuration of a ten-piece train combination. "There are two of these wagons, either side of the armoured locomotive. You will get the opportunity to study these photographs in more detail after the briefing," he added, noticing that some were straining to see as much detail as possible. "I also have shots showing differing views.

"It doesn't end there. On each of the artillery wagon's sides, behind the turrets and facing outwards, are two Maxim 7.62mm water-cooled machine guns. They are armoured sleeve and ball-mounted, so offer good protection for the gunners. Each turret also has a machine gun for additional protection. This unit alone is a pretty tough target. They weigh some seventy-five tons, sixteen metres in length, have a command cupola in the centre and a crew of thirty each. The space inside is pretty cramped as they hold about thirty thousand rounds of 7.62 and five hundred and sixty rounds of 76.2 ammunition. Once on top of this beast, you can hold the crew inside. The commander has a panoramic periscope and triplex glass visors for observation. So, as you can see, these artillery wagons could be a problem just on their own."

Leeb put his hand up to ask a question.

"Not just yet, Ernst,' said Paul. 'The Major has a lot to go through. Once we have the overall picture you will have plenty of opportunity to go through any questions you may have."

"Sir."

"Also in this train combination," continued the Starshiy Major, "on each side of the artillery wagons is an anti-aircraft defence unit. The wagons are armoured, but there is no top cover. When the four-barrelled Maxim machine gun platform is to be used in its air defence role, the armoured plates protecting them from the sides are dropped down, exposing them to enemy fire. They are an effective, low-level air defence. Either side of them, there are two control cars."

Moving to the right-hand side of the montage, the Major pointed to a picture pinned there. "This monster is classed as a rail cruiser and actually has a name: Stremlitelniy-Impetuous."

"It's a battleship on rails!" exclaimed Leeb.

"Yes, Leutnant," responded the Major, smiling. "It is pretty impressive, a force to be reckoned with. Over twenty metres long and weighing forty tons, it was built in the Kirov plant in Leningrad, our ultimate goal. On the one end, you have a single T-28 turret, taken from a Soviet T-28 tank, and at the opposite end it has two staggered T-28 turrets, one higher than the other. It is self-propelled on five axles with a speed of up to one hundred and twenty kilometres an hour. When stationary, for close defence, it has two Vickers machine guns each side just behind the two inner turrets."

He turned towards the group again and continued. "This black and white photograph doesn't show it but it is camouflaged with vertical bands of black and tan stripes over its olive-green finish. Its side armour is sixteen millimetres thick. The turrets are twenty millimetres thick but the roof is only ten. That's its weak point. There are steel rungs protruding from the sides where you can access the guns or the commander's cupola. The tops of the turrets are in the region of four metres high and the cupola six."

He paced the width of the room, head down, hands behind his back, gathering his thoughts. The soldiers took the opportunity to make themselves more comfortable shifting positions. Then the Major approached the table once again and selected a single photograph from a small pile. He held it up, showing it to the watching troopers, sweeping his arm in a long arc so most got a reasonable view. The photograph showed a central platform supported on two rail bogies less than two metres apart. On the low platform sat a tubular frame supporting a bomb, with two vehicle batteries, one either side.

"This, ZhDT-3, a rail-borne torpedo, may seem small and nondescript but it packs a devastating punch. The battery-powered trolley is armed with a two hundred and fifty kilogram bomb, containing a one hundred kilogram charge. It has a top speed of sixty kilometres an hour and a range of ten kilometres. We think that each armoured train may have five of these but we're not sure. Its role is primarily to attack other trains and indeed other armoured trains like itself. Although we're not planning to use any of our own armoured behemoths in this assault, these could still cause havoc amongst our advancing troops and may well be used at the rail bridge itself." He slammed the photograph down on the table. "These and the two armoured trains must be destroyed or at least disabled. Over to you, Oberleutnant."

Paul took the place of the Russian officer and moved to the front, scrutinising the faces of his men, looking for their reaction to this difficult task. All he saw was determination. Max, although probably not fully recovered from his wounds in Crete, looked as solid as a rock, seemingly unbreakable. It gave Paul comfort to know he would be fighting alongside his comrade again, his friend. Max caught his eye and nodded as if to say, we can do this.

Leeb, the commander of the platoon Paul was taking with him, was confident and often outspoken, his chiselled features lined with resolve. This wiry officer had served with Paul in Poland, Eben Emael, Greece and finally Crete. He was glad that they would be fighting a common enemy together again.

The three troop commanders looked on: Fessman, the ex-poacher, eyes like a hawk; Konrad, quietly spoken but confident; and, finally, Braemer, who had assumed command after Jordan's death in Crete. They looked on intently, not wanting to miss anything, knowing how critical and dangerous the mission was going to be.

"The aim of the operation, gentlemen, is the destruction of the two armoured trains and any of these rail-borne torpedoes we can find." Paul gave them a few seconds to absorb the order he had announced. "Insertion will be by crossing the Dvina road bridge at o three hundred on the morning of the 26th. You'll no doubt be wondering how we propose to do this."

He looked at their puzzled faces. They knew that the road bridge would be heavily defended and probably blown up at any attempt to cross it.

"We will cross with the assistance of Starshiy Major Apraxin and his colleague, Kapitan Chernekov of the Russian NKVD. With these two officers and ten of his men, we will be transported as German prisoners of war."

Now the room buzzed; a mixture of disbelief and awe at the audacity of the deception that was proposed. The fact that they would be unarmed prisoners of war, under the protection of men they did not know, or even trust, also filled them with trepidation. Perhaps walking into a trap and end up as real prisoners of the Russians, or even dead.

"Shun," called Max, bringing the briefing back under control.

The noise ceased immediately, not just out of respect for their Company Feldwebel, or because their military discipline dictated it, but also out of fear of the consequences of crossing their most senior NCO.

"Actions: we move out at o two hundred, crossing the bridge at o three hundred driving towards the centre of the town before striking north-west skirting this lake here, Lake Sunuzers." Paul tapped the map. "We go round the tip of the lake, then south-east, down the other side, then east through this forested area which will bring us close to the railway sidings where we will disembark from our transport. They will then leave us as they have other tasks to accomplish." He looked at Fessman. "Unteroffizier Fessman, you will take two men and skirt the edge of the railway sidings, locating the armoured trains. If you find nothing, or other trains block your view, then return immediately and I will send out three two-man patrols to search for them. Then we will plan our next steps accordingly. Clear?"

"Yes, sir, perfectly."

"The assault. This is how we're going to play it, gentlemen. Ernst, your second troop," Paul looked at his platoon commander and Uffz Konrad, the troop commander, "will target the southern end of the armoured train, wherever we find it, and, Uffz Braemer, your troop will be responsible for the northern section."

Both troop commanders nodded their understanding.

"For reasons I'll explain in a minute, both troops are to approach the train from the southern end. Uffz Braemer, you will have to move through Konrad's men to get to your target. Two troop, you will leave an MG34 at the end of the control car covering the southern arc and three troop an MG34 covering the northern arc. Understood?"

"Yes, sir," they both acknowledged.

"You each have three tasks. Blow a small section of track between your respective control car and anti-aircraft wagon, using four hundred gram charges. Take out the anti-aircraft wagon first using a Geballteladungen, six stg.24. Stick grenades strapped together should do the trick. Finally, the artillery wagons themselves. You will need to move beneath the first machine gun, positioning yourself to the left of the turret. There is a runged ladder in the centre for the artillery wagon commander but it's adjacent to the crew entrance door, so we'll be taking ladders with us."

"The height, sir?"

"To the top of the turret, Ernst, it's about five metres. The width is just over three metres and the full length of the wagon some fifteen metres. Once on top, you can use a twelve and a half kilogram Hohlladung hollow charge to blast through. They can punch through seventy-six millimetres of armour so are more than adequate for the task."

"We only have about fifteen millimetres to get through," added the NKVD Kapitan, "so it will cause devastation below. Space is extremely tight inside as it's packed with ammunition. I suggest that you time the AA wagon, railway line break and the artillery wagon at the same time; then get your men away and flat on the ground."

"Thank you, Kapitan."

"What about the locomotive?" asked Leeb.

"The destruction of the two artillery wagons is likely to inflict some damage on the locomotive but the rail line you damage will prevent it from going anywhere," replied Paul. "Right, we come to the armoured cruiser. Let's not forget that. According to aerial observation and information from Starshiy Major Apraxin, the cruiser is usually found at the northern end of the armoured train but about a dozen lines across and further back, hence the need to approach your targets from the southern end. Although they would be reluctant to use their T-28 armament, they are likely to spray you with their Maxims. If that's the case, they could bring the two machine guns on the side facing us to bear. So, Uffz Fessman's troop accompanied by myself and Feldwebel Grun will complete a southern sweep and approach the cruiser end on."

He looked at Fessman. "Set your MG up at the southern end and then assault the train from the top. There is a runged ladder to the right of the command cupola, so nip on top and place a hollow-charge on the roof next to the commander's position. We don't have enough of these to take out the turrets, so just place a four hundred gram charge beneath the turret overhang of the one at the far end. There is a runged ladder to give you access. Then get the hell out of there and head south."

"What if there are soldiers roaming the yards, sir? Asked Max. "Sounds to me like we need a bigger force."

"I agree with you. Feldwebel Grun, isn't it?"

"Yes, sir," answered Max, bemused that he found himself talking to what seemed to be a Russian officer.

"We need to get you through the Russian lines as German prisoners of war. Anymore than the thirty of you will create too much suspicion, so we'll make do with what we have. It is our hope that my rank, which is of General Officer status, will get us through."

"Understood, sir. We'll do the job for you."

"Feldwebel Grun," continued Paul, "you will stay with Uffz Fessman's troop and I will take two men with me and search for these torpedo trolleys."

Paul looked around at his men. "Any questions so far?"

Hands shot up, Braemer's first. "Why don't we just hit them with Stukas, sir? Those cowboys would lap this up."

Paul turned to Major Apraxin. "Sir, do you want to take that one?"

"There are a number of reasons. First, we want to preserve as much of the railway infrastructure as possible. The speed of our advance so far means that we will need a significant amount of supplies sent to the front if we are to maintain the momentum. Those will have to be moved by rail. Also, the armoured trains change their positions regularly, specifically to prevent us pinning them down, and they do have some integral anti-aircraft defence against low-flying aircraft."

"When will we be relieved, sir?" asked Leeb. "When this lot kicks off, we'll bring the entire Russian army down on top of us."

"The rest of the company will come to our rescue," Paul answered smiling, "Leutnants Nadel and Roth have been plaguing me for a task and that will be theirs. The rest of the battalion will be assaulting with the main force but their specific task will be to move south of the lake that we skirted to the north and force a corridor through which Nadel and Roth can move to reach us here at the sidings."

"They had better push bloody hard," added Max, "or they'll have my boot up their arses."

The room laughed, knowing that it was said in good humour, and releasing some of the tension they were all starting to feel. Having said that, they would not advise their colleagues to be late coming to the rescue of their company NCO.

Paul raised his hand for silence. "I'm sure, Feldwebel Grun, that my fellow company commanders are aware of the consequences of failure. I doubt they will let us down."

Laughter ensued again. However, deep down, they were starting to give serious consideration to the task ahead, and some anxiety was setting in. Some were worried about being seen as prisoners of war, travelling behind enemy lines amongst thousands of Russian troops, others the thought of attacking what was effectively a mobile fortress.

"OK," continued Paul, "gather your troops. We're now going to go through the operation in the minutest of detail, from start to finish."

The paratroopers assembled into their troop formations, seeking out their commanders who were dragging photographs across the table to get a better insight into the sidings, the surrounding area and the armoured trains they were up against. They then started to discuss the pitfalls and the best approach to achieve their aims.

Apraxin came over to Paul.

"You have a seasoned bunch of men here, Oberleutnant. I gather they have seen a lot of action."

"That they have, sir, but I have a feeling this is going to be the toughest yet."

"It isn't going to be easy. Getting through the Russian lines without raising their suspicions is not without risk. After that, you've got to take out those trains with only a few men then hang on until rescued."

"It's what we do, sir, it's what we are trained to do. What happens if we fail?"

"The sidings will be bombed, Oberleutnant. We can't afford to allow them to interfere with the bridge crossing. So, you can't afford to fail." With that, the Major moved away towards one of the groups to answer any questions they might have, leaving Paul on his own to reflect. He sensed rather than saw Max approaching him.

"No Tante Ju this time, sir, but we'll still do the job, whatever the transport."

Chapter Seven

Paul was standing next to the Gaz 66 Jeep; a four-wheeled, two metre long, four-by-four utility vehicle, open at the sides, with a canvas-covered roof. It looked very similar to the American Jeep but the bonnet was higher and the mudguards over the front wheels were more rounded. Shielding a small torch, he looked at his watch: it was one thirty in the morning of 26 June, 1941. No more planning, no more preparation. Today, Paul's small unit would carry out the mission they had been entrusted with. Today, they would make their way through the Russian lines, disguised as prisoners of war, cross the main road bridge over the River Dvina, make their way to a major railway sidings and attack two heavily armoured and protected trains, putting them out of action. To leave the trains operable was not an option. Paul knew the importance of their mission but he was also aware of the enormous task that lay ahead. There was no doubt the trains' firepower could seriously damage, if not wipe out completely, the German Army crossing the river. The safety of the men and the taking of the town of Dvinsk lay largely in the success of this operation.

"We'll be there to back you up," encouraged Helmut, "so long as those Burger boys do their bit and open the way for us."

Erich stood on the other side of Paul and placed his hand on his friend's shoulder. "You must be bricking it. I know I would be."

"You're meant to be encouraging him, you idiot," chided Helmut, rapping Erich's helmet. "Not sending him into a depression."

"Into the lion's or is it bear's den," added Manfred.

"Not you as well," hissed a frustrated Helmut. "Ignore them, Paul." He slapped Paul's back, the force rocking him on his feet. "Just lay off the vodka and the Russian women when you get over there and you'll be alright!"

Erich caught the serious look of doubt that flashed across Paul's face. "Look, Paul, get the job done then keep your head down. We'll get to you somehow. Just let the fighting drift passed you."

Paul nodded, thankful for his *kameraden*'s presence and encouragement. However, deep down, he agreed with Manfred's take on it. Although meant as a joke by his fellow company commander, they were heading deep into the Russian bear's territory, and her claws were still very sharp and ready to protect her territory.

They all turned as the Russian Major approached, accompanied by Kapitan Chernekov, Leeb and Max.

"Are you ready, Brand?"

No more niceties. As of now, the Starshiy Major, a Russian officer of the feared GUGB and Kapitan Chernekov, of the equally feared NKVD, were his captors.

"Yes, Major."

"Right, if you'll leave us." He directed his orders to Helmut, Manfred and Erich. They wished them luck and disappeared to make any final arrangements to enable their task of backing up Paul and his men later in the day.

The NKVD Kapitan grabbed Paul's arm and steered him towards the back of the Jeep, indicating he was to get in then sat beside him. In the front, an NKVD soldier jumped into the driver's seat, the Major sliding in beside him.

Another soldier grabbed Max's arm. His natural response was to resist until he felt the soldier's pistol under his chin and an order, in Russian, to move. Max did not understand what was said but the message was clear enough. He allowed himself to be ushered to the back of the lorry, knowing that the act had started. Their Russian escort was now fully in character.

Max jumped up over the tailgate into the back of the canvas-covered, three-axle, Zis-6 truck, already crowded with the other ten men. Two NKVD guards sat either side by the tailgate, their Mosin Nagent1983 Carbines aimed menacingly at the paratroopers inside. All the paratroopers were still in uniform wearing their tunics, combat trousers and boots. Everything else they would need for their mission: their weapons, S-straps, ammunition and explosives were stowed carefully beneath their seats, packed tightly behind their boots. More were secured to the underbelly of the vehicles. They had prepared for every eventuality and they intended to return...

Herzog bent towards Max. "They look bloody serious, Feld."

The response was quick and unequivocal: the soldier to Max's diagonal right thrust the barrel of the carbine into Herzog's chest.

"*Nikakikh razgovorov!*"

"I was—"

The soldier pushed the barrel a little harder; the other guard raised the butt of his gun as if ready to strike the paratrooper.

"*Nikakikh razgovorov!*"

Max gave a Herzog a look that said, shut up you fool, this is for real! After a few moments, the guards sat back down and the one opposite Max leant forward.

"This is the last time I speak German. My life, your life, depends on today and our little charade. If one of you opens his mouth again and puts our lives at risk, I will personally shoot you myself. It would be expected of me."

He leant back against the side of the truck, his comrade offering him a cigarette and, within moments, they were smoking, and laughing and joking in Russian.

Max peered at his men in the darkened interior of the truck, thinking, what the fuck have we got ourselves into...

In the second and third truck, similar levels of discipline were being imposed. Leutnant Leeb and the rest of his men sat in silence. A sense of fear had already started to creep into their stomachs and was twisting their guts.

The driver turned the ignition of the Jeep. The engine roared into life immediately, and the three Russian trucks behind followed suit.

"*Dviggat'sya vpered,*" ordered the Major.

The driver put the Gaz into gear and crept forward, a German Steiner in front leading the way, the Feldgendarmerie escorting them through the German units close by and taking them to the front lines. They moved slowly onto the road, stealthily nudging out of the town of Zarasai. Soldiers looked on suspiciously at the Feldgendarmerie-manned Steiner Jeep, followed by four unfamiliar vehicles.

The convoy left the outskirts of the town moving into more open country, the vastness of Russia hidden under the cloak of night. They passed numerous German vehicles on the way; some were pulled over onto the side of the road, others were hidden, like ghosts, deeper amongst the trees, silently waiting for the order to advance and secure their target, the town of Dvinsk some thirty kilometres away. The air was thick with trepidation and the desire to get on with their task.

After roughly three kilometres, they crossed the border from Lithuania to Latvia. Further on, after passing through eight kilometres of open ground, mixed in with patches of forest, they arrived at the

River Pakrace, the furthest point of the German lines. Here they were stopped by a forward German unit and a heated debate could be heard between the Feldgendarmerie and the officer commanding the control point. The Military Police Hauptmann approached the Russian Starshiy Major.

"They won't let us through unless they are allowed to search the vehicles, sir."

"They've seen our orders?" asked Apraxin.

"Yes, sir, but they still insist."

Apraxin climbed out of the vehicle and accompanied the Hauptmann but was immediately accosted by a Wehrmacht Major.

"Who the hell are you?" asked the Major.

"We have our orders, Herr Major. You are to let us pass unhindered," interrupted the Feldgendarmerie officer.

"I don't care who you are but I do know I'm looking at two Russian officers and a Fallschirmjager Oberleutnant."

Paul had not noticed that Apraxin had slipped his Tokarev pistol from its holster. Quite a tall man, six foot two like Paul, he towered over the infantry Major. In one quick movement, his left hand shot out and grabbed one of the officer's lapels, pulling him close, almost lifting him up on his toes, and he thrust the pistol directly in his face. Rifles could be seen being raised in the background by the officers' soldiers.

In clear German, Apraxin said, "Now listen here, you fucking upstart. These orders give us unobstructed passage through German lines and if you don't follow that order immediately I will put a bullet through your skull. Do I make myself clear?"

The officer, visibly shaking, nodded his head rapidly.

"If you interfere with this convoy, Major, I can promise you the Fuhrer himself will personally order you to be sent to a penal battalion and, if you are extremely lucky, put in front of a firing squad!"

He let go of the officer, the moon slipping through the clouds at that moment showing the man's ashen face.

Apraxin turned to the military police officer. "Get these bloody vehicles from across the road. We've lost enough time already. Once across the river, you can leave us, Herr Hauptmann." Then he stormed back to the Jeep and climbed in while the Hauptmann dispersed the infantry soldiers and pressed them into moving the vehicles being used to block the road. The Wehrmacht Major was nowhere to be seen.

The lorries were moved, along with the lengthy tree trunk which was supported by ammunition boxes at each end. The three soldiers moving the tree were sweating profusely. Was it the effort of the job or the fact that Russian soldiers were close by?

Apraxin rapped the dashboard and, in Russian, ordered the driver to pull forwards following the Steiner making its way past the now dismantled roadblock. After about three hundred metres, the convoy pulled over to the roadside, the Hauptmann coming up to Apraxin's side of the Jeep.

"That's us done then, sir," reported the Hauptmann.

"Once we move out, I want your Jeep across the road. I don't want anything behind us for at least ten minutes. Clear?"

"Yes sir, but—"

"You have your written orders, Hauptmann. This is a top-priority operation. I don't care if a bloody general wants to get past you. They don't."

"Understood, sir."

"That's all."

The Chain Dog left and climbed back into his own vehicle. Checking his watch, Apraxin turned his head and looked at Paul out of the corner of his eye. "We have about forty-five minutes to the bridge, Oberleutnant, but we will no doubt be stopped well before then. There will probably be just a thin screen of Russian troops. Our intelligence tells us that they are pulling back across the river, waiting for the attack they know is inevitable."

Paul nodded his understanding, still reflecting on the ferocity of the Major when confronted by the Wehrmacht officer.

Apraxin ordered the convoy to continue its journey towards the Russian front. The convoy crept forward with the moon in close and silent pursuit.

They had advanced five kilometres through no-man's-land before the driver pulled to a halt, the headlights of a Zis 6 truck blinding the occupants. Two Russian soldiers quickly approached. Paul could immediately sense there were others not far away, weapons firmly fixed on their unexpected night-time visitors. They pointed their rifles at Apraxin. Their loose-fitting pullover tops were shabby and dirty. These were soldiers in retreat.

Apraxin leapt out, closely followed by Kapitan Chernekov, who proceeded to do the talking. The two soldiers, one an NCO, looked at the two officers warily. Another NCO and a senior Lieutenant, who immediately saluted the two unknown Russian officers, joined the group. An animated conversation ensued, the NKVD Kapitan's voice commanding and harsh.

The driver in the front of the Gaz turned and faced rearwards, his pistol hovering in line with Paul's chest and he whispered, "He's ordering them to turn out the lights before they attract the attention of the German Army. He's berating them for their stupidity."

Behind the Jeep, the guards who had been sitting next to the tailboard of the trucks had decamped, their rifles now aimed menacingly at the Fallschirmjager who was still in the canvas-covered cargo area.

The exchange abated after a few minutes and they quickly embarked, the convoy again heading towards its goal: the bridge over the River Dvina.

Apraxin leant back once they were out of sight of the Russian front line unit, his left arm resting on the back of the seat.

"Not a problem," he said, grinning. "The GUGB and the NKVD scare the shit out of them, more than the Germans do. When the secret police are around, they're more scared of their own than they are of the enemy. Once piece of good news: they're all pulling back over the river. Even the screen is making its way to the western bank. That means their controls will be disorganised."

He turned to face the front and checked his watch again as they picked up speed. They still had fifteen kilometres to go and needed to maintain their current pace if they were to meet their schedule.

The rest of the drive was uneventful. The ground they crossed, or what little they could make out in the intermittent moonlit night, was much the same as they had passed through since the start of Operation Barbarossa: wide open spaces with the occasional forest. They passed the odd Russian unit, clearly packing up ready to move back to the river, but each time they passed unhindered. One look at the GUGB officer sitting in the front of the Jeep was enough to send them running. Just before ten to three, they arrived at the outskirts of the town on the western bank of the river. They passed through a narrow strip of forest which took them right to the edge of the river, where they turned right, tracking its western edge, crossing a tributary that fed the river before arriving at the approaches to the bridge. There was some activity but vehicles and men appeared to be crossing unimpeded. No control point could be seen.

They were stuck behind at least a dozen vehicles: a mixture of Russian trucks, intermingled with marching soldiers, Gaz vehicles and even some civilian automobiles, making their way towards the bridge. The Russian moon once again helped Paul pick out the anti-aircraft guns either side of the approach to the bridge, the barrels of the quad 14.5mm guns pointing skywards. He caught a glimpse of a small light flashing beneath the bridge. He suspected it would be Russian engineers placing the explosive charges in preparation for blowing it, preventing the German Army from an easy crossing.

He listened to the guttural Slavic language being spoken around him. Being so deep within the enemy camp was unnerving him. With no weapon immediately to hand, unable to understand what was being spoken, and surrounded by the enemy, all he had was his trust in the men escorting them who, apart from the occasional German sentence, seemed as Russian as the men about them. He saw the curious glances from the dishevelled and tired soldiers that shuffled by, turning to fear and alarm as they saw the two security officers onboard the Jeep.

The jeep stopped and Starshiy Major Apraxin jumped out, Chernekov covering Paul with his pistol. Again, the Russian escort leapt out of the trucks to cover their charges confined in the back of the Zil wagons. Apraxin said something to Chernekov in Russian then walked down towards the front of the line of vehicles that were holding them up, screaming instructions to the soldiers and drivers who recoiled in fear. The drivers of the vehicles in front immediately pulled over to the side. Apraxin could be heard as far as the checkpoint which he had now reached. There were rapid salutes from the officers in charge, panic clearly showing in their eyes, suddenly confronted by a high-ranking, internal security officer. These were men, they knew, that could have them shot in the blink of an eye or, even worse, shipped off to Siberia and the Gulag. Within minutes, Apraxin was back in the Jeep, gesturing to the driver to overtake the vehicles in front and head for the bridge. The guards jumped back onto the trucks and Chernekov reholstered his pistol, while he looked back, checking the rest of the convoy was following behind them.

Once on the bridge, the blackness of the river below them, all they could hear was the sound of the vehicles they were in and the beating of their own hearts. The manoeuvring vehicles and chatting soldiers were left behind on the other bank. They could just about make out the high, diamond-shaped perforated sides of the bridge which soon gave way to a central section of steel arches, before again returning to the high-level barriers on either side.

They drove off the bridge, the ground dropping away either side. At the checkpoint, Apraxin's distinctive uniform and scowl were the only passes they needed. At the end of the embankment, where the ground levelled off, they had three choices: left along the eastern bank of the river; right, which would take them away from the town; or straight on towards the church whose dim tower could be seen in the distance. It had been agreed at the outset that they would avoid the river bank where Russian troops would more than likely be digging in, ready to repulse any attack across the flowing waters. Their convoy might well draw too much attention. So they continued straight on, passing three-storey buildings on their left, two-storey buildings on their right. There was minimal damage from Stuka bombs here, but this was to change very soon. There were some civilians milling about on the street, even at this early hour of the morning, mixing in with Russian soldiers going about their duties.

They motored east, weaving their way through the traffic that seemed to be getting heavier by the minute, turning left just before they hit the railway crossing running north-west to south-east in front of them. The road took them north-west, a minor road tracking the railway line on their right. They continued on this for nearly five kilometres, leaving the built-up area before crossing under the railway line. Somewhere to their left was the Fortress of Dunaburg, an early nineteenth-century military fortification. The construction, started by Tsar Alexander 1 of Russia in 1772, was not completed until the late eighteen hundreds.

Dawn was not far away. Paul watched nervously as troops around them set up anti-aircraft units. Russian infantry could be seen digging in and the odd small Russian tank, T 26s and T 28s manoeuvred into position, close to buildings, ready to ambush any unsuspecting attacker, supporting the lightly defended Soviet soldiers.

A further two kilometres found them opposite the lake on their right, the ground bare and open now, and their speeding trucks clear for all to see; an easy target if they were discovered.

The Starshiy Major was now scanning the roadside on his right, looking for signs and landmarks that had been imprinted on his mind from earlier reconnaissances.

"There, there," he called to his driver, pointing to an exit just up the road on the right. "Turn right, but slow down. Make sure the rest of the convoy can see where we're going."

The driver swung right, off the metalled road and onto a rough, dusty track that would take them closer to the edge of the lake. Paul could hear and feel the suspension creaking as the jeep negotiated the rougher ground. The railway line they had been alongside continued its way north-west.

Chernekov looked back and said in Russian, "It's OK, they're still with us."

After a few hundred metres, the track bore left, running parallel with the lake, taking them through a mass of small garden plots with adjacent buildings of various descriptions and sizes but generally single-storey and no bigger than four rooms; some possibly even single-roomed.

"Dachas," informed Apraxin, "where the locals grow their vegetables and some of the bigger ones are owned by local party officials."

They dropped into a dip, a thick line of trees to their right blocking out the view of the lake, a thinner line of trees to their left. At the end of the small forest, they turned right, cutting across the northern tip of the lake, the size of the gardens much bigger now, the houses of a higher quality, more like permanent dwellings. They entered another patch of trees, the track level but again of poor quality. Clouds of dust trailed behind them. Not difficult for the others to follow, thought Paul, but he imagined the dust playing havoc with the drivers' visibility, and his men in the back of the trucks would be silently cursing the grit that would find its way into the rear of the cargo areas. They continued for half a kilometre and turned south-east. This time a wall of trees was in front of them.

As they entered the forest, Apraxin flagged the driver to slow down as, the deeper into the interior they drove, the darker it became. They were now moving at no more than fifteen kilometres an hour, the convoy close on their tail. The drive became tortuous as they bumped their way down the forest track, deep ruts from where tractors had dragged out felled trees. Their target was less than five hundred metres away.

The driver braked suddenly as they came to the edge of a clearing but the Major signalled him on towards the clearings entrance on the opposite side, checking his watch and knowing time was critical.

Within moments, they had crossed the clearing and were back in amongst the trees.

Apraxin turned round to face Paul. "There is a narrow, metalled road, about a hundred metres away, that runs across the front of us. To the right, it ends up at a number of large buildings. We're not sure what they're used for, but we think it's storage of some sort. It means you will have to cross that road quickly and unseen."

Paul nodded his understanding.

"We're here, sir," said the driver in Russian.

"Stop the Jeep."

The Gaz came to a slow stop, the three troop carriers behind following suit.

"Well, Oberleutnant, this is where we part. It's over to you and your men now. You can return to being armed Fallschirmjager again," the Major said, the whites of his eyes showing strangely in the half-light. "You will need to be quick. Dawn is practically upon us."

Paul, the driver and the two Russian officers quickly and silently jumped out of the Jeep. Paul rushed back towards the trucks where his men were disembarking.

He hissed to Max, Leeb and the three troop commanders, "Offload your kit, but make it quick. We don't have a lot of time."

Max handed Paul his MP40 and the rest of his kit, including his *fallschirm*. "You'll no doubt be needing these, sir."

"Thank you, Max." He placed his machine pistol on the ground and started to pull on his Y straps. "Make sure they offload everything. I want nothing left behind."

"OK, sir." Max hurried off to carry out his commander's orders.

Paul adjusted his Y straps, checked his ammunition pouches, pistol and bread bag. He felt much more comfortable being fully equipped again and, more importantly, armed. He moved along to the middle truck where he found Fessman helping to offload the boxes that had been stashed beneath the wagon's chassis.

"Uffz Fessman, there's a narrow metalled road to our east. Position two men to watch it. Then I want you and one other to cross over and make your way through the trees to the edge of the railway siding on the other side. It shouldn't be more than a hundred metres then come back and report. Take Herzog, Petzel and Stumme with you."

"*Jawohl*, Herr Oberleutnant." He ran to gather his men to carry out a task that was second nature to him, his poacher's skills coming to the fore.

Paul moved amongst the rest of his men, checking they were OK, giving encouragement where needed, cajoling them to get their equipment organised quickly and quietly. All of them now had their personal weapons, along with the unit's three MG34s and grenades, a priority. At least now, if they were caught, they would have a chance to fight their way out. Standing there in the half-light, there was no mistaking they were Fallschirmjager and, had they been seen by the Russians, the look on their faces would have told them that something big was about to happen.

Apraxin approached Paul. "Are you ready, Oberleutnant? We have to go. We have other tasks to fulfill before the morning is out."

"Yes sir. We're complete," answered Max coming up alongside. "The boys are just consolidating the explosives then we're ready to move out, sir."

"You heard Feldwebel Grun Major, we're complete. We'll move to the road first and await the report from the scouts I've sent out before moving to the railway sidings."

"We'll be long gone by then," responded Apraxin. "Good luck, Oberleutnant. It's going to be a very long and memorable day." He shook hands with Paul and Max and quickly rejoined his men, the rear Zis already reversing back down the track, the rest ready to follow suit.

"I wonder what they're up to, sir."

"I don't know, Max, but I wouldn't like to be in the Russians' shoes. I have a funny feeling we have the easier task."

Max raised his eyebrows. "I hope you're kidding, sir."

Paul slapped Max's shoulder. "As you would put it, Feldwebel Grun, it will be a cakewalk."

Chapter Eight

The advanced armoured units of the German Juggernaut, heading east towards their target of Leningrad, came to a halt as they waited for the next phase of the assault on Dvinsk to play itself out. A prerequisite to the attack was the crossing of the Dvina River. The unit commander had seen the four Russian trucks pass his tank column earlier and had been ordered to let them pass unimpeded. He knew the Russian Zis trucks had been captured in an earlier phase of the war when a retreating Russian unit had been surrounded and had surrendered with their vehicles still intact.

The tank commander's head turned as he heard heavy boots stamping along the rear of his Panzer IV. It was his company's second in command, Leutnant Tegeler.

"We just wait for the word now then, sir."

"Yes, Aldrik. We have a little surprise for the Russians."

"I saw them pass earlier. A bit of a gamble, isn't it?"

"It is," responded Oberleutnant Erman thoughtfully, twisting round to face his subordinate, "but if they can secure the bridge it will save time and lives. We could be amongst them before they know what's hit them but you're right: it's a huge risk and I wouldn't want to be them." He picked up his binoculars, focussing in on the approaches to the bridge and the suburbs of Griva. "You'd better get back to your can, Aldrik. When we get the word, we need to move bloody quickly."

"See you across the other side, sir." Aldrik scrambled back down and returned to his Panzer IV tank.

The four Soviet trucks returned through the suburbs of Griva, passing military and civilian vehicles on their way, the bridge in sight very soon. They had passed through a checkpoint earlier but there had been no problems. Their uniforms were perfect and they all spoke Russian as well as any of the locals. Again, the Russian soldiers at this checkpoint were completely unsuspecting and were clearly concentrating on how far away the Germans were. Little did they know that they had already arrived. The Brandenburgers laughed and joked with the guards and confirmed they had seen no sign of the Germans. They thought it was very unlikely they would attack so soon after the last bloody nose they had been given.

The first truck ascended the approach onto the bridge. First Lieutenant Baranski, a member of the Brandenburg Regiment, a special unit formed by the head of the German Military Intelligence Admiral Canaris, struck the truck's dashboard. "Go, go, go."

The driver thrust the truck into a lower gear and accelerated towards the far end of the bridge, a Russian sentry about to flag them down. Failing to stop the first truck, he opened fire on the second one in the line.

"Shit," shouted Lieutenant Glebov, commander of the second truck, as they came under gunfire from the sentry. "Out, everybody out."

He needed to get his men out quickly. Trapped in the vehicles, they would be sitting ducks. They at least needed to spread out and seek cover at the sides of the bridge.

First Lieutenant Baranski's lead truck was now coming under fire from the guards at the other end of the bridge. The windscreen shattered as rounds punched their way through, striking one of the soldiers in the rear of the truck who cried out in shock. The driver, now blinded, swerved into the bridge parapet at the side.

"Out, out," yelled Baranski, knowing they must return fire swiftly or they would be rapidly overwhelmed.

Another swathe of fire forced the Brandenburgers to the ground but their weapons were soon up into their shoulders as they returned fire, their *kameraden* from the third and fourth trucks rapidly joining in the fight. They raced to overcome the sentries, quickly killing them; then seeking out the engineers to overpower them and cut the detonator wires.

Woomph.

Lieutenant Glebov was thrown to the ground as a small section of the bridge exploded, the blast knocking him and some of his men sideways.

The tank commander, with a clear view of the bridge from the high ground overlooking it, saw the flashes of gunfire coming from the bridge itself.

"Forward," he yelled to his driver, dropping into the tank and slamming the hatch down behind him. The tank lurched forwards, the signal already on its way to the rest of his company, the turret now swinging from left to right, seeking out its prey.

At the same time, a signal was winging its way to General Brandenberger, Commander of the 8th Panzer Division and General Von Manstein, Commander of 56th Panzer Corps.

"Dvina bridges secured. Road bridge intact. Slight damage to railway bridge."

The deep thrust into the heart of northern Russia had commenced.

Paul and his men crouched down amongst the trees, a strong smell of pine, fir and alder filling their nostrils. Looking to his right, he could see a few scattered buildings mentioned by Apraxin earlier. They seemed to be made of wood, perhaps workers' huts or storage sheds. Ahead was a narrow metalled road they had to cross. It was only single lane and the clump of trees opposite would soon give them some cover. Diagonally opposite those trees was a small copse. This would put them within twenty metres of the railway line.

Max nudged his shoulder and hissed, "There, sir, looks like Fessman returning."

Paul scanned the trees out front, picking out the two distinctly clothed paratroopers. Prisoners of war no longer but fully armed Fallschirmjager about to carry out what they were good at: death and destruction. The two men scooted across the road and a panting Fessman slid down alongside his company commander.

"They're bloody there alright," he exclaimed, still breathless but his breathing steadying slowly. He pulled out a notebook from his pocket and showed Paul a sketch he had made.

Paul called the other two troop commanders over and, with Leeb and Max, they listened to Fessman's brief.

"On the other side of that copse, sir, about ten lines away is a train with goods wagons, mainly. The doors are open and they appear to be empty, so will provide us with some excellent cover for our approach."

"The armoured train?" asked Leeb, impatient to know where they were.

"Coming to that, sir. On the other side of the goods train, again about ten railway lines away, is another goods train, but this time flat cars; about thirty in total. On the other side of that is our prize, the

80

armoured train. The flat cars will give us some cover but we'll have to keep bloody low if we aren't to be seen. The railway siding seems to be grouped in sections of ten lines. The armoured train is on that second segment, flat cars this side of it. We could see through the gaps; another goods train is on the other side."

"Using it to blend in, by the sound of it," said Max.

"I agree, Feld," responded Fessman, "but it limits their view and certainly confines the side machine guns."

"What about the Cruiser?" questioned Paul, tapping Fessman's sketch.

"We couldn't see it, sir. Although the armoured train is only ten wagons long, the goods train is three times that, so it could be hidden somewhere over the other side. I didn't want to probe any further in case we were discovered."

"You made the right decision, Uffz. Were there any sentries?"

"We could just see the one, on this side anyway. The rest are walled up inside or elsewhere."

"What's the sentry doing?" asked Konrad, commander of the second troop.

"Just walking up and down the line, smoking incessantly. Head down and pissed off, I would say. You wouldn't think that the entire German Army was breathing down their necks."

"What else is there about, particularly north and south?" Paul gestured at the sketch again.

"I can't see beyond the armoured train other than the tops of the trees on the very far side. North and south? To the south, just more railway lines and more goods trains, some of them tankers. To the north, I can just make out what might be a signal box. It's getting lighter, but still not great. We're quite near to the northern end of the siding, so that building may well be responsible for controlling traffic in and out of the town."

"They won't be showing any lights," suggested Braemer of third troop. "They'll be too fearful of the Luftwaffe."

"Right, gentlemen, now is our time. Let's get on with it," ordered Paul as he got up from his crouch ready to move out with his men. "Fessman, you'll need to take out the sentry before we can approach the armoured train. Have you got the kit?"

Fessman handed Stumme, who would be supporting Fessman in this task, a Russian soldier's helmet, a Mosin-Nagant Rifle and a tunic top.

"Who will be the bait?" asked Max. "Let me guess. It wouldn't be Stumme, would it?"

"He volunteered, Feld," replied the grinning Uffz, his hawk-like eyes scanning his *kameraden's* faces.

"Lead on then. Get your men together," instructed Paul, turning to the other two troop commanders.

Leeb gave Fessman the nod and Fessman signalled to his men to move out. Pulling his troop together, Fessman lead the way quickly across the road, followed closely by Stumme. Then came Herzog, carrying two four hundred gram charges. Then Giester with two Gebaulteladungers, six grenades strapped around a central charge; Baader with a light, collapsible ladder; Petzel with his MG34; Beiler acting as his number two in place of Stumme; Rammelt and Geib, each with a twelve and a half kilogram hollow charge; and Barth as tail-end Charlie.

Fessman hurriedly moved diagonally across to the copse, sure that the rest of his troop and the platoon were following. He moved through the copse, traversing left and right around the trees, knowing exactly where he was headed. He quickly looked over his shoulder, satisfied his men were still with him and made his way to the eastern edge of the dozen or so trees.

He crouched down, his men getting into position either side of him. He pulled his binoculars from their battered brown leather case. He scanned a one hundred and eighty degree arc in front of him, checking their route ahead was clear. To his left, he could now make out the signal box. If they were quick, it was not too far away and was still not light enough for them to be spotted. Opposite, the goods train, the first stage of their approach towards the armoured train.

He sensed his commanding officer and platoon commander at his side.

"All clear?"

"Yes, sir."

"Let's go then."

No more needed to be said.

Fessman got up from his crouch and left the safety of the trees, making his way across the railway lines. Paul tucked in close behind, conscious of how exposed they now were. They stepped gingerly over the railway lines, sticking to the thick wooden sleepers, avoiding the stony ballast and steel of the lines. Paul looked up, checking his surroundings, but quickly looked back down as he negotiated the railway lines, fearful of catching his boot and twisting an ankle or, worse, breaking one, and possibly alerting someone to their presence. Crossing the ten tracks finally brought them up against the goods train, the rest of the unit spreading out along its length, placing themselves in the gaps between the wagons, or crawling beneath and moving to the other side.

Paul, joined by Fessman, Max and Leeb, eased himself beneath the empty box car, the distinct smell of oil and soot on the blackened ballast from the many trains that must have passed up and down these lines. He caught his elbow painfully on the hard rail as he crawled across to the other side, manoeuvring himself so he could see out in front. He immediately saw the line of flat cars a further ten lines away, just as Fessman had briefed them. Beyond those, on the very next line, the armoured train.

Paul shivered as he studied the outline of their target, light enough now that he could make out the distinctive shape of the two artillery wagons either side of the locomotive, the silhouette of the four 76.2mm guns visible. He ran his eyes down the configuration of the train, picturing the briefing they had received from Apraxin only days ago. The armoured locomotive in the centre looked just that: a steam train with a smokestack on the far right, the entire length of the engine covered in armour plate. As described, there were two artillery units, one each side, their gun turrets prominent at the end of each sixteen-metre long wagon. They looked dangerous, solid and indestructible; in the centre of each one, the commander's cupola.

On either side of these trains were the anti-aircraft wagons. They appeared to be flat cars with a square steel box on top at either end, the upper section showing armoured panels that had to be lowered before the guns could be brought into action. At the moment, the panels were raised, the tips of the four Maxim machine guns just visible in each box. Next were the control cars, one at each end of the train, armoured goods wagons on wheels, housing more soldiers. Little else was known about them.

"There, sir," hissed Fessman, "the sentry."

Paul scanned the area where Fessman was pointing, the sentry bouncing around in the lens of his binoculars as he steadied his elbows on the cold, hard surface of the steel railway line. Wearing the distinctive steel helmet with its flared ear protectors, his rifle slung over his left shoulder, the guard slowly paced down the length of the line in between the armoured train and string of flat cars.

Head down, dragging on a cigarette, his face was lit with a red glow every time he drew deeply on it, weary of his sentry duty whilst his comrades slept.

"He walks the entire length of the armoured train, turns and does the same again."

"Go when you're ready," ordered Paul.

"The minute he turns and starts walking back ahead of us, Stumme and I will cross. We'll signal once he's dealt with, sir."

"OK, Uffz." Paul twisted his head towards Leutnant Leeb. "Is the rest of the platoon in position, Ernst?"

"Yes, sir, just waiting for the word to cross."

"Watch for the signal from Fessman. Feldwebel Grun and I will take the rest of Fessman's troop and move further south along the goods train, so we can skirt the armoured train and find that Cruiser."

"Understood, sir."

"Right, Max, let's go."

Max signalled to the men from first troop, less Fessman and Stumme, who would be in the team responsible for taking out the Armoured Rail Cruiser.

"I'm going across now, sir," hissed Fessman.

"Good luck," responded both Paul and Leeb. "We'll await your signal."

Fessman crawled from beneath the goods wagon where they had been hiding, Stumme close behind him. With sock-muffled boots, they gingerly crept across, half-crouching as they tried to stay below the line of flat cars across the forty metres of open space. They arrived at the row of flat freight cars, the far right armoured anti-aircraft wagon opposite them on the other side, and dropped down out of sight. The sentry, still with his head down, kicking the occasional stray piece of rail ballast, was now opposite the armoured locomotive, heading for where they expected him to turn and come back their way. They split up: Stumme to the right, heading for the gap between two of the flat cars where he could don his Russian uniform; Fessman to the left, making his way to the opposite end and the second gap. They both crept underneath.

Stumme was now wearing a Russian Gymnastiorka, a tunic based on the traditional peasant's blouse, and a loose-fitting pullover top with a V-shaped front opening extending halfway down the chest, patch-type pockets finishing it off. He also donned the Russian helmet he had been carrying, slung his Mosin rifle over his shoulder and lit up a foul-smelling Russian cigarette. He climbed onto the end of the flat car, facing the path of the sentry, his feet dangling in between the two cars, hiding his Fallschirmjager combat trousers and second pattern jump boots. He pulled out a bottle of vodka, kindly donated by Starshiy Major Apraxin, that had been secreted in his uniform and took a swig, the alcohol biting his tongue and throat, taking his breath away. He looked up, took a drag of the cigarette held in his left hand and could see the sentry was headed back towards them, still between the flat cars and the armoured train, head down, shoulders hunched, rifle slung uselessly over his left shoulder, probably counting the minutes until his replacement relieved him.

Stumme scrutinised the armoured train and surrounding area for any signs of movement. Dawn was gathering, the details of the silent killing machine opposite becoming more distinct. He could pick out the four barrels of the Maxim machine guns poking above the top of the armoured wagon closest to him, pipes from the water-cooling system linking them together. He heard the crunch of the Russian soldier's boots as he got closer, now only a matter of metres away from Fessman's position.

Fessman slowed his breathing, pulling his body in, tight behind the double bogie wheel of the left-hand flat car, as he heard the crunch of the sentry's boots and what could only be the soldier muttering under his breath. He listened intently, his timing was crucial if this was to go the way they expected. The minute the sentry was distracted by Stumme, the decoy, Fessman needed to be in a position to strike. They hoped that the Russian tunic, helmet and Mosin rifle, along with Stumme's demeanour, would distract the sentry long enough for Fessman to complete his task.

The sentry passed the double bogie wheels where Fessman was hidden; then the gap between the two flat cars. Fessman studied his high-booted legs with tucked-in trousers as he passed.

Stumme deliberately clinked the bottle as he raised it to his lips and took a drink. The sentry's head suddenly jerked up in surprise at the sound intruding on his thoughts and the rhythm of his pacing. He stopped in an instant, saw Stumme some twenty metres away, bewilderment on his face at seeing one of his comrades, drinking what appeared to be vodka. Leaving his rifle shouldered, he called out in Russian with a smile on his face, "What are you doing?"

At that moment, Fessman, on his hands and knees, eased himself from between the two flat cars, careful not to crack his head on the heavy gauge metal parts of the rail freight carrier. His helmet had been discarded for fear of it catching on something and alerting the Russian to his presence. He eased himself forward, his ten-inch fighting knife, with its six inches of heavy steel blade, clenched between his teeth, the razor-sharp edge facing away from him, the equally razor-sharp tip well away from the left corner of his mouth. Now in the gap between the two flat cars, the heavy buffers just behind his neck, he peered round at the Russian sentry, fairly short, as were the majority of the Russian soldiers he had seen, but skinnier than most, as he called out to Stumme. He heard Stumme's response, a gurgled nothing, the sound of someone drunk and caring little but for the next drink.

The sentry moved forwards another five paces and challenged him. "What are you doing? You will get shot for this. Get down."

Fessman eased himself up into a crouch, saliva dribbling onto his knife, ten paces away from his quarry, at last able to swallow as he removed the knife, now firmly gripped in his right hand.

"Are you my relief?" the sentry called. "You're too early."

On cue, Stumme clambered down from the flat car, stumbling onto the ground like the drunk he was purporting to be, the sentry making as if to move forward, but unable to see it through as Fessman struck.

There was no more time for the careful placing of steps, ball of the foot testing the ground. This was a mad dash to close in on the quarry.

Fessman grabbed the top of the soldier's tunic, pulling him back and downwards, taking him off guard, before slamming the cold, heavy steel blade deep into his back, using the sentry's weight to force it in deep. The razor-sharp point punched through his kidney, inducing immediate shock. The soldier gasped, his mouth wide open in distress, traumatised, his arms flung wide. As Fessman continued to drag the soldier to him, he extracted the knife and, in one swift movement, executed a cut across his throat, severing the trachea and carotid arteries, sawing the knife deep through the gristle. Pink froth exuded from the gaping wound. Within moments, the sentry's gurgling ceased and Fessman lowered him to the ground, instinctively checking his surroundings, knowing at the moment of the strike he was oblivious to all that went on around him.

Just as he was to give the all-clear, another sentry stepped over the coupling and buffers joining the AA car and control car together, and looked at the scene before him not in surprise but with curiosity. Stumme blocked his view of Fessman so, in the twilight, all he saw was one of his fellow soldiers in front of him plus one other who was on the ground.

Stumme's reaction was instantaneous: he launched himself at the Russian soldier, less than two paces away, propelling his head forwards, the rim of his helmet striking the bridge of the man's nose, a crack as cartilage and bone splintered, blood visibly pouring from the injury. Stumme followed through, pulling the man's head down sharply before he could recover, before the guard's instincts had him raising his hands to stem the flow of blood. He brought his knee up at the same time, striking the man's face, grunting as the force of the blow shot a spasm down his thigh, but the satisfaction that he had temporarily immobilised the sentry mitigated the pain. Still gripping the man's head, he wrapped his right hand around the back and with his left palm facing the soldier's face, grabbed his chin wrenching his head sharply to the right in a twisting motion, the power of the movement snapping his neck. Stumme lowered the lifeless sentry to the ground.

He turned to check on Fessman who was in the process of dragging his quarry to the edge of the AA car. Then he rolled him over the rails and underneath next to the bogie wheels. Stumme followed suit, removing the rifle from the guard's shoulder, hauling him by his armpits towards the side of the rail car, the sentry's head rolling on its broken neck. He too pushed the soldier underneath the wagon alongside his comrade.

They both quickly scouted around, not saying a word. None was needed. All was quiet. They looked at each other in amazement that it had gone so well, surprised that no one inside the wagon had heard the commotion outside. They could only surmise that they were in a deep sleep or that no one was onboard. Fessman moved to the flat car where it had all begun and looked to the goods train opposite, raising his Kar 98 with both hands in the air, the signal of their success. Had they failed then the subsequent gunfire would have given a different message and not only to their *kameraden*.

"There, sir," uttered Max, "Fessman's signal. The little bugger's done it. Good man."

"We've no time to lose. Let's go," ordered Paul.

First troop quickly followed their company commander. Second and third troop, who had also been waiting for Fessman's signal, left their positions beneath the goods train. Braemer and his third troop were up and off, heading at a tangent towards the northern end of the armoured train. Konrad led his second troop towards the southern end. Paul, Max, Leeb and first troop made their way across the intervening ten railway lines to a point at the most southern tip of the armoured train, their task to pass round it, under the goods train on the other side and seek out the armoured cruiser.

Braemer and his paratroopers made their way across the lines, stepping only on the wooden sleepers, minimising any noise they might make, quickly reaching a point opposite the control car at the far end. They arrived at the flat cars, panting breathlessly, laden down with weapons, ammunition and explosives; enough to complete their task and defend themselves until relief reached them – or so they hoped.

"Roon, Sesson, the MG, go quickly."

The two men crawled under the flat car and scrambled to the end of the train where they found the control car. They slid underneath it, a fifty round ammunition belt fed under the top cover of the MG34, a second one close by, ready if needed.

"Go, go," Braemer called to the rest.

Geyer and Ziegler crawled underneath the flat car through to the other side, then stood and leant with their backs up against the anti-aircraft wagon. Its steel plated sides blocked all visibility in or out. They each gripped a Gebaulteladunger and unscrewed the cap at the end of the central grenade, allowing the porcelain ball and string to drop free. All they needed to do now was pull the string, fusing the grenade, and toss it into the open-topped anti-aircraft compartment; the grenades dropping down amongst the four Maxim machine guns.

Two men stood opposite each end of the PL–37 artillery wagon, ready to climb the metal rungs that would take them to the top of the five-metre high turrets: one paratrooper with a twelve and a half kilogram hollow charge; another close by with a light and extendable ladder in case it was needed. Matzger crawled between the control car and AA wagon, ready to blast a small section of track, preventing the train from moving should they fail in destroying its weapons. The rest of the troop remained on guard, ready to cover their *kameraden* should the Russian crew suddenly disembark.

Braemer looked at his men, their figures clearer now in the early morning light. He checked his watch, pleased with the way they had performed. His troop was ready, the northern end of the train secured. They would now have to wait ten minutes while the other units got into position. Any longer and they would lose their cover. Daylight would expose them for all to see.

Konrad too checked that his men were all in position. Duties had been allocated earlier so each man knew where to be and what was expected of him. His platoon commander, accompanied by Pabst from his troop, had moved through minutes ago on their way to the armoured locomotive, to ensure its destruction. He checked his watch: eight minutes to go. He looked about him nervously, the quiet disturbing him, surprised that it had gone this far without a hitch. Although the sentries had been silenced extremely effectively and, more importantly, silently, something did not quite seem right. He had expected more activity.

Paul and Max, along with Fessman who had rejoined his troop, poked their heads from beneath a goods wagon that was situated on the far side of the armoured train. They spotted the armoured juggernaut almost immediately. It was opposite the far northern end of the armoured train, some ten lines distant, its two southern-facing T-28 guns cold and ominous. Even more threatening for Paul and his men were the two Maxim machines facing in their direction. The juggernaut had a line of flat cars on the adjacent railway line, but only running from each end; the train itself was free, giving the side-mounted machine guns clear fields of fire. On the other side, probably two or three lines distant from the MBV-2, was a line of railway tankers.

Paul checked his watch: five minutes to go. In five minutes, the other two troops would be blasting the armoured train and all hell would break loose. Then there would be no more hiding.

He looked across at the armoured cruiser once more: two T-28 turrets to the south, one to the north, two 7.62mm machine guns on each side, a quad Maxim anti-aircraft machine-gun mount on a retractable platform in the roof right of centre. It was formidable. If they were spotted, they would just have to assault as best they could. The attack on the armoured train behind them would go ahead regardless. He wished he had more men.

"Let's do it, Max, we can't wait any longer," he said as he surged forwards, speed now their best ally.

"I'm with you." Max heaved himself up, followed by Fessman and the rest of his troop tasked with the most dangerous element of the morning's mission.

Chapter Nine

They crouched down by the flat cars opposite the southern end of the armoured cruiser, looking even more impressive now that it towered above them. Paul stared up at its enormity. The far-reaching impact of the railroads, on the armies of Europe in the eighteen hundreds, had led to the development of various types of armoured trains. At this point in the war, against the invading German Army, the Russians had over twenty light-armoured trains, eleven heavy-armoured trains and over twenty artillery wagons, as well as the NKVD's armoured cruisers. Paul and his men were up against the mightiest element of that impressive force.

He checked his watch again and nodded to Fessman who, in turn, instructed his men to move into their positions. Petzel and Stumme set up their MG34 at the southern end of the cruiser, the barrel pointing south, sniffing out any potential enemy troops. Stumme pulled the stock into his shoulder, looking down the iron sights, settling down with the weapon that had become so familiar to him. Petzel crouched to the side, lifting the feed cover and placing a fresh one hundred-round belt; two fifty-round belts linked together. Stumme patted the cover down, pulled back the cocking handle, releasing it and pushing a round into the chamber. Next to him were three more fifty-round belts which he pulled close as he scanned the foreground. Their view was fairly restricted. The flat cars to their immediate right extended south for at least two hundred metres and, to their left, their line of sight was blocked by a line of railway tankers a few lines across from them. However, anyone coming at them from their arc of fire would be met by a hail of 7.92mm rounds at over 600 rounds per minute.

Rammelt quickly ran north along the side of the cruiser, stepping with an ungainly stride on the wooden sleepers jutting out from the railway line, heading for the far end of the cruiser. He positioned himself opposite the steel rung ladder that would lead him to the top of the T-28 turret, its barrel pointing north, a twelve and a half kilogram hollow-charge slung over his shoulder. Barth passed him, providing cover at the northern end of the train. Gieb, also carrying a twelve and a half kilogram hollow-charge, had stopped further back opposite the two T-28 turrets at the southern end.

It was light enough now for Braemer to pick out his men and for them to see him. He gave them the nod and they immediately sprang into action, their target the northern end of the main armoured train. Roon and Sesson tensed, Roon pulling the MG34's butt into his shoulder, knowing that all hell would break loose soon. Sesson searched the area in front of them, looking for signs of enemy movement, covering their northern arc. Matzger crawled beneath the buffers of the control car, heaving himself forwards on his elbows until he was up against the furthest rail. He quietly scraped some of the ballast away from beneath the cold thick steel rail, placed the four hundred gram charge underneath and taped it. Pushing a fuse into the charge, he quickly crimped it. The explosive was now set. He looked along the underneath of the train, along the length of its carriages left and right. He had one last look at his work then shuffled back over the rails, cursing under his breath as a splinter from one of the sleepers dug deep into the palm of his hand. His immediate thought, other than pulling the offending splinter out with his teeth, was not to tell his friends as they would only laugh. Back out in the open, he sought out Braemer, signalling that his task was complete. Then he moved beneath one of the flat cars to provide cover for the rest of his troop.

Four minutes to go.

Geyer and Ziegler, still flat against the anti-aircraft wagon, waited patiently, fingering the wooden handles of their grenades, hands sweating as they waited for the signal from Braemer. Theirs would be the last act to be carried out by the troop once they were given the signal.

Ptaff moved to the northern end of the PL-37 artillery wagon, tiptoeing as quietly as possible up to the metal rungs situated at the end. He pulled himself up and over the top of the wagon, the huge turret in front of him, the top of it over five metres from the ground. His Kar 98k was slung across his back and a twelve and a half kilogram charge slung over his left shoulder. He heaved himself up onto the top of the turret, the 76.2 mm and 7.62 mm Maxim machine gun jutting out to his right. He moved over the top, not wishing to make a sound, careful not to slip in his sock-encased boots. Then he lowered himself down gently onto the flat section of the wagon at the rear of the turret. He looked about him, concerned that he may have been spotted now he was so high up, but his splinter pattern smock was helping him to blend in with the disruptive camouflage pattern of the artillery wagon. All was clear. Opposite him, on the other side of the commander's cupola, next to the second turret, he could make out Schneider, nicknamed the 'Dummy' as his name meant 'Taylor'.

Schneider had ascended the extendable ladder, held in place by Vogt, and had climbed up in between the turret and the artillery commander's central cupola. He acknowledged Ptaff with a nod before both got on with their task. Schneider pulled the hollow-charge explosive from his shoulder and placed it gently on the metalled surface of the crew's armoured roof ventilation hatch, positioning it for best effect once it exploded. Behind him was the gun turret maintenance hatch and, below him, their barrels jutting out either side of the wagon, pointing east and west, two Maxim machine guns. Along with these were two hundred and eighty rounds of artillery ammunition and some fifteen thousand rounds for the heavy machine guns. For a moment, he pitied whoever was below him, if indeed it was occupied. Not only would the impact from the hollow-charge weapon be lethal but it would probably ignite the ordnance beneath. He set the three-minute fuse, noting that Ptaff was also complete and already clambering back over the turret top. He moved to the edge, Vogt placing the ladder alongside for him to descend.

Braemer, noting that his troop had completed all of their tasks, passed the word. The MG34 team picked up their weapon and moved further away from the control car, at least fifty metres along the railway line. The rest of the troop, apart from Geyer and Ziegler who still had to toss their grenades into the anti-aircraft car, moved to the other side of the flat cars, ready to exfiltrate back to the wooded area. Their watches ticked through the seconds then minutes as they got closer to their target time for the launch of the attack.

They were joined moments later by their platoon commander, Leutnant Leeb, who had set charges against the armoured locomotive.

"This will be scrap iron soon," Braemer hissed to his platoon commander.

Leeb nodded. "They'll hear this bloody thing for miles when it goes up."

★

Next to the NKVD armoured rail cruiser, Paul and one troop were also in position.

"Right, Fessman, do it. I'm taking Feldwebel Grun and Beiler with me. You'll need everyone else."

"OK, sir," acknowledged Fessman who immediately turned to signal his men to carry out their assigned tasks.

Paul, Max and Beiler hurried away to carry out their assignment, seeking out the rail-borne torpedoes.

Geib from Fessman's troop was the first up, climbing the steel rung ladder attached to the side of the armoured cruiser. Like the others, he was in his sock-covered boots, placing each step carefully, not only to reduce the noise but also to help prevent him from slipping off the vertical ladder. At the top, he stepped off onto a narrow, chamfered platform in a gap alongside one of the two southern facing turrets. The turret to his left was staggered at a higher level than the one on his right, its barrel pointing south directly over the top of it, upwards at a shallow thirty-degree angle. He slipped the four hundred gram charge off his shoulder and wedged it under the bustle of the lower turret and up against the front wall of the left-hand turret. The aim was not to penetrate the thick armour but to damage the turret mechanism and prevent it from turning as well as ensuring that the shock wave caused maximum damage to the troops that might be deep inside. The fuse set, he heaved himself up onto the next chamfered level bringing him alongside the higher of the two turrets. It was difficult to manoeuvre along the narrow ledge. At one point, his foot slipped and he stood, his body frozen, as he waited and listened for signs of discovery. Luckily for him, it remained quiet and he made his way to the rear of the turret and tiptoed onto the two armoured doors beneath his feet, below a compartment housed an anti-aircraft battery, a quad Maxim machine gun mount fitted to a retractable platform.

Between him, the rear of the upper turret bustle and the northernmost turret at the far end of the cruiser was the commander's cupola. This housed the range finders, observation slits and communication links to all the weapons' positions. With three T-28 turrets, two Maxim machine-guns each side and a quad anti-aircraft unit, it was a truly formidable weapon. He pulled the twelve and a half kilogram hollow-charge explosive device that had been slung over his shoulder and placed it gently onto the surface beneath him. Relieved to be rid of its debilitating weight, he placed the device just behind the second level turret and on top of the steel doors of the anti-aircraft guns below.

His comrade, Rammelt, would place a similar charge between the rear of the northernmost turret, on the same level as Gieb's position, and the command cupola. This turret was quite close to the commander's control point, the long nose of the armoured train sloping away at the front, as opposed to the two stepped turrets at the rear. These two charges would punch their way through the train's armour, ripping into the command control and the mechanisms that moved and fired the guns and, at the same time, the ammunition bunkers would ignite, adding to the mayhem. He set the fuse, edged alongside the upper turret, stepped down to the lower platform and descended the steel rung ladder, rejoining his troop commander. He was quickly followed by the rest of the silent paratroopers.

"It's a bloody monster," exclaimed Rammelt as he joined the throng.

"To your positions," snapped Fessman, keen to get his men away. "The whole world is going to come down on top of us soon," he hissed.

His men dispersed, moving a good twenty-five metres away, Petzel and Stumme crawling painfully along the railway line, lugging their MG34 and belts of ammunition.

In the meantime, Paul, Max and Beiler had crept from under the flat cars on the western side of the armoured train, skirting around its southern end. Petzel and Stumme acknowledged them with a quick wave. They ran, at a crouch, across the seemingly never-ending railway lines that knitted themselves in front of them. Looking behind, they saw the shadowy figures atop the armoured cruiser. In front was a line of rail tankers they would need to negotiate. They found a link between two tankers and scrambled over the buffers and connecting chains, crouching down on the other side. Once there they looked about them, searching for any sign of discovery. Ahead of them, there were two more railway line groupings of at least ten railway lines in each group, converging north into dual lanes, passing what seemed to be a signal box controlling access to and from the yard. To their right were more engineless train configurations and, ahead, on the far side of the railway sidings, a wooded area. Earlier, all they had been able to see were the tops of the trees. They crouched down, covering their respective left and right arcs.

"This is too bloody quiet," hissed Max, obviously concerned.

"I have to admit, it does seem to be going all our way at the moment," Paul replied. "Seems too easy."

"But as far as the Russians are concerned, sir," joined in Beiler. "We're supposed to be on the other side of the river."

"You may be right," agreed Max begrudgingly, slapping him on his arm, but the hairs on the back of his neck were starting to tell him differently.

Paul checked his watch. He held up three fingers so his two men knew that the mayhem that would descend was only three minutes away. He quickly pulled his binoculars from their case, the forty-times magnification causing the wooded area and railway lines to leap into view. He could almost reach out and touch the trees. He scanned the southern part of the sidings. Nothing. The railway lines bordering the trees also appeared empty of the destructive weapons they were looking for. However, to the north, a small platform at the furthest junction of the railway line groupings had what appeared to be small trolleys alongside it; at least two, and maybe even three.

He tapped Max's arm and handed him the binoculars. "Take a look, Max."

Holding the lenses up to his eyes, Max searched the area Paul had indicated. "Check this out, sir. There's some sort of small electricity station and a pile of batteries alongside it."

Paul took the binoculars back and confirmed what Max had seen. He checked his watch again: less than three minutes to go.

Max, seeing Paul check his timepiece, said, "We'd best move, sir."

Paul turned to him and Beiler. "The time for silence is over now. We need to get to those torpedoes as fast as we can. Let's go." He leapt up, MP40 moving from side to side, Max on his right covering the southern flank, Beiler covering their rear.

They ran north-east, sidestepping railway sleepers, constantly adjusting the length of their stride as they negotiated their way across the endless railway lines and dashed the hundred or so metres to their target. Halfway there, they heard gunfire behind them.

"Keep going," called Paul. "They will have to take care of themselves."

"What's that over there, Anton?"

Anton Roon picked his head up slightly, scanning the area to their north.

"What, Drugi? I can't see anything."

Sesson pointed beyond the building they believed to be a signal box. "There, beyond the signal box, on the left. Yes, there they are. There must be at least a dozen of them."

Roon pulled the stock of the MG34 into his shoulder, peering down the iron sights, lining it up with the moving figures he too could now see, some two hundred metres away.

"Get Braemer, Drugi, quickly, the shit's going to hit the fan any second now."

Sesson slithered back along the railway line, at least ten metres, before picking himself up into a crouch, skirting the control car and scrabbling beneath the flat car, knowing the ignition of the explosive charges was imminent. He sought out his troop commander, informed him of what they had seen and was back at Roon's side in under a minute, holding the ammunition belt on Roon's left, ready to ensure the smooth feed of the ammunition into the fast-firing weapon. Braemer settled down to their left, Baader left of him and Rammelt dropped down to their right.

They watched and waited, Braemer checking the time.

"Sixty seconds. Get ready to hunker down."

The Russian soldiers were little more than one hundred metres away, oblivious to all around them, chatting, smoking, stepping gingerly over the railway sleepers, the crew returning to man the armoured train, little knowing what was in store for them.

One of them suddenly shouted to his comrades, pointing at the line of Fallschirmjager helmets facing them, raising his weapon in readiness but uncertain of what he was seeing. His eyes were telling him all was not well but his disbelieving brain was countering his instincts.

"Fire," yelled Braemer and he opened up with his MP40, the sound drowned out as Roon squeezed the trigger of the MG, the stock bucking in his shoulder as the rounds shot out of the barrel at over eight hundred rounds a minute, scything into the unwary approaching enemy soldiers.

The young soldier who had first spotted the strange convex lumps on the ground ahead of him was lifted off his feet as three 7.92mm rounds tore through his body. A shocked grunt was all that emanated from his lips as he flew backwards. His head cracked as he struck the steel railway line; his helmet was hanging uselessly from his belt.

"There's no hiding for us now," screamed Sesson above the din as he fed round after round into the fast-firing MG34. The distinctive buzz saw sound was letting the Russians know the German Army was here. The Green Devils had arrived!

Chapter Ten

There was no longer any need for silence. It was close enough to the planned attack time for it not to matter.

Geyer and Ziegler, backed up against the northern most anti-aircraft wagon, pulled the porcelain ball at the end of the string hanging from the wooden handle, fusing their grenades. They gripped the wooden handles of the Geballteladungen, six grenades strapped around a central core, turned to face the steel sides and tossed them over and into the open-topped wagon. The grenades dropped through the open top, ricocheting off the two sets of quad anti-aircraft guns before landing at the base of the pedestals upon which the guns were mounted. Two ticking bombs that would disable this threat to the soaring sons of Germany, the Luftwaffe; two quad Maxims capable of two thousand rounds a minute each.

Geyer and Ziegler ran to the flat cars opposite, scrambling to the other side and safety, throwing themselves to the ground painfully as the two explosions erupted. Flames, components from the guns, their mounts and shrapnel spewed into the early morning sky. The sound blanketed the noise of gunfire to their north. Both of the quad Maxim machine gun arrays were out of action; the supports buckled. The gun barrels were twisted and useless and the working parts damaged beyond repair. The two men had completed their task and it had all gone remarkably smoothly.

Vogt and Ptaff, positioned further alongside the armoured train, looked up from their prone positions on the ground to check out their *kameraden's* work, conscious that the explosives they had laid on the artillery wagon would explode at any minute. As they did so, they heard the spine-chillingly unwelcome sound of the armoured door beneath the commander's cupola opening towards them. Suddenly, it was thrust aside and two soldiers' faces peered out. The heavy calibre bullets from Vogt's and Ptaff's Kar98s quickly propelled them backwards just as the twelve and a half kilogram hollow-charge exploded. The solid cylinder of explosive, with its metal-lined conical hollow, detonated. The monumental pressure, generated by the detonation of the explosive charge and the inward collapse of the cone on itself, formed a high-velocity jet of metal, moving at hypersonic speed, the slug punching its way through the fifteen millimetres of upper armour of the artillery wagon like a knife going through butter.

A Russian soldier, who had rushed into the base of the left–hand gun turret after seeing his comrades shot and killed, was flung back against the turret elevation wheel. The force snapped his spine in an instant. Although still alive, his reprieve was to be short-lived as some of the 76.2mm rounds stowed in the ammunition storage bins exploded, causing a chain reaction, the rate increasing by the second as the heat and violence of the event ripped through the left-hand side of the armoured artillery wagon.

The same fate occurred to the right-hand turret as the hollow–charge weapon behind it blasted through the armour, destroying everything beneath it. The power of the blast immediately shredded the clothes from the teenage Russian soldier who was scrabbling to open the turret's cupola hatch and escape the inferno engulfing him. His torn and burnt legs quickly collapsed beneath him and he plummeted back into the maelstrom below, the intense heat igniting what clothing still adorned him before ravaging his whole body. His final scream was inhuman but, across the miles, his mother who was at home heard her only son.

The artillery wagon rocked with even greater ferocity as the left-hand turret, under an enormous pressure wave from the initial blast and mass explosions from the hundreds of rounds of artillery ammunition, was torn from its turret mountings and launched twenty metres into the air. It teetered at the top of its ascending curve before plummeting back to earth with a resounding crash between the armoured train and the NKVD cruiser. Vogt and Ptaff buried their heads into the ballast, oblivious to the discomfort, only fearing for their lives as the drama played out in front of them.

Paul, Max and Beiler had just reached the platform that they had been heading to when they heard the mayhem behind them. They stopped and turned round to observe it. They watched as the turret of the northernmost artillery wagon was discharged into the air by the force of the explosion beneath, stopping momentarily as it reached the top of its arc, before plunging back down to earth and out of sight of the three soldiers. Although there was a sense of silence after the myriad of explosions, there was still the ongoing crackle of small arms fire from the armoured train's exploding ammunition and the firefight still in progress as a backdrop.

"*Scheisse*, there's no hiding now, sir," exclaimed Max. "The entire bloody Russian Army will be on top of us soon."

"Look," pointed Beiler, bringing them back to the purpose of their particular mission, "those must be the torpedoes."

Braemer and his men involuntarily ducked and burrowed their faces into the ground as the anti-aircraft wagon was destroyed, followed by the first and second hollow-charge weapons decimating the artillery wagon. There was an even bigger shockwave as the turret was rocketed skywards. The four hundred gram charge that buckled the railway line and prevented the train from moving was almost insignificant relative to the other explosions; now this train was definitely going nowhere. The Russian soldiers in front of them had stopped, frozen in their tracks, no longer returning fire, mesmerised by the events unfolding in front of them. What had effectively been their mobile barracks was being torn apart before their eyes. The trains were being turned into nothing more than grotesque lumps of iron and scrap metal.

Roon was the first to recover, opening fire on the Russian soldiers, taking advantage of their dazed state. The slugs tore into them, reminding them that a ferocious enemy lay ahead. His brothers next to him soon joined in, the enemy soldiers falling like skittles as they sought to escape the devastating fire.

Moments later, the southern section of the armoured train erupted. The three soldiers who had been in the artillery wagon, guarding it whilst their comrades took a turn sleeping in more comfortable conditions, barely dragged themselves from their own blanketed sleep amongst the guns and ammunition before being blown apart by the two hollow-charge weapons placed above them.

Now both anti-aircraft wagons were out of action; the two PL-37 artillery wagons, each with their six Maxims and two 76mm guns, had been decimated. The armoured locomotive in the centre was out of action and, even though it had proven to be unnecessary, the railway line at each end had been buckled, making it impassable. Paul's men had done their job. The armoured train would play no part in trying to prevent the German forces who, at that very minute and with the help of the Brandenburger unit, had secured the bridge and were crossing the river.

Rammelt and Gieb were crouched down, fifty metres from the armoured cruiser. Their job was to cover the northern arc of the railway sidings. They both flinched at each of the explosions ripping through the armoured train to their left. They could see very little, their view shielded by the line of railway wagons also on their left. However, the turret that soared up into the sky, crashing down the other side of the goods wagons and the loud sounds of explosions and gunfire gave them a good idea as to the ferocity of the battle in which their *kameraden* were involved.

They then heard the unmistakable sound of coughing and spluttering coming from the front section of the Russian cruiser nearby, indicative of a cold engine being turned over. The coughing and spluttering turned into a throaty roar as the fuel was ignited; black smoke spewed from its exhaust. The pistons were driving the engine to a frenzy as the panicked Russian soldiers inside, desperate to counter the mayhem outside, over-revved the engine.

"*Scheisse*, they've got the bloody engine going," shouted Rammelt above the noise, the exhaust fumes making him gag as he looked back warily knowing they were directly in line with the armoured behemoth behind them. The engine revved again as the driver, frantic to warm the engine ready to move, gunned it again and again. The cruiser was shaking with the latent force from the exploding power plant. The railway lines Rammelt and Gieb lay on trembled and shook beneath them.

"Shouldn't those bloody charges have gone off by now?" yelled Gieb.

Before Rammelt could respond, another dissonance of sound was added to the orchestra of violence that pervaded their every sense: the firefight and explosions to their left; the engine being thrashed behind them; and now a Maxim machine gun was firing towards the goods train that was positioned alongside the armoured train that was now ablaze.

Although the Russian gunner would have been able to see very little, he felt it necessary to make his presence felt as he rattled off round after round. 7.62mm bullets were splintering the goods wagons and sparks were flying as they ricocheted dangerously off the railway lines. Some rounds made it through the gaps in the wagons, careering off the sides of the armoured train. The gunner's actions, however, were overall ineffective and short-lived.

A sudden blast of the hollow-charge explosives directly above the gunner and behind the single northernmost turret put paid to his attempt to intervene in the battle going on about him any longer. The molten slug ripped through the armoured topside of the cruiser and the hot blast immediately peeled skin and flesh from his skeleton, killing him instantly. He had had no time to feel any pain or scream out as his shattered body was finally ripped apart. Searing waves of white heat whipped through the cruiser's narrow, confined corridor expanding and welling up into the commander's cupola, igniting the clothing worn by the gunner's comrade. The young NCO had been frantically turning to the panoramic telescope, desperate to understand what was happening, cursing his officer for not being there and telling him what to do. In that moment, his eardrums shattered from the force of the explosion; his scream was muffled from the rest of the world. In unimaginable agony, his legs rapidly burnt and billowing hot gas engulfed him in its cloud of death. Passing out, he was oblivious to the second charge, further away from the cupola, above the retractable quad. Trapped in between these two opposing forces, his body was crushed, the force killing a third occupant who had been stationed inside the base of one of the two turrets opposite. The engine screamed out of control until its constituent parts destroyed themselves, the engine seizing with a powerful judder as it ground to a halt, now mere pieces of molten steel and chunks of useless metal. The juggernaut was dead, as were its three guardians.

Paul, Max and Beiler watched as the cruiser tore itself apart, the final death throes of the armoured beast. They quickly returned to their task in hand as they scrambled around the torpedoes they had discovered. Whatever happened to Paul and his men now, they had achieved the main part of their mission.

"Sir," called Max, "if we put the charges underneath the torpedoes here, it should do the trick."

Max pointed to the cradle in the centre of the trolley on which the torpedo–shaped bomb was resting, a car battery each side supported by a metal shelf. The whole structure was supported by a spindly axle at each end. The trolley, no more than a metre and a half in length, but the ZhDT-3 was a simple but effective mobile bomb.

"This can go," said Max as he ripped out the wires leading from the batteries to the two small electric motors attached to each of the front bogies, sparks leaping out as he did so. "*Scheisse*". Never liked electrics."

"OK, do your stuff, Beiler. The Feld and I will cover you."

Paul and Max took up a position a few yards away, watching the events unfold in front of them. Now, in the full light of day, they were no longer able to hide behind darkness and half-light. They could not see any of their own firing positions as they were hidden by the rail tankers that ran alongside them but they could see the Russian soldiers falling as they were brought down by a hail of fire from Braemer's troops' fast-firing MG34.

"If we move north and swing west, we could hit them from behind, sir," suggested Max.

"I know, Max, but we need to finish this job first before we draw attention to ourselves. We don't know how many there are and we could end up being more of a hindrance than a help."

"Makes sense."

While they watched, Beiler placed a Sprengkörper explosive charge, two hundred grams in size, at the side of the bomb, taping it to the large double-pointed cylinder and set the five-minute fuse. He moved on to the second one, muttering beneath his breath, "Bloody job for the Bahnpionier this. Where are the railway engineers when you need one." He placed the charge on the second trolley, moving quickly to the third, knowing that five minutes was probably now four, reducing quickly to three. Once complete, he rejoined his company commander.

"Job done, sir. We have about three or four minutes to get away before this lot goes up."

Before either Paul or Max could react, in addition to the cracks and thumps of exploding small arms ammunition and shells within the armoured cruiser and armoured train and the firefight to their west, they heard the distinctive buzz saw sound of two MG34s as they opened up. Beyond the dirty black palls of smoke now billowing up from sections of the armoured train and armoured cruiser, both Fessman's and Konrad's troops were now in contact with the enemy.

"Right," declared Paul, turning to Max and Beiler, "we'll make our way back to a position centre of the armoured cruiser, pick up Fessman, move forward and connect with Konrad, OK?"

"We're with you, sir," confirmed Max, picking himself up off the rough ballast that had slowly been grinding its way into every part of his anatomy that had connected with it.

Straube pulled the trigger of his beloved MG34, Muller guiding the ammunition belt into the feed housing, ensuring it was not allowed to check the pace of the firing as it spat round after round into the Russians advancing on the southern section of the armoured train, one of many groups now closing in on the destruction initiated by the Fallschirmjager. Shock at the sight of their decimated armoured trains, their intention was to punish the German paratroopers for their audacity.

As Straube continued to fire, rumblings, like distant thunder and explosions, could be heard coming from the direction of the river. The main German assault on Dvinsk was in full swing. They would be relieved soon, thought Straube as he picked off the advancing troops – or so he hoped.

Despite the casualties and as their comrades were knocked down like ninepins, the Russian soldiers were still driven forward relentlessly by their officers and NCOs. They were conscripts, barely out of training. Mainly from the rural areas of Russia, they had a vocabulary of less than two thousand words, some not even five hundred...

At least a platoon was advancing on the paratroopers' position and Straube was relieved when he and Muller were reinforced by Kempf and Lanz. The Russian lieutenant in command of the platoon, seeing his men struck down one after the other, panicked. His sergeant pulled him down on top of the cold railway lines. The sudden change in direction of the light breeze wafted the smell of cordite from the firefight and burning fuel from the armoured train. Mixed in with this was the strong smell of burning human flesh. The young Russian lieutenant was involuntarily sick.

The Russian sergeant screamed at the two sections to his left, initially nine men, now down to six in each, to open up with their light machine guns. The junior sergeants came out of their stupor to instruct their men. The two type-B sections, each having two 7.62mm Degtyaryeva Pekhotnii DP light machine guns whose bipods were now extended, were finally returning fire. The lieutenant, recovering his deportment, took control again ordering the other two type-A sections to his right to get ready to move further to their right and outflank the enemy. The two section commanders, junior sergeants, rose up from their positions, screaming at their men, physically pulling some of them onto their feet, leading and pushing them east, quickly followed by their platoon commander and sergeant. The fifteen men, all that was left of the two sections, ran east across the railway lines before turning north, clutching their Mosin Nagant rifles, the seventeen-inch long M1891, cruciform Shtik, spiked bayonet wavered in front of them.

"*Scheisse*, they are trying to outflank us," called Roon incredulously, watching the Russian soldiers running across their front. "If they get the other side of those goods wagons and come around the back, we're fucked."

"Don't just bloody lie there," yelled Konrad, their troop commander who had just joined them from the centre of the train, "get to the other side of the wagons and head them off. I'll get you some support as soon as I can."

Kempf and Lanz looked at each other, a hail of bullets from the four DP light machine guns now rebounding off the railway lines and the armoured control car behind them, splintering the railway sleepers, a shard slicing along Lanz's cheek.

"God, that fucking hurt," he howled, clutching the side of his face.

"Better than a bullet," suggested Kempf. "Come on, we need to scarper."

There was no time to waste. If the Russian soldiers beat them to it, they would be in deep trouble and a wood splinter would be the least of their troubles.

"And watch out for Fessman's lot," Konrad yelled after them. "They'll probably be coming our way."

"I bloody hope so," Kempf hissed to Lanz. "We're going to need their help."

Paul, Max and Beiler ran down one of the lengths of track, the constant sidestepping of sleepers and steel lines playing havoc with their ankles, before making their way towards the rail tankers. The closer they got to the huge bulk carriers, the more their vision of the armoured cruiser on the other side was restricted. All they could make out now was the black and white smoke, flecked with yellows, reds and oranges as the flames flickered skywards, fuelling the swirling mass. They positioned themselves near the huge buffers that prevented the tankers from making hard contact. They moved in between two of the grey tankers, Paul indicating they remained there while he checked out the other side. He climbed over the connecting chains and clambered onto the buffer on the far side, peeking around the bulk of the tanker checking for any sign of the enemy, or even his own paratroopers.

"Look," said Max, pointing to a piece of paperwork attached to the base of the tanker's supporting frame. "It's crude oil, bound for Hamburg."

"We can take delivery here now, Feld," drawled Beiler, grinning, his teeth showing as a white strip through his blackened and dusty face.

"Psst," called Paul, "let's go, it's clear."

Max and Beiler acknowledged his instruction and made their way over the buffers, various connections and the central link chain until they were hunkered down by the side of their company commander, who was also crouching. Opposite was the MBV2, the armoured cruiser, but it looked very different now. Smoke and flames billowed from either end and both sides of the commander's cupola, or at least where it had been. There was the occasional explosion as ordnance was still being detonated by the intense heat, fuelling the flames further.

"There's Fessman, sir."

Paul looked at where Max was pointing and could see Fessman signalling frantically for them to cross over to him, his rapidly waving arm indicating they should hurry.

"Come on."

Paul leapt up; Max followed with Beiler close behind. They ran as quickly as they could, stepping erratically over the railway lines and sleepers, trying their best to look about them for any signs of the enemy, yet having to watch the placement of their feet for fear of catching a boot and tumbling forward, wrenching or, even worse, breaking an ankle in the process. Max swore under his breath and looked forward to getting back onto proper solid ground.

As they got closer to the iron-clad monster, the hotter it got as the fierce heat radiated towards them. The armoured sides glowed red and, in places, almost white hot. They turned south to run alongside it, but far enough away to escape the worst of the heat, a sudden breeze blowing the smoke and fumes down and across their path. With their lungs heaving, they were too late to hold their breath, the toxic smoke and vapour searing their throats and lungs, a coughing fit ensuing as Paul and Beiler struggled to control it.

Paul felt a tug on his arm as Max, a scarf pulled up over his mouth, steered him out of the thick smoke and well away from the end of the cruiser, collapsing on the floor next to Fessman.

"Sitrep," demanded Max, noting that Paul was still struggling to clear his lungs.

"I have Petzel, Stumme, Rammelt and Gieb opposite by the flat cars," Fessman replied, pointing west to the flat cars that were alongside the armoured train. "The rest of my troop is here. There is a firefight southwest, so I suspect Konrad is getting hit hard."

"Braemer is getting it too," added Max.

"We'll join with your men, Uffz," ordered Paul. "Support Konrad then extract back to the woods. Max, take Herzog and Giester with you, find Braemer and get back to the woods. Don't wait for us. You need to move quickly, now."

They exchanged quick glances. Max's reluctance to leave his company commander obvious but he obeyed. Along with the two paratroopers assigned, he headed, at an angle, north-west to the flat cars that would lead them to the northern end of the armoured train where Braemer was holding his own.

"Move," ordered Paul and he and Fessman ran across the lines to join the rest of Fessman's men. Once there, they scrambled beneath the heavy-duty load carriers, capable of carrying heavy tanks and other armoured vehicles, and positioned themselves either side with Stumme, Petzel, Rammelt and Gieb.

Paul studied the landscape in front of him. The locomotive in the centre was black and silent but clearly damaged. To the left and right of the steam engine, the PL-37 artillery wagons were afire; the sharp cracks of the vast stocks of small arms ammunition detonating and the deeper rumble of shells exploding inside. To their right, between the flat cars and the goods wagons opposite, the turret from the far right PL-37 was still smouldering after being flung from its mountings. Three explosions in succession went off in the distance behind them, a gap of ten seconds between the last two.

"That's the torpedoes dealt with, sir." Beiler grinned.

"Sovs," called Petzel, pulling the MG34 into his shoulder. "They're coming along on the outside of the goods wagons."

"They're trying to outflank Konrad, sir," cautioned Fessman. "Shall we open fire?"

The dozen or so Russian soldiers, their long Mosin Nagant rifles flicking left and right as their NCO urged them forward, were unaware of the Fallschirmjager on their right flank watching them, predators waiting to strike their prey. The Russian rifles looked more like lances; at over 123 centimetres long and 166 centimetres with the bayonet attached, they were probably the longest rifles in the European weapons' arsenal. They moved parallel to the goods wagons and were a mere twenty metres away before they found themselves directly opposite Paul and his group.

"Yes, now. Open fire!"

The paratroopers opened up on the enemy soldiers creeping along the railway lines. Shots zipped from Petzel's MG34, tearing into the group of young and exhausted-looking soldiers who looked on in horror as their comrades in front were quickly and mercilessly torn down by the torrent of fire from the MG. The rest of the paratroopers had also opened up with machine pistols and rifles. The Russians huddled together, in the vain hope that getting closer to their friends would somehow provide them with added protection. This only made Paul's men's task easier; it was like coming across a flock of birds on a winter's shoot back home.

The lieutenant, whose turn had not yet come and with remnants of vomit still in the corners of his mouth, stood stupefied, frozen to the spot. The senior sergeant screamed at him and the remaining Russian soldiers to scatter and hit the deck. His last command froze in mid-flow as a bullet smacked into his skull, knocking him sideways. The instantaneous crack from Fessman's Kar98K/40 was the source of the Russian NCO's demise. The lieutenant, recovering from his shock, waved his Tokarev pistol about him, shooting blindly, screaming at his remaining men to pull back. He met the same fate as his NCO. Fessman again took credit for the kill and his friends slapped him heartily on his back.

"Bloody hell, Walter, you've got it in for the officers and NCOs," called Max, grinning and firing another burst from his MP40.

Seeing the senior sergeant go down, his arms flailing as he fell backwards, the rest of the unit panicked and ran blindly as fast as they could. Some tripped over the railway sleepers in their confusion; others threw their rifles away and sprinted to safety. Three more fell to the paratroopers' concentrated firepower, the rounds that missed splintering the wooden sides of the wagons. Then they were gone, out of effective range, lost around the end of the goods wagons, blundering into the fire of Konrad's troop.

"Cease fire! Cease fire!" yelled Paul. "They've had enough. Save your ammo."

It was suddenly quiet, apart from the sporadic firing at each end of the armoured train. Paul scanned the ground ahead. There were at least eight soldiers either dead or wounded opposite, plus the lieutenant and NCO.

"Let's go," ordered Paul. He leapt up quickly and ran across the lines in front, heading for the wagons opposite.

"Don't stop. Leave the Russians, but watch your backs," shouted Max.

They sprinted the fifty metres, across the ten lines, arriving at a gap between two of the now heavily splintered wagons, hitting the deck, panting and catching their breath.

"Thank God you lot turned up," called a blackened-faced paratrooper the other side of the gap. "Sorry, sir, didn't see you there," he added quickly, as he recognised his company commander.

"Open your bloody eyes then, Kempf," added Max with a mischievous smile.

"What's happening?" demanded Paul.

"They have at least four DPs pinning the troop down, sir. We came round here to block their flanking attack."

"You two stay here in case they come back."

"Unlikely, sir, with the pasting they've just had."

"We don't know who's out there. Best have this door covered. Right, the rest of you with me. We'll go and see what Konrad is up to," ordered Paul.

They clambered in between the goods wagons to join Kempf and Lanz, both of them remaining behind to cover the unit's eastern flank, and came out opposite the connection between the control car and anti-aircraft wagon.

"Uffz, take four men the other side of the train. Take up a position by the flat cars where you can cover Konrad's withdrawal."

"I'll take the MG with me then, sir."

"And watch out for a counter-attack from the south on that side," shouted Leeb, the platoon commander who had just joined them.

"Ernst."

Paul and Leeb clasped hands.

"What's the situation, Ernst?"

"Braemer's holding his own at the other end, but not for long. The pressure's building up."

"I've sent Max to back him up and pull his troop back to the forest. Now you're here, I want to consolidate the entire unit."

They all ducked as bullets stitched their way across the side of the armoured control car, ricocheting in all directions

"*Scheisse*, that was close, sir."

"We need to get out of here quickly before we're surrounded. Fessman should be close to being set up and Braemer should be extracting. Ernst, take the rest of Fessman's men with you and ensure the woods are clear for us."

"What about you, sir?" quizzed Leeb.

"I'll pull Konrad back through Fessman's position."

"Consider it done, sir," and with that Leeb called out to his men, before they made their way beneath the control car and headed for the woods to carry out his task.

Paul, now on his own, crept forwards towards Konrad's position, calling for Kempf and Lanz to follow him.

"Uffz, Uffz Konrad," he called.

Konrad and his troop were about thirty metres away from the control car, having edged slowly back towards the train. They had goods wagons to their left, the control car behind them and the flat cars to their right. In front, half a platoon with up to four DPs keeping the paratroopers' heads down.

"As soon as Fessman's MG opens up, I'll throw some smoke. Pull back here then and head for the woods as fast as you can. Leutnant Leeb will be waiting for you. Understood?"

"Yes, sir," shouted Konrad, ensuring all his men had heard the instructions above the din of the firefight. Although the flanking attack on his men had failed badly, there were still four light machine guns trying to pin them down until reinforcements came. However, at the moment there were only two. One had jammed and one firing wildly had run out of ammunition, and the gunner and his second were frantically manually loading rounds into one of the pan-shaped forty-round magazines that, when full, sat on top of the breech.

Now was the time, thought Paul. They needed to move fast if they were to get out of this and prevent a disaster. Only two DPs were spraying fire at that moment. He plucked two, egg-shaped smoke grenades from his grenade bag, pulled the pin from the first, stood on the right-hand side of the control car and lobbed it as far as he could. He knew it would drop just beyond his men but it would have to do. He then threw the second one. That landed ten metres beyond Konrad's troop just as the first one started to splutter out its white smoke. Paul yelled to Konrad to get the hell out of there. Fessman's MG was now adding to the noise, and the accuracy of Petzel's fire took its toll on the machine gunners. While attacking the German left flank earlier, they had neglected to cover their own left flank. Fessman had also lobbed a smoke grenade at the enemy and the area was soon engulfed in plumes of swirling, white smoke.

Paul grabbed Kempf's shoulder. "Let's go."

They sprinted across the back of the control car and headed for the flat car in the direction of the wooded area where they had originally formed up. They scrambled between two of the cars, hearing the clattering of hobnailed boots as Konrad's men were hot on their tail. There was no need for silence now. Now was the time for speed, the sort of speed that makes the difference between life and death.

"Go, go, to the woods," yelled Paul as he checked his men off as they withdrew from the enemy. Once the last one was through, he made his way along the flat cars until he found Fessman, diagonally opposite the Russian force now engulfed in white smoke.

"Get the fuck out of there now," he shouted to Fessman.

"What about—"

"Bloody move now, Uffz."

Fessman did not need any more encouragement. The urgency in his company commander's voice was enough. He gathered his men and they too sprinted for the quasi-safety of the woods now in front of them.

Paul looked across to the other end of the line of flat cars, to the north, and could see the unmistakable bulk of Max sprinting across the sidings, heading for the wooded area, closely followed by Braemer and his men. It is time I moved, he thought and shot off behind Fessman and his troop.

He heard a cry to his left as Barth went down, hit by a bullet from one of the Russian soldiers who, seeking revenge for the death of his comrades, had clambered on top of one of the flat cars and was firing above the smoke. The soldier fired again, but was in too much of a hurry to inflict death on the German soldiers. The round from his rifle missed its target and spun off one of the steel railway lines, whining as it was deflected away, spent. He suddenly lowered his rifle, a red bloom blossoming on the front of his smock as he was knocked backwards, toppling down the other side, his rifle clattering on the wooden slats of the car.

Thank God, Leeb was able to give them some covering fire, thought Paul as he continued to run. He saw Rammelt and Gieb pick up Barth, Gieb throwing him over his shoulder in a fireman's lift, not knowing his friend was already dead. After a forty-metre dash, they all crashed into the wooded area, chests heaving, sucking in badly needed oxygen, legs weak and burning from lack of glycogen.

Paul looked out of the trees, back towards the sidings, hoping he had got all of his men back safely.

Chapter Eleven

The trucks carrying the Fallschirmjager from the rest of Volkman's battalion rumbled over the bridge, thick palls of smoke billowing ahead from burning buildings and armoured vehicles. As they came off the bridge, leaving the embankment and entering the town of Dvinsk, they were met by widespread destruction: premises with their windows blown out, shattered glass strewn across the roads, crunching as the trucks passed over the shards. The church to their right had survived most of the blasts but chunks of masonry were still missing. Miraculously the spire was still intact. They passed a T-26, its turret askew, black oily smoke still emanating from it, the lack of breeze allowing it to pillar upwards. As the convoy passed, it stirred it up further, small swirling trails whipped downwards, as the vehicles hurried past. Drivers and passengers behind Helmut's truck frantically attempted to close their windows as the acrid fumes entered. The passengers in the cargo compartment coughed and spluttered as the stinging smoke attacked their lungs.

Helmut checked his map. Although it told him very little, it was enough to get him to the objective, relieving Paul and his men. He must have looked at it a hundred times but the entire battalion, minus Paul's small force, was behind him, and depending on him taking them in the right direction. First, they would drive through the edge of the town until they came across the railway line, running north-west where they would turn left, tracking it until they came up against the railway line going north-east. At this junction, they would turn right. Then it was just a matter of following the railway line until they came to the sidings where they could extract Paul and his men who would no doubt be both physically and mentally exhausted after their battle to take the armoured trains. He turned to his company Feld Axel Jung who had kicked the Luftwaffe driver out, preferring to drive his company commander himself.

"The railway line can't be much more than a couple of hundred metres now. Keep your eyes peeled."

Jung quickly swung the wheel to the left to avoid a hole in the road, roughly lined with rubble, hearing the curses in the back as the troops were thrown against each other.

"Well, they're awake now, sir," he said, grinning.

"Yes, but you've bloody well made me lose that Bratwurst now," complained Helmut, scrabbling around the passenger footwell of the truck to recover the remnants of his breakfast.

"Sorry about that, but it is your second breakfast, isn't it, sir?" joked Jung, with raised eyebrows.

"Watch the bloody road and less insubordination from you," cursed Helmut, wiping bits of grit from the prize sausage he had filched from the field kitchen.

"There it is, sir, the railway line."

Directly ahead, they could both see the railway line. Alongside it, stationary, white smoke spewing from its engine compartment, was a Panzer II reconnaissance tank.

"Stop just in front of it," ordered Helmut as he opened the door of the still-moving vehicle. Climbing down once Jung had brought it to a halt, he checked the convoy behind him before heading over to the stricken armoured vehicle. The tank commander was wearing his tankies hip-length, double-breasted, black Panzer jacket piped in rose-pink rayon. The national emblem of the Hoheitszeichen eagle in white clutching a swastika clearly adorned his right breast. His ski-type trousers were also black. He contrasted well with Helmut's green, splinter pattern Fallschirmjager smock and green combat trousers. The tank commander's rank showed him to be an Unteroffizier. The commander slid down the front of the tank's turret, past the 2cm L/55 gun and dropped to the ground. Once down, he saluted Helmut.

The square-jawed, stocky Leutnant, his large hands resting on the MP40 slung across his chest, immediately dominated the tanker. "Problem, Uffz?"

"Yes, sir. Bloody engine has burnt out. Not had a chance of a proper refit since France," he complained pointing to the white smoke curling up from the overheated engine.

"What's the situation up ahead?" Helmut asked in clipped tones, knowing time was critical.

"We're pushing them back. We have about half a kilometre bridgehead at the moment. Your guys joining in the fight then, sir?"

"Yes, Uffz. One of our units is operating behind enemy lines."

"So that's what all the noise is about! We thought the Sovs were blowing up ammo dumps before we got there. Weren't you lot in Crete, sir?"

"Yes, but they knew you tankers would need the support of real soldiers to protect your back. Well, good luck, Uffz."

"Thank you, sir. You too."

With that, Helmut quickly returned to the Opel truck and climbed back in, the engine still ticking over.

"OK, Axel, let's get moving."

"Across the tracks, sir?"

"Yes, go left. There's a crossing point about a hundred metres down on the right. The engineers have banked it up with some wooden beams."

Jung revved the powerful engine and the Opel Blitz jerked forwards. "Bloody clutch."

"Yeah, yeah," chided Helmut.

They turned left, tracking the railway line until they came to the prepared crossing point. Turning right, they bumped slowly across the uneven surface, the rest of the convoy following close behind. The buildings had now receded and they were in an open piece of ground, exposed.

"Keep your eyes peeled, sir. We're coming into bandit country now."

Once across, they turned left following the railway line and keeping it on their left until they met the junction some three hundred metres further on. This section of the track curved north to join the mainline that went north-east, deeper into Russia. They followed this until they hit a small sidings that would be impossible to cross in the trucks.

"This is it, Axel, as far as our taxis take us. Get the boys out."

"*Jawohl*, Herr Oberleutnant," and he leapt out of the cab to gather the company ready for action.

Other vehicles pulled up alongside and, behind the now stationary lead truck, troops dismounted noisily.

"Less chatter," commanded Jung. "Get your platoons sorted. Leutnants report to the Oberleutnant."

A Steiner jeep pulled up alongside Helmut's cab. The Raven jumped out, striding his way across to the Blitz, pulling the door of the cab open. Inside, Helmut had spread his map over the vehicle's dashboard.

"Well, Janke?" demanded the Raven as he stepped up on the footplate, his dark, hooded eyes flickering across the map.

"We're here, sir."

"I know where we damn well are. Show me where Brand and his men are."

"North-west of here, sir, is the lake. They skirted around the top of it to get to the wooded area the other side and approach the sidings from the west. They must be five to eight hundred metres north-east of our position, sir."

The rest of the battalion officers joined them and Volkman stepped back so they could all see him.

"This is how we're going to play it. Fleck," he said looking directly at Erich, "I want your company, supported by Brand's two platoons, to move up south of the lake, on the left-hand side of the sidings. Go for the wooded area. That's where Brand should be holed up, assuming he's got his act together. Understood?"

"Yes, sir."

"Janke, I want you straight up the middle of the sidings. You'll need to spread your men out. The sidings seem to be quite full and your visibility is going to be badly restricted. Don't go beyond the line of the woods. If you cross their front, you could have enemy in between you both and you would be unable to open fire for fear of hitting each other. Clear?"

"Perfectly, sir."

"Bauer, I will join you and we'll secure the woods on the opposite side of the sidings but we won't advance further than the end of them. Got that?"

"Yes, sir."

"Once you're all in position, we wait for Brand's signal; then we'll wait for your signal, Fleck. I don't want any cock-ups."

"*Jawohl*, Herr Major," they all responded.

"Where is Hauptman Bach, sir?" asked Helmut.

"He's liaising with 6th Panzer Division. We don't want to get into a firefight with our own men. Any questions? No? Right, move out."

The three officers returned to their respective companies, Major Volkman attaching himself to Bauer's unit, much to the relief of the others. Erich and his enlarged company crossed the railway lines heading for the low, single-storey buildings to their north-west. Some were small industrial units, many associated with the railway;

the ones further to the north appeared to be small plots or summer houses. Once among these, Erich and his men felt less exposed. Now they had some cover, although they were still alert for any enemy hiding in or amongst the buildings. Placing one of Paul's platoons on each flank, he led them and his company towards where they believed the woods to be, their objective, where he hoped he would find Paul and his men safe and secure.

The battalion commander and Manfred Bauer followed the eastern edge of the railway line, first crossing a small siding before arriving at the much larger one where all the action earlier had taken place. They kept to the edge, the forest on their right, heading towards the platforms where Paul, Max and Beiler had earlier destroyed the rail-mounted torpedoes. Within minutes of coming across the main sidings, they came under fire. The company started to disperse and Volkman urged his men forward.

"Keep moving, don't give them a target. Get those bloody MGs working. Bauer, get a troop covering and get the rest of your men forward."

"Right lads, move out," ordered Helmut leading first platoon forward, north, along the centre of the sidings. Erich to his left, Manfred and the battalion commander to his right, it was a significant force. They arrived at the sidings which widened the further they went as more and more lines branched off, until there must have been over forty lines in groups of ten, dotted with formations of wooden-sided goods wagons, flat cars, tankers and locomotives.

They heard the thump of the tank firing up ahead before they saw it. It was a Panzer IV, its grey form dominating the brown of the goods vehicle it was parked up alongside, a gaggle of Wehrmacht surrounding it.

His lead platoon scattered as Helmut went forward to talk to the Landser. The platoons on the other two sides also stopped, keeping in contact with their *kameraden* via the gaps between each railcar.

"What's happening?" challenged Helmut.

"We can't see a bloody thing, sir, just lines of rolling stock. There's been a right battle going on up ahead, but it seems to have died down now."

"That will be our men, Leutnant. They will be clearing the way for you but we need to get to them fast."

"They're waiting for you, sir?"

"Yes, we're their guardian angels coming to the rescue." He smiled.

He looked Helmut up and down. "No disrespect, sir, but you hardly look like an angel to me."

"Now, now, Leutnant, don't get personal," said Helmut with a grin and patting the young officer's shoulder. "So, what's your plan?"

"My platoon will follow this beast up the centre here, with one troop behind and one either side of the wagons. We can use the rolling stock for cover, along with the Panzer, and push straight through."

"Sounds good. My boys will be right behind you covering your arse."

"Great, sir. Let's get to it."

The Leutnant leapt on top of the tank and conversed with the tank commander inside. Moments later, the familiar, sudden spurt of smoke belched out; the roaring engine jerked the tank forward and it rattled over the railway lines, the driver taking it slowly, clearly concerned about possibly losing a track.

Paul peered out of the trees. The Russian soldiers had not followed them, choosing to go to ground and pepper them with fire from a distance. They had learnt a swift lesson and were not keen to take on the Green Devils again just yet.

Max crouched down beside him.

"All done, Max?"

"Yes, sir. Fessman is covering the front and right flank, Braemer front and left and Konrad's covering our backside."

"Casualties?"

"Just two. Barth didn't make it and Kuhn has had a wing clipped. Assuming we get relieved soon, he should be OK."

"Ammo?"

"Not so good. We've been chucking it about a bit, so they've been told aimed shots only. What now, sir?"

"There's nothing else for it, Max, but to sit tight here and wait."

Erich and his men weaved in and out of the various buildings. No heavy contact with the enemy as yet, just the occasional potshot. They eventually came across a small section of soldiers who were obviously retreating, looking wide-eyed over their shoulders as they ran away from the fighting The paratroopers, almost as surprised as the Russians, reacted first and killed two or three before the rest fled. They continued darting from cover to cover, skirmishing forward, section by section, covering each other as they moved closer and closer to their objective.

"We need to push further east, Reinhold," instructed Erich to his Company Feldwebel.

"Want to get sighting of the sidings, sir?"

"Yes, I don't want us to go too far west. We need to make sure Oberleutnant Brand gets sight of us or we could get on the wrong end of one of their MGs."

"Shouldn't be too difficult to find. Just follow the pillars of smoke. Looks like the Oberleutnants have been busy. Shall I bring one of his platoons forward?"

"They're not needed at the moment."

"I was thinking more for recognition purposes, sir. The Oberleutnant's boys will soon pick out their own men, even from a distance."

"Good idea. Bring Leutnant Roth and his lads forward."

They'll soon pick out Leutnant Roth," said Feldwebel Weiss, smiling. Then he left to bring the commander of Paul's third platoon forward.

Oberleutnant Bauer, shadowed by his battalion commander, and his company, had numerous small firefights as they pushed their way onward between the treeline and the eastern boundary of the railway sidings. Most of the sidings were hidden by the rolling stock positioned there, but Bauer used the palls of smoke from Paul's earlier action to track their progress. Once they reached the end of the sidings, they could set up a defensive perimeter until notified that Oberleutnant Brand and his men were safe.

Helmut tucked himself in behind the Panzer IV as its tracks rattled over the steel lines and crunched over the ballast, the turret turning left and right slowly; the tank commander nervous at being hemmed in either side by railway wagons. One shell had been fired at a small Russian unit that had opened fire on them from the confines of a goods wagon. Now the soldiers were dead and the wagon splintered and battered.

The tank ground to a halt and Helmut joined the Leutnant again. "This is as far as we go, sir. Our orders are to sit tight here until we know your men have been extricated."

"OK, it shouldn't be long now."

★

"There, sir," gestured Max towards the buildings on their right. "That has to be Leutnant Roth. You can't mistake his cherub-like face."

Paul pulled his binoculars up to his eyes and focused on the buildings some two hundred metres away, Leutnant Roth's cherubic face jumping into the lens like an unexpected cartoon character. Scanning left, he could see his friend Erich who was directing his men to spread out along the edge of the building complex.

"It is, Max, and don't be derogatory about one of your seniors."

"Who me, sir?" coughed Max with a grin.

"Time, Max."

"It is, sir. Pass it here."

Paul handed over the Heres model 1928 flare pistol. Max checked it was loaded, quickly brushed the large barrel and then, in both hands, held it out in front of him at a seventy-degree angle and fired. The flare soared up into the sky, almost directly above the sidings, reaching a height of at least two hundred metres. The burning flare slowly dropped down, visible for only five seconds, but it was long enough. Erich responded with his flare. Now the entire battalion would know that contact had been made; they were officially back with their parent unit.

Paul turned to Max, his shoulders slumped, suddenly tired. "That's it, Max, we're done."

"Beer's on me this time, sir." His blackened face split into a broad smile.

"Ice-cold water would do me right now..."

Chapter Twelve

The four friends wandered down the streets of Dvinsk. Many of the buildings alongside them were severely bomb-damaged and burnt out, the flames now extinguished. Locals could be seen either scavenging or attempting to put their properties back into some form of habitable order. There was the occasional building that remained untouched apart from shattered windows.

The Raven had released them for some local R and R, rest and recuperation, something that Paul and his men desperately needed after the intensity of their recent battle. They had successfully fulfilled their task with minimal casualties, and the battalion commander was on a high after the unit's triumph. Praise was being heaped on the Fallschirmjager. As a consequence of the now rapid advance of the German Army deeper into Russia, their specialist skills were currently not required, so they had been stood down.

"The cafe bar is at the end of this street then left," Helmut told the others, shaking Paul's arm. "Food and drink."

"How do you know about this place?" asked Erich.

"Some of the rear echelon told me about it. Seems the locals already have a small market going."

"Commerce always wins through," chipped in Manfred.

"The black market, you mean," said Helmut, laughing.

The four Fallschirmjager Senior Leutnants strode down the wide footpath, often having to step out onto the road to avoid the piles of broken window glass and rubble from the damaged buildings. The surprisingly large number of locals going about their daily business viewed the Germans as liberators, not conquerors. In fact, many celebrated being liberated from the Bolsheviks.

They reached the T-junction at the end of the street, a small section of Feldgendarmerie eyeing them and the local population suspiciously, watching Paul and his friends closely as Helmut cracked a joke causing them to burst into laughter.

Helmut guided them to the left. They were now headed east, deeper into the centre of the town, a steady stream of military passing them, hooting their horns at civilians who got in the way. The majority were supply vehicles carrying much needed food and ammunition for the rapidly advancing Divisions.

It was 29 June. 56th Panzer Corps had succeeded in crossing the River Dvina successfully and had pushed through the town of Dvinsk. Uits of Army Group North were already heading for Riga. Army Group Centre's Panzer Groups, on their right flank, had already met east of Minsk, trapping some twenty-seven Red Army divisions.

"There it is," pointed Helmut. "The one with all the flags hanging from the window. Come on, move it."

"They've got tables and chairs outside. It's like a small square," commented Manfred.

"They're all taken though."

"Don't worry yourself, Paul. We're the conquering heroes. They have to find space for us," bragged Helmut, striding through the occupied tables.

As they approached the front of the cafe bar, the proprietor, wearing a white apron, encouraged a group of men, obviously locals, to vacate their seats and table, which they reluctantly did. Seeing the four Fallschirmjager officers heavily armed with Helmut hovering close by looking particularly big and mean, was incentive enough.

The owner fussed around them. In a Latvian dialect, alien to the soldiers, he welcomed them to his establishment. There was no menu. The four friends only spoke German and a little English, so they just sat there looking at each other in silence until Helmut came to the rescue. Gesturing with pinched fingers towards his expectant mouth and a hand tipping an invisible clasped glass, the proprietor got the message. Smiling and muttering, he rushed back into the building: a dark bricked, two-storey structure with tall front windows and double doors.

They peeled off their helmets, relieved to be rid of the restriction and weight and placed them on the floor, their MP40s placed between their feet, keeping them close at hand and ready if needed. The owner returned moments later with four bowls of something pink and placed one in front of each of his German guests.

Helmut picked up his bowl and sniffed at its contents. Then he grabbed a spoon and sampled some of it. "It's bloody cold, but doesn't taste too bad."

"At the speed your spoon's moving, it must be alright."

"You haven't tried yours yet, Erich. Mmmm, tastes a bit like beet. Not bad at all," Helmut added, looking up at them with a smile. "What?" His friends were staring and suddenly burst out laughing.

"It could be dishwater and you'd still eat it," commented Paul.

They then joined in and soon polished off the traditional Latvian dish that had been served to them. Moments later, the proprietor was back with four glasses of beer all expertly held in his right hand, froth spilling over the top as he placed them down in front of the soldiers who had now pushed back their empty bowls of beet soup. He spoke to them in his language, probably asking if they had enjoyed their food. Then he quickly returned back inside.

Helmut smacked his lips then picked up the glass in front of him, sat back and sampled the traditional Latvian beer that had been produced in one of the many local breweries.

There were half a dozen wooden tables outside the cafe bar, situated on the edge of the small square. Trucks trundled by. Locals walked past them, curious, giving them the once-over. Some smiled, others rushed by trying not to make eye contact. The odd Landser went purposely by on the way, no doubt, to fulfil a task.

The landlord returned with a large tray held high in his left hand, ignoring the protestations from his other customers occupying the remaining tables. With his rotund waist resting against the table, he placed more plates of food in front of the expectant and hungry paratroopers. They each had a plate dished up with pot-cooked cabbage, a meat cutlet, pickled cucumber and a side plate of sautéed sauerkraut. A charger was placed in the middle of the table with slices of caraway cheese. Helmut was the first to grab a slice, quickly followed by a second.

"Thanks for leaving us some," joked Paul.

"There's loads left. We can soon get some more," he responded with a mouth full of cabbage.

The owner was soon back, this time with a basket full of freshly sliced, dark rye bread. He clapped his hands, patted Paul's and Manfred's shoulders, still a little wary of Helmut, and then went to serve the other grumbling guests.

"Sod the field kitchen," advocated Helmut, "this is more like it. *Prost*," he added raising his glass, his friends following suit.

"*Prost*," they all responded. Happy to be off-duty, happy to be together, happy to be alive…

They ate their meals, finished off the side dishes, bread and caraway cheese, and drank three more beers. Then they thanked the proprietor, paid him in Reichsmarks and, with full stomachs, sauntered back the way they had come heading for the building that had been commandeered by the Raven to accommodate his battalion.

"God, that was good," muttered Helmut, rubbing his stomach. "We can go back there for dinner later, yeah?"

"If it will keep you happy," agreed Paul.

"What's going on over there?" Manfred pointed.

A crowd had gathered, clearly locals, a few soldiers and Latvian Police, congregating in a semi-circle around what appeared to be the frontage of a garage or workshop.

"Don't know," responded Erich. "Let's take a look, we'll soon find out."

They headed towards the crowd, positioning themselves on the periphery. Eyes turned in their direction, some with smiles, others with wariness.

"Look, something's happening," indicated Paul.

A young man, his sleeves rolled up above his elbows and armed with a crowbar came out of the workshop. He looked at the crowd then focused in on another group standing apart from the main throng and walked over to them. Paul and his friends could see that they were separate from the main crowd, guarded by Latvian police. The young man approached one of the prisoners, grabbing hold of a man of a similar age. The prisoner, his hands tied and raised in supplication, eyes pleading, called to the crowd for mercy. The police didn't interfere as he dragged him over to centre stage, watched by the audience, and pushed him violently down to the ground. The man fell to his knees, his hands stopping his face from hitting the road. The Latvian swung the crowbar with full force, striking his victim on the back of the head. The cracking of the skull was audible to everyone as the man was hit a second and third time.

"What the fuck?" exclaimed Erich. Although a soldier who had seen and inflicted death many times, he was still shocked by what he had just observed.

Another captive was dragged out and suffered the same fate, beaten to death, followed by another and another. The crowd clapped enthusiastically after each entertainment. The four men were mesmerised by what they were witnessing.

"This is fucking ridiculous. Shouldn't we stop it?" asked Helmut finally.

One of the crowd, sensing Helmut's distaste, called out, "Jude, Bolshevik, Jude," and pointed at the events unfolding where the man with the crowbar was carrying out his killings.

"Fuck off." Helmut glared at the individual who chose to lose himself in the crowd for fear of attack himself.

"There's a Feldgendarmerie over there," said Erich. "I'm going to speak to him."

"I'll come with you," offered Paul.

Paul and Erich walked around the edge of the crowd and made their way to the two German military policemen they had seen over on the far edge of the semi-circle.

The Hauptmann, Feldgendarmerie, commander of one of the troops in the area, was smartly dressed in his M36 officer's pattern *feldbluse*, the orange-red, branch of service on the *litzen* of his collar patches. The oxidised-silver braid shoulder epaulettes, with their two gilt rank pips, confirmed his rank. Next to him was a Feldwebel, his MP40 resting in the crook of his arm, butt into his waist, his hand gripping the magazine, barrel pointing upwards.

Paul and Erich saluted the military police captain.

"Can you see what's going on there, sir?" Paul asked him. "This is murder. Aren't you going to stop it?"

He felt Erich, who was standing just behind him and to one side, grip his left elbow gently, a gesture signifying that his friend should tread carefully.

"They are just Jude and Bolsheviks, Oberleutnant. Nothing to do with us."

"But you... we can't just stand by and allow this to happen."

"The Einsatzgruppe are in charge of this fiasco, Oberleutnant...?"

"Brand, sir, 4th Independent Fallschirmjager Battalion."

"Well, I suggest, Oberleutnant Brand, you go about your business and let others get on with theirs."

"But, sir—"

"Look, Oberleutnant, I've heard some good things about your unit. It seems you took out some Red Army artillery that could have caused us a real problem crossing the Dvina and taking the town."

"But we fought soldiers, sir, not unarmed civilians."

"Go find a bar, get drunk, celebrate your success and get ready for whatever task they drum up for you next."

"Sir—"

"I suggest, Oberleutnant," the captain addressed Erich, "you take your comrade away now, or I'll be forced to take him in and I don't want to do that."

Erich gripped Paul's elbow harder and eased him back.

"Come on, Paul, there's nothing we can do here."

"Leave it, Oberleutnant."

With that, the two Feldgendarmerie left, moving past the two men and heading for the other side of the gathering. Paul continued to stare at the scene beyond the crowd, where the gruesome killings continued. Erich cajoled him into rejoining their two colleagues.

Once they were back with their two friends, events outside the workshop took a different turn. The young man, blood and brain matter still dripping from the crowbar, threw it to the ground and, with one foot on one of his victims, proceeded to play the Latvian national anthem on an accordion he had been handed from someone in the crowd. The watching horde clapped and joined in, singing at the tops of their voices, their voices rippling through the gathering as they all joined in the celebration of the event.

"Come on," said Manfred, "let's get away from here. It's making me feel sick."

They slowly continued their way down the road, the sound of the singing dissipating the further away they got. Helmut and Erich were either side of Paul and sensed his distress and anger. They were concerned that he might do something noble, but foolish. Manfred occasionally looked over his shoulder, struggling to accept the reality of what he had witnessed, and dragged his eyes from the macabre episode. As they made their way down the road, crowds, heading for the workshop and wanting to see what the great attraction was, parted for them as they pushed through. Still in full combats, helmets hanging from their belts, MP40s slung over their shoulders, pistol holder at their side, they were a force the civilians did not want to cross.

Chapter Thirteen

They continued to make their way through the milling throng of civilians who seemed keen to get even closer to the gruesome events that were unfolding. Apart from the obvious combat damage to the buildings, the town seemed to be rapidly returning to normal except for the scene they had just witnessed; some of the locals saw the German Army as liberators rather than an occupying force. The occasional distant thunder of an artillery barrage was the only attestation that the battle for Russia was still in progress.

The four friends discussed what they had witnessed as they pressed forward through the ever-growing crowd. Although hardened fighters, having experienced numerous battles and seen their *kameraden* and their enemy blown to pieces, their bodies almost unrecognisable, this incident sickened them to their core.

"I know they were Jews and Bolsheviks but that was inhuman."

"I agree, Manfred, then playing the bloody accordion and having a sing-song afterwards," added Helmut.

"Whatever their nationality, they're still human beings," argued Paul.

"Shall we say something to the Raven when we get back?"

"No, Erich, you know he pretty much toes the party line," responded Paul. "He would only tell us to keep our noses out and leave the SD to do their job."

"I reckon we can cut through here and get away from this mob," said Helmut, as he steered them towards a much narrower street leading off the main thoroughfare. With a shallow pavement each side, it was just wide enough for a single vehicle. There were three-storey buildings either side; some without windows and the odd one missing its floors, having collapsed from a bomb or artillery shell. Paul felt a knot in his stomach, remembering approaching Christa's apartment to find it had been destroyed by English bombers, and both she and her parents had been killed inside. He still kept her letters in his tunic pocket. The romance had been short lived, all because of the war.

"Some bloody route you've taken us down, Helmut. Some of these look as if they might collapse on top of us."

"Stop moaning, Manfred. They're rock solid." Even so, Helmut looked up at the walls, willing them to remain in place.

"I think we should turn left at the bottom there then we will have dog-legged back to the other main road," indicated Manfred.

"There's some sort of small square by the look of it," pointed out Erich.

"More soldiers too," added Paul. "There are more in Dvinsk than there are at the front."

"They're strange uniforms."

"Bugger, you're right Helmut. They look like SD, don't they?" questioned Paul.

At least half a dozen of the soldiers wore the standard field grey combat tunics, whereas the two officers had the field grey Sicherheitsdienst uniforms, characterised by the black collar patch on the right, police-style shoulder boards and the SD diamond and blank, black cuff title.

"You're right," confirmed Erich. "What are they up to? Why is Internal Security here so soon? Shall we turn back?"

"Sod them," blurted Helmut. "They're not real soldiers. A bunch of bloody pen-pushers if you ask me."

"Nobody was asking you," quipped Manfred.

As they approached the entrance of the courtyard, they got a better view of what was transpiring. The two SD officers stood watching as Einsatzgruppe troops pulled men, women and children from some of the buildings bordering the quadrangle. Some of the civilians were being searched and even stripped, one couple being clubbed with rifle butts in an effort to separate them. The scruffy rabble, the best description for the civilians dressed as soldiers, were separating the men from the women and children then forcing the men, at gunpoint and with a booted kick for good measure, into the back of a canvas-covered military vehicle.

"What the hell's going on here?" breathed Paul, astonished. "We're fighting a war and come back to see thugs bullying, beating and killing civilians."

The senior SD officer, a Hauptmann, overheard Paul's outburst and came across to the four paratroopers who immediately saluted their superior.

"What are you men up to?" he asked after he had returned their salute.

"We're stood down, sir," answered Manfred.

"What's going on here, sir?" asked Erich.

"We're just sorting out the troublemakers, Oberleutnant."

"But why are they being stripped and beaten?" jumped in Paul angrily.

"It's not your affair, Oberleutnant. If you are stood down, I suggest you go and find a bar somewhere and get drunk," he answered with a smirk.

"Yes, we will." Helmut stepped in, squaring up to the Hauptmann. "We've been fighting a real battle against soldiers, not women and children."

The Captain's face flushed. "Stand to attention when you address a senior officer." He was joined by a couple of his thugs and a leutnant.

The four paratroopers slowly but reluctantly, their military discipline overriding their distaste for this officer and what he stood for, brought their feet together in a show of being at attention. The scowl on all of their faces clearly indicated their disrespect for the thug in a military uniform giving them orders.

"I will not speak to you again. You are to leave this area and report back to your units. I know where your unit is based and I will be informing your commanders, and my own, of your interference in internal security matters. It is none of your business. Dismissed."

There was a moment's silence.

"It is customary in the German military for junior officers to salute a senior officer when dismissed. Is it not the same for the Luftwaffe, gentlemen?"

They reluctantly threw the Hauptmann a disrespectful salute, turned about and moved away from the square, Erich was behind them, mentally and verbally pushing them towards the narrow street to the left of the square. Every time he sensed one of them was going to stop or look back over their shoulder, he barked at them to keep moving. "We're in deep shit as it is. Don't make it worse, just keep moving."

Behind them they could hear the barked commands of the Einsatzgruppe, shouts, studded boots clattering over the paving slabs, screams of women and children as the tailgate was slammed shut; the sounds slowly diminished the further away they got. Paul's anger was evident, as was Helmut's and Manfred's, but Erich recognised the signs in his friends and knew he had to keep things battened down or they would explode and real trouble would then ensue.

Unfortunately, after only a hundred metres, they heard a scream coming from up ahead and made their way towards the sound to investigate. Paul hurried off first, turning right down an even narrower street, again not much wider than a single footpath. Ahead he could hear the woman's screams getting louder and more desperate. He increased his pace, Helmut close behind.

"*Schiesse.*"

"We need to leave this, Paul," Erich was heard to shout behind Helmut. "This is all out of our control."

"Bugger it is," Paul called back angrily, striding down the narrow passageway. The sound of his studded boots echoing off the walls either side magnified his determination.

They arrived at the entrance of a small courtyard, no more than ten metres square, surrounded on all four sides by two-storey buildings. The only way in or out was the one they were standing in. Objects were being thrown from the upper windows and in the middle of the courtyard, strewn everywhere, were the personal possessions from those living in the flats.

In front of him, in the left-hand corner, a middle-aged man and woman were being forcibly restrained at gunpoint by two Einsatzgruppe goons. In the opposite corner, where the screams were coming from, Paul saw a dark-haired, petite, young girl detained in the corner, her white blouse torn open exposing the pale skin of her breast. One Einsatzgruppe thug was behind her, pinning both her arms behind her back, another pulling her head back by her hair, exposing her neck to his ravishing, his other hand pulling at her clothes and groping forcefully.

The next few minutes were a blur as Paul charged over, grabbing the thug's webbing straps at the rear and pulling him back with such force that he pulled the attacker to the floor, followed by the woman and the other thug standing behind her. All three collapsed in a heap on the ground.

"What are you doing?" screamed a Feldwebel, his uniform showing him to be SD, who had rushed across from the elderly couple.

Helmut stepped in front of him. The sergeant ploughed into his solid form, almost knocking him down as he bounced back off.

The paratrooper garb, size and rank of Oberleutnant, along with the scowl on Helmut's face, was enough to stop the Feldwebel in his tracks once he had recovered from the collision.

"What the hell is going on?" demanded Paul, pulling the young woman up off the ground and helping her to cover herself.

"With respect, Herr Oberleutnant."

"Respect?" growled Paul through gritted teeth, putting his face within inches of the SD Feldwebel's. "You don't know the meaning of the word."

"We need to get out of here, Helmut," hissed Erich. "It's starting to get messy."

They had never seen Paul so vexed and it was clear to his friends that his high morals were pushing him towards an abyss.

"Release those people," ordered Paul, pointing at the elderly couple.

The Einsaztgruppe bully boys let go of them, lowered their guns and stepped back, unsure of how to react on the receiving end of the tall, tough-looking Fallschirmjager officer. In his anger, Paul did not see the Unteroffizier quietly slipping away, making his way down the narrow street they had walked along earlier.

"Now leave them alone, and she is coming with me."

"Oh, so you want some sport for yourself, Oberleutnant. Why didn't you say," sneered the SD NCO.

Paul's MP40 was off his shoulder in an instant, the barrel pointing directly beneath the man's chin. "I ought to take your head off, Feldwebel, but you're not worth the bullet."

"Come on, Paul," whispered Erich, edging closer. "We need to get out of here."

Paul pulled the young woman towards him and was about to move towards the passageway when someone yelled behind them.

"*Stillgestanden.*"

They all turned to see a red-faced SD Hauptmann, the one they had crossed earlier.

"*Stillgestanden,*" he screamed again.

The four *kameraden* looked at each other, some ignoring him, but Paul acquiesced by lowering his gun.

"Let's get out of here," insisted Erich.

"OK," agreed Paul, "but the girl comes with us."

He took her arm gently, feeling her body still trembling beneath his hand. "You… come… with us," he said to her softly. "You will be… safe. OK?"

He nodded and her dark hair fell back from her eyes as she looked up at him and returned his nod. "Thank you," she said.

"You speak German?"

"A little. My father is German."

"She stays, Oberleutnant."

"We're leaving," instructed Helmut. "Let's go, guys."

Helmut pushed past the Hauptmann, a countenance that challenged the officer to prevent his passage. The SD man baulked at stopping him. Manfred followed, Erich behind him with Paul and the girl close on their tail.

The Hauptmann recovered his poise and stepped in front of Paul. "I said she stays. She is an enemy of the state." He unclipped his black leather holster and pulled out his service issue sidearm, a Luger, cocking it then pointing it at Paul.

There was a clatter of MP40s being cocked as Helmut, Manfred and Erich made ready their machine pistols. The Einsatzgruppe also nervously readied their Kar 98s and, within seconds, the Fallschirmjager were surrounded as the SDs hired Latvian guns closed in on them.

Paul looked about him. The situation looked grim and he could feel the girl trembling next to him as she pulled herself in close to his body. They were confined by the four walls of the buildings bordering the small courtyard. The only escape was four doorways, all covered by Einsatzgruppe, and the street they had come down earlier. That too was closed off. It was silent, the occasional clatter of boots on the flagstones and the rattling of weapons against the men's equipment. The elderly couple had disappeared somewhere inside the premises; safe, Paul hoped.

He turned to the SD officer. "We're leaving, Herr Hauptmann, and the girl is going with us."

"The first person to leave here gets shot, Oberleutnant," the officer responded, waving his pistol loosely in the air.

Paul leaned into him, locking eyes. "You forget, Herr Hauptmann, you are dealing with real soldiers. Men who have fought many battles with a tough adversary and won. How many of your toy soldiers do you think will leave this courtyard alive?"

Paul held his gaze, watching the officer licking his lips, looking around at his unit trying to look like tough and hardened soldiers, but deep down he knew they were far from that.

"All they are good for is beating defenceless women and children," he continued, pointing to the motley group that surrounded them: recruits from the local Latvian community, many after revenge now the Red Army had left. "I don't fancy their chances, do you?"

The Hauptmann's eyes flicked over Helmut, the stocky officer looking about as mean as they come. Then at Erich and Manfred, both battle veterans who looked like they knew how to handle their MP40s and, the SD officer was in no doubt, how to use them. He knew Paul's statement to be true. He and his men would be slaughtered, but he needed to save face somehow.

"You can go," he said to the other three. "But he and the woman stay." He pointed at Paul.

"No chance," Erich protested.

"Bottling out, sir?" chided Helmut.

Paul sensed the stalemate needed to be broken or else there truly would be a fight amongst these two groups. Although they may well come out on top, many could get hurt or killed. He ticked off in his mind what had happened and how it would be seen from the outside. They had interfered with an SD operation, refused to carry out the orders of a senior officer, drawn their weapons on a military unit and threatened its commander.

"She goes. I stay."

The Hauptmann looked up at Paul sneering, thinking he had won. "You both stay."

"Think about it," hissed Paul through gritted teeth. "The alternative is a bloodbath... so it's me or nothing."

"You're crazy, Paul," jumped in Helmut, pushing one of the *gruppe* out of the way.

Erich grabbed his arm. "Paul's right," he whispered. "Let's get out of here with the girl. Then we can come back for Paul."

Helmut moved towards the girl, Erich close behind him.

"We'll take the girl. You keep the Oberleutnant but you'd better make sure, sir, that nothing happens to him or you'll have a very pissed off Fallschirmjager unit."

It was not a question but a statement. The officer, nodded in agreement, recognising that it was the only way out of the stalemate and his only chance to save face in front of his men.

Helmut grabbed the trembling shoulders of the girl, prizing her away from Paul.

"It's OK," Paul said softly to her, "Helmut's my friend. He will take care of you."

Helmut steered her towards Erich, handing her over. "Take her down the street. I'll be with you in a minute."

He turned to speak to Paul. "We'll be back for you later."

Paul nodded his understanding and, with that, Helmut strode off, rejoined his two companions and they escorted the girl away from the scene.

The officer indicated to his Feldwebel. "Take the Oberleutnant to the cells we've rigged up and wait for me there."

One of the bully boys and the Feldwebel approached Paul and went to take his weapon from him. Paul immediately slung it over his shoulder. "It stays with me."

"No, you don't," and the thug turned towards his commander for guidance who in turn, recognising Paul's look of determination, just shook his head.

"Leave him with his weapons. We're still near the front line."

With that, they led Paul away, down the narrow street where his friends had just taken the girl, but keeping their distance from the six foot two paratrooper. His stature and presence dominated them all and, although none would admit it, they feared him.

He sat on the edge of the very narrow, wood-framed single bed; a solitary, dirty blanket enveloped the mildew-covered mattress which was stuffed with damp straw. He looked at the walls, a pale green, marred by mould and Latvian graffiti that he could neither read nor understand. The one small window no longer let in any light, but the darkness was partially held at bay by the single low-wattage bulb suspended from the ceiling by a long piece of flex. The bulb was so dim that it barely managed to create shadows.

He placed his elbows on his knees, his head in his hands, reflecting on the events that had unfolded that afternoon. He was foolish doing what he did but he could not leave her to those brutes. The minute they left, she would have been at their mercy again and he knew mercy was not in their line. His error was that he had dragged his friends into it. What would happen to them now; what would the Raven say? Paul imagined he would be livid and doubted he had a future as a Fallschirmjager officer, let alone with the special battalion he belonged to. A court martial would no doubt be held and he would be imprisoned if found guilty. They were at war and accused of interfering with the country's internal security. He could just as easily be shot or, worse, sentenced to a penal battalion.

Although they had locked him in this room, they had left his weapons with him. Although the Hauptmann was senior to him and he tried to exude confidence in front of his men, he was unsure about Paul — for the moment. Paul was sure it was only a matter of time before his weapons were taken from him. A more senior officer would arrive, or even the Feldgendarmerie. Then he would have no choice. However, the Einsatzgruppe appeared to be busy at the moment. From what Paul had picked up from conversations on their way here and from whispers in the corridor outside his door, the fifth columnists, another term for the Jewish men, women and children and the Bolsheviks, were proving harder to round up than originally planned, so Paul had been forgotten for the moment. He had suggested to the Hauptmann that they just let him go and they could both forget about the whole episode but the belligerent SD officer had just sneered and walked away.

He heard the guard patrolling up and down the corridor outside the door of his two by three metre room. It was not really a cell, more of a plain room temporarily adapted to hold suspects. Perhaps previously a boarding house.

What was that? He heard a thump up against the outside wall. He got up off the wooden bed, the slats groaning as he pushed himself up and headed for the window to his right. It was not barred but quite small and high up in the wall; probably one of the reasons the room had been chosen. Paul put his face up against the pane of glass, his chin resting on the sill, the frame not much bigger than his head. Although he could look out over the darkened garden on the other side, he could only look straight ahead, not down. It was too dark to make anything out anyway, other than possibly the dark shadow of some trees at the far end. He heard a clatter against the wall again. This time he was not mistaken and, moments later, a pair of eyes stared at him from the other side of the glass window, making him step back involuntarily. Then he could see the blackened, grinning features of Feldwebel Max Grun.

Paul's eyes widened as he realised Max had come to get him out and he mouthed, "What... is... happening?"

Max mouthed back, "Something... to... hide... behind?"

"Yes, a... bed... and... mattress."

"Get... right... back. Under... cover. Understand? Away... from... the... window."

Paul nodded, getting the gist of what Max was saying.

Paul looked at Max who suddenly mouthed, "Well... bloody... move."

With that, Max's face disappeared from view and it sounded like one of their light metal ladders being dragged off the wall. Paul moved to the bed, pulling the thin blanket and mattress off. He grabbed the edge of the frame and eased it up off the ground as quickly and as quietly as he could and slowly edged it over to the far wall next to the door. He manoeuvred it until, on its side, it was positioned at an angle across the corner of the two adjoining walls. He was as far away from the window as he could get; three metres would have to be enough. Pulling the bed aside, he went around the back, wedged himself in the corner and slid to the floor, gripping one of the slats of the bed, pinching a piece of the mattress he had placed against it on the other side. He tightened his helmet with his right hand, scrunched as far into the corner as possible, tucked his head down, making himself as small a target as possible.

Probably as little as ten seconds later, but to Paul it felt like minutes, the outer wall shot inwards, the eruption plastering the room with chunks of shattered brick, plaster and glass; lumps striking the mattress with force. Paul was engulfed in dust and debris, but safe inside his man-made cocoon. No sooner had the wall been blasted by the explosion than a bulky figure thrust his way through the gaping hole which was a metre-and-a-half wide with edges like jagged teeth. The paratrooper headed straight for the door and the shelter to his left where Paul was sheltering, MP40 at the ready. The light bulb had been shattered and all Paul could make out was a dark form hovering over him.

"Comfy down there, sir?"

He could not see who it was but with the size, shape and unmistakable voice, it could only be the venerable Max Grun.

He picked himself up from the floor, pushing the bed back to give himself room, Max assisting him by unceremoniously heaving him up by his straps. He was not hurt, but his ears were ringing. He could not see Max clearly, but the white teeth indicated a huge grin that adorned his face.

"We need to get out of here, sir. The SD monkeys will be all over us soon."

The door rattled as the guard fumbled with the latch and tried to put the key in the door. In his panic, he dropped the keys to the floor. Max fired a single shot through the bottom of the

135

door, deliberately aiming wide, not wanting to kill anyone. It was enough; the guard was heard running down the corridor screaming for help.

"Let's get the fuck out of here, sir. That won't put them off for long. Reinforcements will soon be on the way."

Max grabbed hold of his still dazed company commander, steering him towards the gaping hole in the wall, pushing his head down as he eased him through, bundling him into the garden on the other side, ably assisted by Oberleutnant Janke.

"Helmut, what the hell are you doing?"

"Getting you out of this shit. We've no time to discuss the rights and wrongs of it now. We need to scarper."

Paul looked back at the hole to see Max emerge from the back wall of what was once his cell. They were joined by Erich.

"Come on, you lot, shift. Nattering like a bunch of old women."

They quickly moved to the end of the short garden, hearing the door burst open in the cell behind them. Fessman appeared from behind a tree at the end and fired off a round in the direction of the building.

"Good to see you again, sir," he offered while loading another round into the breech.

"We haven't got bloody time for chit-chat. The buggers are right behind us," growled Max.

A head popped out of the hole in the wall, calling back to his fellow soldiers, "They must have gone this way." Another bullet from Fessman's Kar 98 encouraged him back inside.

Helmut led the way through a gate the other side of the tree, followed by Paul, Max and Braemer, Erich and Fessman covering their backs. They turned left down a narrow alley way, small gardens backing onto it either side, moving along it swiftly until they came to a street at the end. An Opel Blitz truck, its engine ticking over, was waiting for them.

"In the back, quickly," commanded Helmut.

The paratroopers clambered up and over the tailgate, Konrad inside helping them. Helmut went round to the passenger side and jumped in the cab. Once they were all in the back, Max banged the floor with his boots, the signal they were all onboard.

"Go," Helmut instructed the driver. "Let's get the fuck out of here."

Braemer turned to look at Helmut. "We're gone, sir."

He put the truck into gear, gunned the engine and they pulled away from the alleyway, slowly gathering speed, leaving a cloud of white smoke and dust in their wake.

Chapter Fourteen

A couple of paratroopers each lit up a cigarette, the flare of the matches lighting the inside of the darkened cargo space of the Opel Blitz military truck, the flap secured down to keep out inquisitive eyes. Opposite Paul was one of his troop commanders from 1st platoon and Max, both of them grinning, conspirators together. Max pulled out a torch and shone it around the interior to compensate for the absence of light as the matches burnt down and out. The only other light were the red glows as Max and Fessman drew on their cigarettes. They gave out a satisfied sigh as they expelled the pungent smoke.

"Well, that was a piece of piss, sir."

"You have such a way with words, Max."

The truck lurched as the driver swung the vehicle down a turning, taking them away from the town.

"Hotels just aren't what they used to be, eh, sir?" added Fessman.

Paul looked at their faces, a deep feeling of comradeship welling up inside. These were not just his paratroopers, his men; they were more than that. They were more like brothers and he felt deeply responsible for them.

Konrad sat to Fessman's left, Max next to him with Erich to Paul's left, who nudged him. "Told you we'd come back for you."

Paul's shoulders slumped slightly and he suddenly felt tired, the recent experience draining him as much as if he had been in battle. Now he was away from his incarceration, his body gave in to the weariness that was slowly gnawing at it.

Paul turned to Erich. "Thank you." Then, looking around the cargo space, he said, "Thank you to all of you."

"Someone's got to keep Feldwebel Grun in line, Paul."

"Where are we going now?"

"On an adventure, sir," beamed Max, glad to have his commander and his friend back in the Fallschirmjager fold.

"We're cutting across the edge of the town to the south, between the Dvina and the large lake just outside of the town. Stropuezers, I think it's called. Then east," Erich informed him.

"We have the company billeted in a small village about ten Ks from here, sir," broke in Max.

"The rest of the battalion?"

"They're staying put, sir."

"So you're going back to Dvinsk, Erich?"

"Yes, once we have dropped you all off, Helmut and I will shoot back."

"How come we've been split from the battalion?"

"All will be explained once we get to Naujene," reassured Erich.

Paul closed his eyes, the languor taking control. The rhythmic motion of the truck, as it settled down on the now straight run to the village, made him feel sleepy. He was no different from any other soldier across the world who takes any opportunity to catch some sleep, not knowing when he will be able to do so next. The rest of the journey was completed in silence. Max turned off his torch and the truck was covered in a blanket of darkness.

Paul woke with a start, gripping his MP40 that had been resting on his knees, as the Opel Blitz ground to a halt, throwing him sideways into Erich.

"Looks like journey's end," announced Erich. "You can sit up now and get off my bloody shoulder."

"Sorry," said Paul rubbing the sleep from his eyes. Although only a fifteen-minute trip, he felt a little refreshed after the catnap.

There was a sudden slap at the rear of the truck and the canvas cover was undone and rolled up out of the way. Helmut peered into the dim interior.

"Come on, you buggers, let's have you out. Janke taxi service has ended."

Paul was the first to clamber over the tailgate, dropping down to the ground which proved to be a hard-packed road. Once again, the familiar mixture of single- and two-storey dwellings either side. No lights were showing. The heavy-booted feet of Max landed next to him, closely followed by those of Erich, Fessman and Konrad, Braemer the last joining them from the cab.

"This is the company HQ," said Max. "Let's get inside and see if there's a brew on. There better bloody had be."

He pushed through a door and jerked the curtain aside. Paul was directly behind and they stepped into a narrow corridor, taking the door to the left and entering what had once been a living and dining area. Now it held a small, square table in the far corner with a Torn.Fu.d1, two-way radio receiver. Bergmann and Leutnant Leeb were sitting alongside it, and both stood up and saluted.

"Good to have you back with us, sir."

"What's the status of the company, Ernst?"

"Never mind that now," declared Helmut, slapping Paul on his back. "Give us a moment, Leutnant."

"Yes, sir. Come on, Bergmann, we'll find a brew for them. You too," he said, indicating to Fessman, Konrad and Braemer in the background, overcrowding the small room.

They all left the room, leaving Helmut, Max and Erich alone, sitting round a wooden table and perched on some low-backed, basic wooden chairs. Paul had slumped into a small, battered armchair.

"Well, are you going to update me then?"

There was a knock at the door and Bergmann popped his head through before pushing it open, "Thought you gentlemen might like a drink."

He entered the room, a tray laden with mugs of still steaming coffee and a small chipped plate with a few home-made biscuits on it, probably made by the previous occupants.

"There is some soup for you later, sir, if you're hungry."

Paul's stomach rumbled. He had not eaten since the lunch he had had with his three friends back in Dvinsk and now realised he was hungry.

"That sounds good. Thank you, Bergmann."

"Just shout when you're finished Feld and I'll bring some through."

Max nodded and the company radio operator left the room.

"Well, Helmut, what's the score? The Raven up in arms?"

"Surprisingly, no. He was pissed with you, muttering something about Brand and his high morals but he came up with a solution pretty quickly."

"Does he know you've got me out?"

"Yes and no. He did order that your company should move to here as he had a task for them and suggested that you should join them."

The flickering light of the two lamps cast shadows over the faces of the three smiling conspirators.

Paul reached for his coffee, sniffing it, savouring its aroma then its taste.

"So, indirectly it was his idea. He just wasn't owning up to it?"

"Something like that, sir."

"I knew you three would be involved," Paul said with a smile, looking at Max, Helmut and Erich in turn.

"The Raven was really pissed off with the SD though," announced Erich. "He's no supporter of Einsatzgruppe."

"He wouldn't say that though," suggested Paul.

"No," agreed Helmut, "but he didn't need to. He was waving his crop around like a conductor."

"I thought he was going to snap it in two at one stage." Erich laughed.

"So, why is my company here then?"

"Two reasons, Paul. First, Division has asked for a unit to be attached to them as they approach the Stalin Line. It seems that, after Eben Emael, we are deemed to be the bunker experts."

They all laughed and Paul visibly relaxed for the first time since his release.

"They want you guys to help with the attack plans," added Helmut, "but not actually get involved in the assault."

"And the second reason?"

"Seemed the best way to get you out of town and out of the clutches of the SD, so to speak," said Max. "Major Volkman felt it was better that you weren't around if the SD came sniffing by."

"The Herr Major thinks they will be too embarrassed by the whole issue to want to follow it through," suggested Helmut, extending his arm across the table and reaching for his third biscuit.

"Hungry, sir?" baited Max.

"Just thinking about your waistline, Feldwebel Grun."

"Very kind of you, sir."

"So, what do we know about the Stalin Line?" asked Paul.

"Bloody tough nut to crack by the sound of it. It runs from the Gulf of Finland in the north to the Black Sea in the south. It's not so much a continuous line, more of a series of strong points built as fortified zones or regions."

"What does a region cover, Helmut?"

"Each appears to cover a strategically important sector of the border, against a potential threat from the Baltic States, Poland, Romania and Finland," said Erich.

"What section will we be looking at?"

Max pulled out a map and spread it across the table. Paul got up and joined them, sitting on the fourth seat around the now cramped table. He looked for a biscuit on the tray and, finding none, looked at Helmut, who shrugged his shoulders guiltily. "Sorry."

Max smoothed out the map, tapping his finger just south of Lake Peipus. "Here, sir, the Polotsk fortified region." He drew a line with his finger from the River Daugava to the strategic rail junction situated on the border of Poland and Latvia.

"We're heading here, sir: Pskov. It blocks a key route to Velikie Luki, Smolensk and Moscow."

"How big are these fortified regions?"

"Bloody big. Each fortified region can be up to one hundred and fifty kilometres long and fifty kilometres deep," elaborated Erich. "There are gaps of up to twenty kilometres between them, but we believe the gaps are defended by a Russian Rifle Division."

"Bloody hell," gasped Paul, "they will take some breaching. What is their make-up?"

"Don't forget, the Landser will be doing all the hard work," added Helmut, grinning. "You will just be aiding them with the planning." He pulled a piece of paper from his pocket and unfolded it on the table, automatically reaching for the biscuits that were no longer there. "I made this quick sketch, I'll leave it with you. The front line is made up of battalion defence regions. The Division will no doubt want to punch through one or two of these." He pointed to the sketch. "This is the forward defence zone, about ten kilometres deep, consisting mainly of lightly fortified pillboxes, barbed wire, tank traps, you know the sort of thing." He looked at Paul who nodded his understanding. "That's just to slow us down, dissipate our forces so by the time we get to the main defence zone we're already a bit battered and weary."

"A battalion defence zone?"

"There will be a line of them making up the bulk of the main defence zone. We think they'll cover a front of up to six kilometres and a depth of up to three kilometres."

"Gaps between them?"

"Yes, probably six Ks, but behind the gaps will be a second battalion defence zone."

"Shit, that sounds daunting."

"It is. They have bunkers, mounted turrets, machine-gun casemates. The only positive, if there is one, is we think they may be below strength. When they moved into Poland, it seems they moved some of the guns and troops as well, bringing their defence line forward."

"And they've had a bit of a hammering," suggested Erich.

"When do we have to move out then?"

"Tomorrow afternoon, sir," said Max. "So we have a bit of time to shake the company out a little."

"Thanks, Max. Where are the platoons?" asked Paul.

"They each have a block of dwellings. None are further than three hundred metres away."

"Right," said Helmut jumping up from his seat, "seeing as there are no more biscuits, it's time for us to make a move. We'll leave you two to talk military stuff while Erich and I head back for some local cooking and a decent night's sleep."

Erich also got up reluctantly out of his chair. It had been a long day for all of them. Paul and Max shook hands with them both, Paul gripping Helmut's and Erich's firmly, the message clear.

"Thank you. I owe you both."

"Don't thank us, thank Feldwebel Grun. It was his idea. But, anyway, you'd have done the same for us," said Erich, patting his friend's shoulder.

Paul nodded, knowing it to be true. They left the room, exiting the building. Moments later, the roar of the truck engine disappeared as it left the village taking the two Oberleutnants back to their respective companies still based in Dvinsk.

"Shall I get the platoon commanders, sir?"

"Not just yet, Max, but a second coffee wouldn't go amiss."

"Hang fire then, sir."

Max got up from the table, went through the door and was back in a couple of minutes, followed by Bergmann with a tray with two mugs of coffee and a two bowls of piping hot soup along with a chunks of home-made rye bread.

"Radio quiet, Feld?"

"Not a peep. I'll shout if anything comes through."

Bergmann left. It was quiet now, the occasional crackle of the radio disturbing the silence along with the sound of breaking bread and the chink of a spoon against the soup bowl.

"It's not much, sir. Just a few root vegetables but it doesn't taste too bad and there's plenty of it."

"Fessman been on the scrounge again?"

"As usual, sir. He always seems to know where to look."

"You took a big chance, Max, all of you."

"Do you think we would leave you with those animals, sir?"

"Still."

Paul took a few more sips of his soup, dipping small chunks of bread and savouring the texture and taste.

"You're right, Max, this is OK."

"Once the company heard what had happened, they were armed to the teeth and about ready to tear the town apart looking for you. I thought it best that just a few of us got involved just in case it backfired."

"Thanks, Max. I'm not sorry to be out of there. How did you know where I was?"

"Oberleutnant Janke hung back and followed you while Oberleutnants Fleck and Bauer came back to battalion."

Paul put his spoon down and laughed. "That sounds like Helmut."

"We asked for volunteers initially and they all stepped forward; even the medic, Fink, was up for it."

"Where's the girl?"

"Who, Hana?"

"Is that her name?"

"Yes. She speaks pretty good German. It appears her father was in the 1914–18 war."

"So why are we bloody rounding these people up?"

"Buggered if I know, sir. Anyway, she's safe for the moment."

"Where is she?"

"Here, sir, in the village. Sorry I didn't tell you earlier. We just thought it best to get her out of the town in case those thugs came looking for her again."

"I want to see her."

"She's probably asleep by now. You'll get a chance in the morning. Best wait, eh, sir?"

"OK."

Paul pushed the now empty bowl aside and grabbed his mug of coffee.

"Who do we liaise with tomorrow?"

"A Major Trier will meet us here at ten hundred tomorrow."

"What unit?"

"He's from the reconnaissance battalion of 6 Div."

"Panzer dust again, eh, Max?"

"Seems that way, sir, but at least one platoon can catch its breath."

144

"Yes, they can. We'll let two and three platoon do the bulk of the work for a while."

"By the way, sir, you probably haven't heard the news."

Max got up from his seat, the radio crackling as he walked past. He popped his head through the door and hollered, "Let's have some more of that coffee. We're dying of thirst in here." He closed the door and returned to his seat, grinning.

"The joys of being a Company Feld, Max."

"Got to have some perks, sir." Max sat down, the chair creaking as he lowered himself onto its fragile form.

"Putting on weight, Max?"

"Made of balsa wood, this."

"The news?"

"Oh yes. We've taken Minsk."

"Minsk? That must be a couple of hundred kilometres in."

"I know. It's bloody amazing."

Someone knocked at the door.

"Yes?" called Max.

Bergmann kicked the door open, two mugs of coffee in his hands. "The lads wanted me to tell you that it's good to have you back, sir."

Paul nodded his appreciation. "Anything on the radio, Feld?"

"Still quiet, rest easy. Come back in half an hour."

"Feld."

Bergmann left the room and Max pushed one of the coffees over to Paul, next to the two empty mugs.

"Another one, sir. You've got some catching up to do."

Paul smiled. "Any other news for me?"

"No, other than Panzer Group 4 is pushing for Riga."

They sipped their coffees in silence, words not needed. Paul was glad to be back with his unit; Max was just pleased to have his commander and friend back in the fold. Before they had chance to speak again, there was another knock on the door, Bergmann returning as instructed.

"Sorry, sir, Feld, but I need to do a routine radio check."

"That's OK, Bergmann, the Oberleutnant and I are bunking down now any way."

"Where are we bunking?"

"We've got a room opposite, along with Bergmann here, when he's not on radio stag. The rest of the companies' HQ are upstairs.

I thought it better if we were near the radio and the exit should we be needed."

Max got up out of his seat, closely followed by Paul who was now starting to feel the strain of the last twenty-four hours. They said goodnight to Bergmann and Max pointed to the door on the other side of the hallway.

"That's us, sir. I'm just going to do the rounds."

"I'll come with you."

"Trying to do me out of a job, sir? How can I maintain credibility when you have to babysit me," Max said with a mischievous grin.

"You win. Make sure someone gives me a call at six."

"Will do, sir."

With that, Max pushed through the curtain and the door and left the house to check on the sentries, leaving Paul to bunk down in their temporary billet.

Chapter Fifteen

Paul came out of a fitful sleep. Someone had been trying to push him down underwater, pressing on his shoulders. There was a light; he must still be near the surface. He gasped for breath...

"Sir, sir, it's six. You OK? Here's a brew for you."

Paul opened his eyes to Max's broad face staring down at him, his fair hair spiky, indicative that he had not been up long himself. His big hand was shaking Paul's shoulder. Paul heaved himself up into a sitting position on his straw mattress, parking his back against the wall. He grabbed the coffee Max handed over to him taking an immediate gulp, burning his tongue in the process.

"I thought you might like a coffee to wake up to. It's still a bit hot, mind." Max grinned.

"Thank you, Max. It's a bit early for your humour, thank you." Paul adjusted his position and ran his hand over his head, touching the scar above his left eyebrow. "I could have done with a couple more hours though."

"Couldn't we both." Max plonked himself down against the wall next to Paul.

Paul handed his coffee to Max who took a sip from the tin mug before handing it back. "Not bad even if I do say so myself."

"Anything I need to know?"

"No, all's quiet."

"Nothing on the radio?"

"No, sir. Bergmann's had his regular radio checks. He would have woken us anyway had there been anything of importance. He's pretty switched on."

"Is she awake?"

"Who? Oh, you mean our Latvian guest. She's fine by all accounts, sir. You've no worries there. The boys have been pandering to her as if she was Queen Victoria."

"She's hardly a Prussian Queen, Max. I want to see her this morning."

"Fine by me, sir. I'll take you."

"Have the platoon commanders ready for the briefing with the 6 Div reconnaissance commander, OK?"

"Done, sir. They'll be there for ten."

Paul looked at Max out of the corner of his eye, Max's jaw granite like, but his nose slightly bent as a result of many breaks.

"Can you read my mind, Feldwebel Grun?"

"Just thought that our Panzer guest might want us rolling straightaway."

"He may well, Max. Makes sense to have them join us and saves me repeating myself."

"That's why you're an officer, sir, and I'm a mere NCO."

"Someone has to lead the way, Feldwebel Grun."

"There's some grub in one of the village houses if you're hungry. Should be ready by the time we get there, providing the first platoon gannets haven't eaten it all."

"Anything good on the menu?" asked Paul as he pushed himself to his feet.

"Not sure. One of the local women has agreed to help out and cook for us. The locals seem quite pleased to see us."

"She wouldn't be dark-haired and buxom by any chance, would she?"

"What are you insinuating, sir?" responded Max with a grunt.

"You won't have much time to utilise your charms, I'm afraid, Max. We'll be moving out first thing this afternoon."

Paul, seeing Max's reddening face and knowing he had hit home, laughed.

Max lurched to his feet. "Ready for food then, sir?"

"Where do we go?"

"Out the front door, turn right and it's the next house. Designated the company mess."

"Is there somewhere I can wash first?"

"Through the door here, turn right and there's a small kitchen at the back. It's tiny, but will do the job. There's a *donnerbalken* in the back garden."

"OK, Max, give me ten minutes and I'll see you in the canteen."

"Take a walk around the lines afterwards, sir?"

"Yes."

Max left through the door of the small lounge and headed outside to frequent the local's dwelling they were using for their messing facilities.

148

Paul rubbed his eyes then bent down and picked up the thin blanket that had covered him during the night and threw it over the back of the only chair in the room. He folded the straw-stuffed mattress in half and considered his bed made. He rolled his shoulders, easing the tension in his aching muscles, and shook his legs in an effort to loosen the stiffness. During his night's sleep, the straw mattress had quickly flattened, losing its padding qualities, Paul's body connecting with the hard wood floor. He looked around the small room, no more than three metres square. He had lain under the single window where the shutters were still closed, the gaps letting in the only light filtering across the room. Someone had slept to the right of the window, across the empty fireplace. Probably Bergmann when he was off stag. Max had slept against the wall opposite the window. There was very little furniture in the room and what there was had been pushed into the centre: a small chair and a dresser that had probably been up against one of the walls at some point. Paul suspected the rest of the furniture had been removed to make space for them to bed down. He wondered where the occupants had slept last night; obviously not in their own home.

He pulled on his webbing and adjusted his ammunition pouches so they were not only comfortable but also easily accessible should he quickly require a fresh magazine for his MP40 which he had now slung over his shoulder. He hung his helmet from his belt. It was not needed just yet.

Two strides and he was at the door, pulling it open and stepping into the corridor. Left was the front door where Max had just exited and, to the right, the corridor, narrowed even further by a set of wooden stairs leading upstairs. The corridor ran to the back of the house, probably leading to the small kitchen. He pushed open the door opposite and peered in, the room much lighter with the blinds opened wide. Opposite sat Bergmann wearing earphones and fiddling with the controls of his radio set. He sensed Paul's presence and started to rise from his seat, pulling the earphones off.

"Stand easy. Anything?"

"All quiet, sir, just routine traffic about supplies. Radio checks completed with battalion. Comms are a bit ropey, but we can understand each other."

"Where's your antenna?"

"We've punched a hole in the ceiling," his arm pointed upwards towards the upper corner of the room, "and fed it up through one of the upper windows."

"You won't be popular with the owners."

"Could be worse, sir," he said, smiling. "They could be in Dvinsk."

"Very true. Let me know the minute anything comes through."

"Of course, sir."

Paul shut the door and headed down the narrow corridor, past the stairs and to the kitchen. Standing in the middle, he could reach practically everything without moving from his position. He paid the outside latrine a visit then poured some water from the kitchen's bucket into the small, very low square sink where he washed his hands and face, feeling the thirty-six hours of stubble on his chin. Seeing a piece of broken mirror on the window sill, he picked it up and examined his features. A twenty-three year-old face peered back at him, dark patches under his hazel eyes, a sparkle still evident. He scratched the stubble which, like his fair hair, was too light to see clearly. He took off his gas canister and rummaged around inside until he found his shaving kit. After bending down awkwardly to use the mirror, he scraped off as much of the growth as possible. Rinsing off his face and checking the mirror again, he almost felt like a new man. Some food and more coffee would see him right. He placed his kit back in the container which was no longer used to carry a gas mask. The army as one felt it was a useless piece of equipment to carry around. Gathering his equipment, he headed outside.

As he left the building, a sentry came to attention and saluted.

"Morning, Stumme. All quiet?"

"Yes, Oberleutnant."

Paul turned right, looking up into a clear blue sky. The air on his cheek was already warm as he walked down the dusty, hard-packed road, arriving at the company canteen within a matter of moments.

Making his way through the front door, he was immediately hit by the warmth and slight fug from both the fire in the kitchen, situated at the back, and those paratroopers who were smoking. Both doors left and right were open and the paratroopers from first platoon were milling about, the buzz of conversation and banter fading as Paul stepped into the room, and replaced by calls of "Morning, sir" and "Feldwebel Grun's cleaned us out, sir."

They all stood to attention, any food they had in their hands gripped tightly and arms firmly by their sides.

"Stand easy."

A further chorus of good mornings and greetings issued forth and the buzz of conversation picked up again as the men relaxed, most finishing off the remains of their meal. The room was packed and many had spilled over into the room opposite.

Max and Leutnant Leeb entered the room.

"Morning, sir, some food is on its way for you," Leeb told Paul.

"Yeah, there's plenty of milk. Some bread and boiled eggs along with a tasty cheese," added Max.

"Has the company eaten?"

"They've eaten in shifts and first platoon is the last, so we'll have the place to ourselves soon."

The paratroopers, some still munching at chunks of bread, slowly filed out of the house and back to their duties, leaving the rooms suddenly quiet.

"Like a bunch of nattering old women!" chuckled Max. "Your table awaits you, sir."

He steered Paul to the small table in the centre of the room which was of a similar size to the one where Bergmann now manned the radio. Max pushed some of the breakfast items, left by previous Fallschirmjager breakfasting, aside, making room on the table for Paul to eat.

All three sat down, placing their weapons over the backs of the chairs, helmets by their feet, peeling their other equipment off and placing it in a pile in one of the corners of the room.

A buxom woman with dark hair and in her thirties glided into the room. As she placed a tray of food onto the table, she gave a quick smile at Max, who suddenly looked sheepish in front of his company commander and Leeb. Paul looked at Max and was pleased to see his most senior NCO flustered.

"I need to check on the troops," Max growled, looking at the two wryly amused officers. "I'll be back in twenty minutes."

"OK, Max," Paul replied, struggling to hold back a laugh.

Max left the house and, hearing the laughter behind him, tore into the first paratrooper he saw doing nothing. Word quickly spread: the Company Feld was on the warpath.

"You can get away with it, sir. He'll make life hell for my platoon for a while."

"Don't worry, Ernst. He'll soon find some new targets," consoled Paul, still smiling.

"I need to go too, sir. A few things to sort out."

Once Ernst and Max had left, Paul surveyed the food laid out in front of him. Two boiled eggs, fresh home-baked rye bread and a plate of cheese. A crock of butter and large glass of milk were also placed nearby. Paul called Fessman and Konrad, who were hovering close by, over to the table.

"I won't be able to demolish all of this bread and cheese so you would both be doing me a favour by helping me out."

"Gladly, sir," answered Fessman, pulling up a chair, picking up a slice of bread, spreading it liberally with butter and topping it with thick slices of cheese.

"Can we stay here, sir, even if just for the bread and cheese?"

"I'm afraid not, Uffz Konrad. We'll be moving out later this afternoon."

"So enjoy it while you can," quipped Fessman.

"Do we know where we will be going, sir?"

"East, Uffz Konrad, east," answered Fessman with a smirk.

"Yes, we will need to continue our push east."

"The attack seems to be going well," suggested Fessman through a mouthful of bread and cheese which he then washed down with a glass of milk poured from the chipped jug in the centre of the table. A glass of milk for breakfast, fresh from the cow, was considered a must by the Latvians.

"So far yes, but it is a huge country to cross."

"Yes, but Minsk, sir," joined in Fessman. "To get that far so soon, that's moving some."

"It does seem that way. It's early days though. I don't want to put a damper on your enthusiasm, Uffz, but we caught the Red Army with their pants down. They will be pulling them back up as we speak."

They continued to discuss the progress of the war and the likely end date. Paul asked after their respective troops' health and morale. All the men appeared to be fit and on a high after the battle against the armoured trains.

Twenty minutes later and, on time, Max returned to claim the attention of his company commander, giving a sideways glance towards the two troop commanders which gave a clear message: breakfast was over.

"The Oberleutnant and I will be doing a full inspection at eleven hundred. You might want to spread the word, once you've finished filling your faces."

"*Jawohl*, Herr Feldwebel."

They both saluted Paul and left the house to return to their units and get them ready.

Max led Paul out through the front door, turning right and heading along the hard-packed road. There were houses each side of the road but here most were single-storey wooden structures, all different sizes and spaced erratically along the roadside. Some gaps were as much as fifty metres. They came to the last house on the right: a single-storey dwelling built of logs and looking solid and sturdy. In the distance, some forty metres further along the road, Paul could make out two paratroopers blending in with a clump of trees. Max, noticing Paul's line of sight, informed him, "Leutnant Roth's boys are covering the western end of the village, sir, and Leutnant Nadel the other."

"Leutnant Leeb?"

"His platoon is completing regular patrols of the perimeter, out to a hundred metres."

"Good, Max, good. We're moving so fast there is a danger that pockets of Red Army soldiers are still undiscovered. They might just blunder into one of our units."

"This is the house, sir."

The heavy log structure had been faced with thin planks of wood; two windows to the left and a door to the right. A small picket fence lined the road, but the gate was missing.

"I'll leave you here. You can make your own way back?"

"Yes, Max, but let me know if Major Trier turns up early."

"Will do, sir."

With that Max left, returning to the centre of the village, intending to put a firecracker under the company paratroopers so they were ready to move out at a moments notice.

Paul hesitated momentarily before walking down the small path that led to the pale blue door of the house. He looked about him. A warm, gentle breeze played on his cheek. It was going to be a pleasant morning and probably another hot day, he thought as his senses absorbed the wind's gentle touch. He knocked on the door of the house which was quickly answered by a rotund, red-faced woman whose teeth had long since gone. She was wearing a mid-calf-length, plain dress and her head was adorned with a colourful headscarf which was certainly the most attractive thing about her. She said something to him in Latvian or Russian. Paul's blank response indicated that he did not understand. Realising he didn't have a clue what she was saying, she waved him into her home.

He followed her in, ducking beneath the very low lintel, stepping straight into a large room that ran the full width of the house. Its ceiling was also low and the top of his head was only centimetres from touching it. He was ushered towards a battered armchair next to an open, unused fireplace, against the far left wall. Bits of horsehair, or at least so he thought, poked through the threadbare arms. The woman indicated to him to take a seat and then went into the rear of the house. Paul removed his MP40 from his shoulder and placed it by his feet. He sank down into the chair, feeling it would collapse with his weight at any minute. The creaking of the chair seemed to support his fear. He looked around the gloomy room; the only light came from the two narrow windows behind him but, with the shutters only partially pulled back, it was limited. Opposite him was another armchair, similar in style and condition, but smaller. Its back was higher and its wooden arms not as broad as the ones Paul currently rested his elbows on. To his far right, in between the front door and another door that possibly led to a kitchen or bedroom, or maybe both, was a narrow rectangular table with roughly made chairs tucked under it. They had probably been made by the owner of the house.

The rear door opened and the old woman re-entered the room, followed by the young woman he had rescued the previous day. Paul stood, as the old woman quickly moved a small side table next to his chair and placed a small glass of milk on its surface. She beckoned the young woman over, indicating she should sit herself down in the chair opposite Paul. A few words passed between them in their local tongue then the older woman left them alone.

"Are they...looking after...you?"

"My German is quite good, Herr Oberleutnant, you don't need to speak slowly." She brushed a lock of dark hair from her eyes and pushed it behind her ear, dipping her head in slight embarrassment as she did so.

"Good," said Paul. Memories of Christa came flooding back, coursing through his body, threatening to overpower his senses.

She looked up, sensing his discomfort. "Are alright, Herr Oberleutnant?"

He stared back at her. The similarity was astounding, although Hana was much shorter and slimmer and maybe lacked the high level of confidence that Christa had.

"Yes. How long will you be able to stay here?"

She moistened her full lips and brushed back her hair. It had again fallen across her face. "She is my aunt, so I can stay here as long as like."

"Your mother and father, where are they? Were they the couple I saw in Dvinsk?"

She winced at the memory of the events that had only occurred the previous day. Nearly raped by the Einsatzkommando thugs, bile rose in her throat and she swallowed the bitter acid, hiding her face behind her delicate hands.

"Are you OK?" Paul asked tenderly, leaning forward.

"Yes, yes, I am fine. They were friends of my family. I was staying with them."

"Your parents?"

"They live in Ferdinhandshof."

"I'm sorry, I don't know where that is," said Paul smiling, hoping to help her relax.

"It is near Torgelow, close to the Polish border."

"I'm told your father was in the German Army."

"He fought for his country in the Great War. He was wounded. You know, they even gave him an Iron Cross."

"Sounds like your father was a brave soldier."

"No, just one of many doing their duty for their country," she responded sharply.

"We all have to do our duty."

"But my mother is a Jew, so it seems duty is not enough."

It was Paul's turn to lower his eyes. "Is that why your parents sent you out here?"

"Yes, they thought I would be safe. Will you be able to find out what happened to my friends?"

Paul searched her eyes, seeing the pain of her ordeal reflected in them. "No, it wouldn't be a good idea even for me to go back, or ask questions about them."

"The big one."

"You probably mean Max, my Company Feldwebel."

"He is from Hamburg?"

"Yes, that's him."

"He told me you got into trouble and were arrested."

"He helped free me but it is best if we don't discuss that."

"He seems like a good man. He told me that you saved his life once."

"Like he saved mine," said Paul, smiling.

"You save each other, it seems," she said, laughing. Her eyes which had been so dim earlier brightened up now and the corners of her eyes crinkled slightly. "I bet those thugs will have to answer some questions for letting you get away."

"They will be embarrassed, that's for sure, so it is my hope that they will let things lie. You mustn't go back there, under any circumstances. Understand?"

She reached across the small distance between them and placed one of her slim hands on Paul's knee. "Yes I understand. Thank you, I owe you my life. I don't know how I can ever repay you."

"We are not all the same. Most of us are soldiers doing our duty for our country and don't condone that sort of behaviour."

"I know, your Max told me a lot about you. He said you were one of the bravest soldiers he had ever known."

Paul's face coloured slightly. "Feldwebel Grun talks too much. I shall have words when I see him."

"Don't be angry with him. He was only trying to put me at my ease. I did want to know about the man who rescued me."

There was a thump at the door and Hana started. Paul picked up his MP40 from the floor and stood up. The woman came from the back room, wiping her hands on a thin towel as she made her way to the door, opening it to be met by Max's frame filling the entrance.

He popped his head through the doorway. "Major Trier is here, sir."

"OK, Max, I'll be out shortly."

He turned back to Hana. "Where will you go from here?"

"I will head back to Germany. I will be safer there with my parents. Those beasts won't be far behind you now the fighting is over."

Paul pulled out a piece of paper and a pencil from his pocket and proceeded to scribble some information on it. He handed it to Hana. "This is how you can contact me."

She took the piece of paper, folded it and held it close to her chest.

"Write to me and let me know where and how you are. Then, when I am next on leave, I could perhaps come and check you're OK. Use my name if you have any problems. It may help, but I don't know."

She stood up and, placing a hand on his arm, went up on tiptoes and kissed his cheek. "Thank you."

With that, Paul, completely flustered, turned round and was gone. He was met outside by Max.

"Come on, Max, let's go and find out what this is all about, eh?"

"Something wonderful, I'm sure, sir," responded Max doubtfully.

They walked down the dusty road towards the company HQ where Paul could make out a SdKfz 223, a light radio armoured car, likely to be the transport for the battalion commander of the reconnaissance element of 6 Panzer Division. As they approached, the Major dropped down from the cupola of the vehicle, placing a mug on the mudguard as he hit the ground.

He returned Paul and Max's salute. The skinny Major, his hair cropped very short at the back and sides, very much the style the German Army had adopted, had a broad grin and was clearly on a high after the success of 6 Panzer Division against the Red Army. He wore a black Panzer jacket, plain yet almost flamboyant and the buttons at the top were undone as the air was already heating up. On his left breast, the Iron Cross 1st Class and the ribbon of the Iron Cross 2nd Class from the 1914-18 war, which also bore the silver eagle bar of a further award for the current war, probably earned fighting in France.

"Oberleutnant Brand?"

"*Ja*, Herr Major."

He reached out to shake Paul's and Max's hands. "It is good to meet you both. Your exploits are well known to the Division. You opened the Eben Emael gate for us to invade Belgium and France and helped us over the River Dvina."

"Just doing our bit, sir," said Max.

"Ah, so you must be the Feldwebel Grun I've heard about."

Max raised his eyebrows at the recognition.

"What have you got for us then, sir?" asked Paul. "Have you been offered a drink and some food?"

"Yes, your paratroopers have made sure we were welcome. Berg, pass down the map."

A head popped out of the four-wheeled armoured car, followed by the rest of the driver's body. Leaning over the hatch, he passed the Major a folded map beneath the square antenna that was raised above the length of the vehicle. The Major reached up and grabbed it, unfolding and spreading it out on the angled front of the glacis. Holding it flat with his left hand, he tapped their current location. "We're here, gentlemen."

They heard soldiers approaching behind them and turned to see Paul's three platoon commanders, Leeb, Roth and Nadel hovering close by.

"Come and join us," Paul ordered them. "These are my platoon commanders, Herr Major. With your permission, I would like them to join us."

"Fine, Oberleutnant, save repeating ourselves, eh?" The Major laughed.

The three Leutnants joined the group, saluted, then moved in closer so they could get a better view of the map and listen to the Major's briefing.

"As I was saying, we are here," he tapped the map again, "in this godforsaken hole and our next target is Pskov. We will attack the Stalin Line to the south of the lake here."

"What's the route to get there, sir?"

"Rezekne, north of this huge forested area; then we move on to Ostov before hitting the Stalin Line. That's where you men come in."

"What's the ground like ahead?" asked Leeb.

"Crap, Leutnant. The roads are diabolical, that is, when there are roads. You can expect poor roads, forest tracks and marsh."

"What will our role be then?" asked Paul, wanting to know what was expected of his company and his men.

"Simply reconnaissance, Oberleutnant. I have strict instructions that your men have earned a breather and will only be involved in helping us in a supporting role."

"We have done no more than your men, Herr Major. Your division has been giving the Red Army a headache too."

The Major scratched his chin thoughtfully. "They do seem to be folding easily but not without putting up some sort of a fight. When they do capitulate, it is normally in droves."

"They are up against the German Army, Herr Major," said Leutnant Roth proudly.

"Yes, of course, Leutnant, but there are a lot of them. As for your task, it is merely to help us with the reconnaissance of the bunkers and emplacements ahead of us. Hopefully your Eben Emael experience can be brought to the fore."

"I'm not sure there are many similarities, sir, but we will certainly help where we can."

"Dropping by glider," laughed the Major, "bloody bonkers the lot of you."

"You wouldn't catch me in one of those tin cans either, sir."

"You'd be thankful of it when the bullets start to fly. Anyway, no gliders and no parachuting for you lads this time around, I'm afraid, Feld."

"Foot sloggers then. What's next then, sir?"

"Well, the division is currently split into three: Kampfgruppe Von Seekendorf, consisting mainly of Motorised Infantry Regiment 114; the Panzer Reconnaissance Battalion 57; Panzer Jaeger Battalion 41 and the 6th Motorcycle Battalion."

"Some force that is," attested Paul.

"Well, Kampfgruppe Raus can punch even harder. It has the 6th Motorised Infantry Brigade along with Panzer Regiment II and other supporting units."

"Will we be attached to one of those?"

"No, you will be with the divisional main body, along with Battalion II of the 4th Infantry Regiment, artillery and engineers."

"Where will you want us in the line of march?" asked Paul

"Most of my battalion will be with Kampfgruppe Von Seekendorf, but I will leave a SdKfz 222 to act as liaison and escort. You can then slot in behind the main divisional body."

"Eating Panzer dust, just as I thought," groaned Max.

"Better they are in front and not behind you, Feldwebel Grun."

"Still move out at three?" asked Paul.

"Yes. The unit that will be attached to you is already on its way. Stick with them until your unit is called forward. Any questions?"

"Not for now, Herr Major. We'll just wait to hear from you."

Paul looked around his command group, giving them the opportunity to ask a question and was not surprised when the slim and wiry Leeb piped up. "How long will it take to get to get to Pskov, sir?"

"That very much depends on the Red Army, Leutnant," the Major replied patiently, "but we hope to maintain a continuing high rate of advance." Trier turned to Paul. "I must take my leave now, Oberleutnant. I have a battalion to command."

Paul snapped to attention and saluted, quickly followed by Max and the three Leutnants. "*Jawohl*, Herr Major."

With a quick flick of his hand, the Major turned and clambered up the front of his armoured car, stepped over the antenna and lowered himself down into the confines of the vehicle. A quick instruction to his driver and they reversed down the road, turned around and sped off alongside the ever advancing supply wagons and trucks.

Paul turned to his officers. "I want the company ready to move out within the hour. Once our escort turns up, I want to be ready to pull out immediately, understood?"

He looked at each one in turn. They nodded individually, the cherub-like face of Roth grinning with excitement. His platoon had not been involved in the armoured train action and he was keen for them to get into the thick of it. Nadel was equally eager and his normally pinched, pale face was flushed with anticipation. He nodded eagerly.

"Feldwebel Grun, I want an ammunition, fuel and supply status for the company and any shortages rectified. I know we should be able to get fuel and supplies from Division but we will be in competition with other units and I suggest that we may not be high on their priority list. Right, get going, report when ready."

They came to attention and the group split up leaving Max and Paul on their own.

"Panzer dust, bloody Panzer dust."

"Missing the arms of the cook already, Max?"

He looked up. "Plenty more cooks ahead, I'm sure, sir."

"Let's get this show on the road, Max. The sooner we leave, the sooner we can fulfil our master's desires."

Chapter Sixteen

The seemingly never-ending, hard-packed road had widened slightly and two vehicles could now pass, although still with little room to spare. Thick, round wooden posts had been hammered into the ground along the verge either side of the road, a metre apart. Most of the traffic was heading east with the occasional empty truck going west to pick up more supplies to feed the ever hungry front line. The SdKfz 222 armoured car from 6 Panzer Division's reconnaissance battalion sent by Major Trier, the battalion's commander, led the way. Paul's convoy of Opel Blitz trucks bumped along the rough road, clouds of dust their constant companion. A familiar haze enveloped them and traffic close by. The horses, pulling their heavy loads east along the road, snorted constantly, trying to clear their mouths and noses of the gritty atmosphere.

"The Landser have got a hard slog." Max, sharing the cab with his commander and a driver, pointed to the lines of Wehrmacht infantry marching in broken file either side of the road. Their sleeves were rolled up, helmets were hanging from their belts, and their weapons were slung over their shoulders.

"To quote you, Max, we're all eating Panzer dust," responded Paul with a chuckle. "They seem happy enough though."

The infantry were smiling at the passing Fallschirmjager. Jokes passed to and fro with the occasional jibe or request for a lift. They had left the village of Naujene the previous afternoon, an overnight stop at another almost identical village. They had been travelling since six that morning, stopping occasionally to give the drivers a break or due to a hold-up on the narrow, congested road.

"It just goes on for ever," exclaimed Max as they drove kilometre after kilometre, the *rollbahn* stretching ahead of them. "Just when you think you're about to get somewhere, it seems to start all over again."

"A bit like climbing, eh, Max? Just when you think you've got to the crest of the hill, there is more ahead of you."

"Yes, sir, but this just bloody endless."

Ahead of them, far into the distance and through the sporadic gaps in the dust being kicked up by the armoured car, black clouds of smoke billowed skyward, turning into towering spirals; evidence of a battle in progress or having been recently fought. They passed a broken down Pzkpfw 38(t), what used to be a Czech tank, that had pulled over off the road. The crew were sitting on top drinking coffee and smiling at the passing troops, waiting for the recovery team to get them back into the fight. They raised their hands to the convoy in a gesture of friendship, one fellow soldier to another, a sentiment that could only be experienced at times of war. Not far in front was a medium-sized Soviet tank, a BT7, fifteen tons of armour mounting a 45mm gun on a cylindrical turret. It was upside down and useless. The paratroopers looked on in amazement. These were their first sights of true armoured warfare. Little did they know that this was just the curtain-raiser. The true nightmare of modern tank warfare was still to come.

During their final stop for the day, resulting from enemy resistance holding up their advancing units, they encountered a sight that they would never forget. Walking towards them on the wide, open plain to their right was a column of walking corpses stretching back as far as their eyes could see. As they got nearer, the Soviet soldiers came into view. Exhausted and starving, thousands of them slowly traipsed past, heads bowed, wearing a mixture of ragged brown, green and khaki uniforms. Their headgear was a strange concoction of differing shapes and styles. A German guard walked on each side. The Landser were ten metres away from the prisoners of war and there was a gap of approximately twenty metres between each guard, such was the confidence of the German infantry who could easily have been overcome by the sheer numbers of Soviet soldiers had they had any fight left in them. The line seemed infinite. A permanent cloud of dust eddied around their ankles as they shuffled and stumbled by.

"Christ, they look well and truly beaten, sir," blurted Roth leaning against the Opel's bonnet as he swigged from his water bottle.

"The line is unending. Where have they all come from?" added Nadel.

"They are the remnants of a mechanised corps we surrounded up ahead," Major Trier informed them. He had recently joined them to check on their progress and update them on the battle up ahead.

He turned to Paul. "You'll be stopping at this village overnight. There's a bit of a hold-up ahead."

"Problems, sir?"

"Not major ones, certainly not the enemy anyway. We're just running low on fuel and ammunition. We're waiting for this lot to catch up," he said pointing to line after line of horse-drawn supply wagons.

Many of the supply unit soldiers were riding on the backs of the horses which were pulling the heavily laden supply wagons and the occasional artillery guns. A heavy reliance was placed on horse-drawn transport for supplies and guns. Two hundred thousand horses were needed for Army Group North alone. The workhorses added to the fine dust as they kicked their way past.

Max spat on the ground. "*Scheisse*. Bloody dust, bloody heat."

Trier laughed. "I'm sure we can dig up some local beer, Feldwebel. Then you can slake your thirst and wash away some of that grit from between your teeth."

"You're a man after my own heart, sir."

"What happens next, sir?" asked Paul bringing the discussion back on track, frowning at Max who just raised his eyebrows and reached into the cab of the truck he was leaning against and picked out his water bottle.

"You will stay here tonight, but I need to rejoin my battalion. Schick will let you know when you can continue your journey."

"Any idea when, sir?"

"By tomorrow morning, all being well, Oberleutnant. We are under pressure from up on high to press forward."

"Fine, sir."

With that, Major Trier flicked a salute in return and climbed up into his command car and sped off east to rejoin his battalion and provide them with the direction and leadership they were going to need over the coming months. His unit was key to sniffing out where the enemy was so the Division could get to grips with them. They also needed to ensure the armoured giant was not heading into any ambush set up by the Red Army.

"He's got his work cut out, sir," said Max, handing Paul his water bottle.

Paul took a swig of water before responding. "He's got a sizeable force at his beck and call, Max. He should have up to forty Panzer IIs."

"So, we're in this dump tonight then."

"I'm sure you'll find a soft bed to sleep in and someone to cosy up to."

They both turned towards the road as there was a sudden cheer from the paratroopers lounging by the sides of their Blitz trucks. Jibes and banter were swapped with a rifle company slogging their way down the edge of the road, laden down with their equipment and weapons. One soldier had a large loaf of bread tucked behind the straps just above his mess tins; food for his troop or platoon when they stopped for a much needed break. Their sleeves were rolled up above the elbow in an effort to keep cool. Marching in the dry heat for kilometre after kilometre was debilitating for even the fittest of soldiers. Some of the villagers had also come out of their houses to greet this new batch of soldiers. Young women handed out flowers; the older members of the village handed out home-made biscuits and chunks of fresh bread. Some soldiers received kisses from both age groups – the lucky ones had kisses from the young women. There was clapping further up the road and men were waving their flat caps again, seeing the German forces as liberators, not occupiers.

"This place has suddenly turned into a bloody circus," complained Max.

Paul gave Max a look as if to say, for God's sake, stop moaning. However he could understand where Max was coming from. A hundred metres away, on the far side of the road, the column of Soviet prisoners of war continued to file past with their guards. Horse-drawn wagons continued to rattle by, the horses snorting and shaking their heads. Landser marched along the edge of the road heading towards the front and the paratroopers bantered with their *kameraden* from the army. All this mixed with the squeals of the village girls and clapping from the villagers. Yes, Paul understood exactly what Max was referring to. Oh, for a bit of peace and quiet.

A rumble could be heard in the distance, steadily getting closer. It turned out to be a flight of Stukas overhead, flying towards the front to seek out the targets they had been assigned as the battle for Russia continued.

Paul turned to Max. "Let's get the men together. I'll give them a quick update then they can get some food and rest."

"Still full security tonight, sir?"

"Yes, Max," he replied, looking at the line of Soviet infantry still trudging by. "We're close to the front and who knows what's lurking out there."

Max came to attention. "*Jawohl*, Herr Oberleutnant. I'll round them up now."

With that Max left, leaving Paul to continue to survey the circus.

Chapter Seventeen

27 September 1941

Volkman was talking to the Adjutant, Hauptman Bach, who was standing next to a large board that was leant against a stack of straw bales. Two maps were pinned to it.

Helmut nudged Paul. "About bloody time we were brought up to date. Maybe we'll find out what the hell is going on."

Paul pulled his tunic collar higher around his neck, feeling the chill as someone came in through the doors. At the far end of the barn, a brazier, in a converted oil drum, was being used in a vain attempt to warm the place up a little. Someone threw on a chunk of wood to keep the flames alive, a curse from his fellow troopers as the flames leapt and sparks flew. Although a clear space had been made around the drum, there was still a risk of the surrounding dry straw catching fire from any sparks flying free. Buckets of water had been placed at strategic points around the barn, just in case. The brazier was essential. Temperatures were already dropping to zero and, stepping outside, the cold immediately hit.

"Something's up. The Landser have been running round like headless chickens for days now."

"You're right, Helmut. I reckon we're going into Leningrad," said Manfred.

"Bugger that," announced Erich. "That place will swallow us up."

"No, it's not Leningrad. Look," Paul pointed to the new officer who had recently joined them, "he's brought 50mm Paks with him. That's got to mean tanks, surely."

"Where else is there?" asked Manfred. "Unless it's to the east? Maybe they need our help pushing the Red Army back."

"What, drop behind their lines? You've got to be kidding," jibed Helmut.

"Well, we'll know soon enough, Manfred. The Raven will brief us any minute now," responded Paul impatiently. He was bored of all the speculation. In a matter of moments, they would know exactly what was expected of them, or so he hoped. Paul was as keen as the rest of his friends to know what was going to happen. His company had aided 6 Panzer Division with their crossing of the Stalin Line near Pskov, although they had been specifically excluded from any of the fighting, acting in purely an advisory capacity, giving insights in tackling the concrete bunkers and armoured turrets. Since then they had just been kicking their heels, tailing behind an increasingly victorious army. His men were frustrated that they were being kept out of the fight. In fact, they were so exasperated they would have jumped at any mission put in front of them.

As they got closer to Leningrad, supplies had become increasingly difficult to come by. Paul and his men often found themselves stranded without fuel and had succumbed to scrounging for petrol from any unit they came across as they tagged along behind the ever advancing Army Group North. The Army was supposed to receive thirty-four supply trains a day, but in fact only received half of that and often even less.

Finally, having been joined by the rest of the battalion and moved to the town of Mga, it seemed that Army Group North again needed their services.

His comrades continued chatting as Paul looked about him. A steady buzz of conversation filled the barn as the small groups of officers and NCOs speculated about what the immediate future held for them. Scattered around the large shelter were a group of leutnants; twelve platoon commanders from the four companies; the new tank hunter detachment; the senior NCOs next to the Battalion Oberfeld, and battalion support staff. A gathering of the clan, indeed, thought Paul.

"Gentlemen," warned the Adjutant, bringing the men to attention.

There was immediate silence, resulting not only from the discipline they followed but because of a real desire to know what was expected of them in this continuing war. They looked towards the end of the barn. The only sound now was the occasional rustle of straw as the men adjusted their position on the uncomfortable and prickly straw; a splutter from the wood-burning drum; and the odd crackle from the battalion radio. Paul noticed that the majority of the officers and NCOs present were relatively clean and tidy, despite the primitive circumstances they lived in, billeted in dirty barns and sparse, often mangy village dwellings. However, the battalion commander, Major Volkman, was immaculate. He was not wearing a paratrooper smock but instead his *flieger bleuse*, Iron Cross first and second class on his pocket and his Knight's Cross at his throat. His ever-present swagger stick was glued to his right hand and slapped at his combat trousers as he came forward. He looked around at his command arrayed in front of him, a look of pride; a unit that, to date, had never let him, the Fallschirmjager or the Fuhrer down. He looked at his most senior officers, his company commanders, one by one, sizing them up. He thought about their strengths and weaknesses and how best to use them in the forthcoming battle. He felt sure that the next one could be their toughest test yet and he had an ominous feeling in the pit of his stomach. Some of these brave men in front of him now would not make it back. They would not be there for future fights.

"We are a battalion again," he said softly, smiling, but with an intensity that did not go unnoticed. He slapped his riding crop against his leg, making some of the new, younger officers jump, mesmerised by their charismatic commander. "We have a task to do at last, although some of us have been getting to grips with the enemy already. Oberleutnant Brand, Leutnant Leeb and Feldwebel Grun have already given the Soviet Army a taste of what they can expect from the Fallschirmjager. You have mine and General Student's commendation, Oberleutnant. Please pass this on to the rest of your men."

Leeb and Max stuck out their chests with pride. Paul blushed with embarrassment at being picked out for public praise by his battalion commander.

"First, an update on the situation, as we see it. Hauptmann."

Hauptmann Bach got up from the bale of straw he had been perched on, cleared his throat and took a drink of water from a tin mug, the constant almost invisible haze of fine straw dust particles having dried his throat. He tapped the main map on the board, looked up as a solitary feather floated down from the balcony above him then back to the map. "Most of you can see the map. You can all get a closer look after the briefing should you need to."

Bach's confidence had grown since his appointment as battalion Adjutant and promoted Hauptmann. His face was still tanned, a healthy golden brown tint, even though, like the majority of the battalion, he had been out of the burning heat of Crete for some months now. His tan had been topped up by the warm Soviet weather they had experienced when they first came to Russia.

"My verbal explanation should be enough to satisfy most of you. The gist of our current situation is as follows. From west to east, the 16th Army, along with 18th Army, have effectively sealed up the 8th Soviet Army in the oranienbaum pocket here." He tapped the map west of Leningrad. "The intention is probably to whittle them down until they either surrender or they are destroyed."

He tapped Leningrad. "As for Leningrad itself, it is now ringed by German forces to the south and our Finnish allies to the north. XXXX11 (motorised) Armee Korps has taken Pushkin, Aleksandrovka, Pulkovo, Konstaninovka, Krasnoye Selo, the Dudergof heights and Taitsy."

He tapped the map from left to right as he continued.

"Pushkin was taken by the second regiment of the SS Politzei Division. 1st Panzer Division was responsible for taking Aleksandrovka—"

"Unfortunately," interrupted the Raven, "1st Panzer Division, along with the rest of Panzer Group 4, are being diverted south. The Fuhrer has other plans for our armour. I suspect for the push on Moscow."

There was a groan from some at the thought of losing the most powerful element of the Group's line-up and of what was to be expected of Army Group North in the future. Others were more positive; the indication that Moscow could fall very soon as a result.

"We still have a significant force in this sector and this battalion will still do its duty," interjected the Raven. "Continue please, Hauptmann."

"We have taken the Dudergof heights, hill 157, here," he tapped the map at a point, "between Taitsy and Krasnoye Selo, 6th Panzer Division enveloping Taitsy from the south. Kampfgruppe Koll has cut the Moscow-Leningrad Highway, road and rail, leading south, destroying an entire Russian rifle regiment in the process. Finally, 58th Infantry Division has captured Konstaninovka and Sosnovka and 36th Infantry Division has secured Finskoe Koirovo and the west end of the Pulkovo heights."

"Have the Soviets made any counter-attacks, sir?"

"Yes, Paul," responded the Adjutant, "there was a battalion-sized counter-attack around the south-west of Pulkovo but it

169

collapsed. They did, however, use their new heavy tanks, the KV1 and KV2s, which apparently took some stopping."

"Our Pak 38s will put a stop to them, sir," called out Leutnant Meissner, the commander of the new tank hunter detachment.

"We would hope so, Leutnant. Our 36s have had little effect so far. You will still find them tough and will have to wait until they are within close range, or even hit them from the sides or rear."

"So," prompted the Raven stepping forward, "enough of what's gone. Now to what's going to happen."

He pointed to a bigger map to the left of the chart showing the surrounding area of Leningrad. "This is the area of the River Neva. Our next mission will be here."

He patted the map with his crop, stroking his chin, his hooded eyes staring at the chart as if it was the first time he had seen it. The paratroopers glanced at each other. They had thought their next objective would be Leningrad itself, not protecting a river. Despite their disappointment, there was still a flash between them. They were eager to finally get some real action. The hanging around and lack of activity had been wearing them down.

He turned back towards his men. "With Leningrad effectively blockaded, the Soviets are getting desperate to link up with their forces on the Volkov front. We hold a line east of Schlisselburg, running south. If the Red Army can cross the River Neva in force and link up with their Armies to the east, it would effectively break the encirclement."

He looked at his assembled officers and senior NCOs. "This cannot happen."

He turned to the map again, tapping it with his stick. "The river flows south-west from Lake Lagoda, passing west of Schlisselburg, in between Dubrowka and Wyborgskaja, where it turns further west passing north Petruskinjo before turning north-west through the city of Leningrad to the Baltic Sea. I believe it to be seventy-five kilometres long."

He turned and faced them again.

"Since mid to late September, the Red Army has managed to cross the Neva at Petruskinjo, about twenty kilometres west of here and about twenty kilometres from Leningrad. Several rifle battalions have also managed to cross the Neva, using rafts by all accounts, near the town of Dubrowka. We are holding them there, but they do have a foothold, some fifteen hundred metres long by about five hundred deep. Perhaps more of a toehold…" he added thoughtfully, "but they are there all the same. They are dug into the clay banks of the river and entrenched in along the fifteen-hundred metre line. There is apparently very little cover and they are effectively surrounded on three sides."

"I wouldn't want to be in their shoes," piped up Helmut. "Can't the Landser push them back?"

"Quite, Oberleutnant Janke, but so far our infantry have been unsuccessful and there is a fear at higher command that they may well attempt more river crossings. So, they have asked for us."

"The best, sir."

"Of course, Oberleutnant Bauer. Hauptmann, will you take us through our movement orders and line of march."

"Sir," responded Bach, moving forward as the Raven stepped back into the shadows cast by the lantern suspended from the hayloft. All were conscious that the battalion commander would still be alert, watching their faces and their reactions as the Adjutant continued the briefing.

Bach stood, straight and strong. The Hauptmann had now settled into his new role as Adjutant of the battalion and effectively the second in command. Although a little uncertain in the early days, he now fulfilled his role effectively and with confidence and was trusted by the officers and men of the battalion. A huge duty, thought Paul; he was not sure how he would cope with that level of responsibility. Paul had only just come to terms with commanding a platoon in Poland and Belgium when a full company had been thrust upon him in Greece and Crete. This had tested his command and leadership skills to the limit. But a full battalion? He respected Kurt Bach for taking the role on.

"Our area of operation will be south-west of Wyborgskaja, opposite Dubrowka situated on the western side of the river. The third battalion of Fallschirmjager Regiment 3, will be on our immediate right flank along with the Fallschirmjager pioneer battalion and the third battalion of the 238th Infantry Regiment. Further to their right, we have second battalion of Fallschirmjager Regiment 3 at Gorodok along with one and third battalion of Fallschirmjager Regiment 1, and first and third Fallschirmjager artillery batteries. On our left flank at Petruskinjo is first battalion of Fallschirmjager Regiment 3, along with first battalion of 284th Regiment. Further to their left, next to the bend in the river where it heads north-west towards

Leningrad, is the second Sturmgeschütz Regiment. Fallschirmjager Regiment 3, is the battle group command and they are positioned near the railway junction between Petruskinjo and Mga."

"Sorry, sir," interrupted Paul astounded by what he was hearing, "but that is not a lot of boots on the ground for what must be at least a twenty-five kilometre stretch of river."

"You are quite right, Oberleutnant Brand, it's closer to a two-division front," answered the Raven moving into the luminescence of the lantern, his eyes appearing like black coals beneath.

"I think you need to be aware, gentlemen, that we've hit a bit of a roadblock. The Landser are exhausted, and Panzer Group 4 has been diverted south to no doubt assist Army Group Centre with their push on Moscow. This leaves our Army Group light on armour and infantry. We fill part of that gap, although a gap still remains."

"Who is backing us up, sir?" asked Erich.

"We have 96th Infantry Division to our south-east and the 254th Infantry Division to our north-east. However, they are in need of supplies, and have failed to push these bridgeheads back across the river. Although they are there and still a significant force, we must see to our own to win this fight. It's not going to be an easy task. We have faced tougher ones," added the Raven with a smile, moving back into the shadows.

"To expand on Major Volkman's point, the infantry divisions have suffered quite badly. They have been fighting since mid-June with little respite and a lack of fuel. Supplies and ammunition are becoming an issue. Our supply line is some two thousand kilometres whereas Leningrad and the surrounding Russian forces have a mere forty. The rest of the Soviet Army has an equally short supply line. Army Group North has sent its last reserve division, the 254th Infantry Division, minus a regiment, to Schlisselburg. OKW have released its only strategic reserve in this area: us."

The Adjutant picked up a sheet of paper from the board that had been laid across the bales, acting as a temporary table.

"Line of march. Oberleutnant Fleck, your company will lead, followed by Oberleutnant Brand then Janke. The tank hunter detachment will be next and battalion HQ will be with you, Helmut."

"*Jawohl*, Herr Hauptmann," the three company commanders responded in unison.

"Don't worry, Oberleutnant Bauer, your unit isn't excluded. You will be the battalion reserve."

Bach turned and pinned up on a post a large half-metre square sketch showing the River Neva and the proposed positions of the battalion. "Paul, you will be dug in on the left, right up to the river's edge. They will do their best to dislodge you from there."

The Raven stepped forward again. "You must hold that section, Brand. If the Soviets manage to push you away from the river bank, they could then either advance south and attack towards I/FJR3 or come north behind the battalion and roll up III/FJR3, punching through to the east, linking up with their main army. Whatever you do, you must hold that ground, Brand."

He held Paul with an unwavering look, impressing upon him the importance of this sector and the reason he had picked his most experienced company commander for the job.

"*Jawohl*, Herr Major," responded Paul with pride, recognising the importance of the task entrusted to him and his men. He stood up and brought his feet together.

"OK, Kurt, continue."

"Oberleutnant Fleck, you will link in with III/FJR3, to your right. As for Oberleutnant Brand, dig in and hold."

This time Erich stood to attention and acknowledged his orders. "*Jawohl*, Herr Hauptmann."

"Oberleutnant Janke, you will set up immediately behind their two companies, so you will have a broad front of some five hundred metres. Your role is to pick off Russian troops that break through at any point in the front line and help plug any intrusions."

"I would suggest that you hold a platoon in reserve at all times. They can quickly move to any hot spot and help suppress the enemy," ordered the Raven.

"Sir."

"Oberleutnant Bauer, you've not been forgotten." The Adjutant laughed. The rest of the battalion in attendance joined in, the tension slipping slightly. The Raven looked on, pleased that morale amongst his men seemed high.

"You will help set up and defend the battalion headquarters, roughly three hundred metres back from the front line. It needs to be secure and well protected from artillery and aircraft attack. This will also be a place of respite for the companies in the line. The front three companies will be rotated, so you will get the opportunity to be at the sharp end while the off-duty unit gets some decent food and rest."

"And my boys?" asked Leutnant Meissner.

"Two are being sent to III/FJR3. One of your Pak 38s will be with Oberleutnant Brand, one with Oberleutnant Fleck and the remaining one with fourth company. That is where you will position yourself and you will come under the command of Oberleutnant Janke. Clear?"

"Yes, sir." The tank hunter commander nodded.

"Good, we march tomorrow at o four hundred. Any questions?"

"What about trucks, sir?" asked a perturbed Manfred. "Ours seem to have disappeared."

"No trucks, I'm afraid, and no Tante Ju. It will be boots on the ground tomorrow."

"That must be at least fifteen kilometres, sir."

"It is, Oberleutnant Janke," confirmed the battalion commander. "Well within your capabilities I'm sure."

This brought an immediate laugh from the rest of the attendees and a flush to Helmut's cheeks. Although they laughed, they all knew the consequences of what had just been said. Laden down with their equipment, supplies and ammunition, it would have to be carried on the fifteen-kilometre route march over unknown but probably rough ground.

"Any other questions?"

"What's the bigger picture looking like, sir?" asked Paul

The Raven came around to the front, his cane gently tapping the side of his leg, a sign the unit had come to recognize: their battalion commander was thinking clearly before he answered.

"News is scarce, but I have it on good authority that Kiev has been captured."

There was a buzz around the room. This was a major Russian city and securing it a major triumph.

"We have captured some six hundred and fifty thousand Soviet prisoners. The encirclement was a huge success, proving our Blitzkrieg technique yet again."

"Will we be advancing into Leningrad, sir?"

"No, Oberleutnant Fleck. The Fuhrer has issued a directive stating that we are to lay siege to Leningrad and starve them out rather than commit our troops to inner-city fighting.

"Will we be under Wehrmacht command, sir?" asked Paul.

"Initially, but within a matter of weeks 7th Flieger Division Headquarters will be stationed near us and we will come under their command."

Smiles played across the faces of the men. Although there had been few problems coming under command of an Infantry or Panzer division, the men were much happier knowing that their own command would be watching over them.

"Right, gentlemen, if there are no more questions, I suggest the company commanders remain behind for some finer details while the rest of you get your men squared away and ready."

That was the signal that the main briefing was over and the assembled men were to disperse, leaving the battalion's senior staff to talk over some of the finer details of the strategy and tactics.

Chapter Eighteen

It was four in the morning on the 28 September 1941 and it was a bitterly cold start to the day.

The battalion was gathered, ready. The companies clumped together in their respective assembly areas, dispersed amongst the trees of the forest. The battalion commander and the Adjutant had a last-minute conflab after receiving additional instructions from 7th Flieger's Divisional Command.

The paratroopers were wearing their thin smocks and combats. Some were shivering; all were keen to get moving and generate some heat. Orders were called out and, with the occasional soft clink of equipment and the crunch of boots, Erich's company moved out, heading along the narrow track that led through the thick forest.

Paul signalled to Max and number one company was rounded up. First platoon, led by Uffz Fessman, would take point following on from Erich's paratroopers. The lead elements of Erich's company entered the forest in single file. They made their way carefully along the dark pathway that would take them eventually, four to five kilometres later, to the outskirts of the nearest major Russian town, Mga.

"This is going to be a slog, sir."

"Nothing for a man of your calibre, Max, surely," chided Paul.

"I'll remind you of that when we get there, sir," growled Max, walking off muttering whilst hearing his company commander chortling behind him. Some of the paratroopers nearby got the sharp end of Max's irritation.

The occasional jangle of weapons could be heard reverberating through the forest as Paul's company took its turn to enter into the gloom. The sheer size and density of the trees quickly absorbed any sound before it reached enemy ears. Although Max had been joking about it being a slog, it certainly would not be an easy march. Both Max and Paul had two heavy fifty-round belts of ammunition for the MG34s wrapped around their chests and shoulders. The Raven had insisted that they take as much ammunition as possible with them, even though some limited wheeled transport was available. The battalion commander had managed to acquire three trucks but they would be needed to carry the ammunition for the 50mm Pak 38s, with any other supplies they could cram in around them. The Pak 38s would be towed by Sonderkraftfahrzeug SD 10s, half-track prime movers. Each man had three days of rations.

After about two kilometres, they walked out of the forest and into a clearing. The distant rumble of artillery could be heard, although not for long. The two opposing armies generally hunkered down for the night, choosing the crack of dawn to start any assault or counter-attack. They were still over ten kilometres from the front line.

After crossing the exposed strip for about a kilometre, clumps of grass under foot threatening to topple an unsuspecting paratrooper, they re-entered the blackness. Dawn was still some two hours away. They came out of the trees again briefly as they crossed over another track passing in front of them. They turned north after a few hundred metres. The column stopped for five minutes, not as a rest break, but probably while Manfred checked his map and compass. Paul, however, suspected that the maps were not that accurate or helpful. The paratroopers gratefully took advantage of the pause to drop their heavy loads.

Continuing north, the forest suddenly came to an abrupt end. Having arrived at the edge of the forest, they had at last reached the town's outskirts. It had been agreed at the start of the march that they would continue north, meeting up with the trucks by the railway sidings in the centre of the town. The railway line, the lifeline that had now been severed, ran west towards Leningrad. They would follow the line through the centre of the town before again turning north, where, they were told, the ground would get increasingly wet and muddy underfoot. Moving towards the centre of the town, past the bomb-damaged streets and houses, the level of activity about them steadily increased as did the sounds of battle to their north-west.

"Sounds like the Landsers are taking a bit of a battering, sir."

"Or else we're dishing it out to the Soviets, Max."

"A bit of both, maybe."

"Could be coming from Wyborgskaja or even Schlisselburg."

"Either way, sir, it's in the direction we're heading. Likely there's some business coming our way."

"I hope it's not more than we can handle," said Paul thoughtfully, stroking the scar above his left eye.

Max watched his commander's face and the gesture. Although confident that he and his company would give a good account of themselves, he had learnt to respect his company commander's insight into what may lay ahead of them.

Dawn was rapidly approaching as they arrived at the railway sidings, a melee of activity all around them. Manfred's company was settling down, making themselves comfortable as they waited for the rest of the battalion to catch up with them.

"Hi, Paul," Manfred called over to him, "managed to get comms with the Raven. We're to rest up here for an hour, give the rest of the battalion a chance to catch up, and get some grub before we move on."

"Sounds good to me. Any sign of the trucks?"

"No, but I've sent some of my boys to scout the railway line and look for them. They're bound to be here by now, so shouldn't be far away."

"What's up then, sir?" interrupted Max.

"We're here for the best part of an hour. Have the men stand down and get a bite to eat."

"I'll send the boys out for a scout. See if we can get something hot. I'm starting to chill already now we've stopped."

"Good idea, Max. I'll go and see if I can track down the Major."

They went their separate ways. Paul's company were milling around, merging into small groups finding somewhere comfortable to perch while they waited, passing around cigarettes or sharing their meagre rations amongst their friends and *kameraden*. In front of them, the open space of the sidings brought a shiver to first platoon who had not long ago fought the enemy in a place that was similar, but much larger. Behind them were the battered remains of the town.

The rest of the battalion slowly filtered into the area. They had made the five to six kilometres in two hours; slow for them. Not because they were unfit, or that the ground, although not perfect, was too rough; on the contrary, the unit was at peak fitness. More so because they were laden with so much equipment, ammunition and supplies. Pairs of men were carrying ammunition boxes slung between them, straining their arm and shoulder muscles as well as carrying boxes of Pak and mortar shells, rifle and machine-gun ammunition, grenades and enough personal food and drink rations for three days. The battalion commander had insisted they also carried enough food and supplies to keep the unit going for at least a further seven days than the planned mission.

Despite the weight they were each carrying, the men were far from exhausted and were in good spirits. Laughter could be heard from all quarters of the encamped Fallschirmjager.

Paul found the battalion commander and confirmed they would move out at o seven fifteen taking the same line of march, west, through the centre of the town before turning north-east.

There was a big cheer as a horse-drawn field kitchen came into view, being led by the dependable Feldwebel Max Grun.

"Hey look, it's a Gulaschkanone," someone shouted, bringing a further cheer from the assembled men.

"Hey, the Kuchenbullen, kitchen bull," someone else called in good humour, bringing a further cheer. The smokestack at the centre of the four-wheeled trailer was smoking profusely from the firebox but, more importantly, there was steam billowing up from the large boiler at the rear. The field kitchen pulled up at the centre of the mass of Fallschirmjager. The carthorses snorted as they were led away and tied up close by. A queue quickly formed and the cook started dishing out a thin but piping hot potato soup.

Max sat himself down heavily next to Paul, their backs against the outside wall of a bomb-damaged house, its blackened walls smudging their tunics. He handed his commander a tin mug of the steaming concoction provided by one of the divisional cooks.

"It's steaming because the bloody air is so cold, not because the soup is hot." He laughed as he handed it over.

"Small mercies, eh, Max? Am I to expect a visit from the Feldgendarmerie, or did you use your impressive charms?"

"I just pointed out that there over five hundred Fallschirmjager back here who were cold and hungry and, when marching past their lovely kitchen, they might just pick it up with them and take it to the front."

Paul laughed. "You have such a way with words, Max."

"This place...is in a...bloody mess, sir," said Max in between sips.

"There's been a bit of a fight here, that's for sure."

"Still more to come, looking at that lot."

They looked about them. Crate upon crate of ammunition was stacked up alongside the railway line. Ammunition for small arms, shells for the artillery and armour, mines and grenades. They were stacked where they had been unloaded quickly, allowing the train to return to the west to pick up its next load.

The first appearance of light before sunrise exposed a number of anti-aircraft positions put in place to defend this mass of supplies. It finally gave the drab town a little colour.

Soon there was a roaring sound and the rattling of tank tracks as a column of armour slowly made its way past the Fallschirmjager, the paratroopers giving the Panzer IVs a wide berth. The column continued past, tank after tank, truck after truck, the proliferation of traffic increasing, heading away from Mga, away from Leningrad and in the opposite direction towards the Wolchow Front.

"Where the hell are they going?" hollered Max to no one in particular and in competition with the ever-increasing thunder as the armoured column continued to roll by.

No one responded because no one heard. All were transfixed by the sight of this powerful force and all wondering why it was heading away from the battle.

"That must be 8th Panzer and 20th Infantry Division moving to support the push towards Moscow," said Paul, anticipating the question Max had mouthed.

"Not a good sign, sir," shouted Max. "We're moving into the fight and half the bloody army is moving out."

"We have a full battalion, Max, and the III/FJR3 are on our right."

"Soon bloody swallow up a few men, sir," responded the disgruntled Max.

"Stop being so pessimistic, Feld," added Paul, tapping Max's shoulder. "You've got hot soup and I'm sure they can rustle up some coffee for us."

But it was not to be. Whistles were sounded and the battalion was called to order. The units assembled, ready to move out. Although enjoying the break and the hot soup, the soldiers were slowly getting chilled and looked forward to marching again and reinvigorating their cold limbs. The battalion clustered into its individual units and, in column formation, second company, followed by the first, fourth, battalion HQ then third company, made their way west through the town's battered centre.

There was a constant flow of men and equipment going in the opposite direction. The paratroopers found it quite disconcerting to see such a large force moving away from the area of the very battle they were heading for. What was even more worrying for the Fallschirmjager, about to take part in the fight alongside their Landser infantry *kameraden*, was the look of defeat on the faces of the ones they passed as they marched towards the river. They had transformed from proud warriors to a shamble of dirty, dishevelled, unshaven men wrapped in any tattered cloth they could find to keep themselves warm. They were hollow-eyed and clearly exhausted. It was a shock for the Raven's men, not used to seeing the German Army in this state. When the Fallschirmjager occasionally caught the eye of one of the hunkered down soldiers, the Werhmact infantry quickly dropped their heads, breaking eye-contact with the fresh, obviously proud paratroopers, realising the state they were in and feeling ashamed.

"A song, I think, sir."

"An excellent idea, Max."

Paul and Max, a third of the way along the company's line of march, burst into song: the first two lines of the Fallschirmjager's battle song.

"Rot scheint die Sonne, fertig gemacht.
Wer weiß ob sie morgen für uns auch noch lacht?
Werft an die Motorren, schiebt Vollgas hinein, Startet los,
flieget ab, heute geht es zum Feind.
Red shines the sun, get ready, who knows whether it will still
smile for us tomorrow?
The engines start, full throttle, take off, on our way, today we
meet the enemy."

It was quickly picked by first platoon ahead and second platoon behind.

"Into the aircraft, into the aircraft!
Comrade, there is no going back.
In the distant west there are dark clouds,
Come along, and don't lose heart, come along!"

By the third line, the entire first company was in full voice; by the fourth, the entire battalion. The last verse was sung with gusto and even the Landser watching them pass and the columns going south could not fail to be uplifted by the five hundred voices belting out their unit song.

"Klein unser Häuflein, wild unser Blut,
Wir fürchten den Feind nicht und auch nicht den Tod,
Wir wissen nur eines, wenn Deutschland in Not,
Zu kämpfen, zu siegen, zu sterben den Tod.
An die Gewehre, an die Gewehre.
Kamerad, da gibt es kein Zurück,
Fern im Osten stehen dunkle Wolken.
Komm mit und zage nicht, komm mit!

Our numbers are small, our blood is wild,
We fear neither the enemy nor death.
We know just one thing: with Germany in distress,
To fight, to win, to die the death.
To your rifles, to your rifles!
Comrade, there is no going back."

As they marched through the town along the main street, battered buildings either side, anti-aircraft positions tactically placed to defend the mass of stores being assembled for the advancing German Army, they sang at the top of their voices. They could even be heard above the throbbing engines of the armour as it rattled by, along with the other units going south. Soldiers who before had sat around listless and deflated started to sit up and hold their shoulders back. Perhaps things were not so bad after all if these men could sing like that at a time like this. The Fuhrer had sent some of his best troops into the foray. Maybe now they could make progress against the increasingly stubborn Red Army.

The song over, the paratroopers settled down, the steady tramp of boots, the odd grunt as a soldier hoisted his MG34 on top of his shoulder or shifted the extra belts of ammunition they were carrying. Troopers swapped hands as they carried the heavy ammunition boxes slung between two of them as they marched side by side.

Reaching the end of the town, they turned north-west, entering again the forest that ringed the town of Mga and passing an artillery battery that had been set up in a clearing before the trees swallowed them. The trucks, along with the Pak 38s, took a different route, meeting up with the battalion later at an agreed rendezvous. The drivers and passengers tried to hold back their smiles for fear of initiating the wrath of their fellow soldiers still slogging onward by foot, laden down by their burdensome loads.

Kilometre after kilometre passed by. Tree after tree was passed as the army of paratroopers weaved their way through the narrow passage, the ground underfoot becoming increasingly saturated the closer they got to the river. They stopped every hour for five minutes to bring some brief relief from the weights they were conveying. Although the battalion commander was keen to get his men to their objective as quickly as possible, he was appreciative of the loads they were bearing, so he relented and gave them a few minutes to relieve their aching arms.

Even though daylight had arrived, the tall, closely packed trees let in very little light and what did filter down was reflected off the white mist that was gathering around their ankles as they trod on the forest's rich carpet. Twenty minutes later, the battalion stopped while their commander and the senior officers conferred, agreeing their position, confirming they were a mere three kilometres from their objective; no more than an hour's march.

Explosions erupted in the distance. It sounded as if it was coming from the area of the river; the distinctive, steady *pup turrrr, pup turrrr* of the MG34s and the crack of a Kar98Ks.

"Well, we know what direction to head for now, sir," suggested Helmut.

"Very true, Oberleutnant Janke, the units holding the line have been hard-pressed to retain it." The Raven nodded slowly.

"They'll not be sorry to see us then, sir," added Paul.

"Quite. The battalion will split up here. Brand, you will move to the southern end of the battalion line, locking in with Oberleutnant Fleck on your right. Make sure you lock that intersection."

He turned to Helmut. "Give them thirty minutes before you pull out. Myself and Oberleutnant Bauer will follow you in, understood?"

"*Jawohl*, Herr Major," they all chorused.

"Let's move."

Paul headed over to his company and called for his platoon commanders. They, along with Max and Unterfeldwebel Loewe, the commander of the mortar troop, gathered around waiting for the orders that would send them on their way.

"We're about three clicks away," Paul informed them, tapping with his left hand the point on the map he had pinned to the trunk of a tree. "We're going straight to our positions. The unit we are replacing has already dug some trenches and firing positions, so we will use those initially until we can see the lay of the land for ourselves. Ernst, you will have the right flank. Make sure you tie in Oberleutnant Fleck's left flank."

"Will do, sir."

"I want your sustained fire MG on the left of your position and the other on the right. So, two troops forward and one back, understood?"

"Yes, sir. How far is the river likely to be from the forward slit trenches?"

"We think about four to five hundred metres. Dietrich, you will be on the left flank. You will be the unit furthest left of the battalion so make sure you tie in with that river bank. Your left is likely to be at the point where the river starts to flow away from us into its outward bulge. The Russian soldiers hold this pocket."

"What stretch do the Russians hold, sir?"

"Likely to be one and a half to two kilometres long?"

"Do they hold any of the village, sir?"

"We're not sure at the moment, Feldwebel. III/FJR3 have been in possession a few times but I don't know if they hold it now. So, Dietrich, you basically hold the left. The river is probably no more than fifty metres from your southern position but moving away from you the further north you go."

"Understood, sir."

"Viktor, you will be covering Ernst and Dietrich's back. A troop behind each platoon and a troop in reserve. The reserve troop will be used to plug any gaps in the line, or a counter-attack against any break troughs, OK?"

"Yes, sir."

"Any questions?"

"Mortars, sir?" Max indicated in the direction of Unterfeldwebel Loewe.

"Good point. Unterfeldwebel Loewe, position your mortars behind Leutnant Roth's right flank, close to his reserve troop. You can provide each other with mutual protection. You will also be well placed to support Oberleutnant Fleck if needed."

"Sir," responded the giant of a man. Another paratrooper who was a qualified Fallschirmjager despite his size.

"That leads me on to the Pak 38s. They will be joining us later this afternoon, once we have replaced the Landser and stabilised our positions. When they arrive, I want them in the centre. Dietrich, position them amongst your furthest troop on the right and, Ernst, amongst your furthest on the left. Clear?"

They both nodded in acknowledgement.

"And the company HQ, sir?" questioned Max.

"That depends on the location of the HQ bunker, if there is one. Whatever, I want Leutnant Roth's reserve troop and the mortar team close by. Can I leave that with you, Feld?"

"Of course, sir."

"Also get Fink on organising a company dressing station. There must be something already set up. If it's going to be rough from the beginning, we need to be as prepared as soon as possible."

Paul turned to the Lion. "Get your tubes set up as fast as you can. Have at least one ready for action should we need you in a hurry."

"*Jawohl*, Herr Oberleutnant."

"Line of march, sir?" asked Max.

"Dietrich, you will lead then Ernst, Loewe and Viktor. We'll move in column for the first two and a half clicks then hold whilst Feldwebel Grun, me and a half troop from first platoon scout forward and see if we can meet up with the Landser holding the line."

"They're going to be a bit jumpy, sir."

"I don't doubt it, Ernst, so keep your eyes peeled, all of you."

He scanned their faces, their confidence obvious. They were alert, experienced and battle-hardened soldiers.

"OK, brief your men." Paul scrutinised his watch: ten twenty. "We move out in five. Let's go."

The assembled officers and NCOs broke up, briefed their respective units, hefted their heavy loads and moved out.

They picked their way through the forest which again seemed never-ending, the saturated ground doing its best to seep through their worn boots. As agreed, at the two and a half kilometre point they stopped for a brief conference, where they all agreed their position which was not more than five hundred metres from the front line and a thousand metres from the river. They prepared to scout forward.

Paul turned to Leeb. "It's likely that the forest edge will be right up to the front line so, Ernst, bring up the rest of the company behind us but hold one hundred metres in. Then wait for our return."

They all acknowledged and the company moved forward a further four hundred metres before they halted. Paul's scouting unit continued onward.

Chapter Ninteen

Paul and Max edged their way out of the fringe of the forest, moving cautiously. Although less than an hour from midday, the closer they got to the river, the murkier the atmosphere grew.

Fessman gesticulated to his half troop to split up; Herzog and Giester to the left; Rammelt and Gieb right, positioning themselves just inside the trees. Crouching down. Listening. Watchful for the enemy and their fellow-soldiers who were out there somewhere in the gloom.

He sniffed the air. "The rearmost unit can't be far from here, sir."

"You're a damned bloodhound, Walter. What can you smell?" whispered Max, crouched down next to him, his company commander to his left.

"Cordite, Feld, and the distinctive smell of human waste," he responded with a grin.

"You mean shit? Don't go all posh on me now, Uffz."

They continued to survey the area in front of them or, at least, what little of it they could see. To an onlooker, they would have seemed wraith-like, their faces macabrely blackened with mud for camouflage.

"Let's go," hissed Paul, "but take it slow."

They all rose from their squatting stance and moved forward, automatically falling into an inverted 'V' formation: Max and Paul at point, Fessman and two troopers on the right, and two troopers on the left. They crept forward, peering into the mist, straining to pick someone out before they were spotted.

"*Wer da*?" came a shout from in front of them.

"Fallschirmjager," responded Paul, MP40 held at the ready.

They tensed as a figure rose up in front of them and emerged from the swampy ground. An unkempt Landser approached them. A muddied, festering bandage encircled his head, his rank showing him to be a Feldwebel.

"Fuck, are we glad to see you lot. Sorry, sir," he uttered, standing to attention on realising there was an officer present.

"Stand easy, Feld. Where's your company commander?"

"He was wounded in this morning's attack. sir."

"We heard it," added Max.

"Your platoon commander?"

"None. sir, they're either dead or wounded. Oberleutnant Krause was the last. We've lost quite a few over the past week. We get attacked at least once a day and they're pushing harder each time."

"So who's in command?"

"I suppose it's me, sir."

Paul looked at the Feldwebel. His uniform, although tattered, was patched where possible. He then noticed another bandage around the man's thigh. Despite his injuries, he still looked at Paul with pride, although his relief at having reinforcements could not be hidden. A feeling of deliverance. Paul and his men would be taking over and he and his men could escape this hellhole.

Two more men suddenly appeared out of the gloom, carrying a stretcher which was holding one of the wounded Landser.

"Oberleutnant Krause, sir, he was hit this morning. We'll get him back to battalion but he won't make it. A mortar round exploded within a few metres of him. He's lost a leg and we can't seem to stop the bleeding."

Paul turned to Leeb who had just joined them. "Ernst, bring the rest of the company forward and have the platoons go straight to their positions. The Feld will direct them."

"Will do, sir," and Leeb headed back to the forest to call in the rest of the unit.

"Once we're in position, Feld, you can extract your company and move them back to the rear. How many men have you got left?"

"Not sure of the exact count at the moment, sir, but I'd say about eighty. Some of those are wounded."

"Are they expecting us?"

"You bet, sir. It's the best news they've had since we were stuck in this stinking hole."

"While my men position themselves, I want you to fill me in on what's been happening here and what Popov has been getting up to."

Paul crouched down and conferred with the Feldwebel from the 254th Infantry Division. As they talked, shadows passed them

188

by, creeping forward towards the trenches ahead, the Feldwebel breaking off to give them directions.

Fessman, whose troop was taking the furthest point on the left of the platoon's position, moved forward warily, hunched over, straining his eyes to pick out anything in front of them. He was as nervous of meeting one of the Landser, who were bound to be twitchy, as he was one of the enemy, in the ongoing fog that surrounded them. They had come across the first set of firing positions, likely to be the domain of third platoon when they arrived, to be told that the ones they sought were a further thirty metres on.

Eventually they arrived at the furthest front positions and, after conversing with the occupants, they took over the site the Landser had known as home for the last few weeks. The infantry moved out, grins on their faces that they could not fail to hide, knowing they were finally escaping. Fresh food, showers, undisturbed sleep and, most importantly, survival were their only thoughts.

Fessman allocated his men to their placements. "Petzel, Stumme, set up the MG here. I want it in a sustained fire role. You can have Kurt with you."

"Gotcha, Uffz."

Petzel immediately unshouldered his MG34; Stumme, his number two, peeling off the belts of ammunition wrapped around his body; Herzog covering them while they set up.

"The rest with me."

The remainder of Fessman's troop moved north along the front line until they came to the next trench and again replaced the now happy infantry soldiers.

"Rammelt, Gieb, your new home."

"Thank you, Uffz, but there's no running water."

"Plenty over there," grunted Fessman in response, pointing in the direction of the River Neva. "Feel free to get some."

"Uh, maybe I'll just wait for room service."

They moved on to the final trench. This was the furthest point north that his troop would take responsibility for.

"Giester, Baader, Ullman, yours. You'll tie in with second troop once you can see them. Keep alert. There'll be troops all over the place for the next hour."

"Can't see fuck all in this weather. Bloody kit's sodden."

"Button it, Ullman. The Landser have been defending this piece of ground just so you have a new home," snapped Fessman, who was feeling the icy fingers of cold seeping through his wet tunic now they had stopped marching.

Further to Fessman's right, second troop were also moving into position.

"Can't see bugger all in this shit," moaned Muller.

"Just keep moving forward," ordered Konrad. "If you hit water or see someone in brown pointing a rifle at you, you know you've gone too far."

"*Wer da?*"

"Fallschirmjager," responded Uffz Konrad.

An infantry soldier sprang up out of the ground barely a metre in front of them.

"You fuckers make any more noise and you'll have Popov shoving an artillery shell up your arse." The Unterfeld climbed up out of the slit trench he had been hiding in. "You our replacements?"

"Yes."

"Right, we're out of here. Popov has already hit us once today and will probably have a go at you tomorrow at seven, but with this shit giving them plenty of cover." He indicated with a sweep of his arm the surrounding mist. "They may well have a pop at you before then to welcome you here. I suggest you keep quiet and your eyes well and truly open."

With that, he gathered his stuff, sent a message along the rest of the line that relief had arrived and slowly extracted his men, vacating the firing positions for the paratroopers to take over. Konrad allocated his men their positions amongst the three firing points. They settled into the cold, dank trenches; the comparative comfort of the Russian villages a distant memory. The houses may have been manky, but at least they were relatively warm and dry. The increasingly dispirited troopers shuffled in their firing pits; their new homes for some time to come. Although wet and cold, they remained alert, the message from the Landser Unterfeld still ringing in their ears.

Paul, Max and the Feldwebel descended steps that had been carved out of the clay and ducked their heads as they entered a small chamber big enough to hold four or five men and topped with a roof of logs. The rest of the company headquarters remained outside. Although Paul did not need to duck once he was inside, he did so instinctively, his *fallschirm* occasionally brushing against the log roof overhead.

"It's not much, sir, but it'll stand up to a direct hit from a one-o-five mill shell. Even bigger if they don't land right on top."

The bunker was lit by oil lamps, similar to those used by the Russian peasants and probably acquired from one of the surrounding villages. It had a bunk bed against a wall opposite the entrance, clearly knocked up out of downed trees and branches from the forest behind them, two straw mattresses finishing them off. Next to it was a small round table, half a metre across, with two wooden kitchen chairs; one with a back, one without.

"Home from home, mate," suggested Max to the feldwebel

"With this bloody cold getting worse, you're going to need it."

"Any comms?" asked Paul

"Yes, sir," the feldwebel pointed to a feldfernsprecher 33, set on an upturned ammunition case in the corner; a field telephone, a ground-return phone, in what looked like a slim miniature suitcase with a cranking handle jutting from the side and a handset resting on top of the main works. "It's linked to the three platoon positions. Two at the front and one at the rear. You can also get the battalion command post from here."

"The other companies?"

"No, sir. We've tried but the Russians home in on the wire parties with mortars and arty."

"We need to do something about that, Max. How do the Soviets operate?"

"They generally launch their attacks at dawn, usually at about seven. They kick off with artillery and mortars first then come at us in the hundreds. Line after line of them. It's like pigeon shooting, but the more you kill the more seem to come at you. We've been nearly overrun twice. That was bloody scary."

"How far away are their forward positions?"

"The river is four to five hundred metres from here, depending where you are on the line, and they can be anywhere between us and the river. Dubrowka, across the river, is the main holding area. You can't miss it when this shit clears. It's the centre for their local industry. The chimneys stand out on the skyline."

"OK, Feld, rejoin your men. Max, I want to check the forward line. Can you get Bergmann to check the landlines? I want comms set up with the platoons and battalion as soon as possible."

"Will do, sir."

Crack, crack. The dulled sound of weapons could be heard

firing outside somewhere although, deep in the bunker, any sense of direction was impossible.

"What the hell was that?" hollered Max.

Zip, crack. Ullman grunted as the 7.62mm round struck him, tearing through his unprotected back, throwing him forward. Another bullet hit Baader as he climbed out of the firing position, knocking him back down, blood blooming across the front of his tunic as he slumped to the bottom for a final time. Ghostly figures appeared out of the encircling mist, the long, bayoneted Mosin Nagent rifle gripped prominently in their hands. Giester managed to get off one round, killing the Red Army soldier before the Russian's comrade thrust the seventeen-inch spiked bayonet deep into the paratrooper's abdomen. Giester exuded a guttural sound as he collapsed to the ground, the soldier allowing the bayonet to remain inside his body. He placed a boot on Giester's chest, wrenched the sucking piece of steel from his gut and prepared to strike again, his face full of rage, anger and fear. However, he never got to see it through as Petzel sprayed the area with his beloved MG34, his eyes wild as he gripped the butt firmly under his right shoulder, pumping round after round into the five soldiers who had suddenly appeared out of the mist, hell-bent on getting revenge for the murder of their *kameraden* earlier that day. Herzog, Bieler and Stumme quickly joined in, finishing off the remaining enemy soldiers. Petzel dropped to the ground, bipod open. Stumme threw himself alongside, guiding the belt as Petzel continued to fire round after round in short bursts. *Pup turrrr, pup turrrr,* into the fog at the fleeing Russian infantrymen. The cries of the enemy confirmed that some of Petzel's shots were hitting home, breaking up the attack before it had a chance to evolve into something bigger. Recognising that the Germans had foiled their surprise assault, they withdrew back to their own lines to lick their wounds, leaving behind a dozen dead comrades. The paratroopers had experienced their first introduction to their new enemy in the area, the Soviets, who had had their first taste of the full force of the Fallschirmjager.

Paul, Max, Leeb and Fink were quickly on the scene, finding Petzel and Stumme providing MG cover while the rest did what they could for their wounded *kameraden*. Fink went to give his expert help.

Paul turned to Leeb. "Ernst, check along the entire company

front. Make sure the men are on the alert. We've just had our welcoming party. There could be more to come."

Leeb sped off to carry out his orders while Paul moved forward and crouched down by the firing position, Fink shaking his head.

"He's dead, sir."

"OK, get him out of there," he ordered, turning to Herzog.

Leaving Herzog, Paul ran low over to where Ullman and Giester lay, quickly joined by the company medic, Fink, who checked them both over swiftly, hissing over his shoulder, "Ullman's dead, sir. Giester is in a bad way."

"Let's get him back."

"Any stretchers around here?" asked Fink.

"I doubt it," said Max, "you'll have to carry him. Herzog, Bieler, here."

"No," countermanded Paul, "we need as many men as possible here. Just Bieler and Fink. Max, bring one of Leutnant Roth's troops forward until we've got this position stabilized and let him know what's going on."

"Done, sir."

Paul grabbed his arm before he moved off. "They'll be as jumpy as hell, Max, so be careful."

"Shoot their company Feld? They wouldn't dare, sir," he said with a laugh and sped off.

"Petzel?"

"Sir."

"As soon as we get an extra troop upfront, I want your MG back in position, set up in the sustained fire role. We need to start hitting this lot hard next time they try that. I want an area in front of your position where nothing survives. Understood?"

"*Jawohl*, Herr Oberleutnant."

"Uffz Fessman, with three men down, you will need to reposition your men."

Fessman nodded. Although a veteran of many battles, this sudden, aggressive attack by the Soviets had shocked him. He had lost three good men in less than a couple of minutes.

"Yes, sir."

They heard movement to the right. All were alert, weapons ready in case of another Russian attack.

Leeb appeared out of the gloom. "Our front line is stood to, sir."

"Good, now link up with Leutnant Nadel. Make sure you tie in with his right-hand platoon and take the MG section back with you now. We have an unmanned position back there."

"What about here, sir?"

"I can hear a reserve troop coming forward. I'll stay until they're in position."

"Right, Petzel, Stumme, Herzog," called Leeb to his men.

They picked up the MG, Petzel cradling it in the crook of his arm, butt under his armpit. The end of the ammunition belt was wrapped loosely around the weapon and Stumme was close by with two fifty-round belts thrown over his shoulder, ready if needed.

"Uffz, as soon as things are bedded in here, make sure Petzel gets plenty of ammunition brought forward to him."

"You bet, sir," replied Fessman, determination back in his voice. "We'll be ready for the bastards next time they come back for us."

"Of that you can be sure, Uffz. They will be back."

The troop from third platoon arrived, wary but alert. Still unfamiliar with their surroundings and accompanied by Feldwebel Grun, they were quickly allocated positions along the line by their troop commander.

"How's Giester, Max?"

"In a shit state. Even if he survives, his Fallschirmjager days are over. Sneaky bastards, eh, sir?"

"It's a warning for us, Max. It's nothing more than we would do and they are far more desperate than we are. This isn't going to be a clean fight."

"We'll be better prepared next time."

"We have a lot to do, Max. These slit trenches need sorting out. They need to be bigger, deeper and have a decent firing step. Oh, and some front cover."

"Give them a breather today, sir, then get the boys on it first thing?"

"No, Max," responded Paul firmly, "today. They start on it now. I want these firing positions fit for use by the end of the day. Work them, Max, work them."

Max looked about him then nodded, knowing Paul was right. There would be no rest until their positions were defendable. "I'll get on it right away, sir."

"And make the platoon command posts a redoubt."

"Will we not pull back if overwhelmed then counter-attack with a larger force, sir?"

"You've seen what's happened here. Weather like this, Max, and there is no pulling back. They must hold their positions, or we'll end up shooting each other. Allow the rear units to deal with any breakthroughs."

"Right, sir, I'll get everyone on it now. It's going to be a long twenty-four hours."

"It's going to get colder as well. If battalion have set up, we must see if we can get some hot food or drink brought forward."

"Leave it with me, sir. I'll get Bergmann on it. He should have comms sorted out by now, knowing him. What will you do now, sir?"

"I want to check on all three platoons."

"What about Fessman? He's down three men."

Paul looked on thoughtfully, rubbing the scar above his left eye. "Give him two from company HQ. We can manage with the remaining two."

"OK."

Max placed one of his shovel-like hands on Paul's shoulder. "Bad start, I know, sir, but it has set the scene. There'll be no more complacency. We will be ready when the big push comes."

"We had better be, Max, we had better be, for all our sakes."

Chapter Twenty

Living in a slit trench was no fun and, coupled with the pernicious cold and damp conditions, it was one of those places where no living being, in their right mind, would choose to be.

Stumme placed the Lafette 34, the MG34's sustained fire tripod, on top of the flat surface in front of the slit trench. Describing it as a slit trench was extremely accurate although, since arriving, they had widened and deepened it. It was now just over a metre and a half deep, three metres long and a metre and a half wide. Fessman, their troop commander, was still not satisfied and had ordered them to improve it further. Logs had been placed in the bottom to keep their feet dry and additional ones to act as a firing step. In spite of the work to upgrade their position, they still had to be very alert for any potential enemy attack. They had been informed that Giester had died a short while ago. Three dead in the troop already, replaced by two paratroopers from the company HQ.

They needed to set up the sustained fire MG34. Stumme positioned the tripod to support the spring-loaded cradle that would absorb much of the recoil from the fast-firing machine gun.

"Push it forward a touch, Friedrich," suggested Petzel. "We'll need a bit more room back here."

"OK." Stumme pushed the tripod further forward flush against the wall of clay-filled hessian bags they had stacked there earlier, creating a barrier across the entire front of their trench. The solid bags would give them some protection from small-arms fire but not tanks. It certainly would not prevent a grenade being lobbed over the top and causing havoc.

"That better?"

"Spot on. Just make sure you bed the *spornblech* in well."

Stumme climbed out of the trench and, with his boots, pushed down on each of the three feet supporting the lafette. He made sure they had good purchase and would not move when the weapon was fired.

"Here you go." Petzel lifted the MG34 up to Stumme, who grabbed it and lowered it onto its cradle, locking it into place. Once in position, Petzel adjusted its direction of fire, ensuring its arc pointed towards the enemy. Situated below the stock was the precision traversing and elevation mechanism that would allow him to set up highly accurate, pre-registered fire.

"We'll need some daylight or at least some better visibility before we can set that up properly, Ed."

"Yeah, I know. I was going to say I wish this bloody fog would lift but at least it's giving us some cover at the moment. I wouldn't want to be setting this lot up with the Soviets taking potshots at us."

The MG34, in the sustained fire role, would give the defence of their front line a significant punch but required a larger team than normal to service it. Edmund Petzel was the Gewehrfuhrer, the commander; Friedrich Stumme, the Richtschutze, who carried and fired the weapon. Herzog was now the number two Schutze who carried the lafette 34 tripod, folded up, on his back when on the move. Giester and Bieler carried the trommetrager, small ammunition drums, boxes of ammunition belts and spare barrels. Although Willi Giester was no longer with them, Petzel believed that, when the time came, his firing position would give a good account of itself and give the enemy the hell they deserved. Stumme brushed some dirt away from the top of the gun and lifted the top cover.

"Pass a belt up, will you."

Petzel took one of the fifty-round belts he had slung around his chest and shoulders, and passed it up to his comrade who, kneeling beside the weapon, placed the belt in situ and lowered the top cover with a satisfying click. They were ready.

"Friedrich, take over here and cover us. You too, Rudi, while the rest of us get this place sorted."

"Make sure the ledge for the bed is at least a metre."

"You'll be bloody lucky. Get down here."

Stumme dropped down into the firing position, lining himself up behind the butt of the MG and Rudolf Bieler positioned himself alongside, attaching a second and third fifty-round belt, ready then to guide the belt and attach a new one when required.

"We're only asking for a decent sleeping position," Bieler joked.

"You'll be wanting bloody coffee in bed next," growled Petzel.

Bieler placed his Kar 98K on top of the front of the trench, should he need it; for example, if the MG jammed, or an enemy soldier got too close and potentially overpowerd the position. The rest of the gun team hacked at the position with their entrenching tools, endeavouring to provide the position with even better protection and, just as importantly, more comfort.

As they chopped away at the thick clay, their platoon commander and company Feldwebel, Leutnant Leeb and Feldwebel Grun, joined them.

"Alright, boys?"

"Not the Adion, Feld, but soon will be," joked Petzel, holding up his entrenching tool.

"MG ready?"

"Yes, sir, but we still need to range it properly and we have no pre-registered fire yet. Need some daylight for that."

"The fog's doing us a favour at the moment. Where's Uffz Fessman?"

"Next one along, sir, making sure all the firing positions are up to scratch."

"Good. Before we go, the Feld has a gift for you."

Max unhooked a thermos flask from his belt and handed it to Bieler who was the closest.

"It's only potato soup and has probably lost some of its heat. It's between all of you, so go easy on it."

It did not matter. Although they had been working hard all day preparing the firing position and had generated some warmth, the cold constantly leeched it away, particularly when they were stationary. The soup, whether beef or potato, hot or tepid, would help warm the core of their bodies and was a welcome morale booster.

"It's just what we need, Feld." Bieler thanked him. "I don't suppose you have any cognac to go with it?"

Max's look said it all. "No, but you're welcome to my boot up your arse. That gives a good kick."

They all laughed but cut it short remembering where they were.

"We'll leave you to it. I don't need to remind you to keep your wits about you. We're the new boys here so can't afford to relax our guard for one minute. Some of our *kameraden* have already paid the price for not taking enough care."

They all nodded, acknowledging the platoon commander's warning. He left, closely followed by Max, to go and find their troop commander Uffz Fessman.

Thirty metres away, in a swirl of mist, they came across Fessman helping Rammelt and Gieb improve their firing position.

"How's it going?"

Gieb already had his weapon on guard, covering the other two as they hewed at the clay, but Fessman made a grab for his favoured Kar98K/42, which was close at hand, and looked up startled. "It's you, sir. Scared the shit out of me. We're getting there but we don't half seem thin on the ground."

"Have you got the two men from company HQ?" asked Max.

"Yes, Feld," responded Fessman. "Ostermann and Lang."

"They're OK. You'll be fine with them. Both were at Crete but with another unit. Once the fog clears and you can see the positions either side of you, you won't feel so isolated. Anyway, reinforcements are on their way." He cocked his head, listening. "In fact, this sounds like them now."

They all looked back towards the rear and could just hear the sound of tracks grinding towards them.

"They're moving slowly so they don't bump into you," informed Leeb. "But also to attract as little attention as possible. We don't want Popov sending us a gift from hell."

"I'll go and guide them in, sir. They can see bugger all at the moment. Keep your eyes peeled, you lot," Max ordered.

"Where will they be positioned, sir?" asked Fessman.

"In between this firing position and the next. You'll have a firing position either side to cover them," responded Leeb.

"We expecting tanks then, sir?" asked Gieb.

"Yes, tanks are inevitable."

"Have we no tanks then?"

"Not attached to us. Most of the armour is being deployed further south. You and Rammelt stay here," commanded Leeb. "Uffz Fessman with me."

They headed north to the next firing position. Fessman had the sustained fire MG, these two rifle positions and a Pak 38 under his command. Once they made contact with Ostermann and Lang, they headed northeast to connect with the half-track that was still clawing its way towards them. They came across it just as the driver was swinging it around halfway between the two rifle positions, pulling the trailing Pak 38 parallel with the front line. The crew dismounted as soon as it stopped.

Leutnant Meissner approached Leeb and Fessman. "We've

brought something with a bit of a punch."

They were immediately joined by Max. "You're a welcome sight. What next?"

"We've brought some logs with us. We can use them to make a strong position once we've dug the gun in."

"Is the half-track staying?" asked Leeb.

"No," responded Meissner. "It will make too tasty a target when this fog dissipates." He waved his arm indicating the thick mist that still swirled around them. "Once it's dropped off our ammunition and logs, it will head back, towards the forest and out of sight."

"We'll leave you to it." Leeb turned to Fessman. "Can you watch over them while they focus on getting this dug in? I have a feeling we're going to need it."

"Where will you be, sir?"

"Checking two troop."

"Has three troop finished digging in behind us?"

"They still have some work to do, but pretty much, yes. I've allocated a troop that can be called forward if any part of our front line is threatened with being overrun. Only call them forward if desperate, and with plenty of warning. I don't want them running their arses off and getting shot up in the process."

"Will do, sir."

"Oh, and here's some hot soup for you and the boys," said Max as he handed over a second thermos flask. "Make sure it's shared with Ostermann and Lang."

"Thanks, Feld, this will cheer them up no end."

Leeb headed off to check on his other front line troop. Max headed back to the company command post to organise some more hot food for his men. It was nearly three in the afternoon and the temperature was steadily dropping. He shivered. Then, at a running crouch, headed east towards the HQ.

Loewe drove his men relentlessly. He wanted three mortar pits by nightfall, fully ringed with sandbags, filled with the clay-like soil. There was plenty of it underfoot. They found that the deeper they dug, the wetter the ground became and the harder the job was. However, Loewe wanted his Granatwerfer 36s well protected. Although only 50mm in calibre, the mortar could still influence the battle if they broke up an attack that was about to overrun a position.

Keller stamped heavily on the ground, in between the rapidly growing semi-circle of sandbags, attempting to fashion a hard foundation for the mortar baseplate. The other two mortar pits were equally as advanced in their preparation, the Lion pushing his troop hard. Once Keller had finished, Trommler placed the rectangular baseplate in the centre and pushed it down at the edges with his booted feet, ensuring the narrow blades that ran the width of the plate went deep into the clay and created a level and stable platform. Once in place, Sommer put the barrel into its location and adjusted the sliding collar until he was satisfied with its position.

"What range, Unterfeld?" he called to Loewe.

"Better err on the safe side initially. Set it for five hundred, maximum range. We can always bring it closer later."

Trommler took over, checking the arc that was fixed to the left-hand side and graduated from sixty to five hundred and twenty metres. He swiftly adjusted the elevation by pressing the quick-release lever, unlocking the catch of the sliding collar that was connected to the upper-end of the elevating screw pillar. Once he had the approximate range, he locked the collar in its guide and fine adjusted by rotating the sleeve of the elevating screw pillar.

"Number one ready, Unterfeld," he called quietly.

Loewe came over and checked it, although he knew the crew of number one tube were efficient and reliable. He was satisfied. They certainly would not resent his check. The last thing they wanted was for a bomb to fall short and kill some of their own men.

"Good, start unloading some of the ammunition. Have ten rounds ready for immediate use. With this lousy weather, best keep them covered. Use some of the broken boxes as a base and for covers."

"*Jawohl*," responded Keller the tube commander.

Fessman, joined by his platoon commander, stood watching over the five-man gun crew as they put the final touches to the firing station for their Pak 38. They had dug out an area two metres by three and just under a metre deep. All five had worked non-stop to get the position ready. Even the detachment Leutnant had rolled up his sleeves and helped. They had used logs brought up by the half-track to line the top of the front and sides, giving them a solid, elongated, U-shaped firing position.

The gun, mounted on a split trail carriage, with an armour plate shield at the front, was manhandled into position. The large wheels were butted up against the western front of the U-shaped revetment. The two hundred and eighty centimetre long-barrel jutted over the edge in the direction the enemy was likely to come from. They pulled the split-trail carriage apart, stamping down on the spades at the end, bedding them into the ground. The spades were designed to dig into the ground when put under backward pressure, preventing the gun from shooting backwards when fired. The Leutnant, once satisfied, had the men stack ammunition close by, in a smaller area that had been dug out by the half-track crew while waiting.

They had a mixture of ammunition: armoured piercing shells to take on the enemy's medium tanks and high explosive shells to target soft-skinned vehicles or even infantry. The majority were AP rounds. For high explosive support, the Fallschirmjager would be dependent on their own 50mm mortars or any artillery support from the rear.

The crew formed a line, unloading the shells from the boxes and passing the four kilogram AP and three kilogram HE shells from one to another, stacking some close to the Pak, others in the pre-prepared ammunition bunker.

The Leutnant sauntered over towards Leeb and Fessman. "My boys are just about finished, so we can take on any armour they want to throw at us," he said with a lopsided smile.

"Are they going to dig some slit trenches as well? They'll need somewhere to hide when the artillery comes their way."

"Yes, they've been told. Meissner by the way, Adler Meissner."

"Leeb, Ernst Leeb and this is Uffz Fessman. It's his troop that will be watching your backs for you."

"Sir, my boys will take care of you," reassured Fessman. "You have no worries about that."

"I don't doubt it. I've heard that you were the idiots that landed on top of some fort in Belgium. Mad, the lot of you," he said with a laugh, but secretly glad he had these veterans covering his men.

"Is there a second Pak going in along the line?" asked Leeb.

"Yes, with your second platoon. Nadel, Dietrich Nadel, isn't it?"

"That's him."

Meissner turned towards the gun crew and called over an Uffz who joined them. "This is Uffz Blacher. He's the gun commander. Between the two of you, Uffz Fessman, you'll be able to give the Red Army hell."

They all laughed, although quietly, and after a few minutes' discussion, the anti-tank detachment commander left to check on his other gun positions, while Leeb headed for HQ, a briefing in the offing.

Fessman checked his positions again until he was satisfied they were ready, although not without a little anxiety. He was not actually sure what they could expect. The weather was crap; conditions were far from perfect; they had no idea what the enemy was going to throw at them; and, on top of that, it was cold, bloody cold and getting steadily worse.

Paul was sitting on one of the hard wooden chairs; 'probably knocked up from one of the trees in the forest close by' was Max's guess. It was placed between the bunk bed on his right and a square table tucked in the corner on his left. At the end of the bunk bed, there was a small alcove, a shelf now stocked with a small tin of coffee and some of the meagre rations they had managed to acquire before being separated from the main body of the Army. Tucked under the adjacent side of the small table, another wooden chair, although this one was more of a stool. Behind it, next to the far wall, was a woodburner, the piped chimney disappearing up through the timber-laden roof above. The flickering flames added some additional light to the gloomy bunker and, of course, some badly needed heat to drive out the cold.

The pile of logs, left by the Landser, had already been restocked. To the right of the stove was both the entrance and the exit for the bunker. Steps outside led to the upper level. To Paul's immediate left, a flickering oil lamp was positioned in the centre of the table, adding the smell of burning oil to the smell of damp leaching up through the floor of dank logs.

Between the table and the woodburner, two upturned ammunition boxes, stacked one on top of the other, were being used as a platform to support the field telephone. Bergmann, perched on two additional ammo crates next to it, was keeping a log of the communications between the Company HQ and the platoons and the Company HQ and the battalion.

Max, sharing the table with Paul, was sitting in the small gap between the table and Bergmann's field phone.

"So, the battalion commander's off to see FJR3 then, sir? Oberst Heidrich, isn't it?"

"Yes, it is, Max. He just wants a full update on the situation."

"And knowing our leader, sir, he'll be sniffing around to make sure third battalion don't have any weak points that might leave our right flank exposed."

"True, true, but it would have to be pretty bad for them to fold. Let's just hope it's not us first. He'll be pulling strings to get some more ammunition as well as other supplies. We don't have full communication with 7th Flieger Division yet though."

Max turned towards the bunk bed, his back against the cold bunker wall, his feet now resting on the edge of the lower bunk bed. "MG ammo, sir, that's what we need plenty of. It'll be the 34s that keep the Russian hordes back, but those babies just eat up the belts."

"He's promised to get more, Max. He's never let us down yet. Have the Paks been positioned?"

"Yes, sir, bedded down where you wanted them, although two Paks along our entire front is hardly going over the top."

"Beats having 37s, Max."

"Those door knockers are bloody useless. Can't seem to touch any of the medium tanks the Soviets send against us."

"These new tanks have certainly caught us with our pants down. That's why the two Paks we have will act as a fortified zone in their own right."

"I hope to God we don't get one of those monsters coming at us."

"The KVs? Yes, they will test our front, that's for sure."

Max looked over his left shoulder. "Sounds like the platoon commanders are on their way."

They heard the thud of boots on the wooden blocks used to reinforce the steps down to the bunker, preventing them from collapsing. Then a grunt from Nadel as he hit his head on the low beam of the doorway.

"Mind your head, sir," Max called out to the unfortunate officer who was rubbing a sore spot on his scalp, wishing he had left his *fallschirm* on until he had got inside. Max was barely able to contain a smile. Paul kicked him beneath the table.

"Thank you for your timely warning, Feld, much appreciated," replied the officer, his pinched face even more so after being in the bitter cold outside.

Max got up and moved across to the bunk, lowering himself down on the creaking frame, giving his seat up for the Leutnant and cracking the back of his head against the upper bunk which was only a metre above the lower one.

"Watch your head there, Feld," advised Nadel. The room burst into laughter as Roth and Leeb joined them.

"Pull up a seat, Dietrich, Ernst."

Nadel sat down on Max's now vacant seat and grinned at the Feldwebel who was sitting opposite, rubbing his head. Leeb, after rubbing his hands by the woodburner, took Bergmann's place on the ammo boxes. The radio operator dragged another box over to sit on, although it now meant he was much closer to the cold, open doorway. A blanket will fix that, he thought as he contemplated the telephone, patiently waiting for it to ring, his radio set currently not required. Roth pulled over the stool that had been next to the woodburner and tucked himself between Leeb and the end of the bunk bed.

"Very cozy," said Max leaning forward, rubbing the back of his head, the upper-bunk bed too low to allow him to sit back straight.

"Bergmann, will you knock up some coffees?"

"Feld."

Bergmann got up off the ammo crate and sauntered over to the alcove behind the bunk bed, rummaging around until he found the coffee amongst the supplies there, and a couple of mugs.

"I'll need your mugs," he called to the gathered officers.

He collected the tin mugs, placed them on top of the woodburner and charged them with coffee before topping them up with the hot water from the kettle gently steaming away on top of the stove.

"I won't keep you long," Paul said. "We don't know what tricks Popov will get up to so I want us all on the prowl tonight."

"Chucking us back out into the cold, sir?" responded Leeb, rubbing his hands. "Home from home this."

"Better than the heat of a bullet if the Soviets catch us with our pants down, Ernst."

"Sir."

"We've found a Panje hut in the forest," Max informed them, "about five hundred metres in. There's a small clearing where a few locals have set up home. We're having one of them set up as a rest area for the boys. It's not much and it stinks but we've got a woodburner going and we're certainly not short of fuel."

"Report," ordered Paul once Max had finished.

"Two platoon's ready, sir," informed Nadel. "Pak 38 dug in but the crew is still working on some personal firing positions. More for protection against mortars and arty rather than a frontal assault. They should be behind their gun when that happens."

"Good, make sure they're deep. I don't want shell scrapes. Looking at the ground around us they've been bombarded here pretty regularly."

"The rest of my platoon are dug in. The MG34 SF is on the right and three is dug in at our rear," concluded Nadel.

"Good. Ernst?"

"One platoon is all set, sir. Pak dug in. They seem to know what they're doing. They've built a miniature fortress and they're still going at it."

"Leutnant Meissner is riding them hard, sir," added Max.

"Excellent. We can't afford any complacency," Paul said, maintaining eye contact with each one of them.

"Ernst?"

"That's about it, sir. SF34 on the left. So, between Dietrich and I, we will be able to work our fire right across the front. Could do with some ammo though. The MGs will just eat what we've got at the moment. Oh, and we need to range and pre-register but could do with some visibility and something to fire at."

"Good. As I said before, see the mist as a blessing. It's given us an opportunity to get sorted under cover. Feldwebel Grun is liaising with battalion regarding our ammo stocks and the battalion commander is begging from FJR3 as we speak. In the meantime, units at the front will get priority. Viktor?"

"I have a troop covering Dietrich's back on the left and one covering Ernst's on the right. Three troop is being held in reserve as per your orders, sir."

"Has Unterfeldwebel Loewe bedded in his mortars yet?"

"Yes, sir. His mortar pits have been dug and bagged. He's positioned them close to our reserve troop so they can give each other mutual protection should the Red Army break through."

"I shall check all positions later. Ernst, have you made contact with second company on your right?"

"Yes, sir. I've spoken to Oberleutnant Fleck."

"It looks like we're ready then. All we have to do now is wait. This is a very different situation for us. We've always been on the offensive but are now forced to sit in fixed positions," Paul finished off thoughtfully, rubbing the scar above his left eye. Max noticed and understood that some concerns or schemes were running through his commander's mind.

"Here you go, sirs, Feld." Bergmann placed two groups of mugs containing steaming coffee, that had slowly been burning his fingers, on the small square table wedged in the corner of the room. The coffee's inviting aroma competed with the earthen smell of the bunker. Nadel leaned right to allow him to reach across.

"Thank you, Bergmann, must come to this cafe again," joked Leeb.

"The first one's free, sir, the rest will have a price," laughed Bergmann, moistening his burnt finger with his mouth as he headed back to his ammo box and Feldfernsprecher.

Leeb pulled his seat further forward; Nadel moved his to the left. He tapped the table with his fingers. "The men have some rations that will last them for the next forty-eight hours, sir, but after that... We need to get some hot food for them as well. It's bloody cold out there and getting much worse."

Max leant forward, the bottom bunk creaking as he did so. "We're organising something at the Panje hut. We have a fire and can organise some shuttle runs of flasks of soup. Any meals we can knock up will have to be eaten back there. A local woman is helping out."

"Yes," said Paul, "we'll bring the men back in shifts so they can take a break from the line and have an opportunity for some hot food and sleep. Will you sort out a rota, Feld?"

Max nodded.

"But not tonight. Tonight I want everyone on full alert and stood to at five."

"We've been told the Soviets attack at seven, sir," advised Roth.

"Yes, Viktor, I know, but the Soviets know there is a fresh unit on the line and that we will have been told that. If I were them, I would bring the attack forward and try and catch us on the hop. So full alert tonight; no exceptions. Understood?"

"*Jawohl*, Herr Oberleutnant," they all acknowledged together.

Paul pulled his sleeve back and checked his watch then looked at the entrance to the bunker. Darkness had descended as they had been talking.

"It's now just after eight. I will do a full tour of the lines at nine so let your men know. I don't want to be mistaken for one of the enemy."

They all laughed.

"Right, let's get to it."

The three officers shuffled out of their seats, the confined space seeming suddenly overcrowded as they all stood up. They placed their empty mugs back in their kit, reluctant to leave the warm cosiness of the bunker, knowing what waited for them outside.

"Have the lines been checked between the platoon HQs and here, Bergmann?"

"Yes, Feld, all are working well."

"I want two-hourly checks," added Paul.

"Yes, sir," they all responded and filed out of the bunker, up the steps and out into the bitter cold. The temperature was already hovering around minus-one.

"Sounds like we have time for a second coffee then, sir," suggested the grinning Max, heaving himself up off the bunk bed that threatened to collapse under his weight. He held his hands out to the woodburner, then turned around and warmed his backside. He moved away from the stove pulled all the chairs back into place; returned Bergmann's to him and then made the three of them a fresh brew.

Max turned towards Paul as he picked up the now full mugs. "They'll hit us in the morning, early and hard."

Paul nodded. His thoughts exactly, and he was not looking forward to it.

Chapter Twenty-one

Paul and Max crouched down in the firing position created by Petzel and Stumme, trying their best to stop shivering from the bitter cold. Paul noticed that all the paratroopers attached to the MG34 sustained firing position had wrapped scarves or other material they had acquired around their head, ears and chin. Their helmets were then placed on top of the cloth. The 29th of September, just after six in the morning and freezing cold. The temperature had now hit a low of minus-two. With still no sign of an attack, Paul was beginning to doubt his earlier prediction.

"My fucking feet are like blocks of ice already," cursed Max.

"Be a darn sight colder if we didn't have these logs to stand on," whispered Petzel.

"You've made this place positively palatial," complimented Max.

"We've worked at it most of the night. Too bloody cold to sleep."

"Well, we shall all have the chance to warm up soon," added Stumme.

"Quiet," hissed Paul, his impatience obvious.

There was a sudden silence. Petzel climbed to the top of the trench and knelt down on the left of the platform they had made to support the MG's tripod. He scanned the foreground with his binoculars. Although dawn was still fifty minutes away, early fingers of light were slowly breaking through the darkness, reaching out to the soldiers, straining to encircle them.

The mist had cleared during the night and had not, as yet, reappeared.

"Can't see any movement, sir," he called down softly. "If they're coming, they're treading bloody quietly."

Clink.

"What was that?" whispered Max, cupping his ear, straining to pick out any further sounds.

Clink. They all heard it that time.

"In the trench, Petzel, quickly. Mauer, the flare."

Just in time, Petzel slid down the front of the trench, a cascade of clay and stones following him down, when Mauer, from company HQ, fired off a flare. Its sudden glare blinded them all whilst at the same time lit up the advancing Russian Infantry some two hundred metres away.

Then, the first rounds struck the ground in front and around them.

Crump, crump, crump.

Three mortar rounds straddled the firing point held by Rammelt and Gieb.

Crump, crump, crump, crump.

Artillery rounds landed behind them, hitting the rear of the line and disrupting any attempts to bring reinforcements forward or to man the forward positions after resting in the rear. Helmut's company suffered two casualties within minutes of the barrage starting. Caught out of their trench system: one dead, one wounded.

Two mortar shells exploded not more than twenty metres in front of Paul's position. A plume of earth, debris and shrapnel splayed upwards and fanned out, raining down on them, showering them with dust and debris. A hot fragment glanced off Petzel's helmet as he peered over the top seeking out the enemy.

"Get down, you idiot," shouted Paul. "Wait until the bombardment's stopped."

He grabbed the field telephone linked to his Company HQ bunker and, more importantly, the mortar troop. He wound the handle furiously. Loewe picked it up almost instantaneously, expecting the call.

"Loewe, they will come at us as soon as this lot is over, I want the range three hundred metres beyond us," yelled Paul down the mouthpiece and above the cacophony of sound. "Then work it forward to one hundred."

"Isn't that too far, sir?"

"I want to hit their follow-up troops but also make sure of all our ranges first. We'll mark the fall of shot every time you change your range. Understood?"

"Understood, sir."

"We need to take out their second wave. Our firepower here should cope with the first one."

"Gotcha, sir."

Paul put the handset back on its cradle and watched as Max pulled two grenades from his belt and laid them on top of the trench in front of him, still keeping his body crouched low.

Paul nodded and adjusted his MP40, cocking the weapon, leaving the safety off. He ran through his defence plan in his head. It was simple but effective, or so he hoped. In the centre of his area of operation, he had two MG34s set up in a sustained firing role and one Pak 38. This was his strong point. It could hit the enemy straight down the centre with such ferocity, it should stop the enemy dead in their tracks – or, at least, that was the intention. If the standard MG34 positions on his far left and far right came under a heavy assault, he could switch the two central machine guns' fire in support of them. Once they had pre-registered fire set-up, it would be quick and simple to do. If there was a breakthrough, Roth's men could absorb it behind them then bring his troop forward in a counter-attack. Simple, in theory.

More debris showered them as the barrage continued, a round exploding close behind them. Screams could be heard in the far distance, off to the right. Too far for any of his men, it had to be Erich's position. Clearly some of the weighty explosives being thrown at them were starting to hit home. The mens' screams continued, the shrill sound heard above the bombardment. The Red Army was attempting to shatter the Fallschirmjagers' nerves and their will to fight before they unleashed the full force of their infantry attack.

More agonised screams.

Paul and his small team were unaware that one of their *kameraden* from second company lay out in the open, flung from his trench after a direct hit by a one hundred and twenty millimetre mortar round. His suffering was short-lived: he was bleeding to death, his shattered legs draining the blood from him. There was one last plaintive wail before he joined his two dead *kameraden* in the peacefulness of the afterlife.

Whump, whump.

More heavy calibre rounds, one hundred and fifty millimetre this time, thudded into the rear. The paratroopers there buried their heads deep into their trenches, glad their officers and NCOs had pushed them hard to get them completed.

"*Scheisse*, that had to be Leutnant Roth's position, sir," hollered Max.

"I think everyone's getting a taste.".Paul called over to Petzel, "Another few minutes, I reckon, so get ready with the MG."

"We're on it, sir," he responded, tapping his men on their shoulders. Their helmeted heads lifted up from their hunched shoulders as they acknowledged him.

Crump, crump, crump.

Three rounds landed a few hundred metres in front amongst the middle of the now advancing Russian army.

"They've either hit their own, sir, or the Lion is hitting back."

Before Paul could answer, there was a sudden eerie and unexpected silence. The barrage of mortars and artillery that had shattered the early morning peace had stopped as abruptly as it had started. The quiet was extremely unnerving. The only sound that reached their ears was the voice of Rammelt yelling for a medic. Suddenly there were more rounds from Loewe's mortar team, followed closely by a barrage from Erich's.

"I'll go and check on Rammelt and Gieb." Max started to pull himself up from the bottom of the trench but was restrained by Paul's hand on his shoulder, pulling him back down.

"No, wait, Max. They will have to fend for themselves. The attack is imminent."

Before Max could respond, the *pup turrrr, pup turrrr* sound of an MG off to their far right indicated the Russian Army was close to Erich's company position.

"Up, up," yelled Paul, "they'll be on us any second."

"*Anschlag,*" yelled Petzel, popping his head above the parapet, quickly scanning the slowly brightening horizon with his binos. Indistinct silhouettes appeared out of the shadows less than two hundred metres away. He knew who they were and he knew their objective.

Stumme had positioned himself behind the butt of the MG, testing its swivel and then cocking the weapon, a round now in the chamber. Herzog alongside him on the left held the belt ready to guide it once the firing drew it into the weapon. Behind them was Mauer, a fresh ammunition belt at the ready, along with a spare barrel ready for a quick barrel change. Bieler was on the far left, in a position to provide them with close protection, his Kar 98K cocked and ready. Paul took up a position to the MG team's right. Max was still further right, the barrel of his MP40 resting on a sandbag in front of him as he peered down his sights.

Uurraaaah, uurraaaah, uurraaaah.

A cry went up from the advancing Russian Infantry, now gearing up from a fast march to a run followed by an all-out charge against the German line, spurred on by their officers and NCOs and the armed Commissars behind them making sure they also carried out their duty. Petzel did not need binoculars now to direct the fire of the MG. The mass of enemy soldiers filled the whole of the horizon to their front; an unbroken mass of baying, armed soldiers. It was the most frightening sight many of the soldiers had ever seen in their lives.

"*Stellung, stellung!*" Petzel ordered.

Stumme peered through the x3 power prismatic scope, quickly lining up on the advancing horde. Seeing it was too high, he manipulated the elevation screws and lined up the barrel at waist height.

"*Stellung,* Stumme, for fuck's sake, open up or they'll be doing it for you."

Stumme pulled on the remote trigger and the MG34 did what it was good at: blasting 7.92mm rounds at a prodigious rate towards the mass of enemy in front. The ammunition belt tore through Herzog's hands as Stumme fired groups of around ten rounds at a time, keeping a constant rate of fire of three to four hundred rounds a minute, although capable of nearly double that.

For the Russian soldiers, it was like suddenly hitting a brick wall as the rounds thudded into their soft bodies. Gaping holes tore into their young, vulnerable flesh, scything them down like sheaves of corn. Herzog called for another fifty-round belt as he connected the one he already had onto the one that was rapidly diminishing with Stumme's high rate of fire.

Stumme continued to fire, oblivious of additional belts being added as he cut down the Soviet Infantry in front of him. The centre of mass now disintegrated, tens of soldiers writhed on the floor with devastating wounds. Their fellow soldiers behind were forced to leap over their fallen comrades, many becoming entangled and were brought down, making them easy targets.

"Left ten degrees," called Petzel, fulfilling his role of gun commander.

Stumme swung left cutting down another line of the enemy who were getting too close. The crack of Bieler's Kar 98K and Max and Paul's machine pistols joined the fray. Along the full length of the line, the Fallschirmjager returned fire, bringing the advance to a halt. Russians who turned back were either hit by Loewe's mortars or shot for cowardice by their own Commissars.

Their defence had been a success. On this occasion, only the odd bullet managed to find its way towards the dug-in paratroopers.

"Barrel," yelled Stumme.

The air-cooled MG34 barrel steamed in the still close to freezing temperature and, like most machine guns, this barrel was designed to be easily replaced, avoiding overheating and permanent damage. Stumme disengaged the latch which held the receiver to the barrel sleeve, pivoted it off to the right, pulled the barrel out of the back of the sleeve, placing the new one, passed by Mauer, into the back of the sleeve, rotating it back and locking it in. The delay was a matter of seconds and the MG was quickly back in action, emptying another fifty rounds into the retreating enemy before being ordered to cease fire. The Russians faded away into the distance. Only the wounded and dying were left on the field in front of them, crying out for help; crying out for mercy; crying out for their mothers.

"Max, stay here. Cancel the mortar fire. I'm going to check on Rammelt and Gieb before they make another attack."

"Will do, sir," and Max reached for the field telephone as Paul shot off, accompanied by Mauer from company HQ. They scurried along the fringes of the front line, hunched down as they ran the thirty metres needed to get them to the next position. It was now light enough for them to pick out the firing point manned by Fessman and Rammelt.

"Bloody hell, sir, did you see how many there were?"

"Yes, Uffz, fortunately the MGs made short work of them."

"Just as well Stumme sent some rounds this way, otherwise we would have been overrun. Do you think they'll be back again today?"

"Well, their pre-emptive attack failed."

"So they'll be a bit pissed off with us?"

"That's a fact, Uffz Fessman. How is the rest of your troop?"

"Fink's taken Gieb back to the Company aid post. His leg is shattered. He'll live but his leg is fucked, so Civvy Street for him." He looked at his commander from beneath his arched eyebrows, the normally laughing brown eyes dulled today. "This is going to be a slog, isn't it, sir."

"It's certainly not the walkover everyone thought it would be. If we all keep our wits about us, we'll be OK. Just make sure your men stay switched on and we'll keep them back."

"*Jawohl*, sir."

"Your troop is short again." He turned to Mauer. "Attach yourself to Uffz Fessman's troop until we get some reinforcements. You can slot in here with Rammelt."

"Yes, sir."

They heard a rustle behind them and immediately turned, weapons at the ready. It was Leeb.

"Thought I'd check in with you, sir. Contacted Company HQ. They told me where to find you."

"How is two troop holding up, Ernst?"

"No casualties sir, although I think we were lucky. The main thrust seemed to be against the centre."

"It was. I've given you Mauer to strengthen Fessman's troop."

"You only have Bergmann and Fink left."

"They're better placed with you than me. Anyway, I have no intention of sitting it out in the Company HQ. I'm going to the bunker now though. I'm sure Major Volkman will be demanding an update. I'll be back as quickly as possible."

"OK, sir, I'm going to stick with two troop just in case the next push is against the flanks."

"Good idea. I'll join Feldwebel Grun and stiffen up Rammelt's position." With that, Paul set off towards his company bunker and Leeb went north back to two troop, checking with his men as he hastened along the line.

Paul dropped down into the trench alongside Max, who was chewing on a German sausage, washing it down with a cold cup of coffee.

"We've only a day's worth of rations left, sir," he said, waving the half-eaten knackwurst in the air. "Do we know when we'll get some more?"

"Major Volkman will let me know what is going to happen on that score tonight."

"If this cold continues, they'll need food just to keep warm. How has the rest of the battalion fared?"

"We've been lucky so far, Max. Three dead and one wounded in our company. Oberleutnant Janke has one dead and one wounded, and Oberleutnant Fleck has three wounded and one killed. Oberleutnant Bauer is in the clear."

Max looked at his watch: it was eleven o five. "Although it's daylight and a bit warmer, it's brought the bloody fog back. Do you think they'll hit us again?"

"Yes, Max, I'm sure they will. We've lost the advantage now. They now know where our strength is. Have you spoken to Unterfeldwebel Loewe?"

"Yes, I've had him set the range for two hundred; then we'll pull it back to one hundred. We've done some testing shots while you've been gone."

"Shorter than that?"

"I told him, if we were in the shit, we'd bring it down to fifty. Where do you reckon they'll hit us?"

Paul slid further down the trench and perched on a log. He pulled out a piece of loaf from his bread bag and, in between mouthfuls, answered him. "Here again, Max, here. It's a double bluff. They think we'd expect them to attack our flanks next time which are clearly our weaker points. So, we shift our forces to cover those and they punch straight through the centre."

"So we remain where we are, sir. What about the reserve troop?"

"I've brought the reserve troop forward. They're right behind us, ready to come forward once the fighting starts."

Whoosh, whoosh, whoosh.

"Down," screamed Paul.

Explosions erupted beyond them again. The heavier long-range artillery was again, for some reason, targeting the troops in the rear; maybe trying to disrupt reinforcements or fresh ammunition being brought forward.

Crump, crump, crump.

Three one hundred and twenty millimetre rounds exploded in front of their firing position, showering them with debris and hot metal.

Crump, crump, crump.

Petzel and Stumme brushed away any dust or dirt from the MG and checked the log they had made of pre-registered targets. More rounds struck, closer this time, lifting the sandbags at the far left of the trench up and flinging them aside as if they weighed nothing.

Beiler clutched at his face as shards of hot metal tore into his features and savaged his cheekbone and lower jaw; his lower mandible was severed clean away, leaving a gaping hole. He choked and gasped desperately for air before tumbling backwards into the trench. Petzel sprang up ready to rush to his friend's aid but was physically restrained by Stumme.

"Leave him. There's nothing you can do now. Back to your post," he commanded.

Shells and mortar bombs continued to erupt around them, throwing up curtains of dust and spoilage as round after round struck the German positions. More rounds of high explosive tried to shatter their defences. Some paratroopers curled up in a foetal position in the bottom of their firing positions, hands on top of their helmets, arms covering their ears, their teeth grinding in fear as the horrific barrage continued to fall around them. Screams could be heard amongst the German soldiers as the deadly bombardment hit home.

"*Stellung, stellung,*" screamed Paul as the barrage petered out. "They'll be right behind it."

This time the Red Army Command had put their soldiers at risk in an effort to break the German line and push through by keeping their men as close as possible to the bombardment as they worked the barrage forwards over the German positions. All it would have taken was a battery to have dropped its deadly charges short, or for the Russian Infantry to advance too quickly, and their casualties would have been devastating as their own artillery hammered their tightly packed troops. The Soviet hierarchy cared little for its men. Even civilians, in army uniform, were used in the attacks. Fuelled by vodka, kept hungry by the Commissars, promised all the food they wanted from any captured German rations, they were propelled into battle like men possessed. The regular soldiers too were driven by fear and hunger into battle against the tough German paratroopers holding the line.

Uurraaaah, uurraaaah, uurraaaah, roared the Russian hordes as they ran towards their enemy emerging from the mist and fog. They were demons bent on vengeance and death, and now less than a hundred metres away.

Pup turrrr, pup turrrr came from Petzel's MG34 from the far left, as Stumme fired round after round. The slugs tore into the lines and swept to the right ripping through the approaching troops advancing on the right of Paul's position. He watched as the Russian's left flank crumpled. The vindictive firing continued to shatter flesh and bone indiscriminately before swinging back to the front to cover the arc again.

Crack, click, click, crack, Fessman's Kar 98K/42 firing round after round until, after the sixth round, the magazine follower prevented the bolt going forwards. Fessman always, after loading a five-round clip in the first instance, added a sixth round directly into the chamber, giving him a slight advantage when battle first commenced. He pulled a fresh five-round clip from its pouch, pushed it deep into the magazine, discarded the rear guide and pushed the bolt forward, ready to fire again. *Crack, click, click, crack.*

Max's MP40 machine pistol jumped in his hands as shot after shot spat towards the enemy. The empty shellcases flew up and to the right as they were ejected from the chamber. Even with a constant rate of fire from Max and Paul's MPs, the two Kar 98Ks wielded by Rammelt and Fessman were not enough to hold them back. Max fumbled with a grenade but there was not enough time to unscrew the cap and pull the cord. He cursed himself for his lack of foresight, not having them lined up on the trench in front with caps off. It was too late now; the Russians were practically on top of them.

He clambered up and out of the trench to the right, stood with his legs apart and fired, emptying a full thirty-two-round magazine. His hands gripped the gun, preventing it from pulling up and to the right, firing straight into the group who were on the verge of overwhelming the trench. The senior sergeant leading the Soviets looked down, sure he had been punched in the chest twice, the growing dark patches telling a different story as he fell backwards into the very men he had been leading. The infantryman to the sergeant's right, just about to thrust his bayonet-mounted rifle down into the trench at Rammelt who was fumbling to put a fresh five-round clip into his rifle, suddenly lost control of his limbs. A 9mm Parabellum round, fired from Max's machine pistol, cleaved through his spine, severing the spinal cord. The disruption was enough to allow Paul and Fessman to clamber out of the trench as Rammelt fumbled about the bottom of the dugout for the clip he had dropped. He changed his mind and acquired a fresh one from its pouch slung across his chest.

Max released the empty clip. It dropped to the ground. As he slammed a fresh one into the magazine housing, he unknowingly dislodged a round. He cocked the weapon and pulled the trigger. The working parts shot forward but nothing happened. Recocking the gun, he tried again. Nothing. It was too late to complete any IAs, Immediate Action drills, and the Russian soldier seeing the big Fallschirmjager's plight knew he had a defenceless and easy target in front of him. He raised his empty rifle. The vicious bayonet spike on the end was all he required to kill this hapless German pig.

He lunged at Max's gut but, as large and as heavy as Max was, together with the restrictions caused by his injuries when fighting in Crete, he was still as agile as a lynx from his fighting days when a docker in Hamburg.

As the snarling soldier lunged towards Max with his bayoneted rifle and the full force of his weight behind it, Max sidestepped to the left. The thrust of the rifle passed him and there was a look of despair on the Russian's face as he tried desperately to halt his forward momentum. He was too late. Max raised his machine pistol over his left shoulder and brought it down with a sickening thud on the side of the young Russian's head. The metal butt struck him just below the rim of his helmet, crushing his temple and cracking the side of his skull. The force so great that the metal foldable stock sheered off completely. The soldier crumpled and his momentum propelled him forwards, to lie dead in a heap at the side of the trench.

Before Max had a chance to check on his company commander or any of the others, another enemy soldier leapt at him. The machine pistol useless, Max threw it at the advancing infantryman, forcing him to hold up his left arm and protect his face, distracting him long enough for Max to sweep up an entrenching tool he had spied earlier. He grabbed the wooden handle of the pioneer spade and, knowing his life was in the balance, swung it with all his strength at the Soviet soldier as he fired his Mosin Nagent at point-blank range. The bullet scythed a crease along Max's lower ribs but, before the soldier could follow through with his attack, the metal spade hit the Russian's helmet and, although it protected him from serious injury, such was the ferocity of the blow that it stunned him, forcing him to droop forwards. That was all the opportunity Feldwebel Grun needed as he lifted the spade once more, swung it down, edge on, and struck the soldier slicing deep into his arm. The soldier's screeching was pitiful. Suddenly it stopped as a bullet was punched through his right eye.

More shots engulfed Max as the troop, which Paul had held in reserve, pushed forward as ordered. The additional ten men caused localised havoc. Suddenly, Max heard explosions to the Russian troops' rear as they retreated. Loewe worked his Granatwerfer 36s left and right as the Russian soldiers disappeared.

Max slumped to his knees, the adrenalin that had been holding him up deserting him. The pain raged where the 7.62mm bullet had gouged along his ribs on his right. Inside his body, there was a deeper pain from the older injuries, still repairing themselves after the action in Crete.

Paul came over and crouched down. "Max, are you hit?" He pushed his friend onto his back, stripped off his kit and pulled at his bloodied tunic and shirt. He cut a strip away with his gravity knife until he could get a better view of the wound. A jagged line ran across Max's ribs where the bullet had gouged a shallow furrow, the ivory white of the bone shining through but no sign of an entry wound.

"That was a close call, Max. We can soon get that patched up."

"It's not the bloody wound I'm worried about, sir. Who's going to repair my kit now you've hacked at it?"

Paul laughed and a voice behind them said, "Feldwebel Grun, I'm sure one of your many female admirers would be only too happy to help you."

"Sir." Paul jumped up quickly and stood in front of his battalion commander. Max also made an effort to rise but only managed to get as far as one elbow before groaning with pain from both his fresh and old wounds. He was unable to move any further.

"Rest easy, Feldwebel," ordered the battalion commander. Miraculously, although he had been in battle, fighting alongside the reserve troop that had been pushing the enemy back from the trench, he still looked like he had just stepped off a parade. How did he do it? His helmet was removed showing his jet-black hair, hooded eyes and Roman nose. The Raven was a perfect name for him.

"I thought I would join your reinforcements and give you a hand."

"You came just in time, sir."

"Oh, I don't know about that, Oberleutnant Brand. The Russkies weren't getting it all their own way from where I was standing. Feldwebel Grun was like a demon possessed. Well done, the both of you. They know what it's like to take on the Fallschirmjager and will no doubt be licking their wounds for some time."

"Will they be back, sir?"

"They have no choice, Brand, unless they want the siege to be permanent. They'll be back tomorrow and the next day and the day after that."

"Are they still holding the bridgehead at Petruskinjo?"

"For the moment, Brand, for the moment."

"I'd like to check on my men if you don't mind, sir."

"Of course. Let me know your status as soon as possible so I can keep Division up to speed. I shall be pulling you out of the line shortly. I'll bring Oberleutnant Janke and Bauer's company forward. Your company can be in reserve and Oberleutnant Fleck can replace Janke's men at the rear. I'll leave you to get on with it."

With that, he passed on his congratulations to Rammelt and Fessman and then headed for the battalion HQ to report to 7th Flieger Division Headquarters.

Paul crouched down next to Max again. "Right, you old bugger, stay here until I can get Fink to sort you out. I'm going to walk the line."

"Less of the old bugger, sir. I'm only a few years older than you."

"Very true, Max, very true." But when he looked at his company sergeant, his friend, his face told a different story. He wondered if he too had aged. They had all aged these past two years.

Chapter Twenty-two

They were gathered in the small three-roomed Panje hut. The single-storey structure, made entirely of wood cut down from the surrounding forest, had been allocated as the Company's rest and recuperation accommodation for the troops brought off the front line. Narrow, horizontal planks of rough wood protected the structure on the outside. They were nailed to a basic framework that held everything erect and the hut was topped with a low roof that kept out the rain and snow. A jerry-built porch protected the front door from the elements although, in reality, it looked as if even the smallest gust of wind would be sufficient to blow it down.

The structure contained a sitting room where the company seniors were now crammed like sardines in a tin. A small utility room-cum-kitchen and a single bedroom completed the home. Three girls and a boy, along with their parents, had lived here. But, when the troops arrived, they were also sharing the accommodation with three other members of their extended family. The family had stood outside miserably and watched as the soldiers trailed into their home. Where would they go now? It was already extremely cold and at night they could freeze.

They stood outside shuffling their feet. They were dressed in typical thick bundles of dark clothing. The girls wore huge knitted scarves which they wrapped around their head, ears and neck. However, they were still so long that they nearly touched the ground. On their feet, all the children had thick, fur-lined boots.

The father, standing next to his young son, watched impotently. They both wore a cap. The mother was not present. She had been cooking for the soldiers but, on this occasion, due to the sensitivity of the briefing, she had been ordered to leave the hut.

Rather than a woodburner, this house had an open log fire, situated at the one end of the room, to the left, as you walked in through the front door. An internal chimney above it took the smoke and fumes up and out but, on occasions, a gust of wind would blow it back down, a sudden cloud of hot air and sparks showering those too close to the fire. The room was dark and grimy as a result of this. A line of German Army tin mugs were on the mantlepiece. The lucky ones in attendance were crammed in the middle of the room; the unlucky ones were forced to stand close to the hot fire. In contrast, those at the far end of the room quickly felt the cold seeping through the thin walls and into their bones.

Paul nodded to Max. No words were needed: it was a signal they both understood.

"Right, listen up, pin your lugholes back," Max ordered.

Paul was perched on the edge of a small table next to the doorway. This was the only piece of furniture in the room as the rest had temporarily been moved out to make space for those attending the briefing and to create space for sleeping later on.

Paul cleared his throat. "So far, although we have held our ground, we have been taking a beating pretty much every day. Our casualties, although not too serious at the moment, are steadily mounting."

He looked around the room at his men: his three platoon commanders; each of their platoon NCOs; the commander of the mortar troop; the Pak detachment commander, Leutnant Meissner; Max; and, joining them, the Adjutant Hauptmann Bach.

"Well, tonight we're going to hit back."

There was a murmur of approval amongst the group but they stopped quickly as Paul started speaking again. They wanted to hear more from their company commander and to know how it was going to be carried out.

"Max."

Max held up a large, hand-drawn plan which was visible for all to see, despite the room's gloom.

"These are our current positions," continued Paul. "The river running north to south, bulging west towards Dubrowka. The Red Army, as we know, is occupying that bulge and occasionally they occupy the village of Wyborgskaja to the north which is currently being contested by III/FJR3. With our battalion to the south and third battalion to the north, they are effectively boxed in."

He pointed to the map with a finger. "You make a great easel, Feldwebel Grun."

The room laughed.

"Cut it," growled Max, but there was no seriousness in his voice.

"Our two forward company defence positions are manned by Oberleutnant Janke's fourth company to the south, butting right up to the river and Oberleutnant Bauer's third company in the north, tying in with III/FJR3. Our mission, gentlemen."

He could see their expectant faces, eager to know what was in store for them. A chance to hit back at an enemy that had been pounding them with artillery and mortars day after day then piling into them in an attempt to push them back to the forest behind.

"We are going to infiltrate the enemy positions along by the river bank. We will pass through fourth company's lines, push north along the river's edge and dislodge the Red Army from their hold on it. At the same time, two company will pass through third company's lines, creep up as close to the enemy's positions as possible. Then, on a narrow front, push through to the river and turn south. III/FJR3 will also attack but more as a diversion than a full-on assault."

"Wow," uttered Roth, unable to hold back, "that will certainly wake them up."

"That's the idea, Leutnant Roth, to put the Soviets on the back foot for a change; unnerve them; shake the resolve of their private soldiers. However, this is not a full-on assault. If we manage to kick them out of the bulge, all well and good, but it is not our prime intention. We don't know enough about the size or disposition of their troops, so this is an opportunity to put that right and, of course, give them a fright they won't easily forget."

He picked up a piece of paper.

"Timings. Two platoon will lead off at twenty-three hundred tonight. You, therefore, have at least six hours to get your men ready. Check watches."

They all confirmed that their watches were in sync with their company commander's, which was showing seventeen hundred.

"We will advance on three points. Leutnant Nadel, your platoon will crawl to a position about twenty metres from the river. You will then move north, keeping the river on your left at all times. Your target is their second line of defence. Understood?"

"Yes, sir."

"Leutnant Leeb."

"Sir."

"First platoon is to crawl right up to the river, turning north and tracking the river as far as you can. If you can move both along the river's edge and along the top of the bank, even better. I want you to get in behind the enemy positions, dislodge them from the river and cut them off from the higher command across the river. Just remember, Leutnant Nadel and his men will be to your right, not more than twenty metres away."

"Understood. sir."

He turned to Roth.

"Three platoon will target the first echelon of Russian positions. You will again get as close to the enemy foxholes as you can before discovery. That goes for all of you. The longer we remain undiscovered, the better our chances of hitting them hard. Once you hit their line of positions, push north, but keep your firing arcs narrow, all of you, or else you could be hitting your own men. Keep your fire low. There is a risk of Oberleutnant Fleck's men getting hit by grazing fire, the closer both companies get to each other. Understood?"

"Yes, sir," they all acknowledged.

"How far north do we push, sir?" asked Leeb.

"As far as you safely can, but don't put yourself in a position where you can get trapped and surrounded. I don't have the authority to commit the rest of the battalion to come to our aid."

"Understood, sir."

"Leutnant Roth, your third platoon is to hit the front line of Russian positions, at their most southern point. Your primary role is to harass the enemy. Keep them looking forward, keep them occupied, so they ignore what's going on to their rear. Also, prevent them from forming up a counter-attack and sweeping around behind first and second platoon and pinning them against the river."

"What about the units manning our forward positions, sir?" asked Max. "Will they be expecting to give covering fire?"

"Not initially, Feldwebel Grun. There's too much friendly activity in the area. They could end up hitting them and not the enemy."

"Knowing Oberleutnant Janke's lads, they'd all miss anyway. They're crap shots."

The crowded room broke into a laugh again, Max, as usual, finding a way to release some of the tension he could feel building up.

"And me, sir?" asked Loewe.

"You are next on my list, Unterfeld." Paul looked at the giant of a man, thinking how the Russians might react if they ever came across this particular Fallschirmjager in the middle of the night.

"Leutnant Roth, you will also be the left-flank anchor point. The other two platoons will only pull back through you, nowhere else. Understood, Ernst, Dietrich?"

"Yes, sir," they both chorused.

"Make sure, Viktor, that if you do get the opportunity to push a little way northwards, that you leave at least a troop with an MG to cover that withdrawal. Everybody must come through that extraction point."

He turned to Loewe. "This is where you come in, Unterfeld. Limit your firing to five rounds per tube, fired slowly and worked along the Russian positions. It is only to cover the withdrawal. We need to conserve our ammunition for a major assault by us, or a big push by the Red Army."

"When do we withdraw?" Nadel asked.

"I'll take this one, Paul," interrupted Hauptmann Bach.

The Adjutant eased his way through the crowd of paratroopers, perching on the narrow table next to Paul; his feet braced on the floor, arms folded, still a faint tan on his face from Crete.

"There will be two orange flares for the withdrawal, one after the other. That will be both for your company, Paul, and Oberleutnant Fleck. So, the minute those two hit the skies, you need to pull your men back rapidly or there is a danger you will get left behind and isolated from the rest of your unit and *kameraden*. These will be fired, on my order, as I shall be based at the battalion bunker and will be monitoring your progress as best I can. Most of my intelligence will no doubt come from Oberleutnant Janke and Bauer but theirs will only be an educated guess as to how you are all progressing."

He bowed his head for a moment, reflecting on what he was going to say next. When he lifted his head up, there was concern showing on his face.

"This is not an all-out push. More of a reconnaissance by strength rather than guile. So push the enemy hard, take note of their strength and positions, but don't take any needless risks. Don't lose men when it's not necessary. We'll need all of our Fallschirmjager for when we do decide to go for a big push, or if the Red Army reciprocate with a major attack of its own."

"Why don't we push the full battalion into this venture, sir?" asked Paul turning to the Adjutant, their faces centimetres apart.

"The truth is, Paul, that we don't really know what's there. We could be walking into a huge minefield or a force significantly bigger than ours. If we commit the entire battalion and get trounced, they could counter-attack straight through us and roll up III/FJR3's flank."

"Understood, sir, but it's not entirely off the table for the future?"

"No, Major Volkman would like nothing better than to kick the Russkies back across the river and make us all heroes," he said with a laugh which was picked up by the rest of the room.

"If there are no further questions, Paul, I need to get across to two company. They'll be starting their briefing in the next twenty minutes or so."

"Nothing else, sir. I'll call you at battalion about an hour before we move out in case there are any last-minute changes."

"Yes, an hour before. You will probably need an hour to get right up close to the Russian positions."

The room came to attention as the Adjutant made his way to the door, wishing them all luck as he passed by. Lifting the blanket covering the exit door, he ducked behind it and left the dwelling. An icy blast filled the room and the fire flickered in response, casting an eerie glow across the lightly plastered walls. Sparks flew as someone fed the fire with another log.

Paul looked around the room. "Any questions?"

All shook their heads. There was nothing more to say now; their thoughts had switched to the technicalities of carrying out their task rather than the bigger tactical picture. What to say to their men; what equipment to take or leave behind; how much ammunition they would need; would they and their unit perform well or would they let their fellow paratroopers down? Finally, in their head, they all secretly asked themselves if they were scared, but wisely chose not to think about the answer. All had seen action in Corinth and Crete, but this seemed different somehow. They seemed less in control, the Red Army constantly keeping them on their toes.

"Myself and Feldwebel Grun will be around at twenty-one hundred for a check. I'll confirm all is well with battalion then we move out at twenty-three hundred. Let's go."

Max shouted after them as they slowly moved towards the only exit. "You NCOs make sure your men only take what they need. Make sure you do a proper noise check. Get them jumping until their teeth rattle. If they jump for me and I hear even the smallest clank of equipment, their teeth will be rattling, permanently!"

"Feld," they all called back, acknowledging his order.

There was a mass exodus for the door. The officers and NCOs left one at a time, conscious of not letting out too much light and headed back to their respective units, their turn to conduct a briefing. Max and Paul remained behind. Max headed over to the pot, suspended by a large black hook, that was hanging over the flames. He unhooked a ladle close by and scooped some of the insipid-looking contents into his dual-purpose tin mug, sipping its contents.

"Bah, potato soup again! Don't they know how to cook anything else? What's that thick fat floating on the top? Despite all that, it's not actually too bad. Do you want some?" he said to Paul with a mischievous grin.

Paul shook his head. The thought of the greasy, grey layer lying on top turned his stomach. Later, as the tempature got even lower, well below freezing, they would come to understand why the Russians used so much fat in their cooking. It was a matter of survival.

"I want you to put yourself with three platoon, Max."

"Three platoon. Why, sir? I should be with you surely," responded a slightly disgruntled NCO. Taking his mug of soup, he dragged a stool from the other side of the room and then sat down at the table with his company commander, groaning as he eased himself down.

"You shouldn't be going on this operation at all, Feldwebel Grun. Your wound is far from healed."

"It's just a graze, sir, it's nothing. Anyway, I'm not letting you and the boys out there without me watching your backs."

"And what about your old injury, eh? I suspect that's giving you some trouble as well."

"If I'd wanted a mother, sir, I would have joined the Rot Creuze."

"My responsibility isn't just to you, Max, it's to the entire company. If you're invalided while we're out there, you could put others at risk."

Max sat up straight. "Have I ever let you down, sir?"

Paul looked at his friend thoughtfully. "No, Max, no, never." Paul's stern look slowly subsided and his expression softened as he pushed himself up off the chair and slapped Max's arm as he passed. "I'm off to the company bunker to report to the Raven. Seeing as you're so fit, you can do a check of the platoons in advance of me. And, Max, I wouldn't feel easy going into battle knowing you weren't around somewhere."

Paul turned to leave but turned back as Max called after him. "Will do, sir, but won't you be needing this?"

Max held Paul's MP40 in his hand, laughing as he tossed his young commander his personal weapon who caught it with one hand.

"Fuck you, Max."

Slinging the MP40 over his shoulder, Paul left the building.

Max slumped, gripping his side. Although the wound was not deep, the bullet had scored his ribs badly and the lesion was raw and painful. That he could cope with, but the deeper pain was from one of his older wounds from Crete. He had nearly died there but for his company commander who had literally dragged him back through enemy lines.

Fessman slipped down the gentle tier that led to the very edge of the eastern bank of the River Neva. At the moment, they were still on ground under the control of the German Army but, moving further north, it would soon take them closer to their enemy's positions. His men had to keep tight into the bank. The nearer they got to the river's edge, the marshier the ground despite the bitter cold. The sucking mud was impatiently waiting to trap an unsuspecting paratrooper's boot and drag him deep into the quagmire, leaving him exposed as he frantically and noisily tried to extract his boot.

Fessman led; the rest of the half-troop lowered themselves down gently, moving to catch up with their troop commander. He looked back and, although they were merely shadows in the night, he could make out the gait of his friends Stumme and Petzel behind him. The distinctive long shape of the MG34 barrel was pointed towards the other bank of the river. Petzel was nervous about what might be on the other side and felt exposed to the enemy over there. Behind those two followed Rammelt who was normally accompanied by Beiler, except that now Beiler was a frozen corpse, killed by a mortar round that tore off the lower part of his face.

Gieb, Baader, Barth and Ullman had also been killed early on and had now been replaced by members of the company HQ: Ostermann, Mauer and Lang. They were above them on the top of the bank, being led by Herzog. Their task was to cover the men below who would be unable to detect any enemy trenches above them.

Fessman moved cautiously, thinking about the placement of each step; his Kar 98K/42 ready should he need it. His other half-troop above would probably now be leopard–crawling silently; flat on their stomachs, right arm, left leg forwards. Stop. Then, left arm and right leg forward. Stop. A slow, stealthy movement while searching for exposed earth where they might find mines. It was important they kept low to avoid being spotted by a Soviet sentry. Fessman kept his pace equally slow, knowing they would find it hard going.

He stopped; listened. He could hear his men shuffling forwards behind him but nothing else. The sound of the flowing river helped to mask their movement. He continued forward again, sure they must be close to the Russian lines by now after having moved like this for over half an hour. He prayed that the Russians would be slovenly, sentries sleeping on duty, not someone with an itchy trigger finger. They needed all the luck they could get.

Two metres, five metres, ten metres. He stopped again, sniffing the air. A smell of rotten vegetation from the marshy river bank? Yes, but there was something else. He sniffed again: smoke, he could smell cigarette smoke. Many were the times, when he was out poaching, when the smell of the gamekeeper's pipe had saved him from getting caught and probably fined or imprisoned. On this occasion, it could very well save his life, or the lives of his men. He looked up at the top of the bank, straining to see or hear any movement from Herzog above. Nothing. Then he heard it: a slight clink. He was still in line with the men above.

He continued another fifteen metres, the smell of smoke getting stronger. Twenty metres: he must see something soon. Thirty metres, forty metres. He froze. Was that something ahead? He raised the barrel of his rifle, his extra round in the chamber ready. He crouched down and then lay on the cold, wet ground, soaking through his tunic and combat trousers. At the water's edge the temperature was now close to freezing with just three degrees keeping the ice at bay. He shivered as the dampness reached his skin and finally drew the last remaining warmth from his body.

He got the advantage he was looking for. By lying low and looking up, it aided his forward observation and reduced his own profile. The black silhouette of a Russian soldier standing at the water's edge stood out against the lighter sky. He saw the man's head move and his arm lifting something to his mouth. There was a subtle glint of glass as the Russian raised a bottle to his lips and took a large swig of vodka. He was in his own world of thoughts: he might be driven into battle again tomorrow, the murderous Commissars goading them on from behind, but until that time he intended, in these last hours, to drink himself into oblivion to deaden the pain of seeing his comrades fall which, inevitably, many would.

Fessman saw the silhouette bend down, out of sight, and for one brief moment thought they may have been discovered. However, he need not have worried. The soldier soon stood up again, this time holding a cigarette in his hand. There was the sudden flare of a match as he lit the cigarette now hanging from his mouth.

Options quickly raced through Fessman's mind. He could not crawl any further forward. It would make too much noise, the squelching sound increasing the closer he got to the soldier. A second alternative came into his mind.

He shuffled back, as quietly as possible, until he was alongside Stumme who was also in the prone position, suspecting his troop commander had come across something. He whispered his intentions to Stumme who communicated it back down the line. He started to pull himself up the forty-five degree bank. Once at the top, he stopped and listened. All seemed quiet. He could not even hear Konrad's men that he knew could not be any more than thirty metres away from his current position. Then he caught sight of Herzog, commanding the half-troop, on top of the bank, ten metres to his right and five metres out. Herzog raised his rifle just above his head acknowledging he had seen his troop commander. Fessman indicated they were to hold position.

He turned left and started to leopard-crawl along the top of the bank, heading north, deeper into enemy territory. Right arm and left leg forward. Stop. Left arm, right leg forward. Stop. His beloved Kar 98K/42 was nestled in the crook of his arm. After about twenty metres, his arms and legs ached from the exertion. His body felt a little warmer. He spied a slim tree, more of a sapling, jutting out at an angle from the side of the bank and leaning towards the river. Looking left and slightly forward, he caught a glimpse of a small, red glow as the soldier sucked deeply on his cigarette, the rancid smell slowly filtering up and across to Fessman's nostrils. His automatic response was to sneeze. He managed, with great difficulty, to suppress it, pinching his nose until the feeling eventually passed, knowing that it would mean instant discovery and possible death once the Soviet reacted to the sound.

The Russian soldier bent down again, picked up his prized bottle of vodka and took another deep swallow. The liquid swirled around in the bottle but the sound was masked by the occasional 'plop' caused by the ripples from the river as it lapped against the water's edge.

Fessman's head suddenly swivelled right as he heard a cough, not more than twenty metres away, from where he was crouching next to the young tree. Probably one of the soldier's comrades; a foxhole they both shared.

Tucking himself behind the slim trunk of the tree, he decided what he would do as he saw the first soldier throw his cigarette butt to the ground, toss his now empty bottle into the swollen waters and open his flies to urinate.

Fessman silently placed his rifle by his side, ensuring it was leaning against a low branch, keeping the barrel out of the dirt and wet. He quickly undid and removed his kit, careful not to make a sound. Prior to starting the operation, everything that could make a noise or come loose had been taped up and, as the final test, he had made his men jump up and down violently, ensuring nothing dropped out or rattled. This careful preparation meant he was able to complete this derobing in complete silence.

He pulled the weapon he was going to use out of his pocket and slipped down the bank, keeping low. He noticed bootprints next to a tree. He suspected there would be a worn patch on the tree trunk where they had used it as a natural handhold to pull themselves up the bank. The worn ground, a lighter colour amongst the darker earth, trailed down to the river's edge, indicating it was used regularly as a route to travel up and down. He hunkered down next to a one-and-a-half metre high clump of wild marsh grass and waited. His muscles and tendons ached as he remained still. At just under two metres in height, the awkwardness of his position put a terrible strain on his entire frame. He hoped the soldier would come soon as staying in this position too long would cramp his muscles which could fail him as he tried to spring quickly to ensnare his victim.

He peered through the thick grass. His instincts had not let him down. The soldier fumbled drunkenly with his flies before turning and staggering back towards the bank, heading directly along the worn path that passed close to Fessman's hiding place. Unsteady on his feet, the nearly full bottle of vodka was taking its toll. Fessman was shocked they were allowed to drink so much alcohol. However, when he thought back to their suicidal charges at the German lines, it could only have been alcohol-fuelled bravery that made them throw away their lives so recklessly and willingly.

Fessman's thighs burned. His breathing was as shallow as he could make it as the infantry soldier lurched his way along the path, past the marsh grass, and, with a grunt, reached for the tree trunk, preparing to haul his alcohol-laden body up the slope.

Fessman sprang up behind him. The soldier registered something but, in his vodka-sodden state, could not work out what it was and did not react. This was all the time the German, an ex-poacher, needed. With a wooden toggle in each hand, the forty-centimetre lightweight cord stretched between them, he rose up on the balls of his feet, his arms outstretched. The soldier released the sapling, lifted his helmetless head, an alarm inside his skull warning that something was wrong. Fessman reached upwards and forward, flicked the cord over the top of the soldier's head, crossing his arms as he pulled the cord tight beneath the man's chin and around his throat, pulling it taut with all his wiry strength.

Normally, he would have tucked his knee behind the soldier's leg and then pulled him backwards and down but the man was too high up for that manoeuvre. It was not a problem. Instead, he used the man's weight, gravity and the height of the bank to his advantage. He pulled the soldier back by his neck, the cord held tight by Fessman's crossed wrists, sidestepping to the right and swinging the infantryman round and down. The soldier immediately pulled his hands away from the biting cord that was preventing him from breathing or shouting a warning. He threw them forward in front of him as he lost his balance and plummeted, face forward, towards the ground. Fessman quickly moved to straddle him from behind, yanking back on the cord with all the strength he could muster, almost snapping the man's neck as he gently lowered him to the ground to minimise the sound of any impact and using the man's own weight to further constrict his throat and literally throttle the life out of him. The man tried to reach behind him but the attempt was futile and Fessman pulled back harder and harder, resisting the urge to grunt. The wooden toggles bit deeply into his hands but he could not let go until the body stopped jerking. The spasms slowly died down. The Red Army soldier finally submitted to death.

Fessman waited a full minute before extracting the cord from around the man's now lifeless neck, reminding him of the heads lolling on the many pheasants he had killed over the years. He checked the soldier was indeed dead, releasing the toggles from his grip and rubbing his now numbed hands in an effort to bring some life back into them. He was aware he should be checking his surroundings for any sign of discovery. However, all he could manage was to slump forward, his chest heaving from the exertion, the pungent smell from the unwashed soldier beneath him forcing him to dry heave. Recovering his senses, he again made sure that the enemy soldier had perished before crawling back up the slope to recover his equipment and rifle.

Looking across to where he was sure a Russian foxhole was located, all seemed quiet; their comrade not yet missed. Perhaps they thought he had fallen asleep, drunk. However, it was only a matter of time before someone came to search for him; then all hell would break loose. Mayhem would descend.

Fessman picked up his rifle, his hand shaking – not because he had just killed someone – he didn`t give the soldier a second thought – he was the enemy – but from the intensity of the act itself. Once his cramped hand settled into a more manageable tremble, he ghost-walked back to Stumme, careful where he placed his feet, testing the ground before he allowed his full weight to press down, occasionally peering over his shoulder for any signs of movement behind.

He dropped down the slope again and found his half-troop and whispered to Stumme, "There's a foxhole above, about twenty metres out and twenty metres along. That's our next target."

"Herzog's made contact. He said he'd seen you."

"What's he doing now?"

"He's also seen the foxhole; said he'd cover us while we take it out."

"Let's get it done then," responded Fessman, gearing himself up for yet more killing.

They both turned as they heard movement behind. It was their company commander, Oberleutnant Brand.

Paul pulled Fessman close to him and whispered that the other two platoons were in position and ready and would launch their assault in five minutes. He checked the luminous dial of his watch, tapped the face and hissed to Fessman, "Four minutes, time to move out."

Chapter Twenty-three

Unterfeld Kienitz, Roth's platoon sergeant, pushed his head down. The dank, pungent smell of the waterlogged earth filled his nostrils. The water seeped deeper into his uniform, bringing with it fingers of icy cold that slowly eased their way to his skin, making him shiver now he had stopped moving. Leopard-crawling expended a lot of energy and his body built up a latent pool of heat, making him sweat. Now, remaining still, the heat rapidly dissipated and the rivulets of sweat evaporated, taking the warmth with them.

His lead troop was diagonally opposite the Russian defences along this sector of the River Neva. It was the furthest south and the closest trench to the German front line. The first he knew of its existence was when a head popped up above a parapet of earth, the spoil from when the position had been dug out, built up in front of it. The distinctive silhouette of a Russian helmet with its long visor and flared ear protectors was clearly visible. A breeze was blowing in their direction and the smell coming from the Russian entrenchment was unpleasant; a further indication that they were indeed up against the Soviet's first line of defences. The hygiene standards of the enemy were clearly not as meticulous as that of the Fallschirmjager. Saying that, Kienitz had not had a body wash for a couple of days; the luxury of a hot shower not being available to them.

Roth, his platoon commander, crept alongside him, tapped his watch and held three fingers close to Kienitz's face. Feldwebel Grun joined him on the other side. A time had been agreed when they would assault the first trench, quietly if possible, but an all-out attack if necessary. Max and Kienitz had their MP40s slung round on their backs. Each had a ten-inch fighting knife with a six-inch, double-edged, heavy steel blade in their right hand. Roth held a half-kilogram model 34 stick grenade ready, the cap off and porcelain ball clear, ready for pulling and igniting the fuse. This was just in case the silent advance was unsuccessful and a more direct approach was necessary.

★

Nadel, commander of two platoon and Weidau, a troop commander, had their weapons slung over their backs and knives clutched in their hands ready for use. Unterfeld Fischer, platoon sergeant, had his MP40 cocked, ready to spray the foxhole should his comrades fail in their task to silence the occupants. Their target was a mere four metres away and the Fallschirmjager were astounded that they had got so close without discovery. They suspected it was one of a pair of foxholes about ten to fifteen metres apart, probably linked to each other by a channel cut between the two. A third foxhole lay between the two but some fifteen to twenty metres back, again linked by a communications trench. The rear trench would likely be the target for Leeb's men, thought Nadel, pulling his sleeve up to check his timepiece and shielding it with his hand as he squinted at the luminous fingers: two minutes to go.

Konrad's men lay in wait. He, along with Kempf and Lanz, had crept as close as they could to the foxhole without being discovered. He had Straube and Muller to his right with the MG; Renisch, Lehrer and Meister at his back left; Kuhn and Pabst, rear right. Although Kuhn had been hit during the attack on the Russian armoured trains, he was now well enough to fight again. Konrad knew that Fessman's troop would be covering his left flank. He smiled to himself, a little excitement mixed with an element of fear at the prospect of waking the Russkies up. They were in for a shock! Checking his watch, he noted less than a minute to go.

Fessman had positioned Petzel and Stumme with the MG34, to his right. With a fifty-round assault drum, they could suppress any enemy response, giving the troop time to take cover or follow through on their assault on the foxhole in front. Paul lay next to his troop commander on Petzel and Stumme's left, the battalion's tactics for the foray running through his mind. Tactics was one of his strengths. The Raven and the Adjutant had talked the attack through with Paul, recognising his astute mind. He could imprint a schematic in his head, comprehend the enemy's position and the interrelationship between his three platoons. He could picture the initial assault, anticipate the likely routes of a counter-attack and be ready to direct his unit to block or respond to it. Once it all kicked off though and they were in the full throes of battle, he became more dependent on the leadership skills of his platoon commanders, and the individual fighting skills of his NCOs and men.

He closed his eyes and pictured the position of his men and what they would be doing now...

The river was to his left and a foxhole was ahead, covered by Fessman and his half-troop. Further right was another foxhole, this one the target of Konrad's troop, lying in wait on the other side of Petzel and Stumme's MG position. Leeb's third troop, led by Braemer, held back behind the lead elements of the platoon, in reserve. Leeb would no doubt call them forward to exploit any weaknesses, left or right, depending on where a breakthrough occurred or, if the worst happened, reinforce the front units against a counter-attack. Further right again was more of the Russian's second line of defence. He felt sure Nadel's platoon would be lined up with this target.

The Red Army had been busy. Any attempt at trying to push the bridgehead back and evict the Russians sending them back across the river would not be an easy one. And further east still, the closest Russian positions to the German's dug in across their front, was the responsibility of Leutnant Roth's platoon, supported by Max. Holding that piece of ground was imperative if they were to successfully extract from this venture.

Max and Kienitz eased themselves forward, their combat knives between their teeth, a slight flash of white against their cork-blackened faces. Max resisted the temptation to lick his lips; the double-edged, six-inch blade had been holystoned until it was razor-sharp.

They lifted themselves up on their elbows, easing their bodies forward half a metre at a time. Four metres, three metres, two metres – there. In front was a bank of earth about a metre high; to the sides it was more shallow. Kienitz, on Max's left, kept moving, slowly making his way around to the rear; his target the far side of the trench. The dugout was a shallow, reversed 'L' shape, horizontal and part facing south to help protect the Soviets from an attack in this direction, and, judging by the size, it probably held four or five soldiers. Two of these were likely to be on sentry duty. The rest would be at the rear of the hole ready to run forward if they were attacked.

Max moved round to the side. He pulled himself forward centimetre by slow centimetre and carefully peered over the top. Although not quite pitch-black, visibility was poor. The moon was often hidden from view behind the ominous clouds above. He narrowed his eyes and squinted, trying to make out any recognisable shapes inside. He could not detect anything human but, directly beneath him, there was an unidentifiable mound which filled the bottom of the dugout. Tense, he looked up and across to the other side of the trench and managed to make out Kienitz, in position. Max waved his arm in the air slowly, twice. Kienitz acknowledged in the same way.

Max suddenly sprang from his prone position, grabbed the knife from his mouth with his right hand, and launched himself over the top and into the blackness of the metre-and-a-half deep hole. His boots landed heavily on the mass of blankets that engulfed a sleeping form beneath him. A steel-helmeted head appeared angrily out of the folds and cursed his comrade in Russian. He had only just managed to get to sleep in this bloody cold and now he had woken him up! Max reacted quickly. Not being able to find a clear target for his knife, he thrust it back into his belt. On top of the still sleepy soldier, he took the initiative. He wrapped his left arm around the neck of the unsuspecting infantryman, his helmet rim digging uncomfortably into his shoulder. Gripping the man tightly, Max wedged the soldier's throat in the crook of his powerful arm. The hapless soldier frantically grabbed at Max trying to clear his throat so he could breathe and call for help. The fold of blankets restricted him and his efforts were in vain as Max's steel-like muscles contracted, crushing the man's windpipe. Max's right arm was now on top of his helmet, shaking him violently. He twisted the soldier's head violently from left to right and finished him off with a powerful jerk to the left followed by the satisfying crack of a vertebra as his neck snapped. The soldier slumped forward, only Max's strength holding him upright. There was a minor tremble then one last spasm as the body released its precious young life. Max lowered the corpse and looked down dispassionately at the crumpled form. This was no time for pity. He had a job to do.

He looked across and saw Kienitz wiping his knife on a blanket that lay close by. Max had not even heard the struggle opposite him, so engrossed he had been in his own task, but it was also a testament to the expertise of the Unterfeld: a silent attack conducted by a man who had seen action in Poland, Fort Eben Emael, Greece, Crete and now here, Russia.

Nadel tapped Weidau's arm and Fischer gripped his machine pistol tighter, ready to spring into action and support them should the silent attack fail.

Nadel, the tall, pinched-faced officer, eased himself forward; Weidau kept pace. Both silently moved closer to their target. So far they had neither seen nor heard any movement. Beyond, maybe ten to fifteen metres away, was the sister trench to the one they were approaching and they thought they saw some signs of activity. Shadowy movement had been observed; possibly a soldier popping his head above the soil bank to get a drink or food. Whoever or whatever it was, they had now settled down. A restless Soviet infantryman, thought Nadel confident they had not been seen.

Now he was at the side of the trench. The embankment hid him from the prying eyes of those inside but, equally, restricted his own vision. He saw Weidau's form continue left then right as he sidled to the other end of the firing position. Crawling along the edge of the four-metre dugout, he tried to peer inside. There was no protective berm at the rear, proof of the laziness of the enemy soldiers. Halfway along, he nudged something with his right hand – a grenade put there by the Russian soldiers ready for any German assault. A Russian veteran, experienced and knowing that the Germans were not going to sit around while the Red Army pulverised them, had laid the grenade ready for quick access for when the inevitable happened. The round metal grenade would never be used in anger in this battle. Today, it served another purpose. Accidently knocked by Nadel, it bounced into the trench and the inner darkness. The experienced Russian soldier heard the sound of the grenade rolling and knew immediately what it was. He was instantly awake, and sat up. His Mosin Nagent rifle which had been resting across his chest was immediately placed at the port position as he called out, *"Kto tam?* Who's there?"

Nadel, who had just peered over the top ready to take on his target, realised his game was up. He rose into a crouch, dropped his knife and pulled the sling of his MP40 over his head as the 7.62mm round took him in the chest, throwing him backwards. The small, solid shape ruptured his heart as it tore through his body, the force pitching him backwards. For a few short moments more, his body continued to function, but he was beyond saving. He collapsed awkwardly, death seconds away. It all happened so quickly. He did not even get to cry out.

The crack of the Russian rifle reverberated across the Soviet lines, a more distinct sound than the intermittent firefight from FJR3's positions further north. The game was well and truly up as the Russian front line slowly came to life.

Weidau, initially stunned by the sudden crack of the rifle and the flash from the muzzle, frantically pulled at his Kar 98K strapped to his back. His knife was dropped and forgotten. The veteran Soviet rifleman was quicker. Now fully awake and alert to the intruders around him, he had already recocked his weapon and put a fresh round up the spout. He pulled the rifle into his shoulder, swung it round to his right, aimed at the shadowy figure at the rear of the trench and squeezed the trigger; the barrel not more than two metres from the Fallschirmjager's face. Weidau dropped his rifle as his hands flew to what was left of his shattered face. He screamed but the sound was unnatural. The lower section of his jaw and pharynx had disintegrated. As he rose in panic onto his knees, a second quick shot silenced him forever.

The three remaining occupants thrust back their blankets and scrabbled for the weapons that were somewhere close by as Fischer appeared above the trench, legs apart, bracing his body as he let rip with a full thirty-two-round magazine of 9mm parabellum. He sprayed the dugout from one end to the other, bullet after bullet smashing into the enemy below. A fixed look of hatred marred his normally handsome features. One of his men tackled him and pulled him down as the enemy, still in the foxhole further along, started firing indiscriminately in their direction. A grenade flew past finishing off what Fischer had started. He checked his platoon commander's pulse, confirming what he already suspected: the officer was dead and he was now the senior. He rallied his men, knowing they had to keep the momentum going, keep the enemy on their toes and off kilter.

Konrad squeezed Kempf's arm to his left and Lanz's to his right: the signal to move forward. Konrad had earlier crawled up to the trench and estimated there to be three occupants huddled beneath their blankets on this bitterly cold night. What was currently their home would soon become their final resting place as Konrad and his men swung into action. They had already decided who would target whom and all three fell on their adversaries, knives glinting as they stabbed repeatedly at their targets in an effort to kill them as quickly as possible. One soldier managed to cry out just before the blade slid deep between his clavicle and neck, severing the carotid artery. Lanz stabbed frenziedly again and again, in an effort to ensure the soldier's silence although this no longer mattered. To their east,

Nadel's platoon was already in a full-blown firefight. Silence was no longer a prerequisite.

They heard the crack of the rifle shot to the east, probably Nadel's position, where the assault had now been discovered. It was time to take advantage of the Red Army's confusion before they realised it was not a full frontal assault on their main positions but one from the river bank and their right flank, and that the Fallschirmjager were already amongst their outlying positions. Fessman could hear Konrad attacking the trench to his immediate right. Confident that his right flank was secure, he ordered Petzel and Stumme to open fire on the triple trench system beyond them, half right.

Fessman saw a flash about fifty to a hundred metres ahead; then another; then a third. The sighing moan of a mortar bomb being lobbed across their front, heading east, targeting the German front line. The expectation was that the Fallschirmjager were conducting an all-out attack on the Russian bridgehead.

Paul dropped down by the side of Fessman. "Mortars, Uffz, about seventy-five metres directly ahead of us, close to the top of the river bank. That's your target. You need to move quickly. Go."

"Sir. Petzel, we're moving along the river bank, keeping to your left. Keep your arc above one o'clock."

"*Jawohl*," responded Petzel, pulling the trigger again. *Pup, turrrr, pup, turrrr.* He kept his aim slightly off-centre, to the right and covered the troop's right flank, but not too far right otherwise he would hit Konrad's men who were also pushing forward.

Fessman grabbed Herzog. "We're going for the mortars. Take Mauer and Ostermann with you. Push forward, along the top of the river bank. I'll take Lang and Rammelt with me. The Oberleutnant will no doubt join us," he said with a grin. "We'll drop down below you. Petzel's staying where he is for now and will provide you with cover."

Paul joined them again. "Ready?"

"Yes, sir. OK, let's go," Fessman hissed to his men. He led his half-troop north and in single file, just below the sloping river bank, with Paul immediately behind him. Above he could just make out the crouched form of Herzog as he led the rest of the troop along the top of the bank in the same direction. He looked back and checked that his men were keeping up. His company commander smiled. It was good to have the Oberleutnant with them; it made him feel safe.

Not invincible, but a feeling that they would do their best and do it in the most practical way. He was a good leader and a tough fighter who had earned the respect of all his officers, NCOs and men.

A flare suddenly spluttered into the dark sky somewhere ahead and he, along with Paul and the rest of the troop, froze, closing one eye to protect some of their night vision. Green tracer rounds from Petzel zipped past like demented bees and hit the triple trench system now opposite them and to their right. The flare gave Petzel and Stumme a clear target as the Russian soldiers popped their heads up to look about them. Leaderless and clearly confused, they looked east, the direction where a German attack was likely to come from. Petzel's MG accounted for two. The third Russian soldier was hit by Straube and Muller's MG34, as Konrad and his men pressed forward.

Thunk, thunk, thunk, another three mortar bombs left the tubes now no more than twenty metres in front of them.

"There," hissed Fessman to Paul and pointed at the silhouette of the mortar crewmen and the sandbags which protected their mortar pits, lit up by the firing of the rounds.

"Get Herzog to cover us and we'll come up behind them."

"Sir."

Fessman ran along the bottom of the riverbank, before he climbed to the top to seek out Herzog. He also brought Petzel and Stumme forward to provide added firepower to keep the mortar crew's heads down.

He turned to Petzel. "We'll lob a few grenades into their positions, blindly. That will be the prelude to our assault. Then cease fire."

Once they had both acknowledged his orders, Fessman rejoined Paul and his half-troop.

"We're ready, sir."

Pup turrrr, pup turrrr.

"Is that Petzel?"

"Yes, sir, I've brought him forward to cover the mortar teams while we move. Once we've lobbed some grenades, he will stop and Herzog will join us."

Pup turrrr, pup turrrr. The mortar crews ducked for cover behind the sandbags of their mortar pit and looked for their personal weapons, unable to fire in support of their main line as long as they were being menaced by these sudden intruders. Petzel sprayed each position intermittently and was careful with his ammunition. They had only brought four fifty-round drum magazines with them.

Konrad came up behind Paul and Fessman. "Leutnant Nadel's boys have pushed into the triple trench system to our right, sir. I'm keeping my boys out of the way."

"Good," responded Paul. "Where's Braemer?"

"I'm here, sir," a voice whispered behind Konrad. "Where do you want my troop?"

Paul moved back so he was alongside him. "Once Fessman takes out the mortar team, I want you to pass through our position. I want to see what the Russians have further into their lines."

"Understood, sir, I'll bring them forward ready." With that, Braemer moved off to rejoin his men.

"We need to go, sir," Fessman reminded Paul.

"Let's do it."

His platoon commander dead, along with Weidau. But this was not the time for Fischer to reflect. He was the platoon Feldwebel, the most senior, and he would need to lead the men now. His mind switched into assault mode. If they stayed where they were, the Russians would get organised and hit back hard.

Two paratroopers dropped down next to him, MG34 up and ready almost instantly.

"There's another trench, straight ahead, twenty metres," Fischer yelled.

The MG34 opened fire. A hail of bullets ripped into the berm that had been banked along the sides of the enemy trench for protection. The occupants clearly didn't want to raise their heads above it to return fire. A troop commander dropped down next to Fischer and he immediately tasked him with taking out the dugout in front.

"Get your troop in around the back of them, but watch out – there's a ditch joining it to the next one along. There's also a ditch going west."

The troop commander acknowledged him.

"Don't worry about the position to your left. That will be a target for Leutnant Leeb's mob. But leave a couple of men to cover the ditch in case the enemy retreat towards you and get in behind you. I'll take a couple of men with me down this trench system and meet you there. We'll use grenades. Whatever you do, don't go into the foxhole. Now go."

Fischer clambered over the cadavers at the bottom of the dugout and headed for the cut-out that led to the next trench on the Russian second tier of dug-in positions. He was followed by two other paratroopers. At the end of the trench, they reached the claustrophobic but serviceable channel that led directly to the next position. He pressed forward, ducking, keeping his helmeted head beneath the parapet, MP40 at the ready, fresh magazine loaded.

The first positions were now taken and flares lit up the battlefield. Lines of tracer gracefully arched across the sky; green for the Germans and white for the Russians. Both sides started shooting. The flares not only lit up soldiers on the battlefield but also created ghostly shadows that moved as the flares swept through the sky.

Roth jumped down beside Max. "I'm sending a troop forward to continue the assault. Second troop will provide cover fire."

"Third troop, sir?"

"They're staying here. They can watch the back door for us."

"Good idea. If you don't mind, I'll lead second troop in the assault."

"Fill your boots, Feld," Roth said and laughed. His voice was drowned out by a sudden burst from one of the platoon MGs. "I'll be right by your side."

There was a continuous line of trenches along the entire length of the Russian Front, fifteen to twenty metres apart and manned by up to five men. Roth's platoon had to secure the one facing them then at least two or three of the others facing the main German front. Covering the Company's far right flank, they too pushed inwards, thrusting into the Russians' extreme right flank. His men would also act as the anchor point, covering the other two platoons' withdrawal, which would be directed through this starting point.

Back at Fessman's position, Petzel's MG fired round after round into the Russian mortar positions. The distinctive crack of Kar 98Ks could also be heard as the rest of the half-troop gave additional support to the swathe of fire which kept the mortar crew's heads down. There was only the occasional 'thunk' as the Russian crews managed to get the odd mortar bomb launched from a tube.

Down below, at the bottom of the river bank, Fessman led his men forward, followed by Paul, Lang and Rammelt. The two troopers had slung their rifles over their back, two grenades held ready, caps off and porcelain ball ready to be tugged and fuse the cylindrical charge at the end of the long wooden handle.

Green tracer zipped above them and to their right and struck the sandbagged enclosures which protected the mortar crews from the onslaught. Fessman held up his arm as he heard the 'thwack' of the bullets as they drove into the bags directly above them. He knew they were in the right place. He jabbed his fist up towards the top of the bank, indicating they were in position.

Paul came alongside and Fessman cupped his hand around his mouth and Paul's ear. "I'd say we're not far off being in between the first two, sir."

Paul nodded in agreement. He turned and tapped both Rammelt's and Lang's arms, indicating they could now do their stuff. Lang moved ahead and positioned himself opposite the centre mortar pit above. Rammelt moved back slightly until he was directly beneath the first one. They were ten metres apart. Paul crouched down next to Rammelt and Fessman located himself close to Lang. The two paratroopers pulled the cord on the first two grenades and lobbed them, up and over the top of the bank, immediately doing the same with their second. *Crump, crump*, pause, *crump, crump*.

There was a sudden silence from the half-troop above as the MG34 and Kar 98s ceased firing, as planned. The first grenade on the right bounced off the front of the mortar pit. The explosion was muffled and deadened by the hard-packed barrier. The second landed straight in the centre, in amongst the mortar crew, killing or wounding all four men.

Paul scrambled up the bank as fast as he could, not wanting to give the mortar crew a chance to recover from the shock of the initial grenade attack. He fired blindly into the pit from the rear, his machine pistol rattling as he emptied half a magazine into the tangled mess below him. He turned to face the second mortar pit where, stunned by the two grenades, the Russian soldiers tried to fight back but were ineffective. Fessman shot one and clubbed a second with the metal-protected butt of his rifle. The other two, wounded, surrendered immediately. Once their grenades had been thrown, Rammelt and Lang quickly ran to the third pit and returned with three Russian prisoners.

The familiar sound of German boots thudded behind Paul, and he turned to see Herzog and his men join them. Braemer and his troop passed through, ready to push even further north. Paul ordered Fessman to allocate three soldiers to take the Soviet prisoners back. He ordered him to destroy the mortar tubes and secure the immediate area. Paul left to seek out Braemer and continue the attack on the Russian's rear positions.

Chapter Twenty-four

Yet another flare lit up the night sky. The Russians were desperate to locate the source of the multiple attacks on their dug-in forces.

Paul and Braemer, Uffz of third troop, first platoon and first company, followed by the rest of the Fallschirmjager in the troop pressed themselves flat to the ground, just beyond the third mortar pit. With one eye closed, Paul did his best to scan as far as he could see, using the light from the flare to help him. There, no more than a good ten-second sprint away, stood a large shape with possibly another beyond it. They immediately melted into the darkness as the flare petered out and made its way back to earth. Paul did not need to issue any commands; the paratroopers automatically raised themselves from their bellies and moved forward carefully. They moved closer to the dark shapes until they could see clearly now what they were.

"*Scheisse*, they're tanks, sir," uttered a surprised Braemer.

"*Кто это?* Who is that?" A voice challenged them in Russian from the top of a T–34 dug into a berm. Its iconic turret jutted out just above with its barrel pointed menacingly towards the main German lines. Set up in a defensive position, its job was to repulse any German attack which tried to force them out of their hard-fought bridgehead, or to counter-attack if ordered by the Red Army High Command.

Braemer cut the Russian soldier down immediately with a five-round burst from his MP40. Rounds bounced off the armoured turret and journeyed on into the night to find another victim. The tank crewman slumped over the front of the turret hatch.

Sieler sped past, clambered up onto the front track, and stepped onto the machine-gun housing to the right of the driver's hatch and just beneath the turret. He launched himself on top just as another head popped up, this soldier having just pulled his dead comrade back inside the tank.

Seeing Sieler, he frantically pulled at the heavy hatch cover, hoping to pull it closed on top of him as he dropped back down into

247

the confines of the main body of the tank. Unluckily for him, he was too late. Sieler crashed into the tank crewman and turret hatch. He jarred his shoulder against the metal and forced the Russian back inside. He stood up, pointed downwards and fired two rounds in quick succession. He heard the cry of the Russian soldier as he was hit. Then Sieler grabbed a grenade from his belt, armed it and dropped it through the opening before heaving the lid down and pressing his body on top.

Boooomph! The massive explosion mushroomed inside the confined space of the tank causing instant death and devastation. The force of the blast lifted the turret hatch slightly, even with Sieler's weight on top. He jumped up victoriously, pumping the air with his right arm. Three rounds to his chest and heart from a Russian crewman hidden nearby cut short his celebration and his young but heroic life. His body crumpled backwards and his lifeless body landed awkwardly on the rear engine deck.

Suddenly there was the hack and cough of a cold five-hundred horsepower diesel engine spluttering into life. The sleeping monster awakened, followed by a second and then a third. Warning signals raced through Paul's mind. The initiative and surprise had now been taken away from them. The Red Army were wide awake and would be bringing their full force down on those that had carried out the attack on them. Paul knew that he needed to get his men out of there and now!

Perfectly timed and in answer to his unspoken prayer, an orange flare suddenly shot up into the dark skies, fired from the direction of the German lines. A second immediately followed above the arc of the first. This confirmed his own thoughts: it was time to get out.

"Let's go," he yelled as the Russian tank crews who were not in the process of starting and manning their T-34s gathered to attack the interlopers, confident of victory now their comrades were coming to their aid with their twenty-six-ton charges.

Sesson and Roon brought their MG34 into play; short bursts as they only had the fifty-round drums on the weapon, plus two in reserve. The bullets clanged impotently off the metal giants as the drivers thrust their combat vehicles into gear, swivelled around on their wide tracks and pointed in the direction of Paul and his men.

Roon adjusted his fire, knowing it was wasted on these giants. He switched to the more vulnerable target of the tank crewman who was firing at them, supported by their infantry comrades who were also reacting to the German assault.

The Soviet tankies and infantry dived for cover. Paul took the opportunity to skirmish his men backwards. Braemer pulled back two-thirds of his troop ready to cover Roon, Sesson and Geyer when it was their turn. He knew he had to get the MG team moved soon. Although tracer fire enabled the gunners to home in on their target by watching the fall of the brightly lit shot and adjusting their aim accordingly, it also gave away their position to the enemy. The T-34's two machine guns would soon be homing in and the driver would be ready to steer towards his enemy and crush them unforgivingly beneath their tracks.

They skirmished back; two-thirds of the troop; then the MG team; then the rest of the troop again, until they were back with the rest of the platoon, Fessman and Leutnant Leeb. The sudden roar of a tank bellowed into the night as it made its way towards their position. The darkness slowed the driver down, fearing he might run over some of his own men in his desperation to seek out and kill the German intruders.

Another flare lit up the battlefield. The Red Army tried desparately to pinpoint the invaders for their men to target and attack. The nearest T-34 suddenly lurched forward, heading at an angle and directly for Paul and his men who only had machine guns and a few grenades to try and stop it. Its 76mm gun swung their way as if sniffing out its target. The chassis and turret-mounted DT 7.62mm machine guns spat out a lethal rain of fire towards Paul and the assembled first platoon. Huddled behind the sandbags of the mortar pit they had secured earlier, they fired back as best they could, but the sandbags were immediately shredded by the ferocity of fire as a second tank joined in.

Leeb shouted in Paul's ear, "I have an idea."

Paul listened as he watched the approaching tanks and shouted back his agreement to Leeb's idea.

"Down the bank, now!" commanded Paul to his men. "Move. Quickly. Come on!"

They darted for the edge and scrabbled down the slope to escape the incessant hail of slugs that tore into them. Mauer took one of the heavy-calibre bullets in his shoulder, which immediately shattered; the impact threw him down the slope. Meister and Geyer grabbed him, one each side, and frog-marched him south, along the river's edge. Mauer was still able to run with them although his now useless left arm hung down at his side, numb, the pain yet to come.

Paul kept the rest of the platoon moving while Leeb enacted his plan. Roon and Sesson quickly set up their MG 34 on the upper bank of the river and deliberately aimed their fire in the direction of the armoured beasts whose engines had now warmed up and growled as the tracks churned up the sandbags of the now useless mortar position. Roon kept firing, short bursts, and kept his head beneath the top of the embankment. His task was not to specifically hit anything but to act as a decoy to and let the driver believe he could annihilate the German soldiers if he got close enough.

Roon fired round after round. Sesson quickly replaced the empty drum with a fresh magazine. Roon hit the trigger as soon as he was able. The tank driver revved his engine and used his mallet to shift gear and increase his speed. By day, the driver's view was severely restricted; at night, it was virtually impossible for him to see – a real Achilles' heel! The T–34's speed ramped up as the driver homed in on what little he could see: the tracer fire coming from the enemy position. He knew they would soon be under his tracks or running for their lives.

Up until the last minute, Roon fired off his last bullets causing possible damage to the barrel, but it did not matter. He grabbed the weapon, thrust it onto his left shoulder and slid out of control down the side of the bank, Sesson close on his heels. They turned left and ran as quickly as they could along the river bank, silence no longer necessary, their only objective to survive as the metal giant came charging over the edge.

The driver realised his mistake but it was too late. Although he tried his best to halt the tank, the forward momentum was too great and the right track ploughed over the edge with the left track, still on solid earth, pulling it forward. Now, with nothing but empty space beneath the right track, it teetered on the brink before plummeting down with full force. The driver was flung towards the back of his coffin as it dug into the ground beneath and toppled over onto its side. The tracks and engine ground to a halt.

As Roon and Sesson caught up with the rearguard, Geyer and Braemer ran past in the opposite direction, towards the stricken tank.

"Let's get this bastard," said Braemer as he panted, running alongside his comrade. "I'll cover. You stick them."

They reached the tank in seconds, the huge black underside facing them. Braemer ran around the front of the T-34, the angle so steep that when he got around the other side he could see one of the crew desperately trying to crawl through the narrow gap that was available to him. Braemer quickly fired his MP40, deliberately aiming to miss, but close enough to force the tank crewman to take cover back inside.

"Now," he shouted to Geyer.

Geyer slipped between his troop commander and the glacis of the tank and pulled the cord of his grenade as he did so. He was about to throw it into the gap in the top of the turret when he heard the hatch grate open at the front as the driver tried to force his way out. Geyer quickly changed direction, knowing he had only two seconds left on the fuse, flicked the grenade between the driver and the available gap, and threw himself to the floor. The grenade exploded and tore into the driver ejecting his partly severed torso out of the hatch and into the night. Geyer got up immediately, priming another grenade. He headed for the partially blocked main turret-hatch closest to him and threw a second one inside. He did not hang around for the results as he and Braemer sped away from the scene. They heard the '*boooom*' of the explosion behind them as they rejoined their platoon.

The two troops, led by Paul and Leeb, including the ecstatic Braemer and Geyer, continued in the dark along the river bank. Streams of tracer flew above their heads as the enemy sought them out, seeking bloody revenge for their dead comrades.

"Is Konrad far, Ernst?" asked Paul.

"He's at the first set of trenches ready to cover our withdrawal."

"Good. As soon as we pass his position, send someone to get him to move south, as quickly as possible, and meet up with Viktor so we can get the hell out of here."

"What about Dietrich?"

"He will have seen the flares and won't have as far to move as we do."

Leeb grabbed one of his troopers and raced ahead to carry out Paul's orders. He could hear the grinding of gears as a second T-34 crawled along the edge of the bank seeking them out.

Fischer grouped his men together and they too pulled back once they had seen the double orange flares, the order to withdraw, lighting up the night sky. Just in time, thought Fischer. They had come up against a determined Russian defence. It was only a matter of time before they gathered enough strength to counter-attack, push the

Fallschirmjager back and possibly swamp their small numbers. He sent two troops directly towards Leutnant Roth's position, their exit point, and stayed with one single troop and protected the company's right flank long enough to allow Leutnant Leeb and his company commander to get back along the river and out of immediate danger. After a three-minute firefight, Fischer knew they could not win and sensed that the counter-attack was in progress. His MG34 team informed him that they were out of ammunition. He knew it was time to go. One last burst from his MP40 and he ordered his men to pull out.

Chapter Twenty-five

Helmut and Erich pushed their way past the heavy blanket suspended across the entrance to Paul's company command post. A flurry of snow trailed in after them. It was well below freezing outside.

"Fuck this snow, fuck this weather and fuck this country," Helmut cursed. He headed straight for the woodburner at the far end, pulled off his thick gloves and rubbed his hands together above it. The woodburner sometimes made the bunker too hot but nobody cared. After being out in temperatures dropping to below minus-thirty, sometimes for hours on end, they were just glad to get out of the sub-zero temperatures.

"Grab a seat, Oberleutnant," said Max from the opposite end as he pulled himself up out of a chair positioned snugly between the end of the bunk bed and a table in the other corner. "Coffee, gentlemen?"

"Thank you, Feldwebel Grun," responded Erich. "Have you still got some of that real stuff?"

"There's some left."

"Thank God," muttered Helmut. "All we've got is some of that ersatz rubbish. Tastes like it's made out of bloody acorns!" He sat down heavily on the seat vacated by Max, pulled off his helmet and placed it by his feet along with his MP40.

"Back on the line, eh, Paul?"

"Yes, Erich and I will hold back the swarm while you put your feet up. Where's Manfred?"

"He's checking on his wounded from yesterday. His company got hit pretty hard. Bloody tanks are getting closer each time."

"He lost a Pak, didn't he?"

"Yours is the only position left that has one. We're buggered if that one goes."

"He's lost three men just from frostbite," called Erich from near the fire, pulling off his helmet and gloves.

"You'd best keep an eye on your men, Paul. They don't know

if they've got frostbite until it's too late," advised Helmut as he stood up to remove his white sheet, followed by his great coat.

Bergman vacated his seat next to the field telephone. Erich threw off a white covering, made up of white bedlinen, along with his great coat, before taking the seat he had been offered by Bergmann.

The white sheets had been their attempt to provide some additional camouflage for themselves and their men after the snow started to fall and remained with them. The entire Leningrad front was covered in a blanket of snow and temperatures varied from a manageable minus-five to a life-threatening minus-thirty degrees. They felt sure it was getting even colder each day, if that were possible.

They were not properly prepared. They had no winter clothing, only the uniforms they wore when they fought in Crete in temperatures reaching forty degrees. They had improvised. They wore great coats, scarves for their face and ears, and on top, anything white, such as curtains, tablecloths or sheets to help with their camouflage in the snow. This get-up was cumbersome to fight in and deadly when wet but the alternative was to stand out in the snow, making them easy pickings for their enemy.

Erich placed his now white-painted helmet, another effort to improve their camouflage, down by his feet, next to his trusty MP40, and undid his woollen scarf, a present from his mother, along with the thick mittens that lay on top of the field telephone. There was not a day that went by when he did not quietly thank her.

Max gave a coffee to Bergmann, then placed four mugs on the table. He dropped onto the lower bunk bed. Unable to stop the backward momentum, he cracked his head and then again, against the solid upper tier, as he tried to get up.

"Not broken it yet, Feld?" Helmut laughed.

"No, sir. Not only do you get hot coffee when you come begging, but free entertainment too!"

They all laughed.

"You ready to move back into the line, Paul?"

"As we'll ever be."

"How many will you have?"

Paul looked away from Helmut and straight at Max. "Max?"

His company sergeant pulled a notebook from his pocket and he flicked through the pages. "Including myself and the Oberleutnant, the two remaining platoon officers, Bergmann, Fink, Loewe and his last mortar team. Eighty-three, all told."

"We're probably much the same," said Erich.

"That makes our battalion strength less than four hundred," exclaimed Helmut.

"Nearer three hundred," suggested Paul.

"*Scheisse*, if they make a big push we're going to be hard put to stop them," declared Max, concerned.

"The next time we switch the units around, the Raven's going to shorten the company fronts."

"Are you saying we will have three companies forward and one in reserve, Paul?"

"Yes, Erich," Paul knew what was coming next.

"But that means we won't be able to rotate any men back to the rear. We'll be on the front line, permanently!"

They all looked from one to another. Each understood the consequences of what Paul and Erich had just said. They knew the toll it would have on their men's health, state of mind and morale.

"I hope to God the rest of the bloody army is doing better than us," lamented Helmut. "Come on, Paul, you've spoken to the Raven recently. How is the rest of the army doing?"

Paul took a sip from his mug, the liquid already cooling down. He touched the scar above his left eye as his friends looked on. They could see the stress on his face, the tiredness in his eyes; a look they all shared. They had been relentlessly battling for three weeks against the Soviet Army; against superior numbers, as it tried to push them back from the bridgehead and break out.

Now that the Petruskijino bridgehead, further south, had been lost to the Red Army, the Russians had turned their attention and their resources to this one point of contact, Wyborgskaja, in order to maintain their hold on the eastern bank of the River Neva, and to break out and meet up with the rest of their forces further to the east.

"It seems we've made some progress," said Paul finally, looking at each one of his friends.

"Although it has been tough going, we do hold a line from Novgorod." He drew an imaginary line along the small table top. "The line goes north of Lake Il'men, sweeps north-east to Malaya Vishera, Budogoshch. Then the line goes north-west to the east of Shisselberg, passing through Kirishi."

"So, we're in a bit of a corridor then," suggested Erich. "Nice."

"We've got the 1st Infantry Division holding the line, so we should be OK," encouraged Paul, "and 227th Division is further south."

"But if they do give way, we'll be trapped in a pocket," added an exasperated Helmut. "The bloody river to our west, Shisselberg to our north and the Russkies east and south."

"I agree with Helmut, for once," said Erich. "I thought we'd have pushed further east by now."

"According to the Raven, there will be a push again soon, towards Volkhov and Tikhvin," added Paul. "XXXIX AK will be leading the way."

Helmut looked at his watch. "Well, if I leave my men on the front line for much longer, there will be another war, and I'll be the one who's lynched." He heaved himself up from his chair. Max leaned back as the commander of fourth company clambered over his feet, white helmet clutched beneath his arm, MP40 now swung across his back. Paul also stood up. His men who had been resting in the rear taking advantage of some hot food and a relatively warm and comfortable rest, would already be making their way forward toward the front line. No doubt they would be grumbling the minute they had to step out into the bitter cold, knowing exactly what the next twenty-four hours of hell had in store for them as it had been the same, each day, for the last three weeks.

Erich's men, who had been in the reserve company position, would also be moving toward the front line. They would be moving from one hostile environment to another and, on this occasion, their bitterest enemy was not the Russians but the cold.

As they only needed twenty-five per cent of their force to man the firing positions at any one time, Erich could rotate more men through the platoon bunker allocated to them, giving them respite from the intense cold.

Paul joined Erich and Helmut at the crowded woodburner as they donned their layers of clothing ready to face the bitter cold outside.

"My first batch of men will be at the forward bunker by now. I'll start bringing them up."

"A platoon at a time?" suggested Helmut.

"Right."

As Helmut left the bunker, he was immediately covered in a bank of snow that fell from the roof. He could be heard cursing as he climbed the frozen, slippery steps in front of him. Paul and Erich looked at each other with a knowing smile. Helmut never ceased to entertain them both with his deliberate or unintended actions.

"I'd best follow him."

"You go easy, Erich."

"That goes for you too."

"I bet you wish you'd stayed with the Regimental Headquarters now, don't you?"

"Hmmm, maybe, but then who the hell is going to keep you and Helmut in line?"

Paul clasped his friend's hand and Erich returned the gesture with equal strength and affection. Erich turned and left.

Paul turned to Max. "Time to go."

Max sauntered over, his kit ready, looking more like a giant tennis ball than a professional Fallschirmjager.

"If you insist, sir."

Paul pulled on his winter clothing, now warm and dry. But not for long, he thought. He turned to Bergmann, who had returned to his seat by the telephone. "Let the battalion know we're moving forward."

"Sir. Sir, where do you want me?"

"Find Fink, give him a hand. I've a feeling we're in for a busy day. The Soviets are getting impatient with us."

"Especially after we caught them on the hop," chuckled Max.

"Come on, Feldwebel Grun, no more lingering." Paul laughed.

Paul and Max pushed through the blanket and ascended the steps. The cold hit them like a sledgehammer. Paul was shivering, almost uncontrollably, within minutes. They both dropped into the trench that ran alongside, dug by the engineers to make it safer moving to the front. They hunched down, not just as a defensive posture making them a smaller target but to retreat from the icy cold as they moved forward. They were not far behind Helmut and Erich who had stopped to discuss something. They eventually split up, Erich moving north towards the front line he would be manning soon and Helmut pushing forward to catch up with his men who were manning the battalion's southern flank.

Paul and Max made their way along the narrow trench. It was only a metre and a half high and wide with the odd log laid along the floor. Nevertheless, it gave them a protected route to move between the company bunker and the front line.

They reached a much larger bunker. The engineers had specifically built this to allow the troops on the front line to rotate, giving them some short respite with some warmth before returning to the freezing hell of their front-line positions.

At the entrance, a sentry stamped his feet and pounded his sides with his arms in an effort to generate some heat. He quickly challenged Paul and Max with a croak. *"Wer da?"*

Paul recognised the voice of Rammelt from Fessman's troop.

"Oberleutnant Brand. Who's inside?"

"Most of first platoon at the moment, sir, but the rest aren't far behind."

The bunker was little more than a sunken pit, with a log-covered floor and a thick roof of timber on top. They made their way inside. The doorway was staggered to prevent an explosion from blasting directly into the confines of the shelter. A stove stood in the centre with an L-shaped pipe disappearing up through the roof taking the smoke and fumes outside or, at least, most of it. Despite this basic offering, there were no complaints. The men were pleased to have some heat, fumes or not. Huddled around it currently were the majority of Paul's first platoon. The men in the centre of the hut, close to the stove, were too hot but they did not care. They knew they would eventually, like Antarctic penguins, be slowly eased to the outer fringes of the bunker where the lower temperature would quickly bite into them.

"Sir," called Leeb as he squeezed his way through the throng of men to get to the entrance of the bunker.

"Ready to move forward, Ernst?"

"Yes, sir. It's not going to be pleasant. You only need to be out for half an hour and you can't move. It's that cold."

"I know," whispered Paul in the dim, low-ceilinged bunker. "That's why I want to rotate the men as often as possible. Bring a troop back here for thirty minutes to start with and we'll see how it goes."

"That will only give a troop a break every four or five hours," reflected Max.

"It's all we can allow, Max. We're low on numbers as it is and taking more than a troop out of the line at a time is too risky."

"It's bloody freezing out there, sir. We've got too many frostbite cases as it is," insisted Max.

"I agree with, Feldwebel Grun, sir. We might have more at the front but they'll be in a sorry state."

"A quarter of each troop at any one time," relented Paul, "but the minute there is any sign or risk of trouble then the order is rescinded. Understood?"

He made eye contact with both of them and they nodded their acknowledgement. Paul was damned if he did and damned if he did not. Too many men on the front line and they may not be fit to fight; not enough and they could end up being bounced and overrun.

"We need to keep a steady flow of hot drinks going forward as well, sir," suggested Max.

"Agreed, the ones sheltering here can take a hot flask forward with them each time. Let's move out. Helmut will be getting impatient."

Leeb called to his men, who, with a groan, reluctantly left the warmth of the bunker. Max's watchful eyes hurried them along their way as they shuffled through the bunker exit and headed out into the bitter cold, taking one of three trenches that would take them to their platoon positions.

As they filed out, Paul noticed one of the paratroopers was trailing a foot slightly and stopped him.

"Vogt, what's wrong with your leg?"

"It's OK, sir. So bloody cold I can't even feel my foot," he responded with a grimace. "I'll be OK once I get moving again."

"Sit down," ordered Paul. "Max, get his boot off."

Vogt sat down on the icy, hard-packed earth beneath him. The cold immediately worked its way through his thin combat trousers. He peeled off his rifle and extra ammunition belts for one of the MGs and grunted as he clumsily moved his foot into a better position to take off his boot. Max undid the front facing laces of the number two pattern jump boots. He slowly pulled the uppers apart and pulled Vogt's heel forward to ease the boot off. Vogt suddenly screamed in agony. The pressure of his boot being taken off released a surge of blood to the upper part, the living part.

"A torch, sir?"

Paul plucked his torch from the front of his makeshift white camouflage tunic and shone it on Vogt's lower leg as Max peeled off the cold and now damp sock exposing a white ankle and upper foot. Five blackened toes stared back at them. Max squeezed a couple of them gently; they felt cold and hard. Vogt did not flinch as he pressed them further, slowly working his way up his foot until Vogt yelped as he reached the softer upper parts. However, even they were cold. Max called Fink who was in the process of refilling his first-aid sack with supplies that had recently arrived.

"What can you do?"

"Not a lot, Feld. We just need to get him back to battalion. It definitely needs treating."

"It will be OK, sir, once it's warmed up a little," said the debilitated paratrooper.

"You won't," snapped Fink. "Once that warms up, you'd better hope they have some pain relief back at the rear because that's going to bloody hurt like hell."

"You get him back, Fink. The Oberleutnant and I need to get to the lines."

"*Jawohl*, Feldwebel, leave it to me."

Paul tapped Max's shoulder. "Once we get a breathing space, I want all the men's feet checked."

He turned to Fink who helped Vogt pull his sock and boot back on. "Don't be long though. I have a feeling we're going to need your services today. Bergmann is back at the company post. He can take Vogt back."

"Understood, sir."

"Come on, Max, we need to go."

Paul gave Vogt an encouraging pat on his shoulder. "Fink will get you sorted. You'll soon be back with us."

He followed Max through the exit. Max called back with a laugh, "There're no bloody nurses back there, so there will be nothing to keep you."

The cold hit them full in the face as soon as they stepped outside. Paul pulled his scarf up over his mouth, crystals of frost forming on it from his damp breath. He shuddered involuntarily. Max led the way along the narrow passage. They hunkered down, their heads just below the top of the trench, although Paul's six foot two made it more uncomfortable for him.

They passed through Roth's third troop, the company reserve, then his second troop, directly behind Leeb's platoon. The other troop covered the rear of what was once Nadel's platoon, off to the right. Roth, like all commanders in the battalion, had an under-strength unit in his charge and two of his men were immobilised through frostbite. A quick word with the Leutnant and they again pressed forward, only their movement generating some semblance of warmth in their bodies, keeping the icy cold at bay.

They came to the widespread trenches of third troop, first platoon, commanded by Uffz Braemer; now down to seven men. Wirtz was wounded, Sieler was dead, killed whilst taking out the crew of a T-64 and, now, Vogt was stricken with frostbite. After an encouraging word with his men, Paul moved off, south, to the next firing point. At this point, the trench became even narrower, barely wide enough for Max to push his shoulders through. He often found himself walking sideways in order to make any forward progress. Also the trench was not as deep so they had to duck low as they shuffled along awkwardly. They came out directly behind the Pak 38, four men hunched around the anti-tank gun, the only one along the battalion's frontage. If this was destroyed, their only anti-tank defence would be lost to them. The men acknowledged Paul and Max's presence.

"I hope you've got plenty of ammunition for that thing," said Max.

"Yes, Feld," responded the gun commander, Uffz Blacher. "Resupplied during the night."

"How come there are only four of you?"

"We're it. This is the only gun in service, so, apart from the dead, wounded and those withdrawn to our battalion, we're all you've got."

"Leutnant Meissener?" asked Paul.

"Killed yesterday, sir. His gun took a direct hit from a T-34 shell."

"Well, I reckon we're going to need your gun," Paul responded, "so we're looking to you today, Uffz."

"We won't let you down, sir."

Paul looked at the men whom he hardly recognised as Wehrmacht soldiers. The ubiquitous scarves of varying colours, caked in grime, had lost their vibrancy long ago and were now wrapped around their ears, head and chin. They looked little more than washer women but far more pitiful. Their clothing, bolstered by bits of cardboard and rags stuffed beneath their great coats, made them so bulky the buttons could not meet with the corresponding buttonholes. They had used string to hold their coats together. Their gloves had the tips cut off making it easier to handle their charge and ammunition and reducing the risk of a hand getting trapped in a breech or fingers being severed. Two of them had wrapped pieces of blanket around their boots, tied on with bits of cloth or string; anything to keep out the numbing cold. Their gloved hands were held beneath their armpits in an effort to preserve what little warmth they had.

"My boys will be rotating back to the main company bunker. Make sure you release one of your men at a time and bring some hot liquid back with you."

"Thank you, sir. The sooner we can get Gertrude," Blacher pointed to the 50mm anti-tank gun, "up and running, the sooner we can warm our hands up." He chuckled. "The best hand warmer I've ever come across and it fair warms the heart as well to see her do her job!"

"A better hand warmer apart from a good woman you mean, eh?" responded Max

"Thank you for that enlightening piece of information, Feld," laughed Paul. "Do you see many of them out here? Come on, we need to see to the rest of the unit."

"Sir."

They continued their move south, along the narrow cutting that would link them with the next position in the chain. They were now at the most westerly point of the German front line along the frozen River Neva. Today they expected to receive the brunt of any Russian attack. Paul had serious doubts over whether they would be able to hold them back this time. The Red Army had become more and more desperate to make a breach in their line and was pushing more and more tanks and men into the fray in order to break the spirit and back of these tough Fallschirmjager troopers, the only barrier to their success.

It was six in the morning. If the Soviets kept to their schedule, an artillery strike was only sixty minutes away.

They eased their way past Herzog and Gieb. A three-man sized firing position protected the left flank of the Pak gun and its crew. They confirmed all was OK before they continued south until they reached first platoon's strongpoint.

Petzel grinned behind the bandanna wrapped around the lower part of his face, only his eyes visible. Like the others, a scarf covered his forehead, ears and chin. Clouds of frozen breath formed in front of him as he patted his MG34, mounted on its lafette tripod, and spoke with a muffled voice. "We'll send them all back to hell today, sir."

Paul could not help but smile. First platoon, led by Leutnant Leeb, was his strongest and first troop, the best.

"That will definitely help! Plenty of ammo?"

"Could always do with some more, sir," responded Stumme.

"We'll have some later today," informed Max. "They're

struggling to get supplies through. The bloody road system is diabolical."

"Whatever you do, you've got to protect that Pak. It's all we have left in this sector and, without it, the tanks could just roll straight over us."

"Understood, sir, we'll not let you down."

"We've still an hour left and I've managed to acquire some anti-personnel mines. With your permission, sir, I'd like to put a few in front of our position."

"OK, Max, but do it now and be quick. It will be light in an hour and you know what will follow."

"OK, Ostermann, you're with me. Stumme, let the rest of the boys know what we're up to. I don't want a Pak shell up my arse."

"Yes, Feld."

"Get moving then, Max," urged Paul. "I just want to check on two platoon."

"Leutnant Leeb will have them sorted, sir, and Fischer is pretty switched on."

"I know, but..." With that, Paul moved off quickly to check on second platoon, temporarily commanded by Unterfeldwebel Fischer, but supported by Leutnant Leeb. Paul would look after Leeb's platoon in his absence. There was no trench linking the two platoons. Even though dawn was an hour away, he still scurried as quickly as possible, silently sighing with relief when he came across the first trench. The sustained fire MG, set on its lafette tripod, looked menacingly west. It was the main weapon of two platoon's strongpoint. Paul had deliberately placed these in this way. Both MG34s in their sustained fire role could swivel left or right and maintain a high rate of fire; capable of well over seven hundred rounds a minute. This one, and Fessman's to the right, could lay down a devastating deluge of fire decimating any direct frontal attack. Switching left or right, the two MGs could cover each other or provide additional firepower to their flanks supporting the weaker units in his line-up. Paul had made sure that these two MG positions had the bulk of their belted ammunition, along with spare barrels. There was a cost; there was always a cost. The other MG teams had reduced levels of ammunition, but these strongpoints, so long as they held, could blast at the Russian advance all day long, if needed, ammunition permitting.

The Russian soldiers would soon come to respect the Fallschirmjager defence. Although Loewe had only one operational mortar tube left, his priority was to assist the flanking units, left or right, giving them much needed support. With Roth's platoon behind him and a reserve troop he could call on to plug any gaps in the line, he felt he had done all he could. Paul talked to the men in the immediate vicinity and reassured them that the company was in a strong position and, as long as they held their nerve, they would win the day. Now all they could do was wait.

He reflected on the difference between the Wehrmacht and Fallschirmjager. Regular German infantry were trained to fall back whenever the line was broken and could not be retaken. For the Fallschirmjager, it was different. The paratroopers had been taught, from day one, that from the outset they would be surrounded and outnumbered by the enemy. So, whenever the enemy broke through, the Fallschirmjager would hold their positions and fight on, reserves eventually pushing the Red Army back.

Well, he would know soon. All he could do now was wait.

Chapter Twenty-six

Max and Ostermann inched their way forward, cursing the engineers for providing the mines so late in the day. Max calculated the times in his head. Fifty-five minutes until the Russian bombardment would begin, providing they followed their usual schedule, giving them twenty minutes to crawl the hundred metres where they would lay the mines. Ten minutes to lay them then twenty minutes to crawl back to their lines. Not the sort of leeway Max, or anyone else for that matter, liked.

They eased their way across the frozen, undulating ground. They passed the odd splintered pine tree, shattered by the repeated bombardments by both sides these last few weeks. Dips in the ground gave them some shelter and a feeling of security, only to be taken away as shallow mounds rose up exposing them to the Soviet front line. Darkness was their only friend. Max counted off the metres in his head as they crept forward. He could hear Ostermann to his right, keeping pace with him, the occasional scrape as he caught a piece of his kit on the frozen ground.

The ground, when not frozen, was generally marsh, so there were no stones or rocks to crash into making their approach fairly silent. Unheard by the enemy, Max estimated they had reached the hundred-metre point. He reached out and gripped Ostermann's arm, the signal that they were in the right position. He tapped his arm twice, indicating that Ostermann should lay his first mine. Max would lay one in front of him, while Ostermann would move ten metres to the right. They would each lay a further two, move back twenty metres and repeat the process.

Max started with his first as Ostermann sidled away towards the north. He pushed the snow aside before digging a small hole with a trowel-like implement borrowed from the engineers. He had promised he would return it providing he survived doing their job for them! Initially, it was hard breaking through the icy crust but, eventually, working the small tool carefully and quietly, he ended up with a hole a third of a metre deep and twenty centimetres in diameter.

He carefully pulled a small, cylindrical S-35 mine from his bag and placed it in the hole, prongs uppermost. He fused it so it would be set off by someone stepping on the multi-pronged pressure igniter. Scooping the earth back into the hole, he pressed it down so it held the mine firmly in place. Ensuring the prongs were not restricted, he repacked the snow he had cleared away earlier. He was happy it would be well hidden in the dawn light.

Satisfied with his work, he wormed his way sideways, calculating when he had reached the ten-metre point before laying his second S-mine, closely followed by a third. That completed, he squirmed the necessary twenty metres backwards, on his belly, like a snake retreating from a threat bigger than he was, to complete the process all over again, conscious that it was taking longer than he had hoped. The frozen ground made it difficult but, if they were to complete their mission undiscovered, they had to take their time and do it quietly.

After laying his sixth S-mine, Paul could make out the silhouette of Ostermann off to his right, a clear indication that dawn was rapidly approaching. They had finished roughly at the same time. Max could make out the sweeping gestures as Ostermann pulled snow back over the prongs of the device left to shatter the impending Russian assault. What disturbed Max most was how clearly he could see the paratrooper's actions. It was time to get out of here.

He started to move backwards at a much faster rate than previously, but already knew they were too late. They could not make it back before the early morning Russian barrage. He winced as he wrenched his side; stabbing pains shot up his ribs, the wound still raw, constantly chafed by the excessive amount of clothing that had to be worn to keep the icy fingers of the Russian winter at bay. He looked over to his right. Ostermann was keeping pace with him and he could see that his eyes were wide with suppressed fear. He looked back over his shoulder; the forward trenches were still fifty metres away. He wished he was deep within one of the trenches, knowing what was coming and the unlikely chance they would survive out in the open like this.

Suddenly the whining moan of mortar bombs flew overhead. Max knew instinctively they would land close, very close. He called over to Ostermann, "Down, down, get your head down."

They both hugged the ground. Max kept his legs straight, tight together, boots touching, heels and soles facing away from him. He made himself as small a target as possible as the mortars landed a mere twenty metres behind them. *We're buggered*, flashed through Max's mind.

Thud, thud, thud.

It was their lucky day. The three fifty-millimetre mortar rounds, launched by a Russian company who had jumped the gun and fired their 50mm Rotney Minomyot mortars too soon, exploded with not much more of an impact than hand grenades. Even so, debris and clods of earth and ice still bracketed them both.

"Move, Ostermann, now. They'll be chucking the bloody lot at us soon."

Both of them rapidly pivoted around, up on their hands and toes, and scrambled across the cold, hard ground as quickly as practicable. The adrenalin drove them to speeds they did not think possible. They heard the deeper moans of heavier calibre mortars and artillery shells which pushed them to move even faster towards their lines.

Thirty metres, twenty, ten – they threw themselves into the trench head first. Max landed on top of a cursing Stumme. Not a second too soon.

Crump, crump, crump.

The entire front suddenly erupted and was shaken to the core by a succession of explosions as the smaller mortar's brothers joined in the fray. Fifty; one hundred and twenty; one hundred and fifty millimetre shells pounded the German front line.

Crump, crump, crump... crump, crump, crump.

The men cowered in the bottom of the trenches and pulled their limbs into the foetal position, gloved hands pressed to their ears. Their bodies were battered by the deafening sound of bombs, blast after blast, as the lethal rain descended upon them. The ground shook violently. They felt sure the trench would cave in but they had reached the point where they no longer cared. They screwed themselves up into ever tighter balls, their hands pressed even firmer against their ears in an attempt to shut out the uproar. Someone further behind was caterwauling as round after round smashed into the Fallschirmjager defensive zone.

Ten minutes passed and still the barrage continued unabated. A direct hit by two one hundred and twenty millimetre mortar rounds on Ptaff's and Matzger's position killed them both outright, flinging their bodies into the air like unwanted rag dolls. Their shattered and torn forms were unceremoniously dumped back onto the broken earth having no regard for their heroic pedigree.

Five minutes later, Roth's position took its turn, fodder for the bombs. They took a direct hit and his position was torn apart. Men were hurled in all directions leaving them with torn or missing limbs. Their screams for a medic went unheard.

The Red Army had chosen today to consolidate as much of the artillery they could spare in one huge effort to punish the Fallschirmjager for their obstinacy and blast a hole in their defences. Then they could push through and break out, linking up with their forces to the east and break the siege of Leningrad.

Crump, crump, crump.

Debris, ice and shrapnel hammered down onto the helmets of Pabst and Meister huddled deep in their dugout. A hot shard sliced into Pabst's upper shoulder. Known as the 'Pope', the translation of his name, to his friends, all he felt was a hard thump on his back. He wondered why Meister had tapped him. Maybe he just wanted to connect with him, give him some moral support or seek moral support himself, as they shared the horror of the storm that was breaking all around them. He went to move his arm to reciprocate, reaffirm the close bond they had as Fallschirmjager *kameraden* and friends, but was unable to move. Messages were rapidly sent along his nervous system to his brain; the sharp, unbearable pain telling him what he did not want to know.

He shrieked out loud, desperate to be heard above the chaos of sound, pride no longer an issue as he realised he had been hit.

"Bruno, Bruno, I've been hit for God's sake. I'm hit."

There was panic in his voice as they were showered with yet more fragments. The intense onslaught continued, not slacking for one moment.

"Where?" yelled Meister.

"I don't know, I don't know." Tears formed in Pabst's eyes and fear started to grip him. Shock set in.

Meister pulled his friend down and examined the jagged hole in the back of the white sheet covering his greatcoat. He found it difficult in the early dawn light and so low down in their narrow firing position. There was little he could do. Pulling out his gravity knife, he slipped the blade inside Pabst's uniform and cut back the layers. He made a hole big enough for him to dress the wound. He pulled out his own field dressing – not the right thing to do; you should always use theirs, but there was no time to do anything else. He used it to plug the wound as best he could. He felt the chunk of shrapnel jutting out. It stopped him from pressing down too hard. He could do no more as the thunder of artillery suddenly stopped and was almost immediately replaced by a Russian cry of *uurraaaah, uurraaaah, uurraaaah.*

Chapter Twenty-seven

"Hold your fire, hold your fire," commanded Paul, who had rejoined first platoon, leaving Leeb and Fischer to look after the second.

"Wait until they hit those mines," urged Max

Petzel cocked the MG34 and looked down the optical sight. What he saw made his blood turn cold. An advancing horde stretched out as far as he could see. Fuelled by vodka, raw courage and the threat of the NKVD behind them, they drove forward onto the waiting German guns, their fearful war cries heard by every surviving man. *Uurraaaah, uurraaaah, uurraaaah.*

Petzel checked the swivel of the layette 34. Ostermann, to his left, ran his hands along the one-hundred round belt of 7.92mm ammunition, linked to a further two fifty-round belts. Fessman was to his left, his beloved Kar 98K/42 at the ready. Short of the necessary men required to man a fixed firing machine gun, Fessman would be part of the gun crew. When needed, he would make sure additional ammunition was available. He would provide a fresh barrel to replace the one that would inevitably get extremely hot, to keep the fast-firing MG34 fed and, hopefully, able to hold back the wall of Russians advancing upon them.

To the far right, Stumme, the Gewehrfuhrer, the gun commander, watched the approaching Russians and expertly judged the best time to open fire for maximum effect.

"Steady...steady...let them get a bit closer. Don't want them to have our little gift too soon."

Max to the right of Stumme placed three grenades on the bank of earth in front. The wooden handles faced towards him, caps removed, the cord and porcelain ball dangling free. He would not be caught out this time. His MP40 was slung around his neck available for immediate use but the potato mashers would be used first.

Paul spun the handle of the field telephone, the link straight through to Loewe and his single mortar tube.

"Standby, Unterfeld, they're nearly upon us."

Loewe acknowledged and tapped Sommer on his shoulder. "We'll need six rounds a minute today if we're going to stop them this time. Make sure your weapons are close at hand. Judging by the size of the artillery barrage, this is going to be a big push."

All along the front line they watched the Russians advance; a mass of brown and green. Another deafening roar was heard as the Russians broke into a run and charged at them. *Uurraaaah...* Their adrenalin-driven scream evaporated the fear they had felt and replaced it with pure hate; their eyes burned intensely; they were invincible.

"Wait, wait," reminded Paul.

One, no, two, three muffled 'clicks' went unheard as the Russians charged forward close to the German lines. They needed to close the distance before the Germans opened fire.

There was a short delay of a couple of seconds, after the pressure igniters had been trampled on, before the S-mines were activated. The inner casings were projected a metre into the air before they exploded in a cloud of fast-moving shrapnel. Three hundred and sixty steel balls ripped through the tightly packed soldiers and tore indiscriminately through flesh and bone. Those who were uninjured continued to run forward as two more mines discharged their deadly load, hacking at the limbs of those closest, leaving them writhing on the floor like flies who had had their legs pulled off by cruel children. Even those who were some fifteen metres away did not entirely escape the high-velocity steel balls.

"*Stellung, stellung,* fire," yelled Paul.

The German line erupted. Petzel fired the MG remotely and a burst of twenty rounds spat from the barrel at over seven-hundred metres per second. A slight pause, twenty more rounds, pause, and another twenty as he swivelled the gun from left to right, swathes of bullets cutting the advancing infantry down like sheaves of corn. Men toppled forward as their legs were shot from beneath them and their bodies were thrown back into their comrades advancing behind. They, in turn, fell over the dead and wounded bodies. The accurate fire from Fessman's Kar 98 picked off those who had survived the initial bursts of fire. The crack of other rifles were heard as the rest of the unit engaged the advancing enemy.

Whoompf...

A high-explosive round was fired by the Pak, off to their far right. It discharged amongst the Russian soldiers knocking them out of their drunken stupor. Left of the Pak anti-tank position, Gieb and Herzog fired round after round in support of the gun's position. Rammelt and Lang dug in to the right, doing the same. However, as many as they cut down, there were always more to take their place. Their charge was never-ending. Some picked up weapons from fallen comrades; others ran forward with no weapons at all.

Max pulled the cord of his first grenade and threw it in a wide arc over the top of the trench. It landed just in front of the nearest infantry, now as close as forty metres away.

Boomph...

No sooner had the debris started to settle when he launched a second then a third. The hard, frozen ground acted as their friend and increased the effect of the blast. Shrapnel ricocheted through the rapidly diminishing line of advancing soldiers. The *pup turrrr, pup turrrr* of the MG to his left continued its pernicious effect on the soldiers in front. His MP40 jumped in his hands as he added to the wall of fire that was beginning to stop the Russian attack, dead, in its tracks.

It stopped almost as suddenly as it had started. As the German firing petered out, an eerie silence hung over the freezing battlefield. Only the odd dying soldier's moan or a wounded soldier crying out for help could be heard. Over to the left, a Russian officer was seen to shoot one of his own soldiers who was trying to retreat. Although desperate for the break in fighting, the Fallschirmjager knew that the Red Army had not done with them just yet.

Seizing the opportunity, the paratroopers quickly sprang into action. Magazines were checked and, where necessary, refilled. Fresh belts were linked up for the steaming MG34. New grenades were lined up along the trench and a check was made on their *kameraden* nearby.

"At least that warmed us up a little," said Max, holding the hot barrel of his MP40 with his gloved hands.

Then they heard it. The sound they feared the most: the unmistakable growl of a V2 diesel engine being put through its paces, the crunch of tracks on the frozen ground. The sound increased as a second then a third tank joined the line that moved towards the paratroopers. The German soldiers looked at each other knowing another attack was about to hit them. Two tanks headed straight for Paul's first platoon. The third seemed to be moving further north, heading for where Erich was dug in.

"Max, with me."

Paul ran as quickly as he could along the narrow connecting trench, jarring his shoulders as he ploughed his way along the narrow gap heading in the direction of the Pak 38. Max followed close behind, his wide shoulders colliding with the sides forcing him to make his way crab-like.

Paul's mind raced. If they could stop the tanks, they could hold the line; he felt sure of it. If they could not, the tanks would just roll straight over them and into the thinly defended rear lines of the battalion. They reached Gieb and Herzog.

"Max," yelled Paul, "back up Rammelt and Lang on the other side. I'll stay here."

Max's look said it all. He was reluctant to leave his commander's side where he could at least try to ensure his friend's safety.

"Go, Max, go."

Max obeyed and worked his way around the back of the anti-tank position and joined the two Fallschirmjager on the other side. Paul, after a few seconds with Gieb and Herzog, went to check the Pak crew. The defence of the line was very much in their hands. He joined the crouching Pak crewmen and bent down to talk to the gun commander, Uffz Blacher. The Uffz was watched the approaching behemoths through his Zeiss binoculars, once the property of the late Leutnant Meissner, his unit commander. Paul watched with professional interest, juggling ranges in his head, shell types, et cetera.

His number one was between the split trails directly behind the breech. His number two, the loader and firer, was to the number one's immediate right. An AP 40 shot was in his gloved hands, ready to be thrust into the breech. A further soldier was positioned behind the loader, ready to pass fresh ammunition. They had the capacity to reach sixteen rounds a minute.

"Can you see anything?"

The blackened face of the gun commander, testament to the continuous firing of high explosive shells at the advancing tide and the long hours and days battling the Russian forces, responded. "Yes, sir, two at the moment. T-34s for sure."

Hesitating before he continued his report, he brought his bins up to his eyes again, the front of the lenses resting on the log parapet in front. "Three to four hundred metres away, sir, I'd say."

"When will you fire?"

"Any time now, sir. Greater than three hundred and the

penetration is only sixty mill. Less than three hundred and we can punch through ninety."

Smoke billowed up into the now light sky, blocking out the frozen sun. The two giants powered their engines to push the twenty-five ton Colossuses across the frozen tundra and skirt around the occasional shattered tree blocking their route. The sound of cracking and splintering trees could be heard as the tanks' tracks lurched over those they couldn't bypass, grinding them to a pulp.

Clouds of diesel fumes and smoke danced in the frozen air as the infantry dropped off the top and sides. Some were reluctant to leave the heat of the engines and move onto the cold of the icy ground below.

Blacher was confident that the infantry were not going to charge just yet and issued an order. "AP, load."

The number two thrust the shell into the breech then shut it immediately. "Ready."

Blacher scanned the horizon again. "T-34, two hundred and fifty metres."

The number one peered through his telescopic, three-power, magnified sight whilst operating the hand-wheel on the left-hand side of the carriage. He elevated the barrel until it was on target, and tucked his body into the limited space of the armour-plated shield in front as a round 'clanged' into it. A Russian infantryman had taken a long-range shot, hoping to hit one of the crew.

"Ready," he called.

"*Stellung.*"

The number two pushed the firing button. The attached wire cable activated the lug on the cradle which, in turn, activated the firing plunger.

Crash...

Paul placed his hands over his ears but was too late as the breech shot back. The hydro-neumatic recoil system absorbed the powerful backwards thrust as the shell blasted from the gun tube. A cloud of vapour erupted from the muzzle-break and shot jets of hot gases, left and right, engulfing the crew in its shroud. The shell had left the three-metre barrel at upwards of a thousand metres per second.

Boomph...

The windshield-protected, streamlined nose of the tungsten-carbide core shell struck the T-34.

"It's a hit!" yelled Blacher. "Reload AP."

The armoured piercing shell had struck the turret ring of the advancing tank. The turret was knocked sideways by the force of the strike. Suddenly, as a result of the exploding ordnance within, set off by the penetrating slug of tungsten, the turret rocketed skywards in a spectacular display seen right along the Fallschirmjager lines. A jubilant cheer crescendoed, congratulating the Pak team. The turret landed somewhere behind the advancing Russian infantry. The Pak team cheered, ecstatic at their luck.

"Quiet," ordered Blacher. "AP shot, load."

"Target, T-34, ten degrees right."

Paul peered over the man's shoulder, impressed by his calm control as the second T-34, seeing its stricken comrade, turned towards their position, hell-bent on revenge. Its 76.2mm gun had already turned, seeking them out.

Another armoured piercing round was thrust into the breech. The loader yelped as part of his hand, exposed by the fingerless gloves, adhered itself to the shell casing, tearing a strip of skin away from his already frost-blistered hands. There was no time to worry about the effects or the pain as he closed the breech ready for firing.

"Ready."

"Fire!"

The horizontal sliding breech shot back a second time as a round was blasted towards its target. Paul covered his ears in time on this occasion.

Clang...

They heard the strike clearly above the reverberation of the growling tank as it careered towards them, determined to crush the enemy who had the audacity to challenge Russia's armoured might. The shell struck the turret, on the left-hand side, at enough of an angle for it to be deflected. It ricocheted off with a whine.

"AP, load," called the still calm gun commander.

Smoke and flame shot out of the barrel of the tank as it fired at their position.

"Down!" yelled Blacher.

The shell smacked into their position to their left, lifting the logs they had placed in a U-shape for theirs and the gun's protection. A sharp splinter of wood gouged a thin groove along the back of the aimer's head. Although he could feel the warm flow of blood slowly seeping down the back of his neck, he did not have the luxury of time to check it or stem the flow as he bent his head down to the sight as a third round was slammed into the breech.

"Ready," his comrade called.

"Fire!"

Crash!

Boomph...

The shell struck the tank just below its right track, slicing through the 40mm armour that was incapable of blocking its way. Once through this first layer of the tank's defence, it tore into the crew within. The heat ignited the tank's ammunition load. The crew flung open the hatches to escape the inferno blazing inside the hull. Those that managed to heave their bodies out were immediately cut down by MG fire. The driver slumped forwards, halfway out of his hatch, above the glacis. The second one slipped back inside choosing the Hades' inferno to the enemy outside.

They heard artillery fire to their right, followed by the ringing of the field telephone. Blacher answered it.

"They've taken out the third tank with arty, sir," yelled Blacher.

"They'll be back, Uffz," responded Paul calmly. "There are more where they came from."

Chapter Twenty-eight

The Red Army was in retreat; their nose bloodied by the Fallschirmjager who were determined not to let them pass. The paratroopers, however, had no time to rest. Ammunition was shuttled to the front line on wooden sledges. Casualties were transported in the same unglamorous way. The dead, unceremoniously, would have to wait. There would be time later to show respect for their fallen *kameraden*.

Paul dropped down behind the Pak again, after having scuttled along the entire length of the front for which his company was responsible. He had replaced second platoon, as it had suffered the heaviest level of casualties: five wounded and three dead, with third platoon. Roth brought his men forward. Fischer took his battered unit back to act as the second line and company reserve. On the far right, now back in command of first platoon, Leeb had exchanged second troop with his reserve troop, commanded by Braemer.

"Well, sir, do you think there will be another attack?"

"Oh yes, Ernst, they'll be back. They have the bit between their teeth today. They'll not let up just yet."

"You mean the same as any other day?" he said with a half laugh. He rubbed his hands together, trying to generate some warmth. He shivered violently, his head hunched down into his shoulders as he protected himself from the chill wind that cut across his neck and face.

Paul looked at his young platoon commander; his best one, one who had truly gained his respect and trust. Last year he was an Uffz, in command of a troop. Now he had his own platoon. Young, he thought, he looks like he has aged ten years. He looked tired, exhausted even, just as they all did. His cheeks were blistered and cracked from the incessant cold. His lips were blue and split. A row of icicles encrusted the fringe of his scarf that was wrapped around his head, ears and chin. Splinters of ice, driven by the wind, cut into him.

Max scrambled into the gun pit alongside them. His ravaged face, frost-bitten nose and cracked lips looked no different from Leeb's and no doubt his own, thought Paul.

"Ammunition resupplies nearly complete, sir, although there's not much left back there. I've had to send two more back with frostbite. They can hardly move so will be no good in a hand-to-hand fight. Wenger is going to lose some toes, I'm sure of it."

"*Scheisse*," responded Leeb, "we're losing as many to this bloody weather as we are to Popov."

Max looked across at the bleak horizon, a slight phosphorescence behind the low overcast sky where the sun had abandoned its forlorn attempt at driving away the cold.

"Even the sun's frozen today."

"Can we get the men some warm food?" asked Leeb.

"No, sir, the rear bunker has been hit and we can't afford to send anyone back to the company bunker just yet."

"You're right. Max. We'll have to make do. They will hit us again, I'm sure of it."

No sooner had Paul finished speaking when another salvo was released onto the recoiling paratroopers. Not as intense as the earlier barrage, but just as deadly. This time, one hundred and fifty millimetre shells were causing havoc amongst the German positions. A direct hit on the foxhole manned by Ptaff and Matzger hurled their bodies thirty metres away from their position. Their broken forms struck the ground, torn and unrecognisable. Theirs was the position on Paul's northern wing which protected the left flank of third troop's sustained fire MG34.

Once again, it ended as quickly as it had started. Silence for a moment, when even the wounded held their breath, before the dreaded growl of T-34 tanks shattered the temporary peace.

"Fuck," growled Max, "they're going to make us pay today."

"One of my positions must have been hit in that last bout of shelling. I'm going to check it out and make sure any gap is filled," said Leeb.

"Go with him, Max. We must keep those MGs firing or they'll be all over us."

Max hesitated for a second, not wanting to leave Paul but knowing it was the right thing to do. "Keep your bloody head down, sir."

Paul nodded and grinned back.

Max shot off to join Leeb.

"Well, Uffz Blacher, see them yet?"

"Yes, sir."

He scoured left and right with his binoculars. "Four coming for us but it looks like the bloody nose we gave them yesterday has made them wary. There's another six heading for Wyborgskaja."

"II/FJR3 are in for a fight then," mused Paul.

"There are troops behind them, sir. Lots of the buggers. Seem to be keeping back a hundred metres at least though."

"How far away are the tanks?"

"Three hundred, sir. Load, AP."

The breech of the fifty-millimetre Pak slammed shut as soon as the armoured piercing round had been inserted.

"Ready."

"T-34, three hundred, dead ahead. They're coming for us, sir," he said, looking back over his shoulder towards Paul.

Paul saw concern on the Blacher's face for the first time.

"They know where we are now, sir, and they are coming to finish us off." He peered through the lenses again. "One sneaky bugger is using the hulks from earlier to hide behind, keeping them between us and them."

The two still-smoking carcasses, gutted by the Pak 38 in the attack earlier that morning, gave the tanks some protection.

"Stellung."

Paul whipped his hands to his ears as the breech shot back on its slide. A cloud of gas ejected from the muzzle-break, turning into frozen particles as the round was propelled towards its target. The 'clang' of the round was evident as was the sudden change in the forward movement of the tank, stopped dead in its tracks. The round had pierced the left side of the turret, leaving a hole you could push three fingers through, killing one of the crewmen instantly and wounding another. The rest were gunned down mercilessly as they evacuated the tank before it brewed up. The anti-tank gun crew felt an almighty blast wave as the turret flew off and toppled sideways. The sound of ammunition crackled within the hull.

"Load AP." Blacher did not wait a second.

"T-34, five degrees right. Wait for the side shot."

The Russian tank commander had done well getting his charge so close, protected by the burning hulks, but he had made the fatal mistake of getting too close and had not taken into account the fact that his tank would be exposed when he pulled out around them. As he spun left, moved forward then went to spin on his tracks to the right, bringing him back on course, for a few precious moments the side of his hull, where the armour was much thinner, was laid bare to the German gunners and Blacher chose his moment well.

"*Stellung.*"

The shell punched a hole straight through the side just before the driver had managed to straighten her up. The majority of the crew dead, the driver took it upon himself, knowing he would not get out alive, to get revenge for his fallen comrades. Revving the engine, he accelerated and drove the partly immobilised beast towards the hated enemy with the intention of crushing them and grinding them into the motherland's hallowed earth.

A second tank roared into view, moving quickly towards them. Blacher had two targets, both close, both equally as dangerous.

Paul shouted to the rearmost crewman, "Grab your rifle, you're with me."

He called over to Blacher, "Take out the one on the far right."

The Uffz looked surprised but carried out his orders. "Load. AP."

Paul leapt from his position, closely followed by a frightened anti-tank gunner and ran as fast as he could towards the tank that was now a mere one hundred metres away. A further one hundred metres again and Paul could see the dark line of advancing infantry. The entire German line, in close vicinity, opened up on the Russian troops, giving Paul as much protection as they possibly could. Loewe's single mortar tube, firing six to eight rounds per minute, joined in the fray and tore into the Russian line. The Soviet infantry, seeing Paul and one other race into no-man's-land, apparently isolated, pressed forward, determined to kill their enemy.

Another crewman, inside the damaged tank, realised the threat posed by the two Fallschirmjager and opened fire with the hull-mounted machine gun. Round after round kicked up ice and earth around Paul and Romberg's feet. Romberg went down with a blood-curdling cry. His speedy forward movement caused him to somersault as the two heavy-calibre bullets killed him.

Paul darted left and increased his speed as best he could, despite being weighed down by layers of clothing. He heard his breath rasp in the frozen air. He was out of range of the gun. The driver would have to swivel the tank further right for the gunner to keep Paul in his sights. But he was determined to crush the Pak that was now only seventy-five metres in front of him.

Twenty-five metres. Paul unhooked a grenade from his belt.

Twenty metres. Rounds ricocheted off the side of the tank as the Russian infantry closed, firing indiscriminately, desperate to take him down. Soldier after soldier fell as Petzel fired twenty rounds at a time in an effort to stem the flow. It was a race to see who would win.

Ten metres. Paul's chest heaved. His nose had lost all feeling from the freezing air sucked inside.

He pulled the cap then the cord and placed the grenade on top of the slack track. It bounced precariously as the tank continued to move forward. He threw himself away from the tank, hitting the ground hard as the grenade exploded and sheared a couple of the pins that held the caterpillar together, unravelling as the tank veered to the left and ground to a halt.

He did not waste any time as he sprang up and ran as fast as he could back to the safety of the German lines, oblivious to the cheers egging him on or the explosion of the third tank that was unsuccessfully trying to edge round on the other side.

Chapter Twenty-nine

The remaining Fallschirmjager slumped down in their firing positions, cold, exhausted, hungry. But Max, the Company Feldwebel, despite feeling no better than his *kameraden*, showed no quarter.

He chased the paratroopers to rearm and grab any ammunition they could from the dead and wounded. He drove the platoon Unterfeldwebels Kienitz and Eichel to ensure any battle damage to the defences was repaired. He made sure that men were assigned to take a fifteen-minute breather in the company bunker, a short respite from the bitter wind that slashed at their faces with razor-like slivers of ice. He even pushed the platoon commanders Leeb, Roth and Fischer, acting platoon commander, even harder than the NCOs. They needed to reassign men to new stations, balance the front line and strengthen the weaker positions.

Initially euphoric at holding the Russians back a second time that day, they too had collapsed into their trenches and were happy to chat with their men about the day's events.

At first, they resented Max's determination to get things moving, particularly as Max was junior to them. They soon relented, however, knowing he was right. There was no time to relax until their defences were again in a state that could repulse the next Red Army attack that could come at any moment. The Russian forces appeared to be getting stronger every day.

Paul had gone to the Company HQ bunker to contact the other companies and the battalion commander. The Raven was out and about somewhere, Helmut and Erich out with their units. He had asked Max to liaise with two company who held the right flank, ensuring the boundary between them was secure. He returned to his company. He had to get them energised and ready for the next fight.

Returning to the lines, he dropped down next to Fessman and first troop's MG.

"All quiet, Uffz?"

"Not a dicky bird, sir. I hope to God it stays like this."

"Ammunition?"

"Low, but I assume we'll be relieved by Oberleutnant Janke's company, won't we?"

"Yes, but we've already taken some of their stocks and, if we're in reserve, we still need to get hold of some more."

"We'll be in a sorry state if we can't keep this going." He indicated the MG mounted on the lafette 34.

"Where's Feldwebel Grun?"

"He's not back from...here he comes now, sir."

Max descended into the trench to join them, his face unsmiling, his shoulders slumped.

"What is it, Max. Have you been hit? Is your old wound playing up?"

"No, sir...it's...Oberleutnant Fleck."

"Has he been wounded? Is he being treated?"

Paul was alert now, a sinking feeling in his stomach as he looked at Max's grim face. Max remained silent, steeling himself to break the news.

"Well, Max, is he hurt? Spit it out, man."

"He's...dead, sir...dead."

Paul groaned and his head dropped. "How?"

"One fifty hit the forward bunker. Two straddled it, but the third was a direct hit."

"Oh God, let's go, Max. I want to see for myself."

Max knew there was no point in arguing and followed his company commander to the scene of the incident. They made their way along the forward trenches and talked to the paratroopers as they passed, giving them encouragement where they could, but the men were cold, tired and hungry. They still had some hidden reserves, Paul was sure of it, but they had been battered by the Russian bombardments, tanks and infantry, the atrocious weather and even the German logistics, or lack of it. They smiled at him, responded to his coaxing, but he could see it in their faces: they were near breaking point. They were weighed down with excessive but necessary clothing, probably close to starvation, and he could see that some were little more than shells. The life had gone out of them and all they did now was breathe in and out mechanically. Even that was painful.

They continued north before turning east and coming across two company's forward bunker, or what was left of it. It was now completely destroyed; no use to anyone.

Excavations had been completed and what remained of the bodies had been dragged out and laid in a line, their faces, or where their faces used to be, covered in rough blankets.

The Raven stood next to the dead men, his combat gear covered in a dirty white sheet like the rest of his paratroopers. His face was splattered with blood and dirt, a dirty bandage was wrapped round the upper part of his left leg. His appearance was no longer pristine; he looked just like the others.

He had been a staunch defender amongst two company's forward positions and fought like a demon to stem the Russian tide that had burst upon them. He looked up as Paul and Max approached. For once his swagger stick remained at his side. His hooded eyes were darker than usual, the ever-present scarf wrapped around his ears.

He continued to look down at the bodies lined up on the ground. "We stopped them, Brand, but at a price. Hauptman Bach was in the bunker with Oberleutnant Fleck when it was hit. They were bringing more ammunition forward."

He turned to look at Paul. "He was a friend of yours. He was a fine officer, Brand, who didn't deserve to die at the hands of these scum."

He looked down at the bodies. "Hauptman Bach too, sir?" Paul said in disbelief.

"Yes. I want you to take up his duties, not that we've got much of a battalion left. I want Oberleutnants Janke and Bauer to move their companies forward. Oberleutnant Fleck's company to the rear. Yours will have to fill the reserve positions. Rotate your men as best you can."

"What's happening, sir?"

"We're being relieved tomorrow."

"What then, sir?"

"I don't know, Brand. We have a week to recover and then Command have another task for us, I believe."

"The men are pretty beat up, sir," informed Max

"I know that, Feldwebel Grun, but the battle is not going well. The Fallschirmjager are needed again."

The Raven turned back to face the dead men and stood there in silent prayer. Max and Paul took this as their cue to leave.

"Erich, for God's sake, Max, Erich."

Max placed a hand on Paul's shoulder, feeling it tremble beneath his gloved fingers. Not from the cold but from sheer exhaustion and overwhelming grief.

"I'll sort the company out, sir. You get the battalion moving."

Paul nodded and marched off. Max's eyes followed him as he headed away. He was pleased he had the battalion to deal with. It would keep him busy, keep his mind occupied for a while, at least, or until they could get away from this wretched place.

Chapter Thirty

Paul pulled his men back, deep into the wooded area, along with the rest of the battalion. He stood next to the entrance of a log house, isolated amongst a seemingly endless forest. His lungs rasped as he breathed in through the scarf pulled up over his nose and mouth, the sickly smell of blood and carbolic from within the regimental first-aid post filling his nostrils. Inside, the wounded and dying lay close together in the gloom of the almost windowless interior. The men, their faces white, blistered, unshaven, and exhausted were victorious but personally beaten.

The doctors sent to aid them moved amongst the bodies gently as they set about their work. Low-hung lamps were suspended over the operating tables. The orderlies supplied the doctors with hot black coffee, keeping them awake as they functioned on reserves they did not know they had.

Outside were more wounded and dying, placed anywhere there was a space. There was no room for them inside. The wheels of the trucks were already banked with drifting snow as the bad weather continued unabated.

Paul's friend was neither inside nor out. He had been buried the previous day along with Leutnant Nadel and many others from his company and the battalion, with full Fallschirmjager ceremony, or as best they could manage in the circumstances.

They had trained together as recruits at Stendal and helped each other through the onerous training programme that now, even compared to this, seemed like an outing. They had fought side by side in Crete; shared food, wine and laughs. No more. Tears welled up in Paul's eyes and ran freely down his face, quickly freezing, joining the rest of the icy fringe that encircled his face.

He felt a gentle, familiar hand on his shoulder.

"Come on, sir, there's nothing more we can do here. The trucks have arrived."

He turned. His tears continued to roll but he did not care. Max understood. Max was crying too.